A DARK SONG
OF BLOOD

Ben Pastor

BITTER LEMON PRESS
LONDON

BITTER LEMON PRESS

First published in the United Kingdom in 2014 by
Bitter Lemon Press, 37 Arundel Gardens, London W11 2LW

www.bitterlemonpress.com

A CIP record for this book is available
from the British Library

ISBN 978–1–908524–30-0

Typeset by Tetragon, London
Printed and bound by CPI Group (UK) Ltd, Croydon, CR0 4YY

To Aldo Sciaba
And to all the victims,
Known and unknown,
Of the Ardeatine Caves.

Haec urbs arx omnium gentium.
This City, bulwark of all peoples.

CICERO

Roma caput mundi regit orbis frena rotundi.
Rome, head of the world, holds the
bridle of the globe.

IMPERIAL SEAL

1

Again, the airplane. And again, the animal. Same dream in all details, an obsessive sameness. Russia, last summer. I walk toward the fallen plane making my way through the black stumps of the sunflowers, fearing what I will find there. My brother's voice is everywhere, but I do not understand one word of what he is saying. I only know it's the voice of the dead. A blood trail preceding and following me. Then, the rest of the dream, as always.

I woke up in a cold sweat (this is also becoming frequent), and tried for a long time to stay awake. I only knew I was dreaming again when the sound of the animal behind me filled me with dread. It's a quick, scraping sound, as of a large hound racing up stone steps. I climb and climb and the stairs wind around corners in a wide spiral; a blinding light comes from deep windows to the right. By inches the animal gains on me, and all I know is that it is female, and I will find no mercy with it. Its claws are like metal on polished stone, marble perhaps. I can't climb fast enough to avoid it. Looking back into this diary, I can see the first time I dreamt this was the night before the ambush in September.

Martin Bora's nightmares had been set aside by the time he walked into the Hotel Flora from the wide street, early in the morning. A tiger sky drifted white behind the city blocks, wrinkling here and there with striped, ribbon-like clouds. Via Veneto was filling with light like a slow river at the bend, on a

Saturday which promised to be a cold and clear day. His soul was secure inside, well kept, guarded. Anxiety had no room in his waking hours and, surprisingly, things that had been amusing were amusing still.

Half an hour later Inspector Sandro Guidi of the Italian police stood before the massive elegance of the same hotel, shielding his eyes. At the entrance he presented his papers to a stolid-faced young soldier. While he waited in the luxurious lobby to be let upstairs, he gave himself credit for not getting lost on his way here, but still wondered why the unexpected summons to the German command.

In the third-floor office, another wait. Beautiful wallpaper, hangings around luminous windows. Behind the desk, a detailed map of the city, a crowded bulletin board, three moist-looking watercolors of old Roman streets. Paperwork lay on the desk, neatly stacked but obviously being processed. Several maps were folded in transparent sheaths under a notebook. Guidi had seen German aides once or twice. The crimson stripes on their breeches came to mind, and the silver braid draping right shoulder and breast in the ceremonial dazzle of army hierarchy. What could General Westphal's aide-de-camp possibly want from him? It was likely a formality, or even a mistake. But he could not mistake the voice coming from the door, because its Italian had no accent whatever.

"Good morning, Guidi. Welcome to Rome."

Guidi wheeled around. "Major Bora! I didn't expect to find you here."

"Why not?"

"Well, not after what happened at Lago last month."

Bora smirked, and Guidi was at once familiar again with the good looks, the polite levity and reserve. "Yes," Bora said, "SS Captain Lasser has his friends."

"But here in Rome!"

"I have my friends, too."

Guidi was invited to sit facing the desk, where the framed photo of a woman was the only personal object. Bora did not take a chair. He sat on the desk's corner, loosely clasping his left wrist where it met the gloved artificial hand. "So, how were *you* transferred here?" he asked. "I happened to drive past St Mary Major yesterday, and would have recognized you anywhere – sandy-haired, lanky and ever so proper, coming out of church. You put the rest of us to shame."

Guidi shrugged. This invitation was now flattering and he wasn't sure he wanted that. Ostensibly Bora had no reason to have him here other than friendliness. "I was simply reassigned, but never expected to get the capital. Frankly, big cities daunt me."

He mentally compared his crumpled civilian looks to the smartness of the man facing him, off-putting were it not for the amicable cast on his youthful face. "I understand. Don't worry, Guidi, I know Rome well. I'll show you the sights. So, do you have a case yet?"

"I don't know if I can discuss it here."

"You must mean the Reiner matter, then. It's on everybody's lips, whether or not she was just a German embassy secretary who fell from a fourth-story window. Good, I'm glad it's you they brought here for it. Where do you stay?"

"At a house on Via Merulana."

"You ought to have taken a place closer in. Is your mother with you?"

"No."

"She's well, I hope?"

"Yes, thank you." Guidi felt Bora's attention on him. Their association in northern Italy had been circumstantial, due to criminal cases where Germans had figured in one way or another. This was different, and he was not used to relating to Bora without an immediate motive.

"There's much about the city to like, you'll see." Bora stood, which rightly Guidi took as a sign that time was up. "Let's meet tomorrow, at 0900 hours sharp."

"I'm not sure I can."

"Surely you can." By his brisk stepping to the door, Guidi noticed that – four months after the grenade attack – Bora's limp was less pronounced. He looked remarkably well, in fact.

"My driver will take you home."

"It's not necessary, Major."

"It is, it is. You walked here. Your ears are red with cold." Bora's impatience came through, and this Guidi remembered about him also. "I'll see you in the morning."

After the meeting, Guidi was angry with himself for letting Bora do the talking, and subtly taking over. It'd happened in Lago often enough to annoy him, but Bora's concise forceful-ness was as irresistible as it was disturbing. Devoid of leniency, an odd contrary image of himself, because Guidi was not willing to take risks as Bora did.

City life in the fourth year of war was gray, as the German staff car traveled streets where the few passers-by seemed also spare and gray. Guidi was struck by the naked great size of Rome. Far from the northern province – where "Germans" meant Bora and his detachment – here, after the loss of the south, had flowed Wehrmacht and SS, paratroopers and airmen, their commands ensconced in the best hotels, and the most elegant avenues made off limits to civilians. Rome was under siege from within, strangely. Strange, too, seeing Bora wear his medals. Guidi had never before seen them on the severe field tunic, and yet they told at once all there was to know militarily about him. When the German orderly dismounted to open his car door, Guidi felt the eyes of the neighborhood upon him, curious and hostile.

As for Bora, he did not waste time wondering whether Guidi had been imposed upon by his invitation. Within minutes General Westphal walked in with a slip of paper written in Italian.

"What does this say?"

Bora scanned the words. "It says, 'The women do not love us any more / Because it is a black shirt that we wear / They say we should be carried off in chains / They say we should be carried off to jail.' It's a song the Fascists sing up north."

"Well, it's defeatist. Write a note to Foa and the head of PAI and let them know it's all right for Salò but we don't want it sung in Rome. If Foa complains, chew his ass."

"Sir, General Foa is no Fascist, and he's a war hero. Harshness may not be advisable."

"He's also half-Jewish. Ream him, and don't worry about being unpopular. Aides are never left behind for the dogs to tear."

As things went, Foa was an untoward old man who wanted no interference from the Germans, and Bora ended up making an enemy over the stupid ditty. After the phone call he prepared a memo for Westphal's meeting with Field Marshal Kesselring, which he might have to deliver himself, two hours away in the arid massif of Mount Soratte. Allied fighter planes circled the sky in endless vulture rounds all the way there, where the distant mountain cut against the eastern sky a bizarre stone likeness of Mussolini. Westphal was called in by General Maelzer, commander of the city garrison, and Bora was en route to the field marshal's lair before noon.

He made it back to the city long after curfew. On his desk, a message from the Vatican was waiting with a note scribbled by Westphal on the margin. *Inform the Vatican Secretary of State you'll visit first thing in the morning to discuss matters in person. If it's the Italian cardinal, say no; if it's the German, say that we'll look into it. In either case give my regards, et cetera. Don't fall for Hohmann's philosophical talk. Report to me on Monday on this and the trip.*

9 JANUARY 1944

At fifteen minutes to seven on Sunday, a cold, rainy day that made the cobblestones along the Vatican Wall slick with ice, Bora arrived to meet whomever the Secretary of State had chosen for the encounter. He secretly hoped it would be Cardinal Borromeo, whom he knew less than Cardinal Hohmann and would be easier to lie to. But it turned out to be Hohmann who would meet him; the same old man who, as a bishop, lectured on ethics when Bora was at the university. A spry octogenarian who notoriously did not take no for an answer, he noticed Bora's concern and laughed his small squeaky laugh. "What is this, General Westphal sends me a boy from home?"

Bora leaned over to kiss the cardinal's ring.

"Have you been to Mass?"

"Why, no, Your Eminence."

"Then go to Mass first – there's one about to begin next door."

Bora fidgeted through the service in the chapel of the handsome flat just outside the Vatican boundaries, from which all German soldiers were barred. At his return, Hohmann was eating candy next to a small table. "If you haven't taken Communion," he said with a merry flicker of his blue eyes, "it means you were ordered to lie to me."

"I haven't taken Communion," Bora admitted, "but not for that reason. Your Eminence, General Westphal wishes to inform you that we might look into the matter of preventive arrest of civilians by the Italian authorities."

"That's a lie already, because you won't."

"He also sends his respects to Your Eminence."

"They're not worth a fig, Major." Hohmann handed the dainty plate of candy to Bora, who tensely declined. "What happened to the saucy upperclassman with whom I discussed Glaucon?"

"Things are different now."

"Nonsense. From one Saxon to another, Major Bora, tell your commander that I want more than his word for it. If he doesn't make himself accountable in writing, the Holy Father may request to see him personally, or to see General Maelzer, or the field marshal."

"Even the field marshal has his orders."

"What were you to tell Cardinal Borromeo, had he been the one selected to meet you?"

"I am not at liberty to say."

Genially Hohmann slapped his knee. "Then it's 'no'. You were told to tell *him* no, and 'maybe' to *me*. Well, I suppose that counts for something."

"I urge Your Eminence to accept General Westphal's spoken offer of interest. I'm afraid it's as good as Your Eminence is going to receive."

"Our Eminence will accept it if you will apprise him that he is unto us as Plato's prisoner to his companions."

Bora gave him a frustrated look. "With all respect, I cannot tell my commanding officer that he's *ridiculous*."

The teacher in the cardinal relented enough for him to lead Bora out of the room with a fatherly squeeze of the shoulder. "It's all right, Major, you don't have to tell him."

"I still need Your Eminence's answer to the offer."

"The answer is no."

Later that day, from the baluster of the Janiculum Hill, Rome was hazy with smoke – people were burning cardboard and furniture in their stoves after gas and central heating had been cut off, like most services. The view had the dreamlike hues of a northern place, a Flemish quality of misty perspectives, roof edges suspended, outlines dabbed on. But the cupolas betrayed Rome, and so did the somber heads of the pines, and the white marble slope of Victor Emmanuel's monument, a throne fit for a giant.

"How can you know so much about Rome if you arrived only ten days or so ago?"

Bora was thinking of Hohmann, whose outspokenness had nearly cost him his life in Germany, and slowly turned at Guidi's question. "My stepfather's first wife lives here. I spent many summers with her, down that way." He pointed at an undefined spot in the center of the city, where blocks of venerable brick houses clustered around fat churches.

During four hours of visiting the sights and breaking for lunch, Bora's talk had been inquisitive but superficial, with no sign of deepening now. So Guidi decided to prompt him. "Major, what do you know about the Reiner case?"

"Not much. If there's foul play, we want it solved."

"What else?"

"That's about all. Rumors about boyfriends – and about a girlfriend, too." Bora stood straight, and fastidiously rigid.

"That's news to me."

"Well, it proves how we can keep our mouths shut."

"Three weeks have passed since her death, and not a word in the papers. They told me the body is still here."

"Actually, her ashes are. She was cremated upon her family's request. You understand that after her fall, it was hardly an open coffin matter."

"No word about an autopsy, either. And the key to her apartment has not been made available to the Italian authorities."

"The building belongs to the German government."

Guidi was vexed by Bora's reticence. "So, that's it, Major. They brought me in as a newcomer to sandbag the investigation."

"Whatever you mean by *they*, it isn't the Germans. And what a low opinion of yourself you have. Perhaps *they* think you're the only one who can see through it."

For the next few minutes, Bora pointed out monuments through the haze, discussing them. Guidi, still resentful, was not about to settle for the view. He said bluntly, "Frankly, Major, after the matter at Lago, I thought for sure you'd seek headquarters in Germany."

Unexpectedly Bora grinned. "For safety, you mean? Because of a jackass like Captain Lasser?" But he didn't add how close to asking for that very safety he'd come. "War is not over in Italy, by a long shot. I like being involved."

"I don't know why you keep after war when you might not have to."

Bora took out a pack of Chesterfields. "Why, you're not serious!" He offered a cigarette to Guidi, without taking one himself. "Ever since Spain, I've had seven years of great fighting. The *glory* of it, Guidi, the bloody idea of it. It takes more than a lost hand or a jackass colleague! Spain, Poland, Russia – I volunteered for all. Being in war is as much fun as being in love, when the want's in it."

Guidi saw through the bluster. "Is that the only lesson to be gained from it?"

"No. Spain is where I learned what civil war does to a country, so I don't mind being here at all. I know what to expect. As for Italy, it was Albert who brought me here." Bora meant Field Marshal Kesselring, affectionately, though his face grew hard. "I assure you, Guidi, your king made a mistake when he turned on us. We'll do what we must, but you'll be out in the cold."

"You mean the Italians. I see. Why do you bother with my company, then?"

Bora looked down at the lighter he had taken in hand without using it. "Must there be a motive? This isn't police work."

"Some higher-up found me an accommodation at Via Paganini, *closer in*. I was notified of it this morning, and have reason to think you had something to do with it."

"Why should I?"

"That's what I am asking you, Major Bora." Irritably, Guidi carefully lifted the collar of his coat against the northern wind. It was a good coat, an expensive new one, and he was proud and protective of it in these lean years. Bora looked elsewhere and was rapidly isolating himself. Nothing else would be gotten out of him today. "I think you've shown me enough for now," Guidi advised. In silence they walked across the belvedere to the Garibaldi monument, where Bora instructed his driver to take Guidi back to work.

The first thing Westphal asked on Monday was, "What the hell's going on at Verona? Have the Fascists finished trying their own?"

Bora nodded. "Ciano has been condemned to death."

"Good! I'll give credit to Mussolini for dumping his son-in-law. He shouldn't have left his fat post at the Vatican. Who else, besides Ciano?"

Bora didn't need to look at the list. "De Bono, Gottardi, Pareschi and Marinelli."

"Ha! Two of them are decrepit."

"They're all to be shot as traitors tomorrow at nine."

"Serves them right. Now give me the bad news."

Bora reported on his meetings with Kesselring and Hohmann, adding that he had already requested an audience with Cardinal Borromeo to sample the moderate Vatican wing. "The worst news is that the Americans made it across the Peccia River. They've been at it since Thursday, and now they've done it. The French are still north of Cassino, but they may be there for weeks."

"So, is it still looking slow?"

"It's still looking slow."

Westphal went into his office, from where he called out to Bora after a while, "On Saturday there's a party at Ott's house. I want you to go if Dollmann is going. Have you met him already? Good. Sit by him. He loves to talk, for an SS." Westphal came back in, with an ironical bent of his lips. "You know about him, of course."

"I heard rumors, General." Bora did not say the kindest of them had been *They say Dollmann fucks his chauffeur.*

"Rumors? By God, you were a good choice. Now we only need to find a way to use your *other* talent. That's the one we brought you here for."

"Hopefully there'll be no need."

"Don't delude yourself. We haven't seen the tip of what clandestine activities are yet to come. Ask Dollmann at the party. By the way, we go to Frascati tomorrow, and on the way back let's swing by the shore. We won't leave until 0700 hours, but be here at five as usual."

"I suggest we leave at six-thirty. American bombers become active by 0800 or so."

"We'll do as you say. Any news about the Reiner mess?"

"Only that they have a newcomer looking into it. The official word is still 'accident', but we know better."

"Wasn't her door locked from within?"

"Or from without. Her keys are missing."

In the afternoon Bora prepared two itineraries: one through Frascati to Anzio and along the shore to Lido and back to Rome, and another that rejoined the return route inland at Aprilia, skirting the Alban Hills to the south. Their departure, however, was delayed by reports of new fighting around Cervara.

The sun was almost up when they left the southeastern city limits, and rolling along the horizon by the time they crossed the crowded suburb of Quadraro. Past them went the one-storied little stucco houses, ochre- and mustard-colored, beside postage-stamp courtyards enclosed by fences and paved with cement tiles. Frost-covered cacti sat in pots at the gates of more pretentious tenements, three and four stories in height, belted by unimaginative masonry balconies. Bora was reading from his notes to the general. "The birth rate in this place is huge – over twenty-three hundred a year."

Disparagingly, Westphal glanced away from the window. "Mark my words, one of these days we'll come here and fish out all the men and haul them off. All communists and socialists, ungrateful riff-raff brought here from the slums of the countryside. Now, this is the place where you'll count yourself lucky if you don't get yourself blown to bits!"

Bora had noticed the car lacked the customary sandbags on the floor; a mine would explode the chassis and kill them without hope of escape. But then his car was sandbagged on the day a grenade had been thrown at it, and it had made no difference, really. He simply took note of street names, to be able if need be to find his way around the quarter on foot. Despite his staff position, he wore the ordinance pistol at his belt. His assignments had made him realistic about war exigencies, he had told Westphal, and Westphal had answered that he didn't mind.

Five miles out of Rome, when they passed Mussolini's movie citadel, the general drew back more amiably on the seat. "I don't need to be briefed about this – most of your colleagues' lovers are from Cinecittà." Bora looked up from the topographic spread on his knees. "Maelzer doesn't like it, but there's little he can do about it. There used to be a tramway every twenty minutes each way – now it's all up in the air."

Not far from the road Pius IX's old railway could be now seen penciling a straight parallel line among farmhouses and fields. Past Osteria del Curato, the highway to Frascati and that to Anagni diverged. The staff car bore left at the crossroads and had nearly reached the landmark called Halfway Tower (Westphal was giving Bora his plans for the day) when two British fighters burst into view from the south-east, fast and low and coming their way.

At Westphal's order the panic-stricken driver, who had swerved off the road, regained it and continued to travel. The first flyover was deafening, followed by the whine of engines as they pulled up to bank round and return.

"They'll strafe," Bora warned.

Westphal was stone-faced, but would not order to stop. Over them the fighters swept one after the other, cannons ablaze. A loud dry whipping of shells cracked the air – asphalt flew up around the car and pieces of it hit windshield and side windows, stray metal gouged the doors; the noise was for a moment beyond the edge of hearing, and painful. Against a bare sky the fighters had turned ahead, and were scuttling back with the slick ease of deadly fish. Bora knew a third passage could not possibly miss them. In front of him, in naive self-defense, the driver braked and covered his head. Westphal braced for the explosion; Bora had been holding a pen in his hand, and now absurdly capped it and put it away in his pocket. High grating of engines drowned their thoughts.

Then, before the Germans' eyes, the airplanes widely parted and nosed up, their dull bellies giving way to the sheen of cockpits as they veered to rejoin each other to the east. Fire boomed in quick succession from an anti-aircraft post somewhere, aimlessly enough, but sufficient to divert the pilots from the attack. In the suddenly remade silence, Westphal calmly and distinctly blasphemed to himself.

Bora felt much the same, but chose to note the time on his pad. If either man was shaken, he did not show it. As the car started again, "Forget Frascati," Westphal said. "Let's go directly to Aprilia. I want to talk to some of the commanders. Who's responsible there?"

"Colonel Holz."

Colonel Holz, after uselessly appealing to Westphal, protested that his exhausted men had to remain on constant alert.

"I don't think you have much choice," Bora said.

"That's all because the field marshal has an invasion mania," Holz protested. "We've been watching the goddamn shore for three months, and the enemy hasn't even crept up to the Garigliano River yet, twenty-five miles in all! What good are tired troops going to be?" And, because Bora was unsympathetic, he added, "Look, Major, I see you've been to Russia – you know how weary holding the line is."

"It's worse losing it."

"Goddamn it, you're not listening to me! I'm going directly to Kesselring after this!"

"You do that, Colonel."

Holz had begun to turn away from Bora but changed his mind, and faced him again with a sharp half-turn on his heels. "If Westphal ever leaves you behind, I'll have your ass for this."

Bora nearly lost his temper at the words. "As the colonel wishes."

Much the same scene was repeated at Anzio and up the coast from it.

"They're going to have their way," Westphal grumbled as they rushed a lunch somewhere along the road back. "I won't, but the field marshal will listen, I know." He had a map laid open on the battered hood of the car, and munched on a sandwich as he looked at it.

Bora looked down, partly to conceal anger for the response they had met, partly because crippling pain had awakened in his left arm and he did not want Westphal to notice it. He said, watching him pencil circles over the map, "If need be, the Reclamation Land can be flooded."

Westphal nodded, swallowing the last of his sandwich. "It's the interior that will make a difference at this point." Their glances met above the map. "How well do you know it?"

"I've been to Sora, Anagni – Tivoli I know well." Bora spoke as Westphal pointed out the places. "Impregnable citadels for three thousand years. The monastery above Cassino, too – I wouldn't want to have to take it." Moving back on the map, the general's forefinger drew a circle on the flat area immediately around Rome, and Bora shook his head. "The rest is mush."

Westphal assented gloomily. He was pressing with his knuckle on the resort town of Lido, directly in line with Rome. "God forbid anything from happening there – *Il Duce*'s Imperial Way would deliver them into our lap in an hour's time."

"Would they land so far from the bulk of their forces?"

"With Americans, one doesn't know what they would do." The general folded the map and handed it to Bora. "Let's go. I want to be at Soratte before any of the commanders get in touch with the field marshal."

*

The new address, Guidi had to admit, was more convenient than the decentralized Via Merulana. Now from his doorstep on the elbow-shaped Via Paganini – if the public cars failed – he could manage the walk to his office on Via Del Boccaccio. The owners, Maiuli by name, were from Naples – a retired professor of Latin and his wife, a "remarkable hunchback", as he described her. Given the southern penchant for superstition, Guidi suspected a less than disinterested affection on the part of the professor, who was an inveterate lotto player. He listened to the old couple, lost in the array of knick-knacks and plaster saints that crowded the parlor, inform him of the house rules.

"The bathroom is at the end of the hallway, and the maid comes to clean in the morning."

"Dinner is at eight on the dot."

"Overnight visitors are discouraged. This is a well-regulated house and we pride ourselves in keeping only selected guests."

"… And no more than two at a time."

"Who else is staying here?" Guidi asked.

"An art student by the name of Lippi." Professor Maiuli hastened to say, "You'll have a chance to become acquainted before long."

"Will either of you or that gentleman mind if I smoke?"

Donna Carmela made a face. "We'd rather you didn't, but I suppose that a cigarette after dinner will not kill anyone."

Once in his room, Guidi sat on the bed, staring at the lurid lithograph of St Gennaro's execution hanging above it. It was a beheading in full colors, especially unwelcome as he'd just viewed the photos of Fräulein Reiner after the fall. Guidi planned to ask Bora about her again, since she was apparently well known among the officers. For now, he avoided making conjectures, waiting for clues to roll out of a well-rehearsed nowhere, as they often did. After making sure his door was locked, he reached for the lithograph, took it off the nail and slipped it under the bed face down, where it'd stay until the maid came in the morning to clean.

In the morning, as he was preparing for his first meeting with the head of Rome police, Guidi cut his chin while shaving in his room. Remembering he'd seen a bottle of alcohol in the bathroom, he walked down the hallway in that direction, with a handkerchief pressed to his jaw. Just as he reached the door, a young woman walked up from behind and took hold of the handle.

"Sorry, I've got to use it first."

Guidi was surprised, but automatically stepped back. He was standing a few feet away when she came out. "By the way, what's happened to you?" she asked.

Guidi told her.

"Oh, I thought you had a toothache." So, this was the art student, whom he'd assumed to be a man. In her mid-twenties, Guidi judged, excessively thin. Clothes hung loosely on her. Still, her face was fine and luminous, and she had beautiful dark eyes. "Are you the policeman?"

"I'm Inspector Sandro Guidi."

"And I'm Francesca Lippi. Pleased to meet you." Heading for her room, she added, "I use the bathroom a lot, 'cause I'm pregnant."

The newly arrived head of police, Pietro Caruso, looked myopic. On his long head, graying hair sat brushed in a tamed bristle. He was already occupying his desk at the *Questura Centrale*, a post he was due to take over officially in a few weeks.

"Do you know what my name means?" he asked Guidi, whose credentials lay before him. "It means *apprentice in a sulphur mine*. That's what it means."

Guidi failed to understand why the subject was introduced, if not to enhance the achievements of the man facing him. He was anxious to be given the Reiner folder, but Caruso's second question had no more bearing on the issue than the first.

"Where did you attend school?"

"Urbino."

"The boarding school or the reformatory?" Caruso seemed amused by his own joke. "No, seriously – the Piarist Fathers, eh? Good. And then?"

"The university there."

"How could you afford it?"

"I had a bursary to attend. My father was awarded a gold medal posthumously, and the educational opportunity came with it." Anticipating Caruso's next question, Guidi explained, "He was killed in the line of duty at Licata in '24."

"Was he *carabinieri* or police?"

"Police."

"That's good. Any foreign languages?"

"Four years of school French."

"People should learn German, these days."

Guidi did not know what to say to that, so he said nothing.

"Well, we'll have to do with what we have," Caruso grumbled. With his nose on the paper, he read through Guidi's file. "It says here you have worked with Germans before."

"Well, in a manner of speaking, not really —"

"Did you get along?"

"I got along."

Caruso stared at him from above his glasses. "Before we get into the Reiner case, let me see your Party card."

Guidi took it out, and handed it across the desk.

Cardinal Giovanni Borromeo, better known to his many friends as Nino, had not – despite his saintly ancestry – started out as a priest. He had once been prominent in the useless young society of Rome, when the city was newly a capital to the unified kingdom of Italy. You could travel it then as an archipelago where hotels stood out like islands of elegance and decadent living in the sea of streets being just then widened and modernized. Borromeo had frequented the racecourse and the theater, had "loved much" as he himself admitted, and had been much loved. "But God loved me best of all," he would unfailingly add these days. "He knew. He knew all along, and when He got me, He wouldn't let go. He's the last of my lovers. Of course," he would conclude, "keeping in mind that God is neither male nor female."

Bora's request for a meeting did not surprise him. He knew Cardinal Hohmann well enough to be in competition with him – a friendly competition but one nonetheless; and he appreciated that the German aide wisely tried to take advantage of it. Still a young man as cardinals go, he figured as fifty-five in his passport, though he was a couple of years older than that. Tall and elegantly built, he spoke Latin with the same heavy Roman accent he put into his Italian speech, and the unaffected ease of one who doesn't have to prove himself.

He'd first met Bora at a papal audience for German officers during Hitler's visit in 1938, and they had fallen in to talking about church music and the organs in Roman churches. Today Bora found him at his house office in Via Giulia, sitting at his desk with a pile of newspapers to his right and empty cups of coffee lining the windowsill. The first thing he wanted to know was how the interview with Hohmann had gone, and despite Bora's reserve, he gleaned what the results had been by the very fact that the officer was appealing to him.

"Don't resort to my common sense because I have none," he lightly told Bora. "I'm not German." When Bora accepted the invitation to sit, and took place on a skinny sofa padded with red brocade, Borromeo smirked. "And I'd rather you just called me 'Cardinal'. Let's leave the 'Eminence' to those who'd like to be Pope." He listened to what Bora had to say, frowning now and then but mostly looking outside of the window, over the well-trimmed oleanders of his balcony, still green in the crisp winter wind. "So, why should I answer differently from Hohmann?" he said then. "You ask us to accept that you cannot, or *will not* curb the excesses of the Fascist administration in Rome."

"I believe I'm telling the cardinal nothing new if I assure him that the German Army is not pleased with any interim government."

"You'd rather have the city to yourselves?"

"We'd rather have no interference from PAI and what else remains of Fascist police units."

"That's neither here nor there. We expect you to curb the zeal of the Blackshirts left in town – even though I'm a Fascist of sorts myself. The Church was Fascist long before *Il Duce* planned his 'March on Rome'. We marched on it in AD 64 with Peter and Paul at the lead." Borromeo rang a bell on his desk. At the timid appearance of a cleric on the threshold, he merely gestured. Shortly thereafter, a tray with a coffee urn and cups was brought in. "I don't trust people who don't like espresso." He ensured that Bora should accept the drink. "Your ambassador gets along with us – why shouldn't the army?"

"The army is not involved in politics, Cardinal."

"But the SS is. The Gestapo is. What you're telling me is that you Germans will not curb any excesses by our police forces, or yours."

Bora finished his coffee and put the cup away. "The cardinal could help by making sure that no police excesses are required." He had never smiled during the interview, and now grew a little testy. "By *Rome underground* we mean more than the catacombs, and the Church seems to have a part in all of it."

"This you wouldn't dare tell Hohmann. It's impudent!"

"And true."

Borromeo crossed his legs, with some impatience lifting his robe to free them. "On Sunday, there's a concert at the Evangelical Church on Via Toscana. Hammerschmidt music – if you attend, I'll give you an answer." He shrugged at Bora's puzzled look. "Oh, yes, I go to Protestant services, now and then. Not dressed like this, of course. But it's good to know what the competition is up to, especially if there's good music to be had."

At Bora's return from his errand, Westphal said, "Damn these priests! It takes them forever to make up their mind, and all we want is for them to take back an impossible request."

Bora was handing him some snapshots of Ciano's execution, which the general glimpsed briefly. "Damn him, too."

"Should we allow publication of them?"

"You'll have to phone Gestapo Colonel Herbert Kappler to find out. Might just as well, since you're bound to run into him."

Bora obeyed.

In his bleak office on Via Tasso, lowering the receiver, Kappler turned to Captain Sutor, who sat with a disinterested slump across from him. "I just spoke to Westphal's aide – who is he?"

Sutor lifted his bullet-head, craning his neck to look into his notebook. "Bora, Martin-Heinz – *von* Bora. Of the Leipzig publishing firm. Son of the late conductor, and stepson of that Prussian swine von Sickingen. Was commander of a Wehrmacht detachment up north."

"What else do we know about him?"

"Half-English. Transferred at the request of the SS, for bungling the transport of Jewish prisoners. Can't touch him, though. Has a stellar military record and lots of friends. Looks younger than his thirty years, bright-eyed and tight-assed, especially for one who spent two years on the Russian front. The field marshal is a personal friend of his stepfather. Old boys' network."

"That ought to count for nothing with us."

Sutor shrugged like an unconcerned bureaucrat. "You asked."

"Well, no matter. He sounds smart enough to watch himself. Point him out to me if he's at the party on Saturday."

That evening Guidi noticed that Francesca Lippi had already eaten dinner, although it was not yet eight o'clock. "The Maiulis are visiting neighbors," she called from the parlor. "You'll have to help yourself."

Guidi ate a small portion of potato salad alone. Through the open door he could see the girl read and pay no attention to him. He made a point of observing whether she wore a ring, and saw none. She sat with a leg tucked under her body, curling up. The tip of her tongue showed red when she wetted her finger to turn the pages. His shyness with women didn't help at times like this. Guidi was moodily rolling himself a cigarette when she called out, "You work with the Germans?"

"No."

"Didn't you ride in a German car on Sunday?"

"It had nothing to do with work."

She looked over from her chair, her hungry little face pinched like a young fox's. "I bet you got information on all of us before you moved in."

Guidi sat back, choosing not to smoke. Antipathy for the Germans was palpable not only in this house but in the streets, and even at the police posts. Only those whose immediate power depended on their presence still played the pro-German game, Caruso first among them. Guidi disliked the Germans, too, and resented being identified with them. Politics was only part of the reason. History, national character, behavior had more to do with it. In that sense Bora was a strange animal, so familiar with things Italian as to somehow cross over. Tonight Guidi could excuse the major's battered idealism, and yet resent him, and be envious of his flair and self-assurance without any desire to emulate him.

12 JANUARY 1944

On Friday morning, while Westphal and Bora read glum reports on the second raid over Brunswick that week, Guidi found a parcel of papers on his office desk.

"What's this?" he asked his right-hand man, an eager policeman named Danza.

"It came from the German Command, Inspector."

Quickly Guidi freed the papers from a criss-cross of rubber bands. "Anything else?"

"Yes, sir. The NCO who brought it said you'll get to report to the German Army."

Guidi felt himself blush. "The hell I will."

Danza nodded toward an envelope on the desk. "That also came for you."

In the envelope, bearing Caruso's signature, was a typewritten note. *While you will keep me regularly apprised of developments concerning the Reiner case, my German counterpart will be General Maelzer. Report to him through General Westphal's office, and specifically to —*

Guidi didn't need to read further to know that Bora's name followed. Friendliness and car rides and the tour of Roman sites: it all made sense now. Angrily leaning over the parcel, Guidi turned pages until he met the first and only name in the list of suspects: the Secretary General of the National Confederation of Fascist Unions, now heading its "detached office" in the city. "My God" escaped him.

Next he called Caruso's office in Piazza del Collegio Romano.

"That's right," the head of police said coolly. "That's why we need a newcomer. The suspect doesn't know *you,* and you don't have to be as discreet as others have to. Keep looking in the dossier, there's plenty about His Excellency's goings-on. The Germans will want his neck, so prove he killed her."

"I understand, Dr Caruso. What then?"

"Then we'll show our Germanic allies that we're as good as they are when it comes to administering justice. His Excellency might be the token we must turn in to them. I ordered that you be issued your own car, Guidi."

Guidi stared at the dossier, uncomfortably reminding himself that Caruso had just finished playing his role of headhunter at the great show trial in Verona. "What happens if we find out that Secretary General Merlo has nothing to do with it?"

"You had best have someone else in hand by then."

*

The Parioli district, on this side of the Tiber due north of the great Villa Umberto Park, had for the past decade been favored by the upper class and the nouveau riches. SS Colonel Ott's house sat at the corner of Viale Romania and Via Duse, hugging it with its sleek lines over the manicured boxwood of the garden. When Bora arrived, several guests were already assembled in the spacious living room. Ott met him at the entrance, handed him a cognac and introduced him to his wife, who'd just flown in for their tenth wedding anniversary. Near the grand piano, Bora saw Dollmann conversing with a man in a similar uniform. Both were slim, fair, with slicked-back hair and angular, sly features, and both were looking into the room.

Mindful of Westphal's advice, Bora came to greet the SS officers. Soon Dollmann walked back with him toward the refreshments table. "Kappler was dying to meet you." He smiled.

"I don't know if I should be flattered, Colonel."

"Because he's head of the Gestapo in Rome? Don't be a prude. He's a charming enough man. Here, have some caviar."

Bora looked straight at him, which was a frank habit of his and often unnerved people. "There is much in this assignment I could learn from you – we both like Italian culture."

"Oh, Kappler does, too. Collects art. Ancient things, prefer-ably." Dollmann looked around with his vulpine eyes. "Unlike men who collect young ones, like the Reiner girl. What else do you know about the story?"

"No more than you do, Colonel. The word is accident or suicide."

"But of course you don't believe that!"

"I believe even stranger things these days."

"She dated a couple of ruffians. Speaking of which, the Allies have taken Cervara, and soon will have it all from Ortona to south of Gaeta."

Bora drank slowly, so as not to have other drinks forced on him when he wanted to gather information.

Dollmann suavely upbraided him. "Finish your drink, I want you to taste some real vodka. It came from better days at Kursk." He reached for a square of toast topped with a creamy mixture. "By the way, what was your specialty in Russia?"

Bora was sure the SS knew already. "Counter-intelligence, related to guerrilla warfare," he answered nonetheless.

"And in northern Italy, as we hear. So. Do you have night-mares?"

"Not about guerrilla warfare." Bora finished his cognac. He took from the closest tray two glasses of vodka, and offered one to Dollmann. "To Rome, *caput mundi*."

"Yes. Head of *our* world, at any rate. Does it include the Vatican?" Dollmann held the vodka before his lips without drinking. "You were at its doorstep twice this week."

"It's the army that keeps me devout." Candidly Bora glanced up from his drink. "Please instruct me if there are more people I ought to meet, in this room and around the Vatican. You are the Reich's prime interpreter and man about town, while I'm new to Rome at war. And I'm not sure I know what *ruffians* means in the context of the Reiner case."

"One at least was our own. And that's all you'll get from this round of drinks."

Midway through the party General Maelzer showed up, merry with drink already and eager for conversation. Bora was introduced by Dollmann. The general went through some pat routine of questions and then said, "You're young, Major, you'll get in the thick of things quickly enough – I don't mind if you screw someone, but I don't approve of liaisons with Ital-ian women."

"I'm happily married, General!"

"If you were happily married you'd be with your wife. You're as well married as wartime allows you."

With this, Maelzer moved on to another circle of guests and a new round of drinks. Bora, who'd married in a hurry on his way to war, was not nearly as secure as he showed. A sensitive and in many ways romantic man, he had for five years shown steadfast commitment in the face of rare furloughs and a superficial wife. As for other things in his life, his love for the object might be well in excess of what it deserved, from the same idealistic stance that made him obdurate in his work.

Moments later, Dollmann rejoined him. "What did he say? There's no getting angry at the *King of Rome* when he's in his cups." By then a cold dinner was served, which neither he nor Bora chose to eat. They sat with their drinks in hand, Bora looking at the couples growing intimate with what the colonel judged to be more than just uptightness.

That night Guidi stayed up late to read the dossier. The only noise in the apartment was the snore rising from Signora Carmela's crippled body. Elsewhere in the building, the neighbors were quiet. Guidi had routinely found out about them: middle-class people, employees and shop clerks, students. There was a small child on the top floor, who could be heard crying in the morning. Across the landing, a flashy, cherry-lipped woman in black received visits from noisy male relatives, and a reclusive old fellow Signora Carmela called *Maestro* – he played the piano, well in Guidi's reckoning. Oddly enough, the one Guidi had been least inquisitive about was Francesca, whose small room was at the other end of the hallway. She left for work early in the morning, and was home by curfew. Whether the Maiulis knew that she was pregnant, he couldn't say either. Her pale, drawn face came to him, the careless way she combed her hair away from it with her fingers as she read, so that it drew a brown wave behind her ear. She didn't smile, spoke little at meals, and answered curtly to everyone.

Magda Reiner, instead, continued to live a vicarious merry life in the snapshots of summers past, so different from the last dreadful images. Her blond, plump and smiling countenance against unknown mountains, alongside unknown friends, was forever safe from injury. In one picture, she laughingly embraced another woman.

As for *Ras* Merlo, Guidi didn't know whether to laugh or cry as he read about him. His given name was Radames, though he went by Rodolfo. Born 1900, *bersagliere* in the bicycle troops during the Abyssinian campaign. Married to Ignazia Pallone since 1930, four children: Vittorio, Adua (known as Aida), Libico (known as Lorenzo) and Cadorna (known as Carletto). Had been instrumental in the creation of the Istituto Forlanini ten years earlier, and presently headed what remained in Rome of the prestigious National Confederation of Fascist Unions. Rumor had it that he had conflated his last name and his wife's under the pseudonym *Piemme*, and authored the words of the well-known North African Campaign song 'Macallè':

> *Là nell'arida terra del Tigrè*
> *nel tramonto del gran sole d'or,*
> *solitario, il forte Macallè*
> *pieno di ricordi sorge ancor!*

Ever since meeting Magda Reiner at a party during the 28 October anniversary of the March on Rome, they'd been inseparable, or nearly so, until her death on 29 December. "Driven by jealousy", as the report indicated without other comments, he was known to have roughed her up before witnesses occasionally. And now the provincial policeman was expected to find out whether he'd pushed her over the windowsill.

For the rest, the data were scanty: the death had occurred after a year's end party, at around seven forty-five in the evening, on the sidewalk below the deceased woman's premises on Via Tolemaide. She'd engaged in sexual intercourse at least once in the hours preceding her death, and though her bedroom and apartment doors were locked, delaying the entrance of the authorities, no keys had been found.

*

A few streets away, Bora left Ott's party at one in the morning, under a drizzle that fell askew and began to be weighed down by snow. He often drove himself, especially after hours, taking different routes through the darkened city. He had to face the fact that he was angry with Dollmann, whose loquacity he had repaid to excess by receiving a burden of intrigue with it.

Though that wasn't all of it, either. Melancholy and loneliness, so well laid away for the past year, had been stirred up from their places and looked ugly now. He did not wish to recognize them as his own, did not wish to forsake invulnerability. Still, the heartless gossip made him sick at actors and scenario. Kappler's affairs, Magda Reiner's affairs. What could Westphal want to hear out of this? It felt like mud in his mouth.

Talk of his wife had come closest to undoing him. The thought of her caused him pain – beyond desire, soreness of love, anguish that made him bristle and kept him awake many nights. She was inside him beyond herself, even. He was defensive about his feelings for her, and Dollmann had asked entirely too many questions after Maelzer's crude words.

"Why, Major, you're in love!" The amused comment had come when both of them had grown less reticent. "I'd even call you *passionate!*"

The suggestion embarrassed him. "I'm a disciplined man," he had pointed out.

"Yes, and passions are what discipline is for, aren't they?"

16 JANUARY 1944

On Sunday, Cardinal Borromeo, in a three-piece suit under his tan coat, was punctually to be found in the Evangelical Church, where 'All Praise Be To You, Jesus Christ' was sung by a bespectacled alto. Seated in the first pew, he gave no sign of recognizing Bora and kept him in suspense until the end of the concert. At that time he informed him that the Holy

See was sympathetic to General Westphal's position. Bora was visibly relieved. He thanked the cardinal and began to leave, when the other unceremoniously retained him in the seat.

"On the other hand, Major, I am shocked to hear that your office is even now collaborating with the Italian police."

Bora denied it was so. "My commander would have informed me were we to be embarrassed before His Holiness by accepting a cooperation we specifically decline."

"Check your sources, dear friend."

Only on Monday Bora found out the truth, in a memo from General Maelzer. "I know nothing about this," Westphal said. "Do you?"

"It's the first time I see it, General."

"Well, Maelzer must have his reasons for involving you in a girl's broken head. But you'll have to deal with the Italian police in your spare time."

"There isn't much that can be done after hours," Bora observed. "Not with the Italians."

"Well, meet this Guidi fellow now and then and listen to his reports." Westphal handed him Maelzer's message. "I don't like it any more than you do. Now we can't tell the Vatican we have no say with the Italian police, and that baboon Caruso will get us in trouble yet."

In the days following 19 January, there was more for Bora to worry about than the head of police. His long hours with Westphal – often extending to fifteen daily – practically ran round the clock after the British advanced beyond the Garigliano River and passed Minturno by the coast on their way to the crossroad village of St Maria Infante. On Thursday, a counter-attack was launched from Ausonia on the affluent south of Cassino, by which time nervous talk arose of an imminent landing. Kappler called in to inquire about the number of soldiers available in Rome for immediate recall to the front, if needed. Bora came up with ten thousand. All day Westphal stayed at Soratte and returned late, tired after his conference with Kesselring. Still he spent most of the night before a map held in place by hastily emptied coffee mugs, evaluating enemy positions and the endless coastal stretch marked for stand-to. Waiting.

Kappler phoned again at four in the morning to warn that Gestapo and SS stood ready to requisition drivers and attendants.

"Go ahead," Westphal replied, yawning into his fist. "If that's what we throw before an invading army, we deserve what we have coming." He looked at Bora, who had been reading charts of the shoreline from Leghorn to Naples. "Well, it doesn't look slow any more," he said. "And the field marshal is right – they bombed too much all around us for it not to happen in the Rome sector. Especially as they hit the Littorio Airfield yesterday."

"It ought to be on this coast, anyway, if reports of activity in the Naples harbor are correct."

"But where, and when?" Westphal passed his hands over the bristle of his cheeks. "Be good, Bora. Shave and run by Gestapo headquarters to see what Kappler has in mind."

21 JANUARY 1944

The calendar day celebrated the feast of St Agnes with a Gospel reading from Matthew, the Parable of the Wise and Foolish Virgins. During the light hours, mixed reports were phoned in from the front, and by nightfall the only news of interest pertained to a heavy air raid on London. In a headstrong state of premonition, Westphal stayed up until late. Then, mostly because Kesselring had agreed to relent the alert after three tense days, he told Bora he would go lie down. "Call me if anything happens."

Bora set to keep watch in the dead hours that followed, when even vigilance born of foreboding whittled down under physical weariness. Nothing had happened. Nothing might happen. Around him and this room the whole great building seemed enchanted, bound in silence. Shortly after midnight, he began a letter to his wife, reread it and decided not to send it.

A cigarette later, his mind wandered to disparate and irrelevant subjects, as in dreams. Who was the SS Magda Reiner had dated, and was God really Borromeo's last lover? He wondered if it was true that Kappler collected Etruscan art, like Dollmann said. Was this the time to collect anything? And so through the night. Coffee grew cold in his cup, names on the maps became confused scribbles on mountainsides along wavy seashores. At one point Bora turned the lights off and went to open the window. It was like plunging his face in icy water, bracing and beneficial. Outside, the late hour stood calm, depthless. A thin haze stretched like a canopy of gauze over the city. He sat at his desk in the dark, facing the window. Finally, at three o'clock, the news came. Bora collected himself after leaving the telephone, and on his way to the general's room he took time to straighten his uniform. Westphal didn't need much to be awakened. He stared at the door where his aide's figure stood straight, bare-headed. "Where?" he asked at once.

"*Codename Option Richard.*"

"Anzio?"

"And Nettuno." Bora looked away while the general furiously threw his clothes back on. "They're making straight for the interior."

"Call Soratte at once." Even as he left the threshold, Westphal's voice summoned him back. "Stand ready to evacuate the building and the city."

In the early hours of the morning, the magnitude of the disaster was first assessed. By this time emergency troops had been dispatched to cordon off the landing area, and the void behind them was likely to be overwhelmed any time. But at noon, the line still visibly held.

"If they only hesitate today and tomorrow," Westphal wished out loud, bright-eyed with anguish and hope, "you may yet unpack your trunk."

Bora found it easy not to smile. "It's less than sixty-five miles away. In Russia we traveled them in one hour."

"You were not facing German soldiers. No, no. Schlemm and Herr are doing everything right. The 65th Division is a resurrected ghost, but we'll have the 362nd and the rest soon enough, if only we hold until then. The Panzer troops will." Carelessly Westphal threw his greatcoat on. "I'm off to Soratte, and won't be back until von Mackensen shows up. If Kappler calls for men, give him what he asks."

Bora followed him out of the office. "The power of news being what it is, by your leave I suggest that in the next few days we'll see renewal of partisan aggression in Rome."

"All right, I'll make sure the field marshal hears the voice of experience – and I promise I'll sandbag my car. Speaking of experience, have we heard from Holz?"

"We heard from his staff. He was killed earlier today."

"For shame. Well, get some sleep when you can. Any calls from the Vatican, don't let through unless it's the Secretary of State and up. You know what to do if the enemy breaks through." About to leave, Westphal seemed startled, but immediately turned with a grin to Bora's pale and unmoved countenance. "What do you know? You can hear the cannon from Rome."

2

By Sunday, it seemed the Germans had vanished overnight.
Their field-gray cars no longer patrolled the streets. Even the
fierce mouths of tank guns had retreated from alleys and little
tucked-back squares. Wild rumors of liberation were whispered
and denied, but the deep roll of artillery to the west did not lie.
Guidi was all the more surprised when Bora's well-bred voice
invited him over the telephone to a late lunch.

"It's absolutely impossible, Major." He made up his mind to
refuse. "I have work to do."

"All right. I'll come there, then."

Guidi had no chance to reply, because the receiver had
already been clicked down. He scrambled for the next ten
minutes to clear his desk, knowing that Bora did not have a
long way to travel from Via Veneto to Via Del Boccaccio. Soon
the black Mercedes pulled in by the curb, and there was Bora,
overcoat nonchalantly doubled on his left arm, getting out and
climbing the steps with his stiff, quick gait. "Leave the door
open," he told Guidi. "I have lunch coming."

"Here?"

"Why not?" Bora didn't say he had hardly eaten in the last
two frantic days. "I'm hungry."

The men in the police office made themselves scarce. As
for Bora, he took advantage of the fact that no one would ask
him about the military situation. So he showed far more leisure

than matters warranted, amicably inquiring about Guidi's new address, and whether he could be of assistance, "now that it seems we'll be working together."

Guidi watched him stand by the window with his back to it, in apparent disregard of prudence, and suspected Bora may be trying to hide signs of sleeplessness or worry. He joined him to take a better look at his face. "Do you mean you didn't know as of our first meeting?"

"Why, no, I only found out a week ago. I'm glad, though." In order to face Guidi, Bora turned toward the overcast light of day. On his fine-grained skin, character lines still disappeared after a change of expression. "Why are you looking at me that way?" He laughed.

Guidi shrugged. "I was thinking that it's not a good idea to talk by the window," he simply said. Drawing back into the room, he gestured toward a chair. "Will you take a seat?"

"No, thanks. Working in Rome is sedentary enough."

There was such negligence in the reply, Guidi was tempted to believe there might be less to the invasion than rumored. But Bora did look tired, and there was no denying that.

Over lunch they discussed the Reiner case.

"Rome is ours." Bora dropped the political hint as if he were speaking of real estate. "No murderer will get out – if there's a murderer. We want him."

"The *King of Rome* wants him," Guidi specified mildly. "You can't possibly approve of Maelzer, Major. He's a drunken oaf. The Romans can't stand him."

"Well, I'm not Roman."

"But I think I know you better than that."

Bora ate slowly, without looking up. "You don't know me at all." And while Guidi discovered his own appetite in the presence of good food, the German seemed to have lost interest in the meal. Sitting back, he took a house key out of his pocket, and laid it on the table. "My schedule is tight, so we'll visit the Reiner place right after this."

"If you don't mind, I'll come in my own car."

"Fine. I'd rather go in the morning, but I'm a bit tied up." It was only one of Bora's understatements, since he was due to visit the Anzio front on behalf of General Westphal. But his composure was genuine, because he was not afraid. "Tomorrow after work, however, we're off to a Pirandello play. I'll tell you why later on."

At the Reiner apartment on Via Tolemaide – a side street of Via Candia, in the Prati district – Bora leaned to look out of the window at the sidewalk hemming the street four floors down. "Did anybody see her fall?" he asked Guidi.

"No. Curfew was at seven those days, and it was past that time. As prescribed, all lights were off. A neighbor says he heard a woman scream between seven-thirty and eight, but he's not sure it had anything to do with the incident."

Bora turned. "It's not a cold winter by German standards, but it *is* cold. Why would her bedroom window be open at night?"

"Perhaps for the very purpose of ending her life. Notwithstanding the absence of keys – someone could have picked them up from the street if she was holding them when she fell – we can't rule out suicide, or even an unlikely accident. I'll look into every possibility."

While Guidi began searching the room, Bora remained by the windowsill, moodily observing the minute debris of life on it – a pigeon's silvery waste, lint caught up in it, a cinder speck flown here from God knows where. *How little remains after our death*, he thought. His next question came negligently over the rattle of windowpanes, caused by far away artillery. "What was she wearing at the time of death?"

With his head in the wardrobe, Guidi pulled an envelope from his pocket, and handed it over. "Here are the photos. You may want to take a look between meals."

Bora looked at once. "They're horrible."

"You can see she was wearing a nightgown and a robe. Next you'll ask me if someone was here with her, and I have no answer for that. Out of twelve, only two other apartments in the house are tenanted. There was a seasonal party on the floor below, and enough noise for people not to realize what had happened. A policeman found her at seven fifty-five. Although she was undeniably past help, they transported her to the neighborhood pharmacy. Its owner, Dr Mannucci, had the common sense of declaring her dead for good." As he spoke, Guidi opened drawers and poked into them. "By the way, Major, someone has come here before us. Except for her bed – a pillowcase is missing, did you notice? – this room has been straightened out."

"I will inquire," Bora said.

"It'd help if I knew what reputation the victim had in your community. Twenty-seven, unmarried or legally separated – the reports conflict – and 'not too good-looking but vivacious.' That's how a co-worker described her in the dossier."

"I haven't read it yet."

"Well, it isn't enough to go on. Here's Magda Reiner's passport photo."

Bora glanced at the document Guidi handed him. "Some sources," (he meant Dollmann, who had given him an earful of gossip about the story), "suggest she seemed to be actively seeking a husband, or a similar domestic arrangement."

"Among the Italians or the Germans?"

"Both." Bora leafed through the passport, and gave it back. "As for the lesbian angle, it came up after an office party where things got out of hand." Because Guidi stared, Bora repeated, annoyed, "*Out of hand.* Kissing, touching, and the like."

"How do you know?"

"I was told by a colleague who attended. But you're just making me talk, because from what I understand, you already have a suspect."

Guidi passed his fingers on the dustless bed table. "A fairly untouchable one. He's *Ras* Merlo, one of the last and highest-ranking Party officials in Rome."

"Well, could it be?"

"Judge for yourself, Major. He's a henpecked middle-aged Romeo with a brood of children. His oversized wife is known as 'the Grenadier', and apparently not beyond striking him in anger. Jealousy is hinted at as a motive, whether or not it'd be enough for him to kill. He seems to have a history of roughing up occasional girlfriends. We can't place him in this building on that night, but someone looking very much like him was seen in a distraught state shortly after the incident in Via Santamaura."

"A parallel to this street." Bora closed the window. Facing the room, he stared at Magda's undone bed, and then away from it. "What was he doing there?"

"Throwing up by the open market's garbage cans. But I should add he lives on Piazzale degli Eroi, not far from here."

"Does he realize you're on to him?"

"We've been good about playing the accident card. Merlo might suspect there's an investigation, but he doesn't know for sure. More importantly, he doesn't know me. As long as the official word holds, he'll have no real reason to watch his step."

"Why not call him in and straighten things out at once?"

Guidi remembered how Bora asked questions for the sake of being provocative. "Clearly not even Caruso wants to touch this one directly. Though he may take it from his wife, Merlo has a reputation for vindictiveness with political enemies."

"Ah. Not to speak of what he'd do to *you*. I get it. Anyway, tomorrow night we'll have a chance to see him at the theater. It's a command performance, and he'll be there."

Bora did not follow when Guidi went looking through the rest of the apartment, three rooms in all. At Guidi's return, he was sitting at the foot of the girl's bed, weary or melancholy, or unwell. Likely to avoid questions about himself, he came to his feet at once. "Let's go," he snapped, "I can't stay here all day." As they faced each other in the narrow elevator, however, Bora said without prompting, "The gossip is that she began secretarial work in Stuttgart. She was from Renningen, nearby. Was attached to the German Olympic Committee in '36, took on with a foreign athlete, and there were consequences to the relationship. It appears she was briefly married to an army photographer, served with army headquarters, and after a legal separation managed to find a post with the German embassy in Paris. She'd been in Rome six months, and apparently liked it very well. 'Fun-loving' they told me. No more than a social drinker, not much more than an easy lay."

Guidi had not expected the intervention. "But of course," he thought he should say, "you heard all this from men."

"No." They had reached the ground floor, and as Bora walked through the shady archway leading to the main door, Guidi could tell by the stiffness of his torso that he was in pain. "Actually, my first official act in Rome was to phone her mother. It seems a childless cousin is raising Magda's daughter in Renningen. But it's true that I haven't sat to chatter with her girlfriends. That's policemen's work."

Having parted ways with Guidi, Bora walked to the pharmacy where the dead girl had been brought. It was an interesting narrow building on Via Andrea Doria, with an oval plate by the door that read "Free Medications Distributed to the Poor." Inside, with the pretext of buying a painkiller, he conversed with Dr Mannucci, asking him first about the collection of fine apothecary vases on display, and then about the events of 29 January. The pharmacist – a hale old man with an old-fashioned mustache and a keen interest in the humanities – no doubt understood the reasons for Bora's inquiry, but graciously acted as though it were just a friend's concern. Patiently picking up and setting aside the well-fed cat that played with pen and papers on the counter ("Down, Salolo, down. You know better"), he said, "Yes, I did suggest that she be carried to Santo Spirito's hospital. *Carried*, mind you – not rushed. You understand there was no reason to rush her to an emergency room, as her skull was crushed beyond repair and even recognition."

Bora had laboriously opened the Cibalgina container, and now swallowed two tablets. Showing a soldier's pragmatic empathy, "The incident must have required much cleaning of your beautiful floor," he observed.

"Well, blood is less problematic than vomit – and that, too, we had to clean up on the same night."

"Oh? One of the policemen who brought her in?"

Dr Mannucci looked Bora in the eye, both of them fully understanding the gist of the conversation. "Not at all."

At his return home, Guidi found its small population in a state of hushed exhilaration. Tenants from all floors had gathered in the parlor, where Francesca curled like a cat on the floor closest to the radio. "You must hear this." Signora Carmela grabbed him by the arm. "The Americans have really come!"

Her husband hastened to top the news. "The Germans are pulling out. They say there are none left in the city – they're leaving by way of the Cassia."

Guidi glanced at Francesca, who remained turned to the radio, listening intently with her face low. "Who's saying this?" he asked.

"Who cares? The Americans are here!" The cherry-lipped woman – Pompilia Marasca, known as Pina – was ecstatic. "Just think of it – the *Americans!*"

Guidi stared at the odd circle of people. Smiling, the professor said he'd use today's date as a lotto number. The two students from upstairs – on the uneasy verge of being drafted – nudged one another and cracked juvenile jokes of relief. Signora Carmela blew kisses to the saints in their glass domes. "I hate to tell you," Guidi spoke up. "The Germans have not left. The Americans may be coming, but there are Germans still here. Go see for yourselves."

"It doesn't mean anything!" Angry-eyed, Francesca looked up at him, her paleness stark in the dim little parlor. "It's the end for the Germans, can't you see? It's a matter of time!"

"And," the professor whistled through his false teeth, "how long can it take some seventy thousand fully armed men to reach us? I used to run bicycle races to Anzio and back."

The students swore they had seen the glare of battle in the past nights, contradicting each other as to direction and hour, but agreeing that it was the American advance.

"Let's hope you're right," Guidi said.

"What happens if the Germans don't leave Rome?" Pompilia suddenly considered. "Does it mean they'll fight in the streets?"

"I expect so."

"*Oh, Jesus!*"

"Except that they'll get it from all sides." Francesca stood up to leave, contemptuously. What else she meant to say – and Guidi wished she would not – remained unsaid. She pulled back her hair with both hands, hard, until her features were lifted and she looked like a strange geisha. After she left the room, it was as though the space had grown dimmer yet.

The perspective of a battle in Rome started a disagreement as to whether the Germans would line up outside the walls, or make a stand in the Vatican. "Open city or not, the Allies could carpet-bomb Rome," one of the students said. At the ill-advised words, Pompilia saw fit to slump into a faint at Guidi's feet.

"Someone turn the radio off," he ordered. "No point in worrying ourselves sick until some reliable news comes on the air. Professor, will you help the lady?"

Pompilia remained in a stiff faint despite all gentle slaps and sprinkles of water, and only when Guidi relented enough to say he'd take her by the ankles if someone took her by the armpits, she came to with a flutter of eyelids. "I can walk," she piped, lifting herself and proceeding out of the room.

That night Guidi went to bed early. He slept fitfully, dreaming that the Americans had come and he told them how to get to Bora's office. In the dream Bora phoned him to say that he appreciated having the Americans over, since they would all go to a Pirandello play. But the Americans killed Bora instead.

47

The room was odiously dark and cold when Guidi awoke with a sore neck. Unable to find a comfortable position, he tossed for some time, until his trained ear was alerted to the opening of the door at the end of the hallway. Francesca was going to the bathroom. He heard a second door squeak on its hinges as she pulled it closed.

Guidi sat up to fluff his pillow. Germans, Americans – Bora might have been pretending today, and even now he could be on his way north with a retreating army. Back north, where the partisans had as good a chance of killing him as the Americans. *Good riddance*, Guidi wanted to say, but he didn't really mean it as far as Bora was concerned.

He lay back. What took Francesca so long? He hadn't heard water flushed or running, nor had the door opened a second time. Guidi waited a few more minutes, then slipped out of bed. In the dark he groped for the door, listening. Carefully he turned the key in the lock, and stepped out into the hallway. No candlelight filtered from under the bathroom door. Before knocking, he felt the door for resistance, and it gave way under his hand. "Francesca?" he whispered, forgetting the embarrassment that would follow her answer. But no answer came. A chilly draft prompted him to turn the light on: the bathroom was empty, and the window on the street stood ajar.

24 JANUARY 1944

Monday night, Bora said Pirandello helped him understand Italians.

"You must be joking." Guidi took exception. "His plays are absurd."

"Exactly." From where they sat, now that the intermission allowed a full view of the audience, *Ras* Merlo's pomade-shiny head could be seen bobbing up and down at the side of a bright green hat. Bora looked in that direction with an unkind grin.

"The man has the authorities of two nations at his heels, and he's watching a tale about getting caught."

All evening Bora had been of a merry disposition, scarcely due to the sarcasm of the play, and closer to relaxation than Guidi had ever seen. Guidi could share none of the good cheer. He had stayed awake until dawn, waiting for Francesca's return to the house. Without confronting her directly, he'd called for a routine check on her background. He didn't know what he was looking for, but his heart was heavy.

Soon Bora headed for another box, where Guidi saw him greet an elegant group, kiss the ladies' hands and chat nearly until the end of the intermission. "People I used to know," he explained at his return. "Is Merlo still here? I don't see his gummy head."

"He's just picking up something she dropped."

At the next intermission, Bora left the box again. Guidi saw him below, easily finding his way across the partly empty row of seats to accost Merlo and his companion. Next he was clumsily stepping on the man's foot, and apologizing gave him a chance to make small talk. He was even invited to sit to the left of the young woman, where he spent the rest of the intermission. He rejoined Guidi when the lights – miraculously working tonight – were already off.

"Are you out of your head, Major?"

"Why? Merlo doesn't know me."

"He knows you're a German aide-de-camp."

"There's scads of us, Guidi. I wanted to make sure I got close in case the power fails. Don't be a killjoy. He looks like a chummy ad for Brillantina Linetti, and she's… Well, what can I say. She's half his age."

"Well, don't be misled by his fat innocent looks. If he hasn't done in the Reiner girl, he was directly involved in the Matteotti affair."

"You mean his *murder*?" There was no discouraging Bora tonight. "A nasty way of disposing of socialist opposition. Did

I tell you I was in Rome when it happened, twenty or so years ago? My stepfather's wife told me how they stuffed the poor man in a shallow grave in the Campagna. Yes, I can see Merlo digging it. My first summer here, and everybody and his brother searched for this cadaver that no one wanted to find. How can you tell me the Italians aren't absurd?" He sat back, lowering his voice as the curtain rose. "It *was* Merlo throwing up in the neighborhood of the Reiner house, by the by. How do I know? Not everyone is afraid of telling on a Fascist *Ras*, as it seems."

When they left the theater it was very cold and clear. Even Bora admitted it was cold. A distinct rumble of cannon fire was audible past the expanse of city blocks. Guidi glanced at him in the semi-darkness, and Bora said, "It's a beautiful night." The truth was that after his visit at the front he knew how by tonight the worst was past, and the enemy contained. But he didn't let Guidi have a chance to surmise that much. "I just received a telegram from my stepfather," he told him. "My wife is coming next week."

25 JANUARY 1944

Danza told Guidi, "Looked into all you asked for, Inspector. The girl is actually registered under her mother's name, Di Loreto. No father's name given. Has attended courses at the Academy of Fine Arts, goes by Lippi and calls herself an art student. Has been supplementing her income at a stationery shop by posing for painters, which is apparently what her mother does for a living. Not much else to say – works at this place, this stationery shop on Piazza Ungheria."

"Friends, men and women?"

"Acquaintances. Goes to the movies with them, occasionally. No word of a steady boyfriend. If she's pregnant, we don't know by whom or for how long."

"Try to find out. Anything else?"

"It depends on what you're looking for. We can have her followed, Inspector. In case something turns up."

The cold facts were no more significant than those about Magda Reiner, a parallel that made Guidi uncomfortable somehow. Guidi jotted down the names of the students and the cherry-lipped woman. "No. Look further into these, too."

Danza read, and laughed. "She's a familiar one!"

"What do you mean, is she on file?"

"With the vice squad, she is. Nothing big. Soliciting, mostly. She's behaved for the past two years or so – not so many men around, I guess."

"Politics?"

"Pina? Nothing from the navel up."

Were it not for his uniform, Lieutenant Colonel Kappler would look insignificant. Far from consoling Bora, who'd been invited to Gestapo headquarters to discuss anti-partisan operations, the thought oppressed him somehow. Captain Sutor, after introducing him with unfriendly rigidity, left at once when Kappler walked around his desk to shake hands.

"I'm glad you could make it, Major. I've meant to chat with you since we met at Ott's party. After all, we share a long experience in dealing with trouble. Did you hear that Graziani skipped town?"

With the only window shuttered and the electric light on, being in the office was claustrophobic. Bora kept on guard, careful not to appear tense. This was the time to gauge each other's nature, a careful time of observation and taking of measures. He was aware of Kappler's scrutiny and the need to convey an image of ease. "I'm not attached to Counter-intelligence here in Rome. The military end of guerrilla operations is where my experience resides, and stops."

Kappler laughed. "General Westphal told me of your concern about partisan activity after the Anzio landing. The two bombings on Wednesday and yesterday's attacks proved you to be right. I share your concern, and it seems only wise for us to coordinate our efforts. No matter how long it'll take the Allies to get here, you know, it's a lease we have. Nothing else." Because Bora faced him squarely, Kappler added, "My estimate is two to six months, perhaps less." Again Bora did not encourage him, so Kappler nodded to himself, reaching for a sheet of paper on his desk. "We're terminal, as far as Rome is concerned. That's why we should make our arrangements."

"I've done most of my work in Russia, Colonel. Only some of the principles apply to Rome. It all depends on how ideological the partisans are, and how much community support they receive. Surely they have the advantage of close proximity."

Kappler handed him a list of underground organizations. "They're ideologically a mixed bag, but they all hate us. It comes to the same."

Bora read. Without looking up, he said, "The terrain is as difficult as I can think of, whether or not we move the curfew back two hours. It equates jungle conditions as far as I'm concerned, and we know what portions of the city take the place of impregnable redoubts."

His allusion to Vatican property prompted a response from Kappler. "And sanctuary, literally."

Bora glanced away from the paper, but not directly at Kappler; rather, at the map of Rome on the wall facing him. "No doubt, outside the city weapons are being dropped by the Allies. When I was up north, the number of partisans was estimated at about a thousand nationally. They lacked good weapons. Brixia grenades, cheap pistols, no caches to speak of. How many do you calculate are passive and part-time members now; how many are active and full-time?"

Kappler gave him some figures, which Bora did not dispute. "But there are plenty of foreign agents hiding in Rome. American, British – people who, as yourself, speak the language well enough to be taken for Italians. Some four hundred escaped Allied POWs are rumored to be around. God knows, they may be attending our parties. And, with colleagues like Dollmann…"

Bora ignored the comment. He took a handful of documents out of his briefcase. "I brought copies of army directives we received between the end of November and the beginning of December 1941. You are welcome to them. In Russia partisan units were up to five hundred in number. They had huge land expanses at their disposal, knew the terrain, spoke the dialect and could boast highly indoctrinated commanders."

"Did you hang a few?"

"I hanged more than a few."

"But didn't units like yours grant life to those who surrendered, which was the neat army habit early in the war?"

"I spoke Russian well. The commanders who didn't were at a disadvantage in preparing propaganda leaflets and talking things over with the population. Indiscriminate hangings only make more trouble unless you're ready to keep the pressure on. As you are aware, Colonel, ruling by terror in occupied territory has its drawbacks."

"We're not dealing with illiterate bunglers in Rome."

"Except that one can be literate and a bungler. Our trouble in Italy will be north of here, as in the recent past. We might even see the formation of 'partisan republics' on the Soviet model. As for Rome, I would watch the Fascist calendar of saints – irregulars tend to launch attacks on significant dates, which is ideologically correct but predictable."

Kappler had a strange expression, half-admiring and half-malicious. "In any case, we should make sure trouble doesn't happen. I am talking, I believe, to one who understands what personal toll there's to pay for courage. That is, you must harbor *some* bitterness." Bora's silence encouraged Kappler. "Let me show you how we are doing our part, Major."

What followed was a guided tour of the other floors of the large building, where apartments had been turned into cell blocks. Bora noticed partitioning, bricked windows, and how the stuffiness bore the peculiar mawkish odor of interrogation rooms, male sweat and blood washed over with suds. None of this outwardly unnerved him, as Kappler could tell.

Leading him back to his office, Kappler was in fact engaging. "We have another location near the train station – the Italian branch. It's not as efficient, but it works. These – what happens in this building – are the facts of life, every bit as much as what happens on the battlefield. We all stand to know them and be a part to them."

"Well." Bora thought it was as good a time as any to draw the line. He said, "I may stand to know them, Colonel, but I'm not a part to them."

"Lucky for you that you don't have to deal with the reality my seventy-three men and I face every day. But I'm sure you don't mean what you say. Why else would Kesselring have brought you to Rome?" Kappler grinned. "You're as seduced by discipline as I am. It makes it hard for us to differentiate between personal anger and duty. Didn't you lose a brother in Russia?"

"He was shot down south of Kursk, yes."

"Missing or dead?"

Bora kept steady, by long habit of self-control. "I retrieved his body myself."

"What a blow for your parents. I hope you have other siblings. No? And you'd been in Stalingrad to the bitter end, yourself. I am in awe of your even-mindedness. And I grieve for your brother, as we are *all* army brothers."

Bora was so shamelessly grateful for the words, he felt his critical sense slipping from him. Whatever he answered, it took him until the end of the meeting to realize that he was lost, polluted by Kappler's talk whether or not he'd betrayed himself by agreeing to any of it.

The last thing Kappler told him was, "By the way, we just arrested the half-Jew Foa. Assure General Westphal he won't have to worry about the old man's ranting any more."

After Bora left, Captain Sutor poured out his discontent about the visit.

"I'm *not* being unjust, Colonel. I know the army. He's army, there's nothing to be gained from relating to him, and I don't trust him after what Lasser said."

Kappler waved indulgently. "Lasser has a tendency to go hysterical. It isn't the first time he's tried to burn somebody on flimsy charges. He and Bora had a personality conflict, and Lasser is very loud."

Sutor puckered his face, swallowing spite. "I think you're making a mistake by being friendly to this Bora, Colonel. I'd have shown him nothing of our facilities. It's going right back to Westphal and Kesselring. And Dollmann likes him."

"It's just like Dollmann, isn't it? They'll maneuver with one another like chess players, which is just fine. They're both educated and Catholic – the only flaw from Dollmann's point of view is that Bora's straight."

"All the same, sir, I stand by what I said. I don't like him and you will be sorry you did."

Kappler picked up his cap from the desk and put it on. "I think it makes you uneasy that he may discover you dated Magda Reiner, and that your record with the ladies in Paris is so enviable. Let's go and talk to Foa, Sutor. We know about *him*. He's got enough Jew in him to squeal on his own."

27 JANUARY 1944

"Do you find her attractive, Major Bora?"

"I'm not sure 'attractive' is the right word. She doesn't look much like a wolf. She's more like the abstraction of a wolf, sleek and hairless except for her mane. She's alert and threatening, I'd say. Not loving, or loving in a fierce way."

Dollmann nodded. Alone as they were in the Fourth Room of the Capitoline Museum, he walked around the sandbagged bronze statue, and without touching them, he passed his hand under the skinny breasts hanging from her body. "*They near the She-Wolf's tits, and thrive / On milk never intended for them...*"

"Ovid?"

"Bravo. Still, the late addition of the Twins is much too ornate for her sternness. What would you say she actually represents?"

Bora was thinking of the animal of his nightmares, but smiled. "The tribal totem to be expected of a society of shepherds. You make a sacred symbol out of what you fear most."

"Or a taboo. Note how her stance is firm rather than dynamic, Major. She's surveying a danger which is at a distance or no larger than she is, straight to the side. Protecting the children entails no loving glance but a watchful gaze around for danger. Firmness, watchfulness, a worried threat. You wouldn't get close, and though she isn't snarling – her mouth is not contracted, nor her nose wrinkled – she could bite your hand off."

"She did," Bora calmly said.

Dollmann smiled. "No pun was intended, but there's a connection between her and our being here, at some level. I used to think that ideologically we were her children."

"Perhaps Ovid meant us – we're the danger she's guarding against."

"I think we're both. We fed at her breast and resented it and came back, grown, to worry her. We're as uncivilized, as ungrateful as that."

Bora brought his right hand close to the she-wolf's mouth, fingers extended as if to feed her. "She rules in the end."

"*Caput mundi.* Head of the world." Dollmann rocked on the balls of his feet, watching him. In civilian clothes and a bow tie, he had the groomed appearance of a British professor rather than an SS. In the lonely room of the museum, he said in English, "Kappler is not the one to watch out for. Sutor is."

On Friday, Guidi waited for Francesca in front of the stationery store. If she was surprised, she said nothing, not even when he tipped his hat and began walking alongside her.

"Look," he said, "I don't know if I should be doing you this favor, but it's been twice already that I heard you go out at night."

Her scarf was coming undone, and when he reached for it, she pulled back. "So?" She wrapped the woolen cloth around her shoulders, hardly a protection against the bitter wind. "You're going to arrest me for breaking a dumb six-to-five curfew? *Mamma mia*, you must come from the moon!" And when Guidi began to answer, she squared her narrow face at him. "If I go to see my boyfriend, I'm not about to stop 'cause you say so."

Guidi had no reason to be disappointed by her words. Still he said, tartly, "It's because of sabotage that the Germans just took two more hours out of our day. It isn't just the Italian police keeping an eye on things. See him during the day."

"As if I don't have to work during the day. Besides, he's married." She grinned, but it was an uncovering of lips as animals have, and there was no humor in it. It was for a moment as if her skull were showing through the skin, marring her beauty.

Guidi found himself bluffing; quoting empty police talk, because in the end there was no arguing the point. "I'm warning you. Find another way to meet him, or I'll have to turn you in. I know where you're *really* going."

"I bet you don't." She tried, slowly, but was less sure of herself.

"I followed you," he lied. "What will it be?"

Her lips were pale with cold, chapped. She turned away from the wind, wary or discouraged or just unhappy. Not helpless, but unhappy. "All right," she said, making Guidi wait for the next words. "I'll quit seeing him at night."

Guidi could have left now. Instead, he continued to walk at her side to the tramway stop. There, because she was trembling, he undid his overcoat and put it on her shoulders. Francesca did not react; looking away from him, she seemed already a resentful prisoner, whose friendship might now be impossible for him to gain.

Later that day, at the office, Danza made little of things. "There's a mess of people holed up all over the place, Inspector. Anybody could be meeting anybody. Folks came out of the woodwork in the past months, and went back into it twice in number. Jews, monarchists, dissenters, you name it. Deserters by the score, writers, officers from the Royal Carabineers – all watching out for you, me, the Germans, the Fascists. What can we do about it? Either we play political police or we ignore the whole. She sees her boyfriend at night? If that's what she does, good for her. If that's not it, then…"

"No," Guidi said. "I think that's it." And it weighed on him that he might be twisting the law for a woman, as he had risked doing up north only a month ago.

Danza offered cautious support. "So, ignore it. Since the Americans landed a week ago, we've had assassination attempts, slashed tires, gas depots blown up, and the Germans are taking things in their own hands. With all due respect, I couldn't care less about a girl that cats around."

At his return home, the last person Guidi wanted to meet in the stairwell was Pompilia Marasca. He tried to avoid her, but she managed to keep him there by blocking the stairs.

"A nice fright, you men gave me," she said. "After I came to the other night I was ill for hours and hours, just thinking there might be fighting in the streets."

Guidi shrugged. "Who knows. There may not be."

"Women like myself have to be very careful, you see. I'm all nerves. Since my husband passed away, all nerves – nothing else. What you see is nothing but nerves."

Her nerves were well hidden under the padding of breast and hips, Guidi thought. He faced her, with an ear to the other noises in the house – voices, steps, the halting whimper of the child upstairs. Francesca was just then coming in from the street. She walked by, indifferent to both, bound for the Maiulis' door. Pompilia's cherry lips tightened. "She should be with her nose up in the air, the shameless hussy. Who does she think she is? She's even *showing*!"

It was the first comment that interested Guidi. "Showing what?" he said stolidly.

"Haven't you noticed? My God, you men never notice anything. Even the Maiulis, who are the least informed in the world, wonder whether there's anything amiss with the young lady. Amiss, indeed! I should say there is. Things one wouldn't believe! Pay attention, next time – it's still early, but it's showing all right. Since she came, she hasn't spoken ten words to me, and I've been in this house going on three years now. Well, what can you expect from the likes of her?"

Guidi drove his hands into his coat pockets. "I don't know what you mean."

"Her mother's a Jewish you-know-what, and as for her father – he's a bishop or something. That's how she got to go to school and all that. People heard her brag about it."

With his fingertips, Guidi savored the fleece-lined space of his pockets, where Francesca's chafed hands had burrowed as they waited for the tramway. "Sorry you got a scare," he said. "Let's hope nothing happens around here."

"Nothing? Why, just before you came home there was a big blast at Piazza Verdi."

Guidi didn't bother to say he'd been stopped by a German patrol while he drove past the Mint, and despite his documents the intolerant gendarmes had dragged him out of the car before allowing him to continue.

Pompilia pouted with open hands held up to her face. "See how pale I am? I almost passed out. When you're all nerves, it's a constant struggle just to keep your sanity."

Bora and Guidi didn't meet again until late on Saturday, in front of the Hotel d'Italia, only a street-length away from Guidi's *Pubblica Sicurezza* office, at the other end of Via Rasella. The hotel faced the imposing gate of Villa Barberini, its scrolling metalwork appearing out of the dark and fading quickly as the dimmed headlights of passing German vehicles struck it.

"Let's go to my room," Bora said. "I was able to trace one of Magda's colleagues – you might be interested in what she had to say."

Minutes later, taking advantage of the fact that power was on, Guidi took notes on the narrow desk by Bora's window. A photo of his wife – it was the same woman whose portrait the major had at work, in any case – sat on the desk, with a small snapshot of a German pilot tucked in one corner and a dried edelweiss on the other side.

"Wouldn't she tell you whom Magda was afraid of, Major?"

"She doesn't know. What's for sure is that Magda didn't want friends over, and no longer asked for rides from the embassy. She was drinking more, and 'acting strange', whatever that means. You understand, my informant is the girl who was reassigned after the famous party. She says that everyone was drunk, their kissing was just a lark, and Magda got to keep her job because she had a boyfriend in the SS."

"Any idea who that might be?"

"Not yet. But I can tell you who else lives at her address."

Guidi flipped through his notebook. "Ground floor, a retired soprano, deaf and senile, never goes out. Third floor, three German officers, no longer there. Correct?"

"Correct. The officers are elsewhere now," (Bora meant Anzio, Guidi knew) "but they have an alibi and witnesses. They were celebrating at their place, one floor down from Magda's apartment. The rest of the building is untenanted and used for storage by the embassy."

"Well, whoever had a key to her apartment searched it professionally before we got there. I doubt it was the killer, so – whether they were destroying evidence or merely removing potentially embarrassing clues, the investigation has been impaired from the start. Magda dated Merlo, she dated an SS, she was afraid of somebody. As of today, Merlo is the only one we can place near her house on the night she died, and I must tell you, Major Bora, that the chief of police is convinced of his guilt."

"Maybe the chief of police is right. Or maybe he doesn't like Merlo. I hear that unlike his corrupt colleagues at Braschi Palace, Merlo is true blue when it comes to graft."

For some time, neither of them spoke. Bora sat in the armchair at the foot of the bed, his eyes fixed on his wife's photograph. Following his stare, Guidi, too, observed the image again. An athletic blonde with a discontented air, elegantly coiffed, holding a dog by the leash on some smart city street.

"Her name is Benedikta," Bora said.

"Very handsome."

"She is, thank you. I haven't seen her in a year." Bora fumbled with cigarettes and lighter, with uncharacteristic clumsiness. "She'll be here on Thursday, with a Red Cross train." *As you surely know,* his stepfather had wired, *your wife is coming on the third.* Why he should have known was more than Bora could tell. He put a cigarette in his mouth, in what Guidi was beginning to recognize as an antidote for embarrassment, or shyness. "Care to smoke?"

"Yes, please."

"Good. Here. I do, too." With a quick puff of smoke Bora started his cigarette. "You know, I could have been transferred to a German hospital, back in September, but I didn't want to jeopardize my assignment. They did a good job in Verona, I think. The hand could not be saved regardless. I knew that."

"You seem to be doing fine."

"Oh, I do." Bora smirked. "You should have seen me this morning. All four tires of my car were slashed. Have you ever tried to change a tire with one hand? Well, I changed four, by myself. I manage, I manage." Carefully, though he sat facing it, Bora avoided the mirror on the opposite wall. "I spent weeks learning how to do and undo my breeches, put my shirt on and button it, place the metal band of my watch on the finial of a chair so I can slip it on my right arm, all in record time. I can get dressed now more quickly than I did with both hands. I shave, drive, type, do push-ups and shoot a rifle as before. And yet, strictly speaking I can no longer even wash my *hands*, or clap, or hold someone. Playing the piano is also finished, which sometimes I think is the most difficult to take." He smoked for a time, encouraged by Guidi's silence. "Of course that's not true. The most difficult thing is facing my wife on Thursday."

Guidi had to wonder what the matter really was. "Doesn't she know?"

"She knows. We last spoke by phone in October."

"I'm sure she's dying to see you."

"I hope so." Bora smiled in a self-conscious way. "Anyway, she obviously meant to surprise me. Only because of my stepfather's wire did I find out. She'll stay eight days. I'll be at work, of course, but thank God I'll have the nights with her. I don't need to tell you how unbearably physical it becomes after a year's separation."

Just then, the lights went out. Growing from a plaintive whine, the wail of sirens began to rise in pitch across the dark. Guidi heard himself saying, "An air raid here? I thought Rome was an open city," and Bora replying dryly, "Yes, well. Bombs go awry, too."

"What are we supposed to do?"

No rustle of movement came with Bora's answer. "There's a shelter in the basement of the hotel. In case of a direct hit, you can choose between being blown up outright or being buried under these many stories of rubble."

"I'll take my chances here if it's all the same with you."

"It is. I'm staying."

Outside the door there was a scramble of people groping their way downstairs. Guidi's mouth went dry. In the absolute darkness, the rising and falling wail was a ghost of sound let loose over the city. *I hope Francesca is safe*, he thought, unexpectedly. *I don't care with whom – just safe.*

The flame of Bora's lighter flickered. "Another cigarette?"

"Not now."

Off and on the reviving tip of flame pointed Bora out to Guidi in the moments that followed – long moments, drawn and flattened into strips of time, during which Guidi simply tried to find out whether he was afraid or just nervous. To be sure, the possibility of death made him feel acutely lonely; as if suddenly no rules applied, and all life were vulnerable. If Bora was pondering the unfairness of dying on the eve of his wife's arrival, all that showed were the slow glimmering arcs drawn by his cigarette as he took extended draughts from it. Guidi sat back, chasing thoughts from his mind, so that he would not be attached to anything when the explosions rolled in from one periphery or another.

But the explosions were slow in coming. In the odd silence, Bora said, "I don't know why it's taking them so long." Then Guidi heard him move impatiently toward the window, feel around for the lock and throw it open. The crisp night air flooded in. Searchlights scanned the sky, here and there sweeping the bottom of clouds and becoming diffused or reflecting from them. No sound of engines, no anti-aircraft, not even from the beleaguered neighborhood of Castro Pretorio. The only artillery booming at slow intervals was Anzio's way.

"Just howitzers," Bora observed. "The searchlights may have struck a cloud, or it may have been friendly aircraft." He did not close the window until the sound of *all clear* began winding up. Shortly the lights returned, failed, were on again for good. Guidi felt sheepish, because he'd in fact been afraid, and likely it showed. "Not exactly a baptism of fire, was it?"

Bora courteously pretended not to notice. "Let's count our blessings. How about a cognac?"

"Don't mind if I do."

On their way down to the bar, they met guests returning to their rooms from the basement in various stages of undress, military and civilians alike. One of them was SS Captain Sutor, whom Bora did not expect here in his shirtsleeves and with a woman, but greeted by a curt lowering of his head.

3 FEBRUARY 1944

"Well, why was Foa taken in?" Westphal decided to ask Bora.

"No specific charges other than he did not collaborate with Gestapo officials. It seems he refused to inform on colleagues from the Royal Carabineers."

"He's kept under house arrest, is he?"

"No, he's in the state prison. Frankly, it seems unreasonable to expect him to denounce brother officers."

Westphal took a watermarked sheet of paper and began writing on it. "If he's wise he'll do just that. Of course I wouldn't give the SS or the SD the time of day, but Foa has no choice. Thanks for telling me, Bora."

"Should we ask for some consideration? He's nearly seventy years old."

Westphal was in an excellent mood with the news of the bloody defeat of American troops at Cisterna, and did not grow cross. "No. Why should you care? You were the one he insulted by phone. Here." He handed the signed sheet to Bora. "Two days' leave starting tomorrow. And go to meet your wife at the station, for God's sake. It's three hours from now, but keeping you around is like having a sick calf on the farm. You're useless to me. Unless the end of the world comes, I'll make sure nobody calls you until Monday morning."

Bora raced from the office to the Termini Station.

As he walked in, Colonel Dollmann happened to be leisurely coming out. "Well, well!" He stopped only long enough to remark, with an eye to the flowers Bora had with him, "Are we not dashing this morning! Is it legitimate or illegitimate?" When reluctantly Bora told him, he laughed. "There may be fun in that, too. Enjoy yourself."

Bora had been ceaselessly pacing on the solitary platform when the train pulled in from the right, on tracks white with frost. The station – marble, limestone, naked surfaces – seemed to lose immensity when Benedikta's face, dim behind the window glass, framed in her fairness, showed itself to him. He could distinctly feel the walls of his heart convulsively draw in and release blood as she stepped off the train. Fullness of breast in the gray woolen suit, slender legs, hair loosely pinned under the hat's small shade, met his eyes in that order of anxious scrutiny.

"*Martin!*"

Her obvious unreadiness for the meeting he perceived mostly as a reaction to his wounds, an impediment he had anticipated but could not bear. Suddenly everything – his wounds, the flowers, the very space between them – were in the way, and he took her in his arms, lifting her up to himself. They kissed then, and from the undone fur coat the scent of her clothes rose giddily to him, the touch at once aroused him to the edge of exhilarated pain – blood cried within him as life itself reclaimed, reaffirmed. Running his tongue in her mouth, meeting the quick well of her saliva, the sweet edge of her tongue, flushed him until he felt his ears roar with blood in the kiss.

Her eyes, so unhappy other times, stared at him like hard stars; he read nothing in them but physical joy. "You still taste so good," she was saying, and, "How did you find out…? You're so good about all of this, coming here to meet me." The flowers had been crushed in the embrace, and she laughed. "Why did you tell me you limp? You're not limping!"

They started toward the exit – Bora never could recall afterwards if there were other people on the train, on the platform: there must have been, but he noticed none of them. Dikta filled with anxious little words the silence of his admiration, observing him from under the thin arch of her eyebrows. "Really, I don't know why your father told you I was coming. Yes, they're fine, Mother is fine. Your sister-in-law sends her greetings. Blubo and Ulki had puppies. Are *you* all right, Martin?"

Bora was too aroused to think. He held her arm and smelled her scent and told himself that all was well, because she was here and she wanted him. He spoke back in his intense quick way, and she laughed again. "Well, you are so good about this."

Outside, car and driver waited. Dikta asked where he was taking her, and Bora said, "Hotel d'Italia. That's where I quarter."

She turned to the driver, who was loading her suitcases from the porter's cart to the trunk. "Careful with my hat box, it's not army luggage. Are you sure we should stay at the same address, Martin?"

"Of course it is. I wouldn't dream of doing otherwise!"

"If you say so."

"It's quite safe, Dikta." During the brief ride to the hotel he sat holding his eagerness in, absent-mindedly answering questions about the sights that passed them by. The side of her body, her sportswoman's muscular hip hugged his on the seat, no fat cushioning either, so that he cringed with expectation at the contact. Unchecked longing for his wife drove him, as if he no longer knew himself, and what physically happened to him was wild and frightening. He controlled himself because the driver was here and because he was used to controlling himself, but he ached to touch her through her fine clothing, to be let under the gray woolen dress. As if all suffering were worth this, the pain and closeness to death and danger could be soothed in her, safely locked in her.

"Have you lost weight, Martin?"

"I don't know."

"You're pale, I can see the veins in your temples. Is that a scar on your neck?"

"It's nothing. From the windshield when it burst."

She looked away. As the street curved, sunlight suddenly became caught in the crisp fleece of her neck: the sight of it, the pouting curve of her lips etched against the cold brightness of day, filled his mouth with moisture. Lavish and fair, lavish and fair. He had a shameless want to lick her face slowly, to seek her mouth and unseal it again, crazed into strange images of intimacy that drained his face of blood. Dikta knew, of course, but did nothing about it until they were in the hotel, past the lobby where other officers turned to glance at her. In the elevator she unexpectedly reached for his inner thigh and kissed him, behind the back of the round-shouldered lift boy.

After the bedroom door closed they embraced greedily, speaking over each other's mouth now, but already lips, hands, motions lost kindness, hard body parts chafed raw in the frantic silent grind of clothes until Benedikta let skirt and underskirt drop around her ankles, and her fully dressed torso over near-naked hips was outrageous and irresistible. Bora felt the skin of her thighs and lost his head. He freed himself only of that part of his uniform that was necessary, forgetful of the crude tearing of silk over the moist, deep stricture of her body.

She was amused at his embarrassment afterwards. Carelessly she gathered the rent handful of her underwear at her feet and stepped toward the bathroom. "Don't apologize, Martin. It *has* been a whole year, after all. I ought to keep this as a souvenir, you're always so level-headed otherwise."

Bora stood ashamed in the wetness of his clothes, watching her get ready for a shower. He regretted this mode of encounter, not just the quickness of it, as demeaning. Because he loved her, his heart ached for slower and more accomplished love, but Dikta was fast in and out of her urge. He felt exhilarated and aroused again at the sight of her water-sleek body when she lathered herself and with self-indulgence ran her hands on breasts, thighs and knees. He longingly wondered how her tight belly would grow to hold a child of his blood. By next Christmas, why not? It made him dizzy to consider it may have happened even now, by what translucent moisture had raced from him into her. So quickly, so quickly. The latency of life in his precarious self made all dangers to it bearable, even irrelevant: and she was precious many times over.

He watched her. The silence outside of the room was only broken by the rhythmic step and singing of the SS column daily marching for its training up from Via Rasella.

Emerging as from a warm rain, Benedikta gathered her hair to squeeze out its excess moisture. "Get ready, Martin, won't you?"

As they drove out to the restaurant – she did not want Italian food, so they drove to the Corso for Hungarian fare – he could think of nothing else. When a young pregnant woman walked in the restaurant he blushed hard, though his wife did not notice.

By mid-afternoon they were back at the hotel. Benedikta joked that he should look at her less and eat more. From the suitcase open on the bed she began to take out her clothes, with little buffs of the hands smoothing them and placing them aside. Her perfume rose at each unfolding, as if her motions were scent itself. "Thanks for the beautiful roses," she said. "And for coming to the station."

"How could you think I wouldn't be there?"

She smiled after a moment of silent arraying of clothes. "Well, considering… But I'm glad you didn't mention it at all while we were out, Martin."

"Didn't mention what?" he asked, conscious that she might speak of children, or lovemaking. He lit a cigarette for her, stretching it to her across the bed. "I believe we're both thinking of it."

"But you're so stoic. It's wonderful how you take adversity."

"Oh, that. I have little choice in the matter, Dikta."

She took a drag, and then balanced the cigarette on the ashtray's rim. When she leaned over the suitcase, her torso bloomed in a desirable curve under the blouse. "What I mean is that you're not angry with me."

"Why should I be?"

This time she looked up from the clothes. Her eyelids fluttered, although she still smiled. "Well, considering what I wrote to you, of course."

Bora felt a thin line of discomfort stretch within him, unwarranted yet but noxious. Arousal decreased sharply with it; a state of warning took its place. He said, "I was reassigned suddenly; my last mail hasn't been forwarded. I don't necessarily know what you mean."

The brightness of the dress she was holding crumpled like a bird in her hand. "Oh, Martin." She slowly sat on the bed. "Don't tell me you haven't read it!"

"What is it, what did you write to me?"

"You don't even know why I'm here, then."

A nervous smothering of her cigarette in the ashtray was all that passed before she spoke to Bora again, eyes averted. The room shrank before him as if she were the only thing of notice in it, the most disquieting and terrible one. She dealt him the blow quickly. "I petitioned the Vatican for an annulment. It's almost certain that it will go through, and I understand how you must feel, but there is no point arguing over it."

Bora had no need to convince himself that he had heard right: he knew he had.

"*Oh Christ.*"

She glanced his way, less apologetic. "Of course I know Catholics don't divorce, so I thought that since you're Catholic, this really leaves you free to marry again. I did it for you, Martin. I could have done otherwise, but I was thoughtful, and it's for the best. And anyway, it's your nature to get over things. You'll get over this. You simply will." Because he did not approach the bed, she cowardly confronted him. "The reason is not that you're maimed." She saw the blood rush to his face at her words and justified herself. "Well, you *have* lost a hand." Her voice rose in defense, trembling a little. "I had made up my mind even before that. And it really doesn't matter now, does it? You're the one who is stoic, I'm not. I don't take adversities well, you know I don't. I don't even like them, and walk away from them. You never asked me if I'd grown tired of waiting, and I'm sick of it."

"Do you think I have control over this war?"

"Then you shouldn't have married me. You know I lose interest quickly. Had you any sense, you would have understood." She grabbed clothes out of the suitcase, crushing them in hand. Breathlessly, she gave him no room to speak. "I always had fun in my life, and I always got what I wanted. You knew all that before you married me. You knew it. The war has ruined everything, and you've been in it from the start. I'm sure *you* like it. More power to you, go ahead and like your war, but don't ask me to be a part of it. Why should I be sacrificed, when I don't even believe in sacrifices? Why should I? I have too much to live for, Martin. I do. I can't be caught in a marriage until this is over."

That she could keep from crying was incredible to him, because Bora felt torn apart.

"You wanted to marry!"

"It was something to do. Everybody got married in those days. But the war was supposed to end in months, not five years!"

Bora sensed the intolerable uselessness of words even as he spoke them. "How have I failed you, other than I had to be away – and you knew I would, you knew when you married me that I was a career man and would be gone. I spent every moment of leave with you, I wrote to you every day I physically could, even from Russia. I've been faithful to you these five years, for God's sake. I lived to see you again, no matter what happened!"

He could see now what the hardness in her eyes had meant, what their brightness meant to him. "Well, pity it was all one-sided and I never agreed to it. Or if I said I did, I didn't mean it, which is the same, and you're an intelligent man, you should have seen through it." She stood, staring him down. "And don't say you didn't have lovers; men always do when they go to war. If you didn't, it's still not enough. In five years we spent two or three months together, and not all at once. What kind of marriage is that? I never cared for long-distance affairs. I can't accept them. I realize you love me and it makes it difficult, but it's done and you will just have to face reality as you always do."

Bora could not remember a time he'd raised his voice with her. "How can you tell me I have to face this *well*?" he shouted. "You goddamn well know I'm not going to take *this* well! We haven't even talked it over; what about what *I* have to say? You can't just decide for both of us on your own!"

"I have." She was unfolding a document, and laid it on the quilts for him to pick up. "Mother called from her winter house in Lisbon. That's where I'm going next. I'm only here for the paperwork."

Bora would not touch the paper, nor look at it. "Would you stay had I not been wounded?"

"It's a hypothetical question – there's no such alternative."

"But I must know, by God! Would you stay?"

"Maybe. But that can't be helped, you see?" She again sat on the bed, her altered profile barely visible to him. "It'd have been better had you died. For both of us. Had you died I wouldn't have to go through all this. I'm trying to be nice about it, but you make it so difficult by not accepting it as you should if you were sensible."

"I'm sorry I didn't die."

And it was no use saying more, because logic had nothing to do with this except for what she wanted. What she wanted was not him, and it was all there was. Loyalty and commitment meant nothing if she had never partaken of those. Bora ached terribly at the sight of the framework of her mind, exposed as miserly and uncomplicated, bare, a cheap machine. What Dikta wanted was shamelessly simple, but not his to give.

They spent the next hour in complete silence, she seated on the bed, Bora standing against the sill with his back to the muting glare of the window, until daylight grew faint and relinquished the room. His wholeness was scattered all over, as far as his mind could go – strands of him, loose ends, strange pieces, and he would need to pick them up and braid them back together to reshape his balance.

How the person here seemed different from the person who uttered the words, he thought: they were somehow removed from her, like a cause remote already and no longer assailable. Could a separate peace be made with the woman here? Instead of coming together, certainties fell away from him, a sore shedding as a scab lifted from the wound exposes fresh and raw layers. Guilt entered resentment, and this slid and drowned into an anguished sense of being adrift. He felt lost but for the anchorage of the windowsill. Lost, lost. Immense distance lay between him and the bed, unbridgeable, though he may travel to it. The sill was really a part of the outside, not of the room. *She* was the room, a continent in the darkness – edged with high cliffs and perilous shores, largely unknown. How had his heart not told him?

Only from the rustle of clothes he perceived Dikta was undressing and getting into bed, with the familiar sounds of their nights together. Against himself and the aghast disbelief and bitterness of his mind, he felt a wave in the flesh again creep up his thighs at the memory, decidedly painful this time.

Still he stood until she called out to him. Then blood began to sing its dark song which was like a hum, a wordless sustained note that pushed ahead in the veins, until all veins also sang, and the voices multiplied in him. Known voices of killing, children-making and proving oneself. She cared for none of these. But in his belly the song was black and it fed and fueled and filled him up, and yet it remained hungry. Her summons angered him only because he feared she wouldn't invite him again if he refused. He imagined her nakedness in the sheets, hating himself for being like all men, whose resolve counts for nothing when their body is strongest and crazed.

"Come to bed, Martin."

The song inside strained high. It hammered, but he was heeding an unstrung desperate desire to change her mind instead. Deadly sadness and that unstrung desperate want made him strip and climb alongside her in the great bed, where he suffered her to slide her hands and mouth down the lean fore of his belly.

In the morning, Benedikta lay with the sheet between her legs, and these crossed at the ankles. Propped against the pillows, her torso was pink and opalescent in the early light, the nipples diverged on her young breast, brightly pert and narrow of areolas as in women who have never given birth. A fine blond down lined the seam of her belly under the navel, and to it like a tired narrow wave came the twisted sheet, covering her sex.

"Give me a cigarette," she said.

Bora sat at the foot of the bed, facing her, and still was startled by her voice. Dressed already, he struck a strange image of order on the upheaval of the bed. It was the last time, he was thinking, that it would disconcert him how without foreplay Benedikta sought intercourse, in her callous need for lovemaking – how their lying together was then agile but hard, not a *lying* together at all, wordless, a back-breaking struggle that left them sore in the wet space of the bed.

Some moisture still lined the inner part of her thighs, milky and delicate. Bora felt a void melancholy for it, much like regret. He lit a cigarette for his wife and offered it to her.

"I'm sorry for the way you had to hear it, Martin."

"Up front, you mean?" Pitilessly reflected in the mirror, his face came into a shaft of window light as he sat back, and the expression on it was a stern army mask. "I'd rather." A small contraction of the jaw when he spoke was all she likely could perceive of him. "May I at least know why, really?"

"I told you why. We have nothing in common, *really*."

"And we've been married five years, with nothing in common?"

"What we had together were those few weeks of leave, that's all." She prevented whatever else he was about to say. "I'm not interested in sharing your mind and heart, Martin – I don't care to talk to you by phone, or read your letters from the front. I want someone with me *now*. Surely, you lived for those furloughs – when all was said and done they always came down to what's between your legs and mine, and though you dress it up you need it greatly. It's true." She shrugged, and then relaxed her shoulders. "Even though you're a good lover – I'm going to miss that. You're the best lover I've had."

Her compliment hurt him, whether it was from a merce-nary ground that it came, or because he was sensitive and the animal quality of her assessment of him left him bruised and vulnerable. "I don't want to hear it."

"Well, I'll miss it."

"How can this be all? *I* loved you aside from sex."

"I understand all that. It still doesn't change a thing. There's no room for appeal, since I spelled out to the Church my rea-sons – my faults, if you wish – and the marriage will be more than dissolved. It will never have existed." Her cheeks narrowed as she inhaled deeply. "As for what you wanted this time... People told me you would, since you've been wounded. All you men do these days, whether or not you come out and say so. Mortality makes you frantic to reproduce. I can see you feel the urge for it, poor Martin, but I don't want your children."

"I never even made you pregnant." Bora nervously searched his pockets for the lighter.

She stared at him. Without answering she rearranged the pillows behind her back. "Why do you tell me that?"

"Because perhaps you won't get pregnant, even if we stay together."

She smoked quietly for a while, her face turned away. Smoke twirled up from her mouth and hovered above her head; like a halo it created an illusion of bluish light around her. She nearly exhausted the cigarette before saying, "But I did." Calmly, so deceivingly confident that her husband had time to absorb the blow and recoil and pretend to compose himself. "When you came a year ago at Christmas it was the third time. I almost told you then, but I thought better of it. It made me ill and I didn't want it. I didn't. I saw your brother's wife go through with it, the sickness, all the changes in her body, and then the pain of giving birth for someone who was rotting in Russia already." She removed the sheet from her body and he didn't react to her nudity, but was breathing hard and fast. "I got rid of them, Martin. It's better if you know without wondering. They were just clots of blood, not your children, really. They were just little clumps of meat on the midwife's table."

Bora had a sudden urge to throw up. He rose and made it to the bathroom and to the cold edge of the sink, where he doubled up to retch. There was nothing in his stomach and he merely went through painful dry heaves that hardly gathered spittle, and twisted his stomach like a rag that is wrung without expelling any liquid. Afterwards a paroxysm of anger took him, and likely grief in excess of anger. An extremity of physical agony just like when his hand had been torn off by the grenade, and blood had exploded from it onto him, bits of flesh, bone, parts of him, pieces of him, clots of blood. With his back to the tiled wall he let breathing break fitfully out of his lungs through an open mouth – in and out as he had done before to endure the atrocity of mutilation without screaming, until he regained control by rape-like violence on himself. Spiders of pain drew webs in him, stretched tight and lopsided, then ate the spun drivel and crawled off his limbs one by one, leaving him numb.

From the open window, with no effort on his part, the kind morning air came to dry the cold sweat on his face and neck.

Like veins of muddy water, stockings rained from Benedikta's hands as she began dressing on the bed. Were she dead on it, were he dead at the foot of it, nothing less could pass between them. She put her bra on without looking at him, like a stranger you chance upon in a fitting room. Her fingers clasped the lacy band over her stomach, turned it around and lifted it to her chest. She placed her breasts in the cups, passed the satin straps over her shoulders.

Bora could not bring himself to look at her. He went past her to reach for his pistol and holster on the night stand, girt himself with them and walked out of the room.

Outside the air was clean, the sky high and cloudless. Shadows lay blue carpets across the streets, and on them people were blue. He drove the distance to Villa Umberto and entered the park from the riding grounds, where things were green in excess of blue even at this time of year. Under the fretwork of pine trees he sat in the car. To the policeman who came an hour later to inquire discreetly, he said nothing was the matter, though he had the Walther in his lap; when later another policeman accosted him, Bora simply squared the pistol at him.

All around, light washed brightly in the free spaces of sky, but in the shade it drizzled or tossed coins on the frost-yellow grass, or it made the surface of the car into a leopard-like pelt. In time it turned white and the shadows, still spotted, all moved creeping on the earth. Bora looked at the shadows and remembered how summer skies raced overhead when his brother had died. Children were eating sunflower seeds around the crash site. "*Gdye nyemetsky pilot?*" he recalled asking of them, "Where's the German pilot?", as he parted with his hands the hairy, barbed forest of tall flowers under a cloud of dust, with a crunch of salty loam under his teeth. How the shadows raced even then. Bora looked away from the outside, seeking some neutral surface within the car.

And there was the gash in the Russian earth, as if a plough-share had turned it open to prepare it for sowing, its moist sod evaporating in the heat until the line of sunflowers trembled double, a mirage suspended above itself. Flowers on flowers, and the jagged, greenish tail rudder stood like a fin of dead fish past the flowers.

The boys ate sunflower seeds, and his brother was dead.

It was long before bells tolled deep from Trinity Church and St Isidoro's across the spaces now ruddled and flushed. Longer yet until the air became without shadows, of the dead color of ash. Then a waning moon came up somewhere to grizzle the dark.

Bora did not feel the cold. He was bodily numb and his mind clicked orderly from thought to thought with the rhythm of gears finely serrated. Thoughts of Russia and thoughts of death and thoughts of Benedikta. The dark grew near, until like drapes it clung to the windows, and he didn't know if his eyes were open or closed.

All day and all night Bora sat in the car, thinking.

Icy moisture dressed the twin needles of the pines while he traveled to Via Veneto the morning after, perfectly clear-headed. It was his well-known enclosed world of tightly woven runners and typing noises behind doors, where adjutants had adolescent faces and low voices never echoed themselves. Bora kept his things handy in the desk, and washed and shaved before going to Westphal's office.

"What are you doing back so early, Major?" The general took a friendly look at him.

The answer came remarkably unemotional, as if the startling words bore no relation to the meaning of it.

3

5 FEBRUARY 1944

The weather was still cold, but without hard frost.

"You know about leap years," Signora Carmela told Guidi as he got ready for work. *"A year that leaps / troubles in heaps."*

"It can't get much worse than it's been," Guidi remarked. "Is there anything I can get you at the store?"

"No, thank you. Remember that today is tobacco day, in case you need a smoke. Not that I approve of smoking, but you seem to be good in every other sense." Signora Carmela tugged at the small charm on her chest, a slim gold horn that enjoyed much fondling. "Not that I should ask, but how are things coming with Francesca?"

Guidi was caught off guard. "I'm not sure how they ought to be coming."

"We hoped you might help her open up a bit." Signora Carmela sighed. "Such a strange girl. Speaks so little, eats so little. Seems to have no desire to be any more a part of us than as a boarder. We'd love to be closer to her, if she let us."

With some polite, generic formula Guidi took his leave, and because it was his day to report to Caruso, he went straight to the *Questura Generale.* In the waiting room, with guarded hilarity, he was told about the Chief's mishap, as he'd been mistakenly arrested in a routine round-up of civilians and held for several hours before being able to prove his identity.

"He's still livid, Inspector. Watch out when you go in. He's also furious at the Vatican."

"What for? For resenting his violation of St Paul's extraterritorial rights?"

"God forbid you should mention the operation to him."

Caruso's stubble stood on his head like a ruffled cat's back. He acknowledged Guidi's entrance by a slashing gesture of the right arm in the air, his nose deep in paperwork. "Keep it short. What's new with the Reiner affair?" When Guidi reported, "Boyfriends, girlfriends!" Caruso barked, looking up above his glasses, "What are you talking about? As if you had time to waste! You've been spoon-fed a suspect. All you have to do is prove his guilt. What's this going far afield on your own?"

Guidi kept standing, not having been asked to sit. "Naturally I am looking into Merlo's involvement. Up to now, I haven't found a reason why he should kill any woman."

"Obviously you haven't read the material I've given you!"

"He chases skirts and he's jealous, Dr Caruso, but — "

"Here!" Out of his drawer, Caruso pulled a leather case, which he tossed on the desk. "I didn't think you'd need this much help, but these spectacles were found in the Reiner bathroom, complete with his initials on the case. Not mine, not those of her supposed German boyfriends – Merlo's own."

Guidi could not believe his eyes. "But when…?"

"Never you mind when! They were found. Follow your leads, instead of going off on a wild chase. This office isn't afraid of prosecuting one of our own. *You* shouldn't either."

"It would have helped greatly had I known about this. I assumed we did not have access to the apartment."

The chief of police gave him a hateful stare. Folded on his desk lay *L'Osservatore Romano*. No doubt he'd been reading Vatican reactions to his night raid on St Paul Outside the Walls. Daringly, Guidi said, "We all know you aren't afraid of consequences, Dr Caruso. It's a great lesson for us that you arrested not only Jews and conscientious objectors, but army and police officers as well."

Caruso missed the irony. "It was a brilliant operation, yes. The Church squawks, but that's what the Church is all about anyway. I've done my duty. Now get out of here and do the same – Merlo is guilty and should not be protected."

Guidi took the glasses, and left the office with a spiteful need to sneer, which the men in the next room – having overheard the exchange – precipitated by grinning from ear to ear.

Countess Ascanio looked green in the light that filtered through the spaces of the folded shutters – green and striped, she looked, and in front of her Bora's figure also stood dissected by those lines of alternating shine and darkness. "Donna Maria," he said.

She drubbed her rubber-tipped cane hard on the tiles, before opening her arms in a demanding invitation. "What are you waiting for? Come!" Her embrace was long, strong; she pushed him back only enough to hold his face down and kiss him on both cheeks (her lips were cold, soft). She added in a choked voice, "Handsome, that's what you are. Step back. *Fammiti vedere, quanto sei bello.*"

Bora let her survey him unresistingly, though he knew how close her scrutiny had always been.

"How long have you been in Rome? Five weeks? And you haven't visited me before? Bad man, bad man!" Her only mention of his injury was, "And to think I had the piano tuned for you, hoping you'd come." That was all. "I don't know why I hoped you would. I knew. You belong to this house, and must come back to it eventually."

Bora let her talk, oppressed by grief, uselessly struggling against it. "You heard about Peter," he said.

"Yes," she said. "Your stepfather wrote me. Poor Peter, with a baby on the way. God tries us, Martin – God tries us hard." Bora only nodded. "Sit down," she urged. "Tell me everything. You're well, are you? Are you well?"

"I'm well, Donna Maria."

"There, sit down. It's been five years, and the last time you were in a great hurry to go home and marry." Smiling multiplied the wrinkles on her face. "Your wife? No babies yet?"

Bora sat down, feeling as if he were sand, and her kind words came to erode him piecemeal. "She's in Rome," he compelled himself to say next. "She went to the Sacra Rota."

Donna Maria set her jaw firmly, with her hand palpating the handle of her cane. Her lids winked once or twice. "Why, what's happened?" And at once, "I must ask Nino about this."

"I doubt Cardinal Borromeo keeps tabs of annulments, Donna Maria."

The cane's tip drummed, irritably. When she spoke again, she had composed herself to placidity once more. "So. How are you taking it?"

Bora found the question merciless but necessary. He had been preparing for it. "Not well, I'm afraid."

"Do you love her?"

"Yes."

"Do you have a picture of her?"

How many times people had asked him. He took out and showed the photo he carried in his wallet. The old woman looked. "Hm," she said to herself. "Hm. Does she love you?"

"Donna Maria, she's leaving me."

"Sometimes you leave people to set them free, as I did with your stepfather. Of course it was impossible, in our position, to stay married after Sarajevo started the Great War. It worked out for the best. He found your mother and married her happily, and I fell in love with D'Annunzio." She complacently digressed. "*I* was the woman he called *Chiaroviso* in his *Faville*. Not La Boulanger. But you – what are *you* going to do?"

Bora felt the words escape him, with great shame for pronouncing them.

The old woman reacted by one more imperious tap of the cane's rubber. "*Che sciocchezze!* What nonsense, Martin."

"It's true."

"Look at me and tell me it's true, in my face."

"It's true, Donna Maria."

"Because of her? Because of five missing fingers? Nonsense. Look at yourself, you're a strapping young man. I shouldn't be hearing this nonsense from you, Martin! When the war is over – and you're going to lose it, just as His Holiness lost Rome to Italy in 1870. You are, you are. It's lost already, it doesn't merit talking about it. Why, then you'll find someone to make children with." She watched him without blinking, without smiling. "You've got plenty of them tucked in, there where you men keep them. You're young! When you wrote me from Russia, I saw pictures of you in that godforsaken place, snow up to your waist. If you didn't want to die then, what's this nonsense now? Don't you play German with me."

Bora smirked despite himself, because of her misunderstanding. "It's not suicide I had in mind, Donna Maria. I want to be sent west to the front."

"To Anzio?"

"As soon as possible. General Westphal can't use health reasons to hold me back. I'm fine. I feel fine."

"And you'd do this to your mother? She's already lost the other one, your stepfather's own. This is all nonsense." More patiently she looked him up and down. "Do you at least have a lover? If you don't have a lover, these days must be really hard for you."

Bora had a great desire to crumple in the armchair, to let go. And yet fear of losing control held him sitting straight, unrelenting in the effort to keep check on himself. Slowly, Countess Ascanio shook her head. Propping herself on cane and tea table, she stood. As she left the room, she said, "I'm not coming back for an hour, Martin."

Bora held in his grief until she pulled the door shut behind her.

Francesca asked for a ride at breakfast, as they made the best of thin bread slices and watery coffee on the starched linen cloth Signora Carmela laid out every day. Guidi stared at her, and so did the Maiulis, who had hoped the two of them would get along amiably. The professor buried his nose in the cup, and his wife reached for the horn-shaped charm under her shawl.

Her careworn youthful face looked white behind the swatch of dark hair, so much more delicate than the tone in her voice. "It's cold today, and I have a delivery to make at Piazza Venezia."

Guidi frowned. "The piazza is closed to civilian traffic."

"I know that. Why do you think I asked *you?*"

The Maiulis were trying so hard to be inconspicuous, they seemed to be sinking in their chairs. Impatiently Francesca pulled her hair back. "I have to take a batch of envelopes to one of the offices there. I figured that since you have permission to travel freely, I could take advantage of it. I guess not."

"I didn't say I wouldn't take you."

Outside, frost laced the windshield of Guidi's little Fiat. While he scraped the glass with a piece of cardboard, Francesca stood by in her long shapeless coat, sniffling in the cold. They first drove by the store, where she picked up a mid-sized parcel, and then she directed Guidi to take Corso Umberto toward Piazza Venezia. Halfway down the wide Corso, they were stopped by German guards, who looked at Guidi's documents and let them go.

After Francesca delivered the package, Guidi offered to drop her by the store. Because in his awkward attempt to make conversation he mentioned his mother, whose birthday it was, "Your mother was a schoolteacher? Mine is a model," she carelessly spoke back. "There isn't much to it; all you have to do is take your clothes off and let painters look at you, not necessarily because they want to paint you. She's a whore, really."

Guidi was certain he had mistaken her words. "What?" he mumbled.

She laughed. "Why, does it scandalize you that I call my mother a whore? Well, she is. She sleeps with men for money. Germans, mostly, because they have the money, and when it comes to getting into something warm, who cares if the whore's Jewish?"

With an eye on her bitterly amused face, Guidi found himself driving at a snail's pace. He said, "Your father?"

"He put me through school. Sends checks now and then. Turn at the next corner, there. No, there. I met him a couple of times, when I was younger and he passed himself off as an uncle. He's a handsome man. A *man of God*. But I'd rather take his money than Mother's, all things being equal. I make barely enough for room and board." She relaxed her shoulders, with a hand on her belly, palm spread. "And it's too late to do anything about this, so – well, it's got a right to be born in this wonderful world of ours – I'll have to go through with it. I didn't even realize I was pregnant until last month. I haven't menstruated in two years, what with the lousy diet and all."

There were times when Guidi wondered how he'd managed to stay naive, despite his job. Unused to women's talk, he said clumsily, "What will you do then?"

"Give it up for adoption. Any better ideas?"

"I wouldn't know."

"Well, it's starting to show through the winter clothes. I figure I'm due in late May or early June. My only problem is telling the Maiulis. They're so close-minded. But I don't think they want to lose a tenant."

"Wouldn't your boyfriend – that is, wouldn't he take care of things?"

"Well, aren't you nice. No, it's not likely he would."

"Oh, right. I forgot, you said he has a wife."

Francesca merrily tossed her head back. "And you a police-man! Do you believe everything they tell you?" In front of the stationer's, she got down quickly. Before slamming the car door, she said, "I may not come back tonight," she said. "Just tell the Maiulis I'm staying at a girlfriend's house."

At noon, Guidi – getting lost only once – drove to German Army headquarters at the Hotel Flora, with the intent of discussing the unexpected appearance of Merlo's glasses. A cool-faced young woman in uniform informed him that Major Bora was out, and not expected back soon. Guidi thought better than to say he'd seen Bora's Mercedes parked below.

"Would you take a message for the major?" he asked.

"Yes, certainly."

"Simply write this – *Must find out who got there before us.*"

The young woman gave him a curious look, but jotted down the words. Behind her, Bora's door was open onto a full view of his desk: papers stacked, maps. Something was missing from the array of objects, though Guidi could not say what.

All along Via Veneto, armored cars and nervous, gun-toting patrols discouraged him from staying around until Bora showed up. But had Guidi waited ten minutes more, he'd have seen Bora leave for the *Questura Centrale*, bound to deliver a withering reprimand to Pietro Caruso of the *Polizia Repubblicana* on behalf of German Army Command South.

That evening, the first news the Maiulis related was the radio item of a Canadian airplane that had crashed in the periphery. The second was that Francesca had not shown up. Guidi reassured them about her, and while dinner was being prepared, went to his room to scribble the latest in his notebook. The notes were actually questions. Had Caruso just received Merlo's glasses? If his men had gained early access to Magda's apartment, why had the key not been made available to him? Had the Germans taken it back? What did Merlo's glasses actually prove, other than he'd visited Magda at one time or another?

Bora's help, now that it was needed, couldn't be counted on. *Sure, he was "away from work". I bet he was in the back room with his wife. And he got the secretary up front covering for him.* In his jaundiced state of mind, Guidi was more than a little envious of the German, his handsome wife, and to what use "the nights with her" were undoubtedly being put. He compared that to Francesca's lack of interest in him – as if she ought to be interested in him. *But then – she says she has a lover. Does she? Is he the father? Maybe she has no lover at all.* At the moribund glare of the bed lamp, Guidi realized he'd been scribbling Francesca's name all over the page of his notebook. And he recalled, with sudden clarity, that what was missing from Bora's desk was the photograph of his wife.

On his way out of the office, General Westphal said, "*I'*m not telling you anything, Bora. I never waste time advising grown men who tell me they know what they're doing. It's the field marshal who says you're a fool." He sat with arms crossed, nodding toward a short message on his desk. "Does it read, 'Tell Martin he's a fool', or not? It's fine with me if you get your head blown off at Anzio. It will look damn good on the second-last page of the Leipzig paper that my aide was killed at the front."

Bora kept silent, because he did not wish to sound contentious and decrease the likelihood of a transfer.

Westphal suspected it. "You know, most men smash furniture and get drunk when this sort of thing happens to them. You shaved and came back to work. It's no good. When it comes out it's going to be much worse than smashing furniture."

By now Bora had such control over himself, his own image in the mirror would not betray his thoughts. "I assure the general that nothing will *come out.* And the general is in error if he thinks I want to leave Rome because my wife's here. Her presence is not why I wish to resign my position now. However, had the general given me permission, I would have left last Saturday."

"I knew better, didn't I."

"Except that I still wish to be ordered out."

Westphal gave him a critical look from over his arched nose. "Don't bother the field marshal with your wishes. He's in a foul mood after this morning's mess at Castel Gandolfo, though it works for us. Five hundred dead refugees in the Propaganda Fide villa, and no Germans around to blame for Allied bombs! I'm off for the night, and expect you to have forgotten about reassignment by tomorrow. If you wait long enough, I guarantee that Anzio will come to you."

Everyone else in the office, even Bora's secretary, had left by the time Dollmann strolled in with an invitation and placed it on the desk.

"An informal get-together at my place, Major, and I dearly hope you'll come. Am I to understand you are, so to speak, back on the market?" When testily Bora said nothing, Dollmann drove the point home. "I just had occasion to escort your charming wife to the train station. Oh, don't worry. She's been taken care of these past days. I even took her dancing a couple of times. Come, come, Major. Before you get hot under the collar, think about it. Better myself than someone else. You can trust *me*."

"If it's all the same, I'd rather not discuss my wife."

"Very well." Dollmann smiled vapidly. "Whenever you feel like it, you know you can. Good Lord, I'm not going to tell you I sympathize. I think you're better off single in Rome." His face, without warning, hardened into an unkind sneer. "I noticed your car running in idle outside and your driver waiting. You'd be a fool to give in and go to see her off now."

The nib of Bora's pen bent against the paper, bleeding ink all around. "I wish you'd mind your business, Colonel."

"You know I won't. Saturday of next week at 1900 hours sharp, undress uniform." Dollmann flicked his glove in a salute and left the office.

Bora did not look up from his work again until ten at night, when whatever distraction he'd hoped to get from his bureaucratic duties gave way to blank weariness. Disastrously, all that stayed when everything else was stripped off in clean layers, was the thought of his wife.

By dinner time, Francesca was back. At the table, Professor Maiuli informed everyone that he would soon be giving private lessons. "The name is Rau, Antonio Rau. He's a boy who wishes to hone his Latin skills, Inspector. Only this morning I was thinking how nice it'd be to teach again, in the comfort of my own house, and this worthy woman," he said, pointing at his crooked little wife, "comes into the room and says, 'May the angel fly by and say amen.' Well, what do you think? By noon I had a student. Just like that. I tell you, if the Americans had this woman as a mascot, they'd be here already."

Guidi smiled. "Well, take comfort in the fact that the Germans don't have her either."

At the other end of the table, Francesca laughed. Her large, hungry mouth was so attractive to him that for a moment Guidi forgot everything else about her, as though that red, laughing receptacle were meant as a message of friendliness toward him.

"I'll tell you something else," Maiuli went on. "My wife was sitting by the radio, wishing for all these bombings and attempts to end, and the news came this evening that they found a bomb at the Caffè Castellino in Piazza Venezia, and defused it in time. It was supposed to go off at ten o'clock, when German officers frequent it. Knowing their penchant for reprisals, it was a blessing that nothing happened. And all this remarkable hunchback had to do was wish for it."

Francesca was still smiling. But, quickly as a cloud modifies the light of day, the intensity of her smile was obfuscated. Guidi noticed the change, without passing judgment. He was famished, and the soup steaming in his bowl received most of his attention. Only when Francesca excused herself did he wonder whether Maiuli's words had anything to do with her behavior. Was she thinking that she and Guidi had been at Piazza Venezia earlier today, and could have been caught in the blast? Was she afraid? After dinner Guidi stayed up to read, in case she should show up again. But Francesca was in bed for good, and he went to his own room eventually.

Hours later, a knock on the door roused Maiuli long after he had gotten his dentures off and pajamas on. There was no electricity, and at the weak twilight of a candle he stumbled down the corridor to the threshold, where the sight of the German uniform made his scanty hair rise. Although he tried to dominate himself, the flame swayed so that medals and silver cord ran glinting streaks before him.

"Inspector Guidi, please," Bora said.

The extent of Guidi's impatience showed in that he came out of his room buttoning his trousers. "Major Bora, really —"

"Get dressed, Guidi."

"I'm sure that whatever it is, it can wait until the morning."

"Get dressed."

The half-light did not allow for reading of expressions. Guidi could only see that Bora stood with his usual wary stiffness. "Does it have to do with Magda Reiner?"

"Yes, of course. What else? I'm not in the habit of getting people out of bed to chat with them."

"All right. But I must ask you to wait outside. You scared the wits out of these poor people." Walking back to his room, Guidi heard the Maiulis' stifled talk behind the thin wall, and caught a glimpse of Francesca's contemptuous white face through a crack in her door. He threw his clothes on and angrily grabbed Merlo's glasses, carelessly shoving them into his new coat's pocket.

At the Hotel d'Italia, the lobby was deserted except for two German officers dozing over their drinks. Guidi, who hardly drank at all, downed two cognacs at the bar before feeling sociable enough to converse about the latest evidence.

"This is what *I* found out, Major, and I hope you have something important to add to it." It galled him that Bora should seek company tonight, when he'd just spent a week with his wife and could very well sit cat-faced and calm without touching the liquor in front of him.

"To be honest, I didn't realize you had left a message for me until this evening." Bora fueled his vexation. "My secretary gave it to me, but I paid no attention."

"Well, you had other things to do."

With his thumb, slowly, Bora turned the gold band he wore on the ring finger of his right hand, a small steady gesture that seemed habitual and did not alert Guidi. He said, "I received a packet from Magda's parents, and spoke to them by phone earlier today. I think you should hear what transpired. But first," Bora took a note out of the cuff of his army tunic, "here is what I scribbled in response to your message."

Guidi read the slip of paper. "What do you mean, *Not once, but twice was the room searched and cleaned up before we arrived?* How do you know?"

"A copy of the key was made for the head of police on 13 January. The German Security Service had gotten inside on the night of Magda Reiner's death."

Emboldened by the drinks, Guidi had no desire to agree. "Leaving a pair of eyeglasses behind is not what I'd call 'cleaning up'. What are you implying, Major?"

"I'm not implying anything. You're the investigator. I'm just a soldier who comes along for the ride."

Bora's arrogance came through too obliquely for Guidi to respond. He placed the oblong leather case on the counter, saying, "You read this time. See if it is more likely for you or me to track down Merlo's optician."

Bora glanced at the name embossed on the case. "Sciaba," he read under his breath, and then, again, "Sciaba," he said. "Great. Of all the opticians in Rome, he had to use a Jewish one."

"Well, Major, Rome *is* yours. The man's shop is locked up, and there's no one at his home. No information as to where he is, or went."

Bora copied down the optician's name. "I'll try, but I make no promises."

"Did the Reiners tell you anything new?"

"They unwittingly confirmed the image most people seem to have of their daughter – ambitious, somewhat light-headed, frivolous without being mercenary. But as for her being unlikely to brood over unhappy thoughts – that's another story. In the packet they sent me there was a newspaper clipping. Here, you can see it's a notice of army casualties. Magda had apparently taken up with this fellow, who went missing in action on the Greek Front last summer and is presumed dead. Her mother glosses over it, but I gather that at the time Magda thought about, if not attempted, suicide." Musingly Bora smoothed the article with his fingers. "Her work record shows a three-week medical leave shortly after the fellow's disappearance, no details given. If she had any suicidal thoughts, surely she kept them under wraps, or else she'd have lost security clearance."

Suddenly free of drowsiness, Guidi's mind was going a thousand miles an hour. "What else was in the packet?"

"Letters and photographs. They're in my office safe."

"Damn. I was hoping – but why in the safe?"

"Because that's the appropriate place for them." Bora's words came as always, polite and discouraging further inquiry. What he meant by that, Guidi could not say. He could read nothing into the German's composure. But he had to wonder whether Bora ever lost control, or swore, or went one day without shaving twice. "I brought the photographs," he was adding now. Out of his pocket he took several snapshots, which he lay on the counter. "She, and occasionally her relatives, identified date and place on the back."

Guidi studied the pictures. In the batch there were several from the last two years – Magda posing with a variety of friends of both sexes, sitting in a horse-drawn tourist buggy in front of the Colosseum or sunning at the beach.

"This was taken at Ostia last November." Bora pointed to the last one. "Three months past, twenty miles away. And if you pay attention, the man standing behind her with a magazine is *Ras* Merlo."

"Wearing glasses, no less."

"Yes. The rest are photos from the past – the Olympic Games, Paris, the fellow from the Greek Front, Christmas at home." Bora took a sip from his drink and put it down. "I am in the process of reading the letters. I'll let you know if there's anything in them worth noting."

Guidi yawned, glancing at his wristwatch. "Look, Major, it's nearly two o'clock, and I have to be off to work by seven. Was it really necessary to bring me here?"

"It was. I'm celebrating."

"Really. Celebrating what?"

Bora took another sip from the amber-shaded cognac. "I was at the Caffè Castellino at ten o'clock today. Worth celebrating, I think."

12 FEBRUARY 1944

Francesca sneered as Guidi walked from the bathroom past her door on Saturday morning. "The Germans must really like you if they come to get you in the middle of the night."

Guidi stopped. Forgetful that he already had his shirt on, he whipped the wet towel over his shoulder. "We're lucky they didn't come to ask about Piazza Venezia."

She laughed. In her nightgown, she sat cross-legged on the bed, and hair like a dark limp wave hung about her face. "I don't know what you mean."

"On the contrary, I think you do."

"Is that supposed to be policeman's talk? Because if it is, you'd better be ready to act on it. All I did is deliver a package, *and you drove me there.*" Carelessly, with no regard to his presence,

Francesca pulled the nightgown over her head. Suddenly her torso bloomed bare, breasts bluish at the tips and engorged by pregnancy, her belly rounded but still small. "You can be sure *that* would take some explaining." She reached for a cotton slip at the foot of the bed, and smelled the armpits before putting it on. "Do we both turn ourselves in?"

Guidi opened his mouth, and closed it again, having said nothing. He could remember exactly – exactly – the last time something like this had happened, a year, six months and two weeks ago. It was her name that he didn't remember. Blood rose to his face there where he stood, on the threshold of her room, with the wet towel across his shoulder. Legs dangling from the side of the bed, Francesca was now covering the slip with a plain woolen dress. Finally she looked at him. "*What?*" And, "What is it, haven't you got a girlfriend you see naked now and then? Why, you turned red!" She burst out laughing, with her face in the black bundle of her cotton stockings. Guidi stepped back from the threshold, breathing hard. The clicking of keys in the front door warned him that Signora Carmela was back from early Mass at the Bellarmino Church, and her husband from his snail-paced constitutional around the block.

That evening, he was back at Magda's address. The limestone-framed main door let him into a now-familiar arched passageway, looking on to the paved dark well of the inner courtyard. There was no porter, and taking the stairs to the left of the entrance Guidi climbed directly to the fourth floor.

With Bora's help, he had gathered a partial list of people who had attended the holiday party on the evening of her death. The German officers among them were off to Anzio or Cassino, and German civilians had already left Rome on 9 January. Guidi had since traced two Italian guests, from whom he learned that Merlo was not at the party. They had never heard Magda Reiner's name, and couldn't tell whether she was expected or not. Tonight, for an hour, he went through every detail of the bedroom. He knew he could not necessarily trust the clues left behind by those who had preceded him in the search. Her dress – one button missing from it – and stockings lay on the armchair, as she had left them when preparing for bed, or readying to go out again. All he came up with were store receipts, a scrap of crumpled white paper wedged between the bedstead and the wall, and a handful of dust from under the bed. Cloth fibers were caught in the dust, a hair, fine ash-like impalpable bits, bread or cake crumbs, a bit of dark chocolate.

His skimpy file on *Ras* Merlo had grown steadily, mostly thanks to Danza's knack for burrowing through papers and getting folks to gossip. It included dated reports of rough carousing in army brothels up near Vittorio Veneto back in 1917, a couple of serious injuries to political adversaries in his Matteotti period, and the frustrated, petty overbearing typical of local Party officials. Details that Guidi (but not Guidi alone) now so much associated with fascism. But the man seemed indeed honest when it came to money. As for his relationship to Magda, Bora had gotten out of her girlfriend that she'd come to work twice with bruises on her arms, and had taken to wearing a neck scarf lately. It was something, but not enough. Bruises are nameless. Having placed his flashlight on the bed table, Guidi stood in front of the window, tried its lock, opened and closed it, measured the two steps between the window and the bed. There was no escaping the conclusion. Why would the window be open on a late December night, if not to throw herself out?

On his way out, floor by floor, Guidi stopped by every locked door in the apartment building. No name tags, no tenants. What were the Germans storing in those empty spaces? He tried his key in several locks, without success. Through the soprano's door on the ground floor, exceedingly loud sounds came from a radio. The news reported how the American 34th Division had been halted below the town of Cassino.

Bora heard the same news at Mount Soratte, where he spent the day with Kesselring and General Westphal. Dusk was spreading over the city at his return, sheets and streaks of violet drawn across a clearing sky; he drove past the dark expanse of houses at high speed, bound for the mud-clogged Anzio front.

13 FEBRUARY 1944

In fact, Bora only made it as far as Aprilia. He'd managed to reach it by a miracle, along country lanes spared by shelling and bombs in the convulsion of craters, upheaved earth, trees splintered as they began to bud. Past a disused railway bed, at dawn he reached the station of Carroceto, where cannon fire was still being exchanged, but fighting had stopped enough for troops to crawl out of foxholes and gather the dead. A gray-faced, high-strung lieutenant showed him around and began to cry with exhaustion when Bora commanded him to sit down. American dead and English dead lined the streets on quilts of bloody mud, face up where they fell; medics looked like butchers. "Watch out, live wire!" someone yelled, and the gray-faced lieutenant was still sobbing with his face in his hands when Bora rode off in an army truck toward Aprilia.

Smoke hung in pallid layers over the town. All around lay disabled vehicles, dead mules, overturned carts, civilian dead pasted with dust and ashes, worn embankments, a geography of war Bora had learned by heart elsewhere, until he could move through it with a steady, heavy heart. Artillery fire came in fits from the direction of the sea, beyond fruit trees not even ten years old and zigzags of whitewashed orchard walls. Under the wraiths of smoke, Aprilia bore the name of its birth month and, like other towns in the Reclamation Land, showed its usual handful of factory-like brick buildings: city hall, church, *casa del fascio*, a few blocks of workers' housing. Hard to tell what was what right now. Fitful artillery fire came and went.

The improvised field hospital, crammed with enemy casualties not yet interrogated, was Bora's target of opportunity for fact-finding. It occupied a two-floored square house of ugly bricks – the whole town was bricks and two-floored square houses – packed with beds and pallets among which an army surgeon moved wearily.

All day Bora had smelled and recognized the odors of battle, and walking into the hospital dismayed him with the realization that he'd missed them: sweetish, intimate, sour and hard, the odors of wounded and dead flesh, painful and offensive but a part of him for so long that even their offensiveness was welcome. The surgeon – a Captain Treib, bleary-eyed, with some days' worth of blond growth on his face – stared at the Polish and Russian campaign ribbons on Bora's chest, and let him do the rounds of the crowded floor. Artillery fire, coming from somewhere westward (Bora knew where: the flat and muddy stretches reclaimed and planted forcibly, Mussolini's claim to greatness) had started up again full force. A closer blast caused the incongruously ornate ceiling lamps to swing; windowpanes rattled, plaster crumbled and fell. An amputee from across the room said in English, "My God," and then cried out the words again at the top of his voice. Bora turned to look at him.

And at that moment, even as he straightened from leaning over an American's bedside, a direct hit reached the corner of the building. Space, time, words seemed to explode. A metal basin came flying, smashed into a shelf, glass and iodine and phenol erupted all around. Pieces of masonry, tiles and stones jettisoned downwards, one of the lamps dropped with an armful of plaster and wires attached to it, the windows were obscured by the roof crashing down in sheets. Through their shattered panes a fury of debris burst in. Dust, glass, metal bits shot inside, rubble cascaded from the upper floor in heaps that clogged the stairs and blocked the door. A fretful high-pitched howl screamed into a second explosion, and the shock wave rocked and broke through the debris of the stairwell. Choking clouds of smoke and pulverized plaster flew into the room with it. The ceiling caved in from the center out.

This time Bora was thrown back against the wall, pinned to it by a rage of collapsing lumber. Through the wreckage, he saw flames leaping high from the truck parked outside the blasted window and a storm of plaster dust circling the room, where the one lamp still hanging swung like a censer in its own smoke. He tried to free himself and couldn't, to stretch enough to reach for the half-crushed bed and couldn't. Steadying his breathing was all he could do, guarding nausea was all he was able to do. Fear had no place in this. It was physical revulsion at being caught, his neurotic body response of the Stalingrad days, where the hopelessness of having no way out made him throw up before action, as if his animal shell had to empty itself to claim autonomy from starvation and defeat. He knew it well and it threatened to rack him out of control even as he stood there, the nape of his neck driven against the wall to keep check on himself and his breathing.

Other explosions followed, with the banging and cracking of things that break and trundle and fall in. Bora found enough room to slide down and crouch on the floor with his back to the wall, so tightly in control now; even panic was preferable to this being crammed inside by discipline, possessed by it and unable to let go.

"Oh my God!" the voice was crying from the ravage of the room.

Billows of dust rose and fell, obscuring even the closest object. In the extremity of his tension Bora was hardly aware of pain in his left leg, but when he groped for his knee, his hand met blood. The warm stickiness had had time to soak the cloth and leather of his breeches. His left boot was already filled with it. Pain was slow in coming, traveling through his stunned body. Bora wondered how he could have not noticed, though he had, his breathing had been affected by it. He fingered the blood and smelled it, that private touch and odor of self, frightening and known. Cold sweat beaded over him as in his Russian days, but fear did not follow. His mind neither elaborated nor anticipated things, so that each moment was its own disastrous self, bearable in its brevity, done with, and what came next was what came next.

It'd have been better had you died, his wife had said. And long ago – long ago, it seemed to him now, as far back as Poland, and her first silence – his heart had told him that she was out of love with him.

Airplanes were tearing overhead. Bora recognized the sound of mid-range bombers, deadly accurate. All around, bombs came down in clusters, devoured each other's echo until one felt no obstacle of skull or flesh between the wracking noise and one's brain, and the din grew beyond hearing. With a bone-cracking effort Bora reached for the bed through the lumber, and grasped the frantic hand of the man lying there.

Bora's cool-faced secretary looked uninterestedly at Guidi. "The major is not in, and is not expected to be in today. He left no message for any civilian."

Guidi took her dryness and accented Italian in his stride. "Has he set aside a packet for me?"

She gave him an annoyed look. Under the military cap her hair was accurately combed in two rolls on her temples, shiny as if cast in metal. "Guidi, you said?" She extricated her shapely, silk-sheathed legs from under the desk and stepped into Bora's office. Guidi heard her shuffle some papers, and return empty-handed. "I'm sorry, there's nothing."

Guidi took a deep breath. "There ought to be a bundle of letters."

She had again sat at her desk, with a pretended air of absorption, placing a blank sheet in the typewriter. "Letters? Then you should have said you were seeking letters." From a drawer she took out a sealed manila envelope, marked *Briefe* in Bora's handwriting. Without wasting time in further conversation, she gave it to him and began typing.

Inside the envelope were the translations of Magda's letters, and a note from Bora which Guidi chose not to read before leaving the building. Nervous after the early-morning air raid on the railway across the Tiber, the Germans were rude and inquisitive, and Guidi especially disliked the Gestapo uniforms gloomily staining the hallways.

Bora had written down the first names of two men mentioned in Magda's recent correspondence. One, Emilio, was Italian and "very young, now out of town." The other was German, still in Rome, and his name was Egon, a captain in the SS.

I believe it's Captain Sutor, but don't know how useful my mediation with him would be, the note concluded. *If needed I will put you in touch with him. Should things not work out in the next couple of days, get in touch with SS Colonel Eugene Dollmann, whose phone number my secretary is instructed to give you.*

Guidi read through the lines that Bora had at the time of writing entertained at least some doubts about returning from wherever he was about to go.

14 FEBRUARY 1944

The heads of fat, brown-faced sunflowers rose and fell in waves over the black earth, swinging back and forth on endless stems. Deep sky, whitewashed farmhouses under roofs like trimmed haircuts of straw. Birds and airplanes stitching the sky like wounds, hands parting the shafts and hairy leaves, and no one stopping him. A yellow laughter of light seemed to run through the sunflowers even as they bent and fell over to uncover more sky and earth – they cheered and clapped with their bearded leaves. They billowed and tried to overwhelm him in black and yellow on the way, but there was no stopping Bora from what he would find.

The fin of the tail rudder stood, stark and green, high against the sky.

If only the sunflowers would close again and trap him as one who wants to drown. But they rose and fell away, and no one stopping him, no one stopping him.

"In God's name, Bora, are you alive?"

Bora had to stare at the man shaking him before he recognized General Westphal at his bedside. He had no idea of where he was, though obviously Westphal had found his way there. The general kept shaking him. "I've been knocking on your goddamn door for ten minutes, and finally got the concierge to open with a skeleton key. I thought you had given up your damn ghost! When did you get back, and what in God's name…? There's blood all over!"

With much effort Bora pulled himself up against the headboard. He felt empty and nauseous, but was starting to remember. "No time to change," he apologized, "I know I'm late," and other words that were nonsense even to himself.

When he tried to get off the bed, Westphal prevented him. "Don't get up, you fool," he said, and to someone on the threshold, invisible to Bora, "Get a physician right away."

16 FEBRUARY 1944

In Guidi's reckoning, the "boy" Professor Maiuli had started coaching in Latin was well past high school age. He was likely a university student, since classes were not running these days. Home early by coincidence, after crossing Rau on the stairs Guidi asked the professor, "How did he avoid the draft? It's remarkable that the Germans haven't taken him as forced labor."

Maiuli touched his chest. "Bad lungs. You needn't worry about Antonio, Inspector. I saw his university papers – all's in order. He lives with his parents near St Lawrence's."

"A fine place to get bombed. And he comes clear across town to be coached?"

"He heard how good the professor is," Signora Carmela spoke up. "There's nothing strange about that."

Francesca had stayed home with a headache, though she hardly looked in pain. With an undefinable little smile she'd been listening to the exchange. "He has a beautiful profile," she said. And when Guidi turned his attention to her, she added, "Well? He does." She filled her mouth with a piece of bread and put her coat on. "I'm going to see my mother. Don't any of you wait up for me."

There had been several air raid alerts in the past few hours, and only the day before the police station at Monteverde had been hit by errant bombs. "Why don't I drive you there?" Guidi suggested.

It was raining, dark and close to the curfew when they reached the address. Little was visible of the house except that it looked like every other house front along the Via Nomentana, a lonely spot where the remains of a brick kiln marked the old city limits.

Guidi rolled his window down. "Who really lives here?" he asked.

"My mother, I told you. Why?"

His resentment was up. Guidi didn't know what to do with it and grew bold. He said grumpily, "I just don't want to be driving you around to your lover."

Francesca was a melancholy presence in the small car, faceless but for the glare from an incoming truck's headlights. The headlights were blackened into slits by paint, and only cut a sliver of murky yellow across her cheek. "Why, what would that be to you? It's not like I have to answer to you about my life."

After she stepped out, and the house absorbed her, Guidi remained in the car. Chilly rain came in through the open window, and still he looked out toward the house. Francesca knew Antonio Rau well, that was clear. A look, a word half-said, the way they brushed past each other in the hallway. Three times Guidi had seen him, and he did not like him. Rau was her lover, or her contact with the underground, or both. Three times he'd been about to face him, and only the awareness that Francesca was involved dangerously, to the immediate risk of the household, and he'd have to act upon it, had held him back. The Germans were the enemy, now more than ever – it wasn't that. But where *that* put him with Bora, Guidi didn't even want to think.

Back at Via Paganini, Pompilia Marasca, candlestick in hand, met him on the stairs as soon as he walked in. She said, "I've been meaning to talk to you," one hand on her hips and hard to avoid.

"It's almost ten o'clock. Can't it wait?"

"As a good citizen, I don't think so."

In the semi-darkness Guidi looked without interest at her skin-tight black dress. "Well, what is it?"

"It's that new, Jewish-looking visitor that you have at your apartment. Three days now he's been coming and going freely, whatever he comes here for, or whomever. Don't you think the neighbors watch? People are being turned in to the Germans for less than that." Her eyes narrowed and she spoke through graciously rounded red lips. "You ought to tell the young lady to mind her acquaintances, before somebody does something unneighborly."

"I appreciate your concern," Guidi said dryly. "Continue to keep an eye on things."

Careful to keep her candle steady, Pompilia took a reticent step back. "If nobody acts on it, what good is my observing things?"

17 FEBRUARY 1944

On Thursday, Bora, back at work for the past two days and limping again, phoned SS Captain Sutor to invite him to lunch.

Sutor sounded wary. "What's the occasion?"

"Other than rejoicing about our parade of Anglo–American prisoners yesterday? I'm headed to see what damage the Allies did yesterday to the Colosseum and the Protestant Cemetery. Since I'll be passing by on my way to St Paul's Gate, I thought you might want to join me."

"Why should I want to join you? I don't give a fig about those old ruins. And you, I thought you'd have little taste to see what bombs do after Aprilia."

Bora kept his temper. "I hear Montecassino was far worse. Well, don't let me take you away from your job. If you change your mind, I will be at the Colosseum at 1200 hours."

And indeed, at noon it did not surprise him to see Sutor's Kfz 15 drawing near his Mercedes on the Palatine side of the Colosseum. "I'm glad you could make it after all," Bora said, pointing to damage on the venerable archways, and to the pumice-packed scaffolds around the Arch of Constantine.

"What are you going to do, tell me the story of the Colosseum?"

"If you wish. It was not my intention, however. We don't know one another, I thought, and probably should. Our positions in Rome are similar enough."

Sutor removed his cap long enough to slick his blond hair back. "You get around much more than I do, it seems to me."

"Only because I speak the language. But I don't fraternize much."

"Well, what's keeping you?"

"Force of habit." Bora looked straight at Sutor, and neither man had his mind on the ruined walls. "After five years of married life it's awkward to start again."

"Why are you telling me all this? I'm not your confessor."

"No, but you're well introduced." They began walking around the formidable arena, unhurriedly. "Let's face it, Captain. You're about my age, have been here longer than I... There's a party, the day after tomorrow, at Dollmann's house, and I'm sure we're both invited."

"So, you're looking for a lay. Why, don't you trust Dollmann's judgment in the matter?" Sutor grinned at his own joke. "Maybe you should try your secretary, Major. She's a nice piece." Seeing that Bora kept a friendly mien, however, "I *do* know most of the women who'll come to the party," he ended up boasting. "What are you looking for?"

Bora shrugged. "A well-built woman. Athletic, you know. Not fat, but nicely built."

"Is that all?" Sutor laughed. "I can't believe you're so simple in your tastes!"

"The physical is all that matters when there isn't to be more than that, Captain."

"Blonde or brunette?"

"I have no preference." Bora kept silent a while, wishing he could believe a small part of what he was saying. His left arm hurt. He still ached from the bruises of the air raid, and the shrapnel fragment in his leg had reawakened all the pains of his September wounds. Letting Sutor prod him, he did not rush to answer. "Since you insist," he said when they'd come nearly full circle around the Colosseum, "speaking of secretaries, I was thinking of someone like the poor Reiner girl. As you know, I've been handling the paperwork for her parents. I had a chance to see photos of her. One can't judge her personality, but the appearance was attractive."

Sutor's wariness was up, and immediately down again. His feline blondness made him look smarter than he was; of this Bora was convinced. "She was a damn pleasant girl," he said.

"Well." Bora stepped away. "Here's my car, and there is yours. Should we continue on to the English Cemetery or go to lunch?"

"Wait a minute, Major. What's the last word on how she died?"

Bora walked to his car. "You heard the doors were locked. She must have killed herself after all. Cemetery or lunch?"

"That can't be all." Sutor held him back. "You know something else you're not saying."

"I don't. And I'm truly sorry I brought up the issue."

"Then there is something else. Look, I knew her *well*; I think you ought to tell me."

"It's not my place to tell. Please forget the matter, and if it's all the same with you, let's drive to St Paul's Gate."

Sutor kept Bora from closing the car door. "No. Lunch. You said lunch, and lunch it is."

At the restaurant – he had insisted on going to *Dreher*'s – he resumed the argument. "Now that you brought it up you must finish it. Come on, what has emerged from the investigation?"

"I am not the one in charge of it. It's Inspector Guidi, of the Italian police."

"How do I get in touch with him?"

"You embarrass me, Captain. Why would you want to become involved in an ugly story? You know policemen and their stupid questioning."

"So what? Do you think I couldn't handle questions by him? *I* may have information he's interested in. I have nothing to hide. Hell, I've got a career to think of!"

Bora looked down, with the excuse of unfolding his napkin. He thought of the sad rooms of Via Tasso, and his heart was sick at Sutor's words. "I will give you Guidi's number. But kindly do not tell him how you got it."

That evening Guidi stayed at work until late. At his return home, Francesca was the only one still up, reading *Città* in the saint-strewn parlor. It was as good a time as any, and Guidi reported the gossip he'd heard from Pompilia the night before.

Francesca slapped the magazine on her knees, her bony cheekbone like a blade against the dark upholstery of the armchair. "Why don't you listen to the gutter, since you're at it?"

"If gossip creates danger to the Maiulis, I'll listen to the sewer."

"Ha!" She regained some humor. "Can't you tell she's jealous? Just as you are."

"Why in the world should I be jealous?"

"Because I haven't told you whether I like you."

"Neither have I."

It was clever of him. Francesca lost the advantage, and for a moment they stared at each other without a word. Then she took up the magazine again, turning the pages in haste. "Anyway," she said, "if it's Rau who bothers you, he's neither Jewish nor the *father*."

"But you do know him. Should anything go wrong, the Maiulis will be in trouble."

Francesca teased the magazine's first page, tearing little pieces off it. "Is it forbidden to know someone who comes for his own business? You're the policeman. If anything goes wrong, it's because you'll make it go wrong." Her voice, not cold but distant somehow, Guidi would remember many months later, when all this was already a part of the past forever. "And how much do you report to your German friend about us?"

"He never asks."

That, too, would change.

18 FEBRUARY 1944

On Friday morning, Guidi noticed the renewed stiffness in Bora's walk. Other than that, he was his usual self. No trace of worry about the battle for Cassino, raging in the nearby south.

"Major, I got a call from Captain Sutor, through his interpreter."

Bora smirked, walking to close the door of his office. "So, will you meet him?"

"Next week. While you were away, I also visited the Reiner apartment again. So far, the strongest evidence that someone went through it is that we found no letters, no scraps of paper with notes or numbers or scribbles on them. Only receipts from a couple of stores."

"Not everyone keeps correspondence around," Bora intervened. "*I* don't."

"Just hear me out, Major. They might have removed evidence, though we don't know for example whether the pillowcase was missing to begin with, or what a missing pillowcase means. But there were still minute bits of ashes here and there in her room. People are burning anything they can find in their stoves, I agree, but only in her bedroom did I find these." Out of his pocket, he showed a small clear glass bottle, in which were dust-like remnants. "They aren't just cinders from the outside. I think paper was burned in her room at some point."

Bora remembered the impalpable ashes he'd noticed on her windowsill. "If that's the case," he said, "it can only have happened *before* her death. A third party would have disposed of any documents elsewhere."

"Well, let's assume that for some reason she decided to get rid of letters, addresses, whatever else. Prudent, you might say, for an embassy employee. But it does point out her desire to *hide* something, or her fear that her belongings might be gone through."

Bora sat on the corner of his desk, his left leg extended – bandaged, from what Guidi could tell through the tightness of breeches at the knee. He took from a manila envelope a batch of letters, holding them up for Guidi to see. "These are the originals from which I translated for you. Even when writing home, she was careful not to mention her boyfriends' surnames. Was it correspondence she received from someone else that she worried about?"

"Possibly. And there's something else, too. I'm just curious, but what is stored in the vacant apartments up and down from her own?"

"Office supplies of some kind." Bora replaced the letters in the envelope. "Nothing of importance, or else we would not keep them in a house without porter or security. I expect I could gain access to those spaces."

"Please try. So far, all we really know is that she came home some time before seven o'clock on 29 December, changed, and by eight she was lying four floors below her window. If she killed herself, for whatever reason – fine, we'll have to be content with that. But if someone did her in, he wouldn't be so idiotic as to leave his glasses behind."

"Or damning correspondence."

"And even if it were true that Merlo left his glasses, Major, on that night he might have just been headed for the apartment to retrieve them, and ran into the scene of her death. It'd have been enough to make anyone sick." Guidi watched Bora walk to a plainly visible wall safe and put the letters inside it. He said, "Either way, I'm being squeezed. I can't openly pursue Merlo, but can't exonerate him either. Whatever is going on between the head of police and Merlo's faction, I'm in the middle. The other cases coming my way are chicken manure, *nothing*. I make work by handling small black-market rings, spiteful neighborhood disputes and the like. They got me here for one reason only, as far as I can tell – to prove Merlo's guilt and take the rap for it."

Bora took his place on the desk corner again. "Which does not exclude that Merlo might be guilty. I will check into the vacant apartments, and so much for not making promises. I will stick my neck out and locate Merlo's optician, too, one way or another."

19 FEBRUARY 1944

"Sciaba?" At the party, Kappler repeated the name pronounced by Bora. "We have no one in custody by that name. It's a bit impertinent of you to assume that because a man has a Jewish surname he'd be with us." But he seemed amused that Bora had asked.

Bora was fairly sure that Sutor had mentioned Magda Reiner to his superior at some point, and gambled on it. "I'm seeking him in relation to the Reiner case."

Kappler's eyebrows rose enough to show surprise, or interest. "Scratch a Jew, you find a womanizer. Why don't you try the state prison?"

Bora said he would. As Dollmann had promised, this was a cozy and informal get-together, SS and Security Service men mostly, with a token number from the army and Air Force. Maelzer was not here, and Westphal was expected later.

American music was being played on a gramophone, some swinging, wistful love tune that one could well dance or weep to.

"You know," Kappler continued, "you could have asked me to acquaint you with the ladies. I believe my tastes are closer to yours than Captain Sutor's. You don't come across as someone who'd have trouble getting what he wants. There's a wayward persistence about you. But that's how it is with us military men. Women are an entirely different kind of catch."

As for Dollmann, he had been floating from guest to guest. "Why on earth have you asked that bunglehead Sutor to play matchmaker?" he whispered to Bora as he passed by.

"I had other things to discuss. It was a credible excuse."

"He's boasting about it to everyone, and now you're stuck with having to take a woman home."

"I'm hardly stuck to anything any more."

Dollmann changed subject. "We heard about your gallantry at Aprilia. Digging through the rubble in spite of your own injuries and on behalf of wounded prisoners, no less."

"Being caught like a rat is nothing to brag about."

"We know that, but for the world we must say that it was bravery." Dollmann winked. "Enough said. Here comes one of Sutor's prospects. I'll leave you to her."

Bora took a glass from the closest tray before the woman reached him. An oversized blonde with sequined ribbons in her hair, she had a friendly, dense look. Her name was Sissi or Missy or other such, and over the generous cleavage the accent was Austrian.

"So, Major, where do you quarter?"

Bora had done some rather hard drinking, but still watched his words. "The Flora," he half-lied, since his office was really there.

"So do I! Curious. I never saw you there nights."

"I often spend my nights out."

"You could spend them at the hotel and miss nothing of what's available outside."

"That may be. But you don't know what I'm looking for."

Her smile widened. Traces of lipstick smeared her teeth as she did. Though she was still young, a weariness of men and yet desire for them came through to him. "It can't be so far-fetched that I can't guess it. I'm a pretty exotic guesser."

Across the smoke-filled room, Dollmann caught his eye and toasted him with a glass in his hand. Bora gulped a shot of bourbon. "I can be, too."

"*Really!*" Her face upturned, she seemed to be judging from his expression whether or not he was aroused enough for a decision. "I hope you're not the kind who plays hard to get, Major."

"I am. You should see me when I haven't had a drink or two. I'm pig-headed and impregnable. And what could you teach me that I don't know?"

On tiptoes, she whispered in his ear and Bora laughed. "I learned that in Spain."

"Not the way I do it."

By the time Bora knew he was reaching the stage of dangerous candor, safer company was in order for the rest of the night. He eventually came to join Dollmann, who said, "You seem to be doing all right with the ladies. I counted five so far."

"Yes, and I have it up to here."

"It's probably the drink, not them. But you're nearly as good as I am at keeping them entertained. Charm is what they love, and providing that you give them heaps of it, they may leave the rest alone. But you probably don't want that either."

Bora let the statement go past him. With a remarkably steady hand he lit Dollmann's cigarette and his own. He was uneasy, and distressed with the superficial excitement that came from talking to available women. "Did my wife tell you why she sought an annulment?"

"I thought we were not to discuss her."

"As you see, I ask."

"She touched upon it."

"And what do you think?"

"Unlikely match – no loyalties. Very unlike you. I'm puzzled as to what brought and kept you together, even though I suspect what it might have been." Dollmann's stare was like a ring around Bora, who did nothing to elude it. The answer slipped from him with great bitterness.

"No great virtue, Colonel. I could lay her harder than the others."

"I bet you could, too." Dollmann laughed at his own words, and at Bora's quick apology. "No offense taken. Only, don't let these women know."

At half past midnight, merrier music blared from the gramophone, guests were dancing, and it took Dollmann a while before he even noticed the valet waiting with telephone in hand. A moment later, he was calling on Westphal, whose face went suddenly white. The general found his way amidst the dancing couples to Bora, who was leaning against the wall between two talkative actresses. "Bora," he said quickly, "come. They've just started firebombing Leipzig."

Within minutes the Saxons were bound to the Flora for further news. Standing by the phone in his office, Bora felt entirely sober. It was as if no alcohol had entered his bloodstream while he waited to hear what districts and suburbs had been targeted. Westphal paced the floor. "It has to be the airplane works, Bora."

Bora glanced at him without removing the receiver from his ear. "Let's hope so."

"Where do your parents live?"

"Lindenau."

"I have in-laws in Moeckern. Keep trying."

Bora needed no goading. Long-distance communication, halting, crackling in from Air Force commands somewhere, led to other calls, other heavy pauses. He thought of Thomas Hardy's verses, broken into the bits that mattered and were full of anguish right now. *Upon Leipzig's lawns, leaf-strewn,* and,

Whereover a streak of whiteness swept – the Bridge of Lindenau... To Heaven is blown Bridge Lindenau... Westphal paced the floor, and Bora stubbornly manned the phone. By the time confirmation came that only the Leipzig fighter and bomber factories had been hit, it was Sunday morning, and even the last of Sutor's girls was in her beauty sleep.

20 FEBRUARY 1944

On Sunday morning, small and twisted in her kitchen chair, Signora Carmela knit her brow. "The professor is good enough to say that I'm no gossip, and I take pride in that. Of course he's too good to me, and many of the compliments he pays me I don't deserve. All the same, a gossip I'm not. I wouldn't even mention this to you, Inspector, if I didn't worry about Francesca. The professor and I are old. We've had our life – whatever God wills for us now, it's well done. But she is young, and the times are hard. I *have* to tell you that I worry about her."

Guidi chose not to ask for details. "Did you speak to her?"

"It's like telling the wall. The wall won't say yes or no. What made my blood run cold, though, was seeing her last night handing something to Antonio Rau. I wasn't looking on purpose, but it was a big roll of money she gave him." Signora Carmela squirmed in her shawl. "Where would a young woman get so much money? Why would she give it to a man she just met? I'm afraid for her, I tell you. I wish you'd watch over her, so that she won't get in trouble."

Guidi nodded unthinkingly. His wristwatch read seven in the morning, it had rained buckets, and Francesca had not come home the night before. He promised to "do something about it," and out of a paper bag he pulled the side benefit of a raid on black marketeers the night before, in the shape of a full loaf of bread.

He and the Maiulis were readying for an unusually luxurious

breakfast when Francesca returned, soaked and pale with cold. She stopped by the kitchen door, crying out, "White bread? Great!" Ignoring the elders, she singled out Guidi, who sat with a piece of bread in his mouth. "Just the time to change," she said, "and I'll join you." Moments later she was back in her nightgown, a breach of decorum in the well-run house. "I hope you don't mind if I make myself comfortable." She stood by the table to cut herself a slice of bread. Through the corner of his eye Guidi caught the old people's dismay at seeing the swell under the loose flannel cloth. The professor's face had an apoplectic tinge when she merrily said, "Well, and good morning to you all, too! Did the cat eat your tongue?"

1 MARCH 1944

It was still pouring ten days later when Bora drove across the Tiber to the "New Prisons" of Regina Coeli, like a dam of bricks facing the bridge straight on. He'd been away from Rome for a week, visiting the troops engaged in the attempted retaking of Anzio, sitting with them at Cisterna and other threatened inland posts, interrogating prisoners of officer rank, and generally seeking danger. Life at headquarters was "getting to him," he'd calmly told Westphal, and Westphal had cut him loose for a week.

Now he walked into the prison with a permit signed by Maelzer. Aldo Sciaba, it turned out, was detained in the German-controlled Third Wing, where Bora also expected to find General Foa. He did not, but Sciaba was taken out of his cell to meet him in a bare windowless room. He listened without a word while Bora explained his reason for being here. When handed the case containing Merlo's glasses, he took them out and studied them.

"Well?" Bora urged him. "Are they your work?"

"Yes, they are."

Bora dismissed the Italian guard. "Tell me more."

"Can you get me out of here if I tell you?"

"No. What I can do is arrange for your wife to visit you."

"And have her arrested too?"

"Why? She's not Jewish."

Sciaba was a short, patient-looking man with a waxy complexion to which the long prison stay had given gray undertones. "No, no." He waved a tired hand. "Let's leave her out of this. Just let her know I'm alive." For the next minute or so, Sciaba turned the glasses this way and that, looked through them, lifted them to the faint electric bulb. "These aren't anything His Excellency could use today," he concluded. "They're the pair I fitted for him two years ago. His eyesight was never good, but lately it has grown worse. I had to refit him frequently. He wouldn't carry these around. Where did you find them?"

Bora chose not to answer. "When did you fit him last?"

"In October, before they brought me here. He might still be wearing the last pair I sold him, though it's been about six months."

"Is it your policy to take back used glasses?"

"Yes, sir, it is. These were in my store. That's why I wondered where you found them."

"I did not find them. And that's all I want for now."

Seeing that Bora was about to leave, Sciaba spoke up. "Please tell my wife not to worry about me. Tell her they treat me decently, and all that."

Bora nodded, safely inscrutable under the shade of his visor.

"I mean, I was born an Italian citizen. That must count for something, right?"

Bora took the glasses back. He returned them to their case, slipped it into his breast pocket and took a step toward the door. Before knocking to be let out, he pulled from the cuff of his left sleeve a tightly folded piece of paper. His hand met the prisoner's only for the time necessary to effect the exchange. "From your wife," he said.

Back in his office, Bora gave his secretary the afternoon off, and called Dollmann's work number. The colonel would not give him an answer. Rather, he asked, "Why must you find out where Foa is, Major Bora?"

"Because one Cavallero 'suicide' is enough."

"And what would you know about that?"

"Only that Italian generals who refuse to cooperate don't shoot themselves in the right temple twice, especially if they're left-handed."

"From what I hear, Foa is alive." Dollmann dragged his words, clearly unwilling to give out the information by phone. "I cannot tell you where he is. I think you ought to adhere to your sightseeing schedule and visit the *Domus Faustae* instead."

The receiver was clicked down, but Bora had caught the clue in Dollmann's advice. The Latin name of the Lateran basilica undoubtedly pointed at Kappler's jail on nearby Via Tasso.

He stopped by Westphal's office on his way out. "The only reason I'm letting you go," Westphal warned him, "is that I don't like the idea of SS informants turning in army officers, not that I give a damn about Foa. If you do see him, you are to convince him to talk. As for the rest, all you'll get from me is a signed request to transfer the optician to the Italian section of the state prison. And that's purely for pragmatic reasons relating to the Reiner case."

"Shouldn't General Foa be transferred back, too?"

"He won't be, so don't ask."

Sutor was not at Via Tasso. It was Kappler who received Bora, and – having read the request for transfer – promised he would look into it. "If there are no specific political charges against him, Sciaba can be transferred, probably as early as the end of the month." He invited Bora to sit across the desk from him. "Didn't I tell you he was not with us? Sit down, don't be in a hurry. Tell me, what do you think about the attempt on the Fascist vice-secretary two weeks ago?"

Bora sat. "That if he persists in celebrating the Party saints he'll get more of it."

"Yes. I told him in no uncertain terms that this is no time for parades, but he doesn't want to hear that. Has other shindigs planned for the tenth and the twenty-third." Pointing to his own collar, Kappler asked, "When did you get one of those?"

Even without looking, Bora knew he meant the Knight's Cross with Oak Leaves. "Stalingrad and Kursk. The Oak Leaves caught up with me last week."

"Garish but telling. It helps to compensate you for past sufferings, and now they'll make postcards with your portrait for children to swap."

"On Monday, Field Marshal Kesselring visited our command." Bora spoke in as neutral a tone as he could, eyes leveled at Kappler. "He believes the fate of officers like Foa to be a key to the loyalty of what Italian troops are left in the north."

"Really? Has he talked it over with SS General Wolff?"

"It's on the field marshal's agenda. After all, Foa readily collaborated with German authorities. His arrest was only due to unwillingness to reveal the whereabouts of other officers."

Kappler had been listening coolly, but now had a troubled laugh. "The *other* officers are precisely those who refuse to serve alongside you and me."

"I'd just as well do without them."

"So, you've come to see Foa. Who told you he's here?"

"No one, actually." Bora looked away from Kappler for the first time when an ambulance passed outside with siren blaring. "Is he?"

Kappler did not say. He was fingering an ashtray with quick strokes, muscles contracting on his narrow jaw. The ashtray was an antique dish. "You'll have to come back for him."

Across the paper-strewn surface of the desk, Bora looked at the hands around the unpainted, frail dish. Shoulders relaxed, breathing relaxed, he was doing better than Kappler at the game of disguised control. "I would, except that I am to try to convince Foa to accede to your demands, and report to the field marshal tomorrow morning."

Kappler's hands left the ashtray. "Well, then. You'll see him as he is. He's a troublemaker. You dealt with troublemakers in Russia."

"I also heard he made a scene at the state prison and must be kept in isolation. I quite understand, Colonel."

Bora had never met Foa, but had seen photographs of his sharp-featured face, with a shock of white hair swept back over the forehead. What he made out in the cramped room upstairs from Kappler's office – unspeakably stifling and foul – was a skull emerging from the thin skin of the cheekbones, strangely drawn and empty. The eyes alone were alive in it, round and deep and awake and following the visitor's motion toward the mat in a corner.

"General Foa, I come from Field Marshal Kesselring."

Foa neither moved nor acknowledged him. Only his eyes flicked about Bora's uniform. He sat crumpled against the corner of the room, as if one wall were not sufficient to hold up the broken lassitude of his frame. When his sight adapted to the twilight of the room, Bora made out dried bloodstains on the man's shirt and the front of his trousers. Blood drops and small sprays of it had dried on the wall as well. Bloody feces and urine from pain-induced incontinence had been released in the corner least visible from the door in an absurd attempt at privacy.

Bora took a step forward, startled when Foa mumbled, "And who the hell are you?"

"My name is Bora." He leaned over. "I spoke to you over the telephone in January, about a Republican song." The inane stupidity of words broke his thoughts like strings of beads that rolled off and were lost.

"So, you're the army hard nose I yelled at over the phone." When Foa stretched his lips in what Bora was unnerved to recognize as a smile, his swollen gums and missing teeth showed;

his tongue, too, was black, like a strange sick muscle grown in his mouth. A gray, caked growth of beard matted the old man's chin; at the corners of his lips nested dry blood clots.

"Sir." Bora crouched by the mat. "I must speak to you."

"If you think I'm telling you anything, go back the way you came." Still, Foa did not move. It was a horrible immobility in life, if this was life, in the stench of body glued to bloody cloth. Bora could not suffer that crushed inertia, and extended his hand to lift the prisoner, rearrange him, help him sit up.

"Don't touch me," Foa growled, and his eyes were terrible and imperious, alive in the dead face.

Bora drew back. Somehow he had to deny his own past suffering in order to accept this, shamed that the undefiled flowing cleanness of blood once issued from him had nothing to do with this extracting of matter from the flesh by torture, hideous as a profanation of form, impure. It revolted and condemned him by association, and both men knew so. Whatever sentence he built next was flimsy to his own ears, and to it Foa said no. Not listening to himself, Bora continued to speak anyway, angry at his senses for crowding him with sight and smell and the dreadful imminence of death. "General, I beg you to give us leave to help you. This is an untenable outrage, it must not continue —"

"Give me a smoke."

Bora had to make his hand firm enough to place a cigarette in the prisoner's mouth and light it, lowering his face not to stare. "I urge you to reconsider, General."

"Leave me alone."

"A man of your age —"

The fierce bloodshot eyes riveted themselves on him. "Of my age, of my age! I was a colonel when you hadn't yet grown hair between your legs. Leave me alone. If you must kill me, kill me, and get it over with. There's nothing I want to tell you, or Kesselring or Kappler. Nothing. Nothing. Nothing."

"Give me enough to help you."

"Help me? This is *my country*. None of you belong here, not you, not the Americans. I spit on your help. Tell Kesselring that."

"I will tell him what I see fit, General Foa."

"Then go to hell with the rest of them."

Bora stood up slowly. That he could not bring himself to leave proved nothing other than a mortified sense of shame. He turned away because he knew Foa's eyes were on him, and he had nothing to cover his shame. "I cannot go without some assurance from you."

"So that you won't be troubled, maybe?" Foa did move a hand, weakly. "No. I need to piss, lift me up."

Bora did so. By the elbow he raised him and supported him to his feet, had to all but carry him to the corner where he held him up forcibly as Foa fumbled to undo his trousers. He meant to avert his head, but the flow was stark blood and Foa passed out, crumpling so that Bora nearly lost hold of him and had to gather him up in his arms to take him, half-dragging him back to the mat.

At his exit from the room he learned that Kappler had left for the day. It was just as well, because all his safeguards of discretion had blown, and a wrangle now would compromise what he planned to do next. When the massive door opened at the bottom of the stairs, the fresh bracing air of the street welcomed him and Bora gulped it in deep drafts. Across the street, his car waited, driver at attention next to it; his pasty boyish face seemed nearly blank after seeing Foa's injuries and ordure. Bora ordered him to return to headquarters alone.

He walked under the pelting rain, avoiding the safety of wide streets and squares; he kept away from the mighty churches beached on wet strands of cobblestones, walking where Germans did not, thinking of what he should tell Kesselring that could if it pleased God conceivably *fit*.

That evening, he happened to call Guidi while the police station was in turmoil over the shooting of a German courier at Via 23 Marzo. Bora, who had not yet heard about it, recalled the sound of the ambulance in Kappler's office, and how the colonel had left the building in haste. He asked if there was a description of the killer.

"Some children were playing in the street. We're questioning them now." Guidi did not add that a woman had been seen hurrying off with the soldier's briefcase.

Bora was gone from the telephone for a couple of minutes, presumably to brief Westphal; at his return he told Guidi of his visit to Regina Coeli.

"Major, can you guarantee Sciaba's availability in case of a trial?"

"I cannot even guarantee that I won't be shot as I walk down the street. What makes you think I can guarantee anything in this damned city?"

Guidi knew when to let go of a subject. "I'm meeting Captain Sutor tomorrow afternoon," he said, "and will be in touch with you afterwards."

"Do what you want."

Until half past nine, Bora worked at a complete record of Foa's military achievements, to pad Kesselring's case with General Wolff. He seldom had headaches, but tonight tension cramped his shoulders and neck until it felt like a rod driven at the base of his nape and knots tightening all around it.

His secretary prepared to leave. She poured herself out from behind the desk like a liquid, taut and long-legged in the closely fitting uniform. Bora watched her approach the desk – which she did every night, to ask for orders and permission to retire – hands folded in front of her.

"Good night," he said. Eyes back on his papers, still his peripheral vision showed him her hands, like a white stain on the dark of the skirt. There was a thin scent in her; Bora knew it by now and it was somehow familiar, a part of the office. Her nails were clipped closely but well rounded; at the grazing light of the table lamp a delicate sparse fuzz was visible on her wrists.

Bora looked up. Her cool face was in the shade of the lamp, utterly poised. There was safety in the quiet of features. Not friendliness or support: safety.

As for her, she kept on him the controlled glance of a woman who is not invited to come further. The major seemed very young tonight, battered like a wall that stands tougher because of it, but unsafe to her. "Will there be anything else, sir?"

Bora read in her face words and motions, and it was like a brief drunkenness trying to work its way through him, thick and quiet. Her hands were safely folded on the nest of the hips, bare of rings. Bora felt the heat of the lamp on his face, gentle but *on*, and pain coiled down from his neck, down his spine. He pulled back on the chair and she sensed the avoidance of his mind, not his body. Motionless, she feared losing him quickly and irretrievably for this hour. Already arousal in him became something else, *was* something else. His eyes traveled back to the papers before him. "No, thank you. Good night."

At the Maiulis, meanwhile, "No, no, Inspector. She's been home all day with a sore throat, poor thing." Unaware of Guidi's relief at her words, Signora Carmela served him supper. "I wonder why she didn't tell us she got married – we could have given her a little gift or something."

"Married? What do you mean?"

"Well, how else could she be expecting a baby? Go and ask her how she feels."

Guidi said no. He did not want to see Francesca after last night, when she had shrugged off his questions about Rau. "I owed him money, and paid it back. So what?" At his insistence, she had risen from the armchair, and impulsively kissed him on the mouth. Which was very much an answer, but not *the* answer.

4

At Mount Soratte, Bora was disappointed to find that SS General Wolff had already come and was closeted with Kesselring. He was forced to leave his documentation without a chance to further Foa's cause. Back in Rome on Thursday morning, he was summoned to the Propaganda Fide Palace, where the unusual coalition of Cardinals Hohmann and Borromeo gave him an earful about the overnight bomb damage to the Vatican's inner courts and railway station.

"Is it your doing?" Hohmann asked with a teacher's pointed stare.

Bora tried not to resent the question. "Why would we bomb the Vatican City? Piazza Bologna was bombed the other night – definitely not our doing. It shook us rudely on that side of town, Your Eminence."

"An open city ought to be free of military occupation, Major."

"Not by definition. By definition, it merely has to be demilitarized."

"And I suppose your uniform does not denote military character."

"It depends whether one considers 'character' as a distinctive trait or inherent quality."

"So, as long as you're in Rome you subscribe to your accidental rather than metaphysical militarism. A soldier on the outside only, eh?"

"I am not involved in offensive actions, Your Eminence."

"Only if you speciously narrow your definition of offense."

Borromeo intervened. "Speaking of Scholastic definitions, Major Bora, why don't you come and view the books we salvaged from the ruins of the Bishop's palace at Frascati?" Quickly he led the officer to the next room. "Are you out of your senses, trying to equivocate with Hohmann? He'll make field-gray mincemeat out of any rationalization your army can think of. He's exasperated at what happened today at the labor prison."

Bora politely freed himself. "I don't have enough details to discuss the incident."

"Peace of angels, Major! What is there to discuss when a poor woman is shot for asking to see her husband?" The books were kept in crates inside a small laboratory, where the cardinal preceded Bora. "You will be pleased to know that a surviving eighteenth-century set is from your family firm at Leipzig, complete with your *Fidem Servavi* motto. Cardinal York knew good commentaries on Aquinas when he saw them."

"Ours were not as good as Grotius'," Bora replied. He doubted Borromeo had taken him aside just to separate him from Hohmann, and his forced geniality disturbed him.

"I must agree that your critical edition of Spinoza was much better."

They began leafing through the venerable pages, with Bora less interested in the survey than in Borromeo's reason for not speaking his mind. "So, the annulment has gone through," he prompted at last.

"Yes, it has."

Bora put away the book. "It's amazing how five years are quickly disposed of."

"The Church ties and loosens as it judges proper, Major."

By the noon hour, the Roman sky was again thick with the roar of airplanes bombing the outskirts, likely the railyards to the east. Thundering from the western quarters indicated that ammunition dumps might be the primary target. Flak artillery boomed now and then in response, as if unconvinced of its effectiveness. For all that, Bora was unruffled when Guidi met him in front of Magda Reiner's house.

"Sorry for being late, Major. The street is blocked."

"You're not late, I'm early. Here are the keys to the vacant apartments. Should we go up?"

There was no power, so they had to climb the stairs. Because of Bora's limp, Guidi preceded him to the first landing. He said, "We are at an impasse, Major. Merlo's glasses surfaced from a requisitioned store only when I did not seem quick enough in pursuing the official lead. Is Caruso doing it to harm Merlo, or to protect someone else?"

When Bora joined him by the door, and leaned forward to fit the key into the lock, for the first time Guidi noticed a gray hair here and there in his dark crop. "When you find out, you'll likely be relieved of the case. But is Caruso the only one who'd have an interest in muddying the waters?"

The door opened on an entirely dark, small waiting room. Guidi went in first, with his flashlight. "Well, Captain Sutor comes to mind. He drove her home that evening, and says he left her at the door no later than seven fifteen. But I did find a witness – an African police officer – who remembers seeing a car with a German license plate parked by the curb at least until seven forty. So, theoretically, Sutor might have been still around when Magda died."

Except for the waiting room, each room in the apartment was packed with boxes nearly to the ceiling. Guidi heard Bora rummage around at the glare of his own flashlight, and say, "You assume that was Sutor's car. Remember there was a party in the house that night, attended by Germans. And Sutor volunteered to talk to you. He *insisted* on it."

"He knows I can't check his alibi if I wanted to, Major. The fact remains that both he and Merlo were in the area. Evidence might have been removed by the SS as much as by Dr Caruso's office. Say, can you tell what's in these boxes?" Guidi asked, and Bora showed blank ledgers, reams of typewriter paper, blank envelopes. "Is someone covering for Sutor or just protecting his innocence, and doing the opposite for Merlo? No tests for alcohol or other substances were run on the victim, so we don't know whether Magda was drunk or drugged, let alone suicidal. I'd be reconciled to continuing to investigate and ask questions for which there are no answers, but I'm being pressured to conclude."

"If you want, I'll come down on Caruso."

"And the SS, too, who may be behind him?"

Bora replaced the office supplies in their boxes without answering. They went from room to room, and from one uninhabited apartment to the next, and everywhere stacks of boxed, unused paper items, enough to serve a century of bureaucracy. In the last apartment – 7B – they found more of the same, but from the kitchen Bora called, "What's this? Shine some more light in here, Guidi."

Guidi complied. The combined beams of the flashlights revealed what Bora seemed to have stepped on: crumbs and crusts of bread, a desiccated and brown apple core. The floor space was small, no more than a six-by-four-feet clearing among boxes, which Guidi explored on his knees. They'd been careful not to open the windows, but now the inspector walked to the stacks obstructing the kitchen window, took them down and opened the shutters. Little more evidence appeared – ash residue bearing the imprint of a shoe's tread, lint from a blanket – but Guidi studied it, then gathered everything according to its kind in the envelopes Bora held out to him.

Afterwards, they sat in Bora's car to discuss matters.

"Even without racing to draw conclusions, Major, we have to admit it's odd that someone might be picnicking in a German-owned untenanted apartment, and in the same building where a death occurred."

Bora watched Guidi pull out a nearly empty box of Serraglio, and quickly offered his Chesterfields instead. "It took me some time to obtain the keys from the head of Supply Services, too. He made me sign for them, and told me none of the apartments had been opened since mid-October. Let us suppose, for the sake of argument, that someone was squatting in 7B. Is there a connection to the death? And would a killer stalking his victim – in a *German-owned* building – leave evidence of his being there?"

"Not unless he had to leave in a hurry." Having accepted the longer cigarette, Guidi placed it sideways in the box of Serraglio, for later use. "I'll have these scraps analyzed, and see if we can make some sense of them. I might be able to tell you more later."

Bora lit his Chesterfield. "It may have nothing to do with anything, but the fellow from the Greek Front, it turns out, did not exactly fall on the field of honor. And if he went missing, it's because he deserted. I have it from unimpeachable sources in Berlin. Of course, no word on where he might have ended up, if he's even alive. Which is more than I can say for him had he fallen into our hands after his exploit."

On the sidewalk, over the precise spot where Magda Reiner had fallen, a well-dressed young woman went by, holding a bouquet of evergreens. Neither man turned to look at her, but their eyes followed her even as they spoke. For Guidi, who'd walked in a haze since Francesca's kiss, all things were warped by his heightened interest in her. He glanced at Bora's hand on the steering wheel, at the wedding ring on it and what it meant, and the question came quickly and unchecked. "May I have your opinion on a completely different matter, Major?"

"Certainly."

"What – that is, how much restraint would you advocate in a relationship?"

Bora was not surprised, or else guarded his surprise well. He put out the half-smoked cigarette. "That depends on the people involved. Are you both free to pursue it?"

"Possibly. I met her recently, but I know she's not married."

"Well, the next question is, is she willing?"

"I think so." Because Bora had an expression that Guidi read as mild curiosity at being chosen as an advisor, he felt he should add, "Knowing you've been married for years, Major..."

"I know how it is to grow up Catholic, too."

"I assure you it's less a religious issue than one of confidence. I'm a shy man, as you may have noticed." Guidi blushed as he said it, but as Bora kept straight-faced, with his thumb slowly turning the gold band around his finger, he went on. "She's aggressive but I can't tell whether she truly cares. She's fierce in some ways, and yet I know she has fragility also. We have spoken always superficially, but there's another dialogue happening between us at all times. I believe you know – motions, a turn of the face. I feel it without being able to give a name to it."

"Are you in love with her?"

"I don't know. By the way, she's pregnant."

This time it took Bora a moment to react. "And you want to hear from me whether you should make love to her? I am obliged to you for deeming my opinion even relevant."

"Well, you *have* a wife."

"Guidi, my wife left me." Bora said it kindly, as an urbane correction rather than a call for sympathy. "Your trust in my advice might be misplaced."

Guidi was caught entirely unawares. Of a sudden, he was deeply ashamed for envying Bora in the past weeks. "Major, I had no idea."

"It doesn't matter. I have to get used to the thought. But as for you, why don't you ask her? An aggressive woman will tell you exactly how she feels – that is, if you do want to hear it." They were looking at each other in a very unpretentious way now – their differences for once smoothed over, worn small and flat and insignificant. Bora was the first to lower his eyes, to protect some private aching space of his own. Slowly he drew a cigarette out of its case and laid it on the dashboard as if he had not decided what to do with it. Only when Guidi lit a match for him he placed it in his mouth and inhaled. "Next Thursday there's a reception at the Excelsior," he said. "It's an official Party holiday, and you should come. General Westphal ought to meet the man who is directing the investigation of the Reiner case. It'll be good political leverage for you in the event Caruso decides to give you trouble."

"I am embarrassed to say I may not have the required attire, Major."

"I've seen odd combinations of clothing lately, but we can have a garment store open up – all you have to do is pick what you want and take it."

"You say it as if one didn't have to pay." Guidi smiled.

"You don't." By contrast Bora was severe behind the faint barrier of smoke. "Christ knows those store owners no longer have use for money."

9 MARCH 1944

In the next three days, daylight bombing of Berlin began. The first to be hit were the textile plants south-west of Greater Berlin, and by Monday (Westphal had flown to meet Hitler that day) a major raid of 1,400 aircraft reached the city. On Tuesday, the Roman marshaling yards were hit again, and the popular districts beyond the Tiber heavily damaged. Cardinal Hohmann called the Flora to complain about the lack of adequate air defense. Bora took the line.

"The Church of St Jerome's was demolished, not to speak of the agony of hundreds who have been thrown out in the streets. What will be done about it, Major?"

Bora said, "I don't know. What will be done about the Catacombs of Priscilla?" And his oblique reference to a location where people were in hiding cut the conversation short.

When ten hostages were shot on Wednesday in retaliation for the attack on a fuel depot, Hohmann called again. Again Bora told him he knew nothing about it, adding that the Gestapo were the people to contact.

By Thursday Guidi had managed to find a suit. Not in a Jewish store, as Bora had suggested, but in a second-hand hole in the wall. It was of gloomy black cloth, and the sleeves were so long, Signora Carmela had to stitch them at the cuffs. She told Guidi the suit made him look like a mortician, and that it'd bring no good to wear black at a party.

The Excelsior, with its turreted mass, stood at this hour like the much ornate prow of an enormous ship ready to be launched, so huge that its hull was lost in the dark. Cars were parked up and down Via Veneto and Via Boncompagni, a full display of diplomatic license plates and chauffeurs in liveries and army uniforms. Security was absolute. Bora, who met a dazzled Guidi at the entrance, was impressive in dress uniform and with an array of ribbons, medals and badges that had begun to spill onto the right breast of his tunic. Guidi remarked on the Knight's Cross, and the German laconically replied, "I should hope so. It's all I'm worth."

In the hall up from the conciergerie, at one glance Bora judged the import of the reception, which he communicated to Guidi. Maelzer was here, and so were Westphal, Dollmann, Kappler, Sutor, Luftwaffe officers, SS officers, Fascists, diplomats, some prelates and many civilians. Borromeo stood out in a crowd of gowns like a Renaissance prince, chatting with women in his unrepentant old way of charm. Bora went to greet his superiors, and introduced Guidi. Maelzer paid little attention, but Westphal stared Guidi down. Guidi was stunned by the rank and beauty present. The women seemed to him unreachable and alien, a different race from the gray numbers of housewives one saw in the street, waiting for hours just to fill a jug with water from a fountain. Any of these outfits would make Francesca glow like a princess. Most of the die-hard

Italians present were in Party uniforms – those whom Bora knew, he was introduced to. Guidi was glad neither Caruso nor Merlo would attend.

This, he realized, was seeing Bora in his environment. The major moved no differently than he did outside, with wariness but altogether a confident attitude. From one group to the next, before long they came to Dollmann, whose fine smile stretched his lips rather than parting them.

"It's good to meet you, Inspector," the SS said in Italian, already looking away and toward Bora, who stood beside him. "I'm glad the major brought you as a guest. Don't let our brass intimidate you, we're quite friendly under the eagles and stripes." With that, Dollmann began inquiring about his career, so personably that Guidi was tempted to believe he was interested.

Bora had meanwhile begun to circulate. He acknowledged by a nod the presence of Kappler, who was speaking to a colleague but waved a curt little gesture to detain him. "One word with you, Major Bora." When Bora neared with a polished expression of neutrality, he said, "I understand you had scarce success with Foa."

"I had no success at all."

"I told you he's a troublemaker." Coming close to provocation without stepping into it blatantly, Kappler looked past Bora at Guidi. "Who's the fellow you came with? Ah. I see. Sutor told me about him. Is he any good?"

"I think he's good, yes."

And meanwhile Dollmann was telling Guidi, who looked as awkward as he felt, "It's an odd lot tonight. Do you realize there may be partisans and foreign agents among us, brazenly eating our cakes and eavesdropping?" He laughed a mean laugh. "Yes, they *would* dare. I keep an eye open for them, but who's to say, really? That's why I love Rome. The intrigue is splendid."

In due time Bora faced Cardinal Borromeo, beside whom was the wife of an American diplomat, "presently out of Rome". He had already noticed from a distance how her dress was exquisite in its simplicity, an off-white set of sculpted lines. Now he saw she wore no jewels but a thin chain of worsted gold. Her face was that youthful Anglo–Saxon face, open and clean and attractive. In his bad English, Borromeo introduced her as *Signora Moorfi*, and Bora bowed to kiss her hand, unaware that Dollmann had meanwhile drifted from behind and was speaking to her.

"Major Martin-Heinz Douglas Freiherr von Bora, Mrs Murphy. Major, Mrs Murphy, née Carroll, of Baltimore, whose husband is attached to the Holy See. The major is a Russian Front hero, Mrs Murphy. He's a terror on the enemies of the Reich."

Glancing up from her hand, Bora saw her expression grow cool, and it was no use being vexed at Dollmann for spoiling his chance of dialogue. Damage done, the colonel had already moved on. Mrs Murphy's hand drew back, and slackly hugged her left elbow as if to bar the space between them. "Well, Major, are there any redeeming qualities about you?"

He did not expect the question. The first answer that came to mind was, "Well, I like children."

"Oh. In which sense?"

"In the good sense, Ma'am. I would like to have some." And because of his wedding band, Bora felt he could say so and not sound forward. The fact that she was tempted to smile at the British form of his address made him relax. Moderately straddling the floor in front of her, he physically opened up to her, but without impudence.

"You speak English extremely well. Most Germans have a dreadful accent."

Bora laughed at the comment. "Actually, I was born in Edinburgh. And I'm Scots on my grandmother's side." She smiled this time, which he found seductive enough to feel his blood search the veins of his belly. "I'm often in the Vatican's neighborhood. I regret not having met you there."

Wisely, her eyes stayed on the medals and ribbons across his chest. "It's unlikely that you would or will. I am not fond of army get-togethers. The only reason I'm speaking to you at all is that Cardinal Borromeo thinks well of you. He told me of your generosity toward wounded prisoners – enemies of the Reich such as they are."

"I'm indebted to the cardinal," Bora said, meaning it. He was not often taken by a woman's presence as he was now. He'd quite forgotten Dollmann and Guidi and the party around him. Standing here was wonderful. It was wonderful. He'd thought himself unable to revert to an elemental stage of delight in someone else's nearness. "How do you find yourself in Rome?"

"I don't. I live within the Vatican City. *You* have Rome. And do you have an idea of how many children – since you say you like them – would enjoy the delicacies on the tables here tonight?"

"We all give according to our kind, Ma'am. It isn't exactly candy your compatriots are bombing them with, either."

She observed him, and it seemed to him that she could see right through the knot of insecurity and grief he had inside. He returned the scrutiny in his frank way, but with some effort. She appreciated the glance, he could tell. Without tenderness her lips questioned him, small thoughtful questions carefully answered. And Bora felt tenderness instead, and an impulsive need to be liked by her. "So then, Major, what else do you think of my countrymen?"

"I find your men superficial, but I admire American women."

"And I dislike German men."

"Ma'am, it's most assuredly my loss."

It was only because Borromeo resumed his place by her and overtook the conversation that Bora had to ask for leave, with regret continuing his rounds of the hall.

Dollmann placed a buttered canapé in his mouth as he said casually, "You're aroused," and at the startled look he received, "It doesn't *show*. I can tell." His eyes trailed up Bora's uniform in an innocent, candid way. "Do you like her?"

132

"Very much."

The colonel's attention wandered to where Mrs Murphy stood, speaking to other women of the diplomatic corps. "She's inexpugnable."

Bora took a long sip from a glass of mineral water. "I honor that, too."

"Why, what a good man you are!"

"Or stupid."

"No, no. True-souled, that's the word."

"Some good it does me, Colonel. It gets old when virtues are their own reward."

"Did she accept your offer to drive her home?"

"How did you know I asked?"

"I thought you might."

"She did not accept."

"Pity. At the end of the party I'll give a lift to your secretary, if you're not interested. Poor girl, she has eyes only for you, but I fear she may be getting ready to settle for less." And since Bora was discreetly looking for Guidi and how he was faring, "I like this associate of yours, this Guidi," Dollmann continued. "A decent chap. Do you get along?"

"Yes and no. We're very different."

"That's your fault, if you think of it. It's dangerous looking for a brother."

Bora took the blow, but not well. He'd lowered his defenses while speaking to Mrs Murphy, and now precipitously tried to rebuild them around himself, not quickly enough to answer Dollmann. By the time he'd regained his composure, an already drunk Egon Sutor came ambling his way with another SS officer by the name of Priebke.

"Are you having fun, Major, or do you still keep your tail tucked between your legs?"

Bora smirked at the equivocal joke. "It's a hard, cold world, Captain Sutor."

"So, you just let it hang?"

"The alternative is to let it stand. And a wagging tail gives the dog away."

"He's a good sport, isn't he?" Sutor turned to Priebke. "He doesn't swear, doesn't get plastered, is faithful to his estranged wife. He'd be awfully boring were he not such a bastard in the field, with all that he goes to Mass on Sunday."

Priebke grinned widely. "I see you brought along your police dog, Major. Is it for company or security?"

"I had an extra invitation."

"He's Magda's investigator," Sutor explained. "Asked *me* questions about her. As if I'd talk to a greasy Italian about the women I fuck. How's the inquiry going, Major Bora?"

"You'll have to ask the dog."

In his corner of the hall, Guidi was wondering if his eyes deceived him. Better dressed than usual, with his unruly black hair slicked back and his attractive profile cast against the blank space of a drawn curtain, Antonio Rau stood chatting by the refreshments table. Racing thoughts clogged Guidi's mind. The only one he salvaged from the garble was that Francesca ran a deadly risk if Rau worked for the Germans. Quickly he discarded the idea of asking Bora about him. Because Dollmann was within earshot and fussily looking at the sweets on a tray, he turned to him and resumed the conversation. Before long, he managed to approach the subject sideways. "Who is the officer that dark-haired man is talking to? I seem to have seen his photo somewhere."

Dollmann looked. "I doubt it. He's just a liaison officer in one of our offices. Gephardt is the name. And he's talking to one of our Italian translators."

So, that's what Rau does. Guidi tried to curb his anxiety. "I would think that with interpreters such as yourself your army would not need the aid of translators."

"I don't do low-level work. You must have people who can put messages and warnings for the population into simple Italian. Do you see the girl in red? That's Major Bora's secretary."

"I had occasion to see her at his office. She's a fine-looking woman."

"Isn't she?" Dollmann seemed to be asking him idle questions, without a real motive. "More's the pity, she doesn't interest our good major. As you know, he's very eligible." Curiously Guidi followed Dollmann's admiring glance toward Bora. "Very likable, too."

From his place by the table, Rau had seen Guidi, but continued to chat. Still, every time Guidi chanced a look at him, an attentive glance came back in his direction. They had been surveying one another for a while before Bora rejoined Guidi.

"Well, what do you think of the party?" Unlike Dollmann, Bora never volunteered information, and his questions were intended.

"I had never met so many SS officers in one spot. Colonel Dollmann tells me there may be spies and prisoners of war and even shirkers mingling with us."

"It's possible."

Guidi noticed that Bora carried around a full glass to avoid unwanted refills. His glass had already been taken and substituted three or four times, and he was starting to feel a pleasant but dangerous effect, with great leaps toward carelessness. When he looked toward the table again, Rau was gone.

"Who are you looking for?" Bora inquired. "You're searching the hall."

"Me? No, Major. I'm just being provincial." But Guidi was relieved to see that Rau was still here. With his back to the hall, he circulated among the Italians now.

A few steps away, Bora rejoined the elegant woman Guidi had seen him approach earlier. Whatever he was telling her, she listened with a skeptical cast on her face, though she very much seemed to want to smile.

Moments later, the electricity failed, but there were candles already in the chandeliers, and at once valets lit them. In the muted glare the decorations of skulls and seal-like sheen of belts and boots darted sinister. Bora was still talking to Mrs Murphy. Dollmann had turned to a group of his own, and Rau spoke to a fat civilian, both of them holding a plate with food on it. General Maelzer was helping himself to drink; Westphal eyed Guidi, which put him at unease, since he could not intelligibly communicate with him.

After the party, Rau left early and alone, which meant he had the privilege of a safe conduct. Guidi regretted not having brought his car, which would give him freedom to tag him. Facing him in the lobby a few minutes later, Bora was nonchalantly pulling his glove on the right hand with the help of his teeth. "Let's take a walk, Guidi. You need to clear your head. So do I, and I haven't even gotten drunk."

Soon Bora was preceding Guidi down the high-banked canal Via Veneto resembled at night, shored by large buildings and trees and leafy gardens. "So, what came of the scraps we found? You never mentioned them once all night." Hearing no answer from Guidi, Bora turned to look at him. In the moonlit cold air, impatient clouds of vapor formed around his uniformed figure as he breathed. "Well?"

"Nothing came of them, Major. I sent them off to the *Questura Centrale* and somehow they were *misplaced*. I'm confronting Caruso about it tomorrow, and you should know I may be dismissed from the case as a result."

Bora smiled, and Guidi could see how women might find him *charming*, as Dollmann said. "Caruso means nothing," he said, not so amiably, "and I'll remind him of it."

"He *is* chief of police, Major."

"Because we let him be. By our grace. I will come down on him and there's nothing else to be said. Don't irritate me, Guidi. Why do you resent being helped?"

"For the same reason you do."

"That is incorrect." Bora stopped on the sidewalk, and Guidi with him. "I accept assistance, from some. My injuries have taught me that humility. I hate it, but I learned it. How could I not, when I had a nun help me relieve myself because I was too weak to stand? I could die with shame, but there I was, thinking, 'She's a nun, and look what she is doing.' No. There's a time to accept help. And in any case, don't place much stock in anything Captain Sutor might have told you. Tonight I had the impression he didn't take the interview with you seriously."

Guidi loosened the knot of his tie. "I'm a step ahead of you, Major. I suspect Captain Sutor was in Magda's room the night she died. Why else would he be so anxious to discuss her with me? He was in no way a suspect and, as you said, he *volunteered*. I might have lost some of the evidence to Caruso's machinations, but I haven't been idle in the past three days. I traced one more guest at the holiday party that night, an Italian. It seems he arrived late and, since the power was on, took the elevator. In his haste he ended up on the fourth, rather than the third floor. Even though he didn't turn the corner to see what it was about, he heard a violent altercation between a man and a woman, speaking German. This was at seven-forty. I submit to you that Sutor was very much in the building just before Magda died."

By the cessation of quick clouds in front of Bora's face, he might be holding his breath. In fact, he said nothing whatever. Guidi looked down the dark, wide emptiness of the street. He smelled the night air, bitter and already green. He said, "So, you see, Caruso may be working for the Germans after all, and your intervention might make a worse mess of things. I cannot prove Sutor killed Magda Reiner, but Merlo was framed – this I know. You may have been as much a pawn as I have, Major Bora. Only, your own people may be behind it all. I'm not about to help convict an innocent man. And, whatever happens, I will continue to look into that woman's death until the result satisfies *me*."

"What about the man hiding just three doors down from Magda Reiner's?"

"Well, what about him, as you assume it was a man? Since

I came to Rome I've been told that spies and informers are hiding all over, and even showing up at elegant parties!"

Again Bora fell silent. He'd taken Guidi's words in a way undemonstrative of frustration or resentment. Now he walked alongside him, but nearly at the edge of the sidewalk, close to the curb. For all the world, the night sky seemed to interest him more than what had been said.

"That's *Capella*," he said eventually, pointing up. "The 'Little Goat', in the constellation of the Charioteer. A beautiful star, don't you think? It's so distant that the light it shows now was emitted when my mother was seven years old. Its light today will shine on us when we're seventy-two." He had a subdued, friendly laugh. "When you're seventy-two, anyway. I wouldn't gamble on numbers for Martin Bora." The star seemed alone in an empty and dark region of the sky. "I'm much preferable as a friend than as an enemy, Guidi."

"It's probably true of most of us."

"Some people make ineffectual enemies."

"Some circumstances make ineffectual friends."

Bora lifted his collar against the night wind. "You mean the war? The difference between you and me is that you don't look at it as a contingency."

Guidi did not know why he was angry at Bora. All he knew was that he wanted for him never to meet Francesca, never to have anything to do with her. He was afraid for her, though on the surface there was no motive to worry about Bora, who never invaded his privacy. It was Rau he had to worry about. And Rau dealt with Bora's friends.

They continued to walk. Bora had a sore want to share some of the anxieties that beset him, but checked the desire at once. Because it couldn't be done, or shouldn't, which came to the same. So he walked alongside Guidi, listening to his own steps as he took them: steps that grew regular as his leg healed. And once more strength was within him as it always had been, but with nearly neurotic intensity, as if after being injured his body had to compensate for the forced interruption. It was hard, wholly physical. A great sense of manhood went with it, whether or not Dikta wanted him, a hope that like the war she was after all incidental to him, and he did not need her.

And yet the structure inside was flimsy, thin. The supports of it did not stand trial. And the American woman, tonight – he'd been attracted to her in an irresponsible way, which she had no doubt noticed but decided not to use against him, merciful as fine women will be at times. He was grateful for it. The loose, liquid sound of the English language was still in his mouth like slowly melting candy, good to savor, soothing, fresh. Carelessly he said, "I've been promoted to lieutenant colonel."

"Congratulations."

"Thank you. I'll add a stud to the shoulder braid on 1 June."

Guidi walked with hands in his pockets, driven deep into them and thinking thoughts of his own, which to Bora were yet unrevealed, though Bora had a keen attuned mind and perceived things and moods, and this was why in the end he refused them and his wife could tell him, *Didn't you know?* or *You should have understood, you're an intelligent man,* as if intelligence had anything to do with knowing in the way he knew most of the time, whether he accepted it or not. It seemed to him at times that the world was thick and he thin, transparent, going through it as a glass needle into porous, thick wood, affected by it but still getting across.

And it was perhaps meaningful that since Dollmann had asked him whether he had nightmares (and he had answered, "Not about guerrilla warfare"), he had nightmares nearly every night now. The nameless animal chased him endlessly. And even now that they walked in the city street – the full moon had risen above the roofs and was erasing the stars, shadows were long and as rolled-out carpets before them – he could see the sinister triangle of the airplane rudder, and the nightmare was never to reach it, knowing well what was there. It was unthinkable to tell Guidi what was in his heart.

"Had you been home yesterday, I'd have given this to you then."

Francesca looked at the flat parcel in Guidi's hands. "Why, what was yesterday?"

"Your name day."

"Was it?" She took the gift and began unwrapping it, smiling at first, but only until she saw what was in it. Then her face grew earnest. "Silk stockings. God, are these *silk* stockings?"

Guidi, who'd spent a fortune on them, and on the black market to boot, said, "I hope the gift is not too personal," though he was eager for them to be taken as a personal gift.

Francesca licked the base of her nails to wet down the cuticles, before slipping her right hand into one of the delicate woven tubes. "They're beautiful, that's what they are."

It was Friday morning, and they were alone in the apartment. The Maiulis had gone to the San Giovanni Hospital to visit an acquaintance injured in one of the recent air raids. Even now the windows rattled with the hammering on distant railyards. Guidi wanted to alert Francesca about Rau without spoiling the moment, and as a result he stood irresolutely in the middle of the kitchen. She thought it was something else entirely. "All right," she said, and kissed him, less hastily than in the past week but not deeply, not with open lips. Guidi returned the kiss the same way, and then kissed her fully. "My, my... They teach you that much in Catholic school?"

"I'd like to make love to you, if you let me."

"Ha. And what about my lover?"

"You haven't got one."

"Well, whatever." Francesca carefully returned the stockings to their wrapper. "You'll be late for work if you don't get going."

Her lack of response was an irksome letdown for Guidi. "Look," he said with a sudden lack of diplomacy, "are you aware that Rau is connected with the Germans?"

Again, she surprised him. "Yes. He's gutsy, isn't he. He told me he'd attend this big party you went to last night. It's amazing what he learns by listening. Don't worry about him. He won't be coming here this week."

"Why, has he had enough Latin lessons?"

"He just won't, that's all."

In his office, Bora was reading reports on the three-day air raid on Berlin. The weather in Rome had turned bad overnight, and he doubted bombers would strike here: but he heard them fly over, and Mrs Murphy surely heard them from the Vatican, like a beautiful prisoner in a maze. Did she have children? He should have asked her. What a wonderful thought, to make children with her. He could not think of it without trepidation of body and soul. And all the while, down he went through the dreadful list of losses in Berlin. The Daimler-Benz airplane engine plant had been hit, and the Bosch Works; he read about those and the secondary targets, preparing to brief Westphal.

By telephone, confirmation came from Fascist headquarters that today's parade was about to begin at Via Tomacelli. Yes, he knew where that was, and no, he would not attend. No Germans would attend. Could he at least send a representative? No. No Germans would attend.

Actually Westphal had told him, "Avoid it like the plague." Bora cast a glance at the wall map of Rome. More and more like an island, its irregular outline was eroded by daily raids. The ancient roads fanning from it – Aurelia, Flaminia, Cassia, Salaria, clockwise to the southernmost Appia and Ardeatina – could be made impassable any day. And the claustrophobia of army and SS was on. He heard from the next room that his secretary had arrived and engaged in her routine of morning motions. Removing her coat, nearing the desk, moving back the chair to see what orders had been left for her. Reading them. He came to the door of his office, and she stood at attention. "Why don't you take the day off?" he said.

"The day off, Major?"

"You deserve it. Take the day off."

She put the papers back on the desk. "Thank you, Major."

"You looked very charming at the reception."

She saw through his courtesy, still. "Thank you, sir," she said.

Shortly Westphal came in with a cigarette in his mouth and newspapers under his arm. "Where's your girl going?"

"I gave her the day off."

"Relenting, are we?" The general smiled. "Are you taking her to bed?"

"No, sir."

"I was just joking. As if there were reasons. Well, what about Berlin? I bet you'll get me out of good humor quickly."

What happened in Caruso's office could be surmised by the occasional barking shout of the old man, and the crash of his fist on the desk, and the liberal use of the word *merda* in what already resembled a diarrhea of insults.

Guidi found himself uncannily calm under it. He let the barrage crest and wane and flush down to a grumbling sewer, only worried that spittle from Caruso's vituperative mouth would leave stains on his typed copy.

"Do you know what this is? This is shit! These are big, round pieces of shit you're handing me, expecting me to gobble them down!" Flung from his hand, the report fluttered like a wounded bird across the room to the floor. "You have the murderer, you *have him*! The proofs are there, if you have eyes to see! What's this nonsense about *reasonable doubt* and *the possibility of culprits unknown*, who do you think will buy it?"

"The Germans will."

"The Germans will do as I recommend to them!"

"That's good, Dr Caruso. Westphal's aide will be here at ten."

Caruso swallowed, bilious with contempt. "I won't receive him. And as for you, no further investigation is allowed. Get out of my office." Guidi leaned over to retrieve the report. "Leave that alone!" Caruso shouted. "That stays here, and no one sees it but me! It goes to the trash along with you!"

Guidi dropped the report. "If you would read past the first page, sir, you'd see how I arrived at my request for more time. I intend to find Magda Reiner's killer. The only thing I have not yet figured out is why Merlo is being framed, but that may emerge eventually." And, though Caruso had grown fearfully congested, veins knotting on his temples, he added, "In the end, exposing a possible conspiracy is as important as finding how the woman died. I am modeling the readiness to 'prosecute one of our own' you insisted on, Dr Caruso."

Silent and motionless, Caruso sat in the chair with his eyes sunken under the contracted brow. The only sign of activity on his body was the flicking from marker to marker of the gold hand on his bulky wristwatch. It seemed hours before he said the words. "You are fired."

Suspended is what he should have said, but he said *fired*, like an outraged employer. As Guidi went without comment to the door, he growled after him, "Someone else will take over for you. Out. Out. Out. Do you think you're clever? You don't know what clever is!"

In the next office, the policemen were silently standing behind their desks, and when Guidi went by, they clapped a mute applause to him without letting their palms meet.

Knowing that Bora was not one not to be received, Caruso went home indisposed by nine o'clock.

By this time Guidi had driven back to Via Paganini. Frustration and anger were catching up with him quickly, in excess of what they would be had he vented them somehow during the argument. His head throbbed hard when he stepped inside. The apartment was cold, quiet. The Maiulis had not yet returned. From their glass domes in the parlor, only the saints were staring out. Guidi tried the radio, but the power was off.

The more he tried to nurse his spite, the more disgruntled and vengeful he became, sick of his ways. Having been shouted out of a room mortified him, as though his composure were not a strength. Hell, he had unobtrusively gone through life this way. He was sick of it.

In the cloudy day, the hallway was dark, and only Francesca's door, slightly open, afforded some light at the end of it. *Is she home?* he wondered. *Why is she home?* Guidi walked to the door, reached it and was about to knock but didn't; he simply pushed the leaf inwards.

Francesca sat on the bed, sallow against the white of the sheets, bare-breasted as he had seen her once, except that she had removed blouse and drawers this time. Only the cotton stockings sheathed her legs still, up to the widening of the muscle of her thighs. And on her pale flesh the contrast of black cloth made an impression on Guidi, as did the unexpected triangle of dark fleece between her legs, which the growing belly did not hide yet, but would soon.

She had in her nakedness the oblivious immobility of the model who removes her mind from matters at hand, such as nudity and being watched. The lack of emotion that went with the display of her body was perhaps what emboldened Guidi into starting to unbutton his shirt, plucking each with fumbling energy. Halfway through the buttons on his chest Francesca lay back, resting her elbows on the mattress, so that her belly was lifted and flattened by the position, and more visibly the triangle draped dark in the thighs was revealed. Then Guidi was quick with his clothes, undid his trousers and removed those, shoes and socks followed, and he was long and lean and white at the foot of the bed. His skin felt like candle wax, and was clear and hairless and of the kind that seems to glow opalescent in the light. Last came his shorts, which were tensely molded around the painful knot of his groin. And he could not have borne it had Francesca laughed or looked away or moved in any other way than she did, calmly drawing her stocking-sheathed feet to the edge of the bed and parting her knees like a beautiful animal.

144

Guidi half-kneeled between them, but it was uncomfortable, so he took her by the hips and moved her back and lay on her, too timid to use his hand and energetically, nervously trying to enter her by driving his belly against the lower bulge of her belly in the right direction. He did at last, soon enough, and it had been so long it seemed since he'd gone into a woman and yet it turned so familiar again, that sliding in by a little chafing force, now rubbing the sides of the narrow fleshy depth, now the top, until it was all in and the flat whiteness of his belly was against her entirely, and he could angle his arms and relax before starting to move on her.

Her arms were at ease in a circle over the head, her breasts large and dark-nippled. The angle of her face drew itself in the lavish, crisp darkness of her undone hair. Guidi took her breasts and felt their firmness, the shift of glands under the skin, with his thumb he followed the curve of the flesh until her armpits, where a tangle of hair in each was soft and had a thin wild odor of life in it. And he was already moving, his body had quickly begun to shake and vibrate on her, in her, he was saying soft words to her and tried to kiss her. She wouldn't kiss him back, though her thighs tightened around him and made his motion more insistent, blood riding his veins in frantic jolts. Pleasure came in waves up from rubbing inside her, until he grew so rigid and hard he thought he could cry, and cried out, too, at frantic speed jerking over her, buttocks and thighs and the small of his back up and down driving him. Then a new rigidity, the need to cry out again, and he arched his spine then and drove his knees on the mattress when semen came out of him in a spurt that repeated itself and seemed to him a grand pouring out of thick discharge, after which what had been divine for a while left him, and he lay quite inert between her legs.

His desire was fast becoming an incomprehensible but no less strong need to weep, to accompany the emptying of his body with the emptying of the soul by tears. He conquered the

145

need, and already Francesca propped herself on her elbows with a smile neither mocking nor ecstatic – a pleased smile of the flesh. With a quick pat on his shoulder she let him know, nicely but without giving alternatives, "You can get off now."

Great shame came over Guidi then, Adam-like in the discovery of his nakedness, all divinity stripped from him, and only the white limpness of flesh left behind, which of its own accord slipped out and was his once again, unflatteringly attached as an appendix and that was all. He turned around to slowly put his shorts on again, on which moisture drew a stain right away, while Francesca sat up and was mopping between her legs with her blouse, which she then threw in a corner of the room, asking, "What time is it?"

Back from his useless errand at the *Questura Centrale*, Bora was on the phone when an orderly rushed in with the news that the Fascist parade had been attacked by partisans.

"Was Pizzirani hurt?" Bora put down the receiver.

"No, sir. It's unclear what happened, but the parade was broken up. The PAI are there now, and the SS are on their way."

"Well, there's nothing we can add to that. I'll inform General Westphal."

Westphal had overheard from his office. "The fools, I knew it! I knew they would get in trouble. Just wait until General Maelzer hears this! Get in touch with Kappler, Bora, and get first-hand information from him."

Bora dialed the Via Tasso number. "Just the man I was thinking of!" Kappler said. "You heard about Pizzirani. No, only his ego is bruised, but this is it for ceremonies. *We* knew that, didn't we? Sure, the *republican guard* charged, but it was my boys who gathered a handful of suspects. I'm going to the site to take a look. Why don't you meet me there?"

Via Tomacelli ran straight into the Cavour Bridge, past which Piazza Cavour sat under the gigantic, cake-like monstrosity of the Palace of Justice, set at an angle from it.

"Typical." Kappler spoke to Bora with his foot on the runner of his car, as a hunter stepping on his kill. "Grenades and some gunfire, and they were gone. The Fascists panicked. It would have never happened to us."

Bora took the dig personally. "Allow me to disagree. It can and does happen to us, with all that we don't hold parades. How much do you expect to learn from those arrested?"

"Who knows. They probably had nothing to do with it. The trouble is that there's open abetment of terrorism in the Roman upper class."

"Well, then, we make things worse by going to dinner parties with them and toasting their health. All this catching the small fish amounts to little."

"Why, thank you," Kappler said acidly. "And here I was, thinking I was doing a good job. The biggest offenders are your skirted chums in the Vatican. The attackers could leisurely walk to Castle Saint Angelo from where we stand."

"Some of the biggest offenders are our drinking partners and the women we take to bed."

"Oh. In that case you and Colonel Dollmann are safe."

Somehow, Bora showed no umbrage. "Pizzirani has already informed us there's another ceremony planned hereabouts for the twenty-third. He wishes to celebrate the Founding Day of Fascism up the street, at the Teatro Adriano."

"He must be crazy, there's no security there."

"Don't let it trouble you, Colonel. We ought to worry about our own, and let the Fascists get themselves blown across the Tiber if they're stupid enough to sit on bombs."

Kappler laughed. "I can't believe you're the same man who's got a soft spot for Foa."

"I have no quarrel with Foa."

"Other than he's Jewish, I presume."

Bora did not answer. He looked beyond the bridge, toward the squat statue of Cavour looming from its high pedestal in a forlorn oasis of meager palm trees.

Afterwards, skipping lunch for the day, he went instead to St Mary of the Orison and Death, a sinister church at the end of the old street that ran into Via Giulia. Bora stopped by it for no other reason than it was the anniversary of his father's death. He had no intention to pray or to look over the relics of the old Brotherhood that had once made it its mission to bury the forsaken dead. He went in and out in the way visitors in Rome dip into churches and seek the outside again – just the time to whiff musty incense and plaster, feeling they've done their duty.

Next he stopped at Donna Maria's on Via Monserrato. If there was any place he called home now, this was it, a *palazzetto* almost Spanish in its elaborate entryway and wrought-iron balcony, where a potted oleander had been sitting ever since Bora remembered. Donna Maria, with a cat on her shoulder, had seen him from the window of the dining room and rapped on the glass with the head of her cane for him to notice. Bora saluted her and went in.

"*Ma come,* Martin! You find flowers in Rome, when most people can't even find turnips!"

"Donna Maria, the day I do not bring you flowers you'll know something is very wrong."

"It's been a long time since you've seen *my* flowerbeds at *The Seagull.* I'm afraid they've all gone wild the past season."

"Do you still go there in the summer?"

The old woman shrugged. "Now and then, and not for two years. Country houses are made for young lovers who want to get away. Time was, Martin. The house still looks like a beautiful white bird, with D'Annunzio's verses on the halcyon days over the door. But he's dead and I'm old." With her face in the flowers she looked up at him, coyly. "I want you to have the key to it."

Guidi was putting his feet in his trousers when the main door lock clicked and Signora Carmela's squeaky voice came next, complaining to her husband about something or other. Guidi froze. How had he not thought they would be back soon? For a moment he was totally unable to think of a way out.

"Just don't say anything," Francesca said under her breath, and it seemed to him she had a commiserating irony in her tone. She slipped her house dress on and left the room, closing the door behind her; Guidi overheard her tell the Maiulis that the inspector had stopped by – she had to justify his briefcase on the kitchen table – and had left again. He would not be home for lunch, and not to worry about him. Back in the room, she wiped the sheet with a wet face cloth. "They may be stupid, but the maid isn't," she whispered to Guidi, who stood by looking sheepish. "Now wait until they take their afternoon nap, and pretend to come in from the outside. They'll never know the difference."

He sat on the small armchair in the corner, with nothing to say. The orgasm and the scene with Caruso had taken all he had in him, and he felt cheap in the measure Francesca seemed comfortable and even amused by the circumstances. Cross-legged on the dry side of the bed, she began reading from a *giallo*, without as much as looking at him.

So Guidi sat there, watching her read. Everything was different now and his grudge was useless. She *had* him. He'd let her do it, and it was now, hiding in her room, that he realized she had him, in more ways than one. He tried to feel righteous, but that too was a sham. He watched her flip the pages, wetting her finger with the tip of her tongue. The *giallo* was called *L'Inafferrabile*, a title that in another moment would seem laughably ironic. He needed to roll himself a cigarette, but she did not smoke, and he feared the Maiulis would smell it and grow suspicious. Francesca, who never helped with chores, seemed oblivious to the clatter Signora Carmela made by preparing lunch in the kitchen. Hating himself, Guidi watched her.

11 MARCH 1944

On Saturday morning, Pompilia Marasca was polishing the knocker of her door when Guidi left the apartment to buy a newspaper. "Not at work, Inspector?" she called over her shoulder.

Guidi didn't look up. "I'm taking the day off."

"My, you all get time off in your house. Signorina Lippi hasn't been to work in ten days."

Giving up, he decided to humor her. "How would you know she hasn't been to work?"

"I went to buy envelopes yesterday, and the hired help at the store told me."

"Maybe she's taking a few days' vacation. Ask her."

The woman rested her oily hand on the pear-shaped knocker, holding it in a fondling grasp. "I'm sure that's how it is."

12 MARCH 1944

On a rainy Sunday afternoon, the fifth anniversary of the coronation of Pius XII was observed in St Peter's Square. Maelzer forbade all ranks to attend, and sentinels placed at the bridges ensured compliance. Bora, who'd have loved seeing Mrs Murphy again, listened to the Pope on the radio, translating for Westphal his speech as well as the occasional anti-German slogans yelled out in the crowd of three hundred thousand. When an orderly came to deliver one of the leaflets found in the Square, he translated that as well. It was signed by the communist group *Unione e Libertà*.

18 MARCH 1944

Despite the unusually severe pain in his left arm, Bora had been at work five hours when the air raid siren sounded before noon.

Westphal was at Soratte, and on the desk lay stacks of reports from the crumbling line at Cassino. As usual, Bora planned not to leave his office, though he urged his secretary to join others in the shelter. Through the doorway, she looked up from her typewriter and said she would stay also. The bombs fell very close this time. The roar of motors and din of explosions made it difficult to identify where they came from. Bora assumed the eastern rails were being targeted, but the charges seemed to be exploding even outside that perimeter, no more than six hundred yards away. There was nothing to do about it. After Aprilia he had a more than fatalistic view of air raids. He lit himself a cigarette and continued to work.

At one point the whole German Command seemed about to sink into its foundations. Open city or not, Bora thought the Flora may very well be next in the bomber's sight. His secretary came in, paler than she was cool-faced, and simply sat across the desk from him. Bora handed her a cigarette; when he saw she was not steady enough to light it, he did it for her. So they sat for an hour, and then – it was half past noon – Bora climbed to the roof terrace to see which neighborhood had been hit. When he returned, Dollmann was in the office, looking no worse for wear. Blandly removing his overcoat, he asked, "What did you see from above?"

"There's a billow of black smoke due west, outside Porta Pia. It seems they struck Via Nomentana and the university hospitals. We must organize some help."

Dollmann stared at him. "The only thing we can do for the Romans is getting out of Rome, and we can't do that just now. Actually, Via Messina has been hit, and so has Via Nomentana, Piazza Galeno and at least one entire wing of the Policlinico Hospital on Via Regina Margherita. It's a mess of broken glass and masonry, water mains are gushing all over. Whole lines of people queuing for groceries were blown to shreds. I don't know how many people wounded. It's the worst I've seen in Rome. We'll be seeing migrations through the streets in the next few days." With his foot, gently Dollmann pushed the office door shut. "I'm actually here on my own mission of mercy. I'll get your old friend Foa out of Kappler's hands. Even Caruso's hands are better in this case." He winked without friendliness. "Now you owe me one, Major Bora."

20 MARCH 1944

On Monday, when the head of police least expected it, Bora walked into his office unannounced, with a copy of Guidi's report in hand.

"It has come to General Westphal's attention how attentively the investigation on the death of our compatriot Magda Reiner is being pursued by your office. I am here to express the general's appreciation to Inspector Guidi for a job well done."

Caruso seemed to be gulping a distasteful lump of food. "This unexpected visit, Major…" he began, but Bora's attitude dissuaded him from continuing on that tone. "I regret not to be able to share your commander's opinion," he said then. "I assigned someone else to the Reiner case. Inspector Guidi missed some of the important clues. Egregious oversights were committed. I'm sure you want to see justice done. Justice will be done."

Bora took Sciaba's written deposition out of his briefcase. Without handing it over, he held it before Caruso's face. "We fully concur. Naturally any wrongdoing within the ranks of the Italian police makes it unlikely for us to trust anyone in it. I am under orders to take a more active role in the investigation at once. Accordingly, I am here to collect all pertinent evidence and paperwork."

Caruso was still reading. "What is this?" he then blurted out in anger. "Has Guidi been begging at your door?"

"Hardly." Bora put the document back in his briefcase. "I haven't seen the inspector in over a week. Can you tell me where he is?"

"At home, I expect. He's been suspended."

"I see. We expect him to be reinstated, of course."

With his usual bluster, Caruso slapped his hand on the desk. "Look here, Major, I hold general rank, and I'm reminding you of your place!"

"My place is to represent *both* General Westphal and Field Marshal Kesselring, whose wishes I have expressed. If you prefer a direct order, I can do that as well. Kindly telephone Inspector Guidi with the news of his reinstatement, while I secure the Reiner material."

Caruso jumped to his feet. "This is an outrage! You would not dare get into our files!"

"No. I have two men outside doing it for me."

Moments later, Signora Carmela called Guidi to the phone. "It's for you."

The last voice Guidi expected to hear was Caruso's.

The second last was Bora's, who called less than half an hour later to invite him to lunch.

Guidi found the coincidence unlikely. "Major," he said irritably, "I was just reinstated after being dismissed from the case. Did you have anything to do with it?"

"God forbid. I've been minding my own business. And I'm only calling because I don't like eating alone."

In the end, Guidi was grateful for the invitation. At the Hotel d'Italia, every other table was occupied by men in uniform. Bora good-naturedly remarked on it. "I hope you don't mind my staying in the family, so to speak. These are unfriendly days, and we have one disadvantage over the Romans – we get bombed from the ground, too."

Guidi sat, glancing round to see if by any chance Rau was here. True to Francesca's words, he had not shown up since the tenth, which was the day of the attempt in Via Tomacelli. He'd rather not draw conclusions from that. Across the table, Bora appeared sedate and fresh, but when the waiter brought drinks, he took three aspirins with a glass of water. "I must tell you, Guidi, you look different."

"I do?" Guidi cringed at the words, thinking that Bora would ironize about sexual relief. "I can't imagine why."

"I don't know, you seem preoccupied. Caruso must have really chewed your backside."

Guidi nodded eagerly. "I didn't mean to sound rude on the phone, Major. The thing is, as of tomorrow I'll be back at Via Del Boccaccio. I thought you might have a hand in that."

Bora repeated that he didn't. But his friendliness turned inwards and became guarded. They ate speaking of trivial matters, until Bora returned to the subject. "Well, will you keep your resolution to pursue Magda's case to the end?"

"Not only. Relieved of duties as I was, I checked on the receipts from Roman stores found in the Reiner apartment. One is from a shoe store at Via del Lavatore, and the other from a clothing store named Vernati."

"So?"

"Well, the first establishment, whose motto is *From death – to strong and hardy life*, referring I expect to the leather they use, makes shoes for men and women. There she bought a pair of men's rubber-soled shoes. Vernati – there are three stores with this name, and she went to the biggest one, Alla Primavera! on Via Nazionale – is a men's clothing store. She bought trousers, a shirt, and a sports coat on 15 December. Good quality stuff."

Bora looked intrigued. "Really? What size?"

"Not Merlo's and not Sutor's, from what I can judge. Closer to yours, I'd say." And because this time Bora seemed half-amused, half-vexed, Guidi added quickly, "That is, taller than most. And I found ample proof that for all of his private flaws, Merlo has been a regular terror on party graft in Rome. It explains things, doesn't it?"

Bora, who had difficulty using fork and knife, impatiently let go of both. He sat for a moment with frustration on his face. "Only if we can connect with her death the mysterious recipient of the clothes, who may or may not be the secret tenant," he said afterwards. "You can't expect much collaboration from us if you start exploring the Sutor lead, or another German lead."

"I know. And we have no reason to assume she knew there was anyone hiding in 7B."

At that very moment, as they sat across from one another, Guidi had the bizarre temptation to tell Bora the real motive for his preoccupation – that he loathed lying to the Maiulis, that Francesca had been as indifferent to him as before, and that last night he'd managed what amounted to masturbating in her, smothering every sound, fearful that Signora Carmela might walk in on them. Even had they been friends, it was hardly what he could tell Bora over lunch. He watched the hard shaven faces of the Germans at their tables, hair shorn to expose pink napes and bony temples. Would Rau go after them? Sitting here suddenly repelled him. Bora's trust especially made him sick with guilt but with enmity, too. He saw the fragility of human life in that relaxation, and the impossible task of alerting him, because he did not want to. What if, he thought, what if... What would he do were Francesca to tell him that Bora was to be killed next?

"You know, I thought things over." Bora's calm voice came to him. "I reached at least one conclusion for myself, if it comes to it. To the Americans, I will surrender. To the English, I might. To the Russians or the partisans, never. The only way they will get me is with a fresh hole through my head, which I won't mind putting there."

Guidi looked around significantly. "Major, people might hear..."

"So? We have to think of possibilities. I'm sure the Americans do the same. I *know* the partisans do."

5

On Wednesday the first issue of *Il Messaggero* was withdrawn after Bora translated for Westphal the editorial titled "Why Rome Is Bombed", indirectly suggesting removal by the Germans of targets for further Allied bombing. The second issue was published without the article, but Francesca had already secured several copies.

The day went by slowly. It was overcast and cool, though greatcoats were no longer necessary and women had started wearing brighter colors. Guidi once more made himself at home in his office on Via Del Boccaccio, at the foot of Via Rasella.

Bora had a working lunch with Dollmann, and took the chance to mention that General Foa had not yet been transferred to the Italian jail.

Dollmann groaned. "Why are you obsessed with the old man? Forget about getting him out of the *Shambles*. He's done for."

"You assured me, Colonel. I can't stand seeing him abused for doing what you or I would do under the same circumstances – protecting our brother officers. He's as old as my father."

"Oh, stop it. Your father was a famous orchestra conductor, and he's dead. As for your foolhardy stepfather, you'll be lucky if he doesn't land you in trouble, which is just like those Prussian monarchists who began keeping spinsterish diaries at eighteen in Lichterfeld and never quit."

"I keep a diary," Bora said. "And mostly in English besides."

"Anything political in it?"

"No. I'm afraid it's a spinsterish list of impressions of people and places."

"That, too, can be political." Dollmann played derisive, but pleasantly. "Am I in it?"

"Yes. Will you speak to Himmler about Foa?"

"Absolutely not. What do you say about me?"

Bora took a sip of water. "That you are a man with the threefold soul."

"I am, am I? And which one dominates, the intellectual or the irascible?"

"Actually I was thinking of the concupiscent, though I didn't put it on paper."

Dollmann drew back on the chair, and if there was annoyance in him, he disguised it as one who puts a trim on plain metal. "I do like my comfort. Don't you?"

"No. My wife thinks I'll self-destruct."

There was an icy, cautious offer of alliance in Dollmann's next words. "Just be grateful that you have the aide's guardian saints – *die hochheilige Lampassen*." By which he meant the crimson stripes on Bora's breeches.

"I pray to them often."

"Well, keep a big white page in your diary for tomorrow – we're both invited to the Fascist celebrations, are we not? Your entry will be a regular bestiary."

Bora poured wine for the SS. "General Wolff would be sympathetic if you introduced Foa's case to the Reich Commissar. He's liaison to Himmler, but you're Himmler's friend."

"I do think you're doing this just to spite Kappler. If that were the reason, and *nothing else*, I might consider it."

"Well, what else could it be?"

Dollmann laughed. "Hohmann taught you right. We'll see. But here's a word of advice, Major. If you don't do so already, keep your diary under lock and key, and be kinder to me in it."

23 MARCH 1944

Long before dawn, Bora awoke in a sweat.

It was still pitch dark outside, and the room was an unintelligible void for him to stare into. The nightmare had been much the same, but details had been so vivid he could smell the burning metal, and feel the resistance of the cracked, blood-lined cockpit under his fists as he tried to open it. Yet he could not see his brother in it. And then the spiral staircase, the animal bounding behind, gaining on him, with no hope of escape.

The phosphorescent hand on his watch marked five o'clock when he sat up. *A wolf,* he thought, *that's what the animal is.* He shaved under the shower (the water was nearly cold, and not much of it), dressed and went downstairs to have a cup of coffee. *And it's a she-wolf.*

No one was at the bar at this hour except the woman who made him an espresso, and she looked like she had had a bad night.

His schedule for the day was long and busy. He scanned it while the hiss of the espresso machine seemed to be the only thing to keep the woman from falling asleep again. The entries began at six, when he was to be at the office; by seven-fifteen, briefing General Westphal on new business; at seven thirty he was to meet General Maelzer at the Excelsior; between eight forty-five and nine he was expected at Centocelle where the Air Force was assessing damage caused to the airport by the latest air raids. At noon a quick lunch with Westphal before the general left for Soratte, and critical reading of the Roman press. Before two, he was to attend the celebrations either at the Ministry of Corporation, where the Germans had convinced the Fascists to congregate instead of Teatro Adriano, or at the Palace of Exhibitions. These over with, he'd leave for Soratte to join Westphal there and wait for Kesselring to be back from Anzio.

He drank the coffee and was met by his driver in front of the hotel. As they left in the pre-dawn gray light, Bora glanced down Via Rasella, where cobblestones like fish scales ran down to the police station and the offices of *Il Messaggero*.

By the time Bora was done briefing Westphal, Guidi arrived at Via Del Boccaccio, around the corner from Via Rasella, and began to work. At the Excelsior, the *King of Rome* was not yet out of bed at seven thirty, so Bora waited with an eye on the people who populated the hotel in the morning. He recognized the Minister of Interior among others, several officials who cropped up every time there was free food, and at least two movie stars, who he'd heard took drugs, and looked accordingly glassy-eyed. General Maelzer received him at seven fifty in the unfriendly mood of a hangover.

And while Bora was getting a flat tire on his way to Centocelle Airport, Guidi called Signora Carmela to find out if Francesca had come home.

"No, she hasn't. But she phoned just a few minutes ago and I'm worried sick. Said she couldn't say where she was calling from, and not to expect her any time soon. It's not the first time she has done it, but she sounded so *strange*."

Guidi put the receiver down with a bitter taste in his mouth. Before him were the sketchy notes he had gathered on Antonio Rau. Born at Arbatax on the coast of Sardinia, single, officially unemployed. His father had been a miner in Austria, where he had married, which explained Rau's facility with German. He'd never attended the university and his parents lived nowhere near St Lawrence's. Was Francesca with him today, and what for?

"How's security at the Palace of Guilds?" he asked Danza.

"Tight as a fist, Inspector. There's also to be a Mass at St Mary of Mercy's. The Fascist Republican Guard is keeping watch there. On Via Nazionale they have something else going on, and there's PAI blocking all entrances to the street."

"Fine." Guidi left his desk and walked to the window. To the left, he could see the steps leading to Via dei Giardini.

In the moist spring sky, the first swallows flew like shuttles on a loom.

At Centocelle, the combination of badges on the Air Force uniforms was too much like his brother's for Bora to look at it. He listened with his eyes low to the pilots' requests for labor to repair the runways and took notes.

At eleven thirty one of Guidi's colleagues left for the movie house down the street to watch a foreign film. "It's cheaper than lunch, and there's nothing good to eat anyway."

At noon Westphal grumbled to Bora that they should close *Il Giornale d'Italia.* "That's what happens when you have a founder who's half Jewish and half English! 'Obstinate defense of the Gothic Line', eh? I want you to call the editor and ask him who wrote that."

The *Mostra della Rivoluzione Fascista* had until recently had its seat in the Palace of Exhibitions on Via Nazionale, the long stretch connecting Diocletian's Baths to Trajan's Market. Bora went there directly at one o'clock, noticing the security checks at every intersection.

Militia Guards lined the steps in their black uniforms. Inside there were already several guests. All were inevitably treated to talk of past glories, for want of present ones, and Bora was just grateful that he hadn't had to attend the official swearing in of Pietro Caruso at the Ministry of Corporations. And he fared better than those who had after that ceremony overindulged in food and wine at the Excelsior. He tried to attend tedious functions on an empty stomach, and – having limited his lunch with Westphal to a mouthful – from long practice of political rallies could hold yawns in by nothing more than a quick swallowing.

The two o'clock speaker, worse luck, was a one-legged elder whose nobility of sentiments was affected by slurred Southern speech and unbearable long-windedness.

"Jesus, this is boring," someone whispered behind him. The cramming of similes, hyperboles and quotations continued for more than an hour, by which time Bora followed nothing of what was being said. Left wrist in hand, he had assumed a lock-kneed immobility that allowed him to think of something else entirely. As always when he was under tension or stress, his left arm ached dully, a warning of pain that might unpredictably rise high from the severed muscles and nerves. Before him drifted thoughts of the trip to Soratte and of Mrs Murphy, and of the kind of pain a man with a leg amputated at the groin must have gone through.

"I wish somebody would pull the crutches from under his armpits." This time Bora recognized Sutor's voice behind him. He looked back to see if Dollmann was here also, but he wasn't. Sutor whispered, "What the hell is the old prick saying? Someone ought to cram a foot in his mouth." But they all had to endure the speech to the end, and clap, too.

Afterwards, Bora was about to leave when Sutor told him of a party at the German embassy in Villa Wolkonsky.

"If it's tonight, I can't."

"It's tomorrow night, and it's the aftermath that counts."

"I have no objection. Where's the *aftermath?*"

"At Lola's house, in the country, and it's an all-night affair because of the curfew."

Lola was Sutor's present lover, Bora knew. "How do I get there?"

Sutor gave him directions. "Nineteen hundred hours, sharp. There'll be intellectuals and movie people, and you can count on several of the women being high." He grinned. "By morning they won't know what got into them, or who."

They had drawn close to one of the windows, talking. Both were alerted to the shaking of glass panes by four distinct, close explosions. By habit, Bora checked the time: three thirty-five. His first thought was that the anti-aircraft was firing at enemy planes. A disorderly flight of pigeons rose from the Ministry of Interior garden. Sutor crowded him to watch. "What happened?" By this time the militiamen were in turmoil, looking over to their right and grasping their rifles. "Something's been blown up back of us!" Sutor shouted, and withdrew precipitously from the window. Before everyone else, both officers rushed from the hall, Sutor to find a telephone and Bora out of the building, where the militiamen spoke agitated nonsense.

"They blasted the Excelsior!" they told Bora, who got into the car and urged the driver down Via Quattro Fontane to Via Veneto. His car careened past the unstrung troops of the security checks, beyond the American Church and the block of the Ministry of War. Here it became clear to Bora that neither the Excelsior nor the Flora nor Ministry of Corporations had been targeted. Dark smoke was coming out of Via Rasella at the Hotel d'Italia end of it, where a bus lay on its side and people were crawling from it. Bora ordered the driver to bear left and approach the street from the opposite side by the parallel Via dei Giardini.

Even as he left the car, a burst of machine-gun fire filled the steps leading to Via Del Boccaccio. Blindly Bora fired back. From here he could not see the top of Via Rasella. Midway up the incline, rags of smoke obscured the explosion area. A red froth of blood and sewage water ran down from it, and against that slippery waste Bora climbed to the screaming gate of hell.

The blasted pavement resembled a slaughterhouse. Gore splashed on the walls of houses seven and eight feet high, torn pieces of human bodies emptied themselves on the cobblestones. Men crawled screaming in their blood. The cries, smell and sights briefly overwhelmed him in an agonizing flashback. It was the continued shooting that kept Bora in control.

"Block the west end!" Bora ordered some dazed soldiers who were spinning around and firing at windows. Shouldering past them, he entered one of the houses at random. Before the terrified tenants, he grabbed a phone and sent word to Soratte that an SS battalion had just been decimated near Via Veneto.

When he stepped back into the street, Maelzer and Dollmann had joined in from the Excelsior. Maelzer was drunk, ranting for revenge. Medics knelt in the blood and called for stretchers.

Sutor had also come. He stood blankly, rooted to the spot where a man's intestines had bowled out onto the pavement. "Help me out," Bora said, unbuckling his belt. "I can't do it with one hand." Together they tied a soldier's leg, blown off at the knee. Their sleeves and cuffs and the hems of their tunics became drenched with blood, shreds of flesh stuck to their fingers. Hunching over, Sutor had barely time to turn away before starting to vomit. Bora thought it cowardly, though only an empty stomach kept him from doing the same. He overheard Maelzer's hysteria and Dollmann trying to speak sense to him. Army and SS were pouring into the street. They forced their way into the houses scarred by the blasts. Loud crying and shouts soon came from the houses as well.

"Get some more medics!" Bora heard himself shouting. "Block the goddamn streets!"

Dollmann rudely turned him around, and Bora could see he was exasperated. "Try to speak to that Maelzer windbag instead, or the whole block goes up in the air. There are engineers coming at his orders with enough charges to do it."

Bora came close to panic. "What can I tell him that you haven't, *Standartenführer*?" But he went to the place where Maelzer mopped his face, exhausted with screaming at the German Consul. All it took was for Bora to address him and he reverted to his ranting until saliva sprayed all around him. "Don't you tell me what Kesselring ought to know and not know, Major!" and upon Bora's insistence, "Shut up, I'm telling you! If you don't shut up I'll have you sent to the Russian front!"

"I've been there."

The rashness of his answer struck Bora only after uttering it, but Dollmann stepped in to deflect Maelzer's anger with a timely objection of his own.

Confusion reached an extreme. The engineers had come. Bodies were moved to the sidewalk, sometimes piecemeal, while

163

crowds of detainees were herded with hands clasped behind their heads to Via Quattro Fontane, and lined against the gates of Palazzo Barberini. The last to arrive at Via Rasella, with a face of chilly composure, was Lieutenant Colonel Kappler.

At a quarter past five Bora was back at the Flora, where he spoke by telephone with Westphal. The general, just arrived at Soratte, glumly informed him that orders had already been received from Hitler's headquarters at Rastenburg. "He's asking fifty to one," he said. "How many died?"

"Twenty-five at least. Several were badly injured and will probably die overnight. It could be thirty and more."

"It comes to fifteen hundred hostages. Too much, Bora. Too much. Were any of the attackers caught?"

Bora removed his tunic, and was in his shirt. The blood-spattered cloth was wringing wet with perspiration and clung to him. "Unless they were grabbed among the local tenants, I doubt it. It was bedlam and no one cordoned off the streets for ten minutes or so. I'm sure it was TNT, yes, at least twenty kilos' worth. It damaged the walls badly, and there must have been some other charges also, hand-thrown. Clearly several people were involved. They must have been at the corners of the streets perpendicular to Via Rasella, where they could get away quickly."

Westphal went silent at the other end, or else was speaking to someone with his hand on the mouthpiece. "Has General Maelzer calmed down?" he asked then.

"Somewhat."

"Who else is with you?"

"Colonel Dollmann stepped in a moment ago."

"Try to talk to him."

Dollmann stood on the threshold, his narrow, ugly face blotched and weary. "You'll have enough to fill the rest of your diary with this." He valiantly tried to make light of things.

"Colonel, you must agree that this will be most unfortunately army business, whether or not it was an SS unit that was targeted. So far we've had politicians, diplomats and SS giving recommendations, and it should be our own General Mackensen's decision."

"It will be General Wolff's, I'm thinking. But I agree."

Bora had not expected the quick assent and was disarmed by it. "What weight will Mackensen carry in the decision-making, then?"

"Don't know."

"The field marshal is due back to Soratte at seven. If you must contact Germany, I hope you will delay until his return."

"I'm going to the embassy now, Bora. You realize there will be a reprisal."

"I understand, Colonel."

Eyes closed, Dollmann inhaled deeply. Bora was self-conscious of his sweat and bloody smell, but Dollmann filled his nostrils with it. "Do you?" he was saying. "*I* don't." The colonel dragged his fine hands over the red blotches on his cheeks. "It was done to make us react, and if Kappler doesn't see through it, we deserve whatever trouble will follow. As for you, Major, if you really wanted to make Maelzer angry you should have answered that there's no Russian front left to send you to." After a moment in which they looked at one another, listening to telephones ring throughout the building at long, lugubrious intervals, he rapped Bora's shoulder with his knuckles. "Now comes the killing time. God help us all."

Signora Carmela expected Guidi to come through the front door. It was Francesca instead, breathless, wide-eyed, who rushed past the parlor to her room.

"Are you all right, dear?" With cautious small steps the old woman approached Francesca's room and looked in.

Doubled over on the bed, Francesca was sobbing. Signora Carmela made out that German soldiers had followed her for a stretch of the way and nearly caught her. They had lost her only when she had turned into Via Paganini and stepped into a doorway.

"Why would they follow you, poor lamb? A young woman with a baby on the way!"

Francesca went from tears to laughter at the words, a frightful voiceless laugh that stiffened her into rigidity. Signora Carmela couldn't get her to stop. Scared, she called her husband in.

"Her nerves are shot," he gravely said. "This requires *Aurum*." In the Maiuli house the aromatic liqueur was the ultimate resource, and what there was of it in a bottle was jealously kept under lock and key. Now the professor poured a generous dose in a glass his wife held before Francesca. "This is so unlike her, the poor girl. Now we'll get the doctor to come."

Francesca gulped down the drink. "No." She coughed. "No, doctor. Nobody. I'm not home for anybody. No one, no calls. Nobody, do you understand? Not even my mother. Something went on downtown, the Germans are berserk."

"Goodness." Signora Carmela wheezed. "And Inspector Guidi hasn't come home either." She drew away from Francesca, who was regaining her self-control and angrily wiped the tears off her face. "Where could he be, do you think?"

"Don't ask me where he is." Shivering, Francesca kicked her shoes off. "I'm tired, I want to sleep." And even as the old couple stood there, she climbed into her bed and covered herself, turning her back to them.

Shortly after seven that evening, Bora called Guidi to confront him about the shots fired from the police station. There was no answer there, so he tried Via Paganini. Timidly Signora Carmela picked up the phone. Bora's Italian reassured her, and – assuming he was a friend – she shared her worry about the inspector, who hadn't come home from work.

"Did he say he might be late?"

"On the contrary. It was his turn to buy bread and he's always been good about that. He's a thoughtful man and wouldn't let us go without bread for supper."

Bora hung up with a queasy feeling.

At nine Westphal called back from Soratte: Field Marshal Kesselring had just deliberated with Hitler and the head of the 14th Army, General von Mackensen. The reprisal would stand at ten for every German killed. Bora called the embassy in hope of finding Dollmann still there, but was told that he had left for the Vatican. He phoned the Vatican next and learned that the colonel was no longer there. So he waited until nearly ten o'clock to call his apartment.

Dollmann answered, and when he heard the final number, he cried out, "What a mess! And I haven't had time to speak to General Wolff yet!"

On his way to the hotel Bora stopped at the foot of Via Rasella, blocked off and eerie in the dark. The houses around it were empty and silent. At the corner of Via Del Boccaccio, the Public Security office was barred shut. Guidi's little car was still parked at the street corner, with the windows smashed by gunfire.

24 MARCH 1944

The sun came up in a glory of little clouds, but Bora felt a noxious darkness inside. He had not been able to sleep all night, and today he ached dully. He decided against taking painkillers because they might make him drowsy, and he didn't need that. Westphal would not be back from Soratte today, which he had expected. Kesselring was taking grave military decisions, and likely would visit the Anzio front again in the next few hours.

Despite tales of overflowing death cells, Bora knew there were not enough capital punishment inmates in Roman jails to make up the number of hostages to execute. The SS death toll had risen overnight to thirty-two, and from Dollmann he heard that until late at night Kappler and Caruso had been discussing quotas. He still wondered what to make of Guidi's disappearance, and it was with some hope that he called again at his workplace and at home. The police phone still rang empty. Signora Carmela began to weep when he asked her the question. Next, he was debating whether to contact Kappler, to whom he had not spoken at all the day before. Once Kappler had his orders he would carry them out with unshakeable thoroughness, and there was nothing to gain by irritating him. Uneasily Bora sat by the phone with an ear to the relentless cannonade from Anzio, resting his forehead in the palm of the right hand.

At seven thirty he went to report to Maelzer. As yesterday, he was told to wait. When, half an hour later, the general had not yet left his breakfast table, Bora was curious to see Caruso come in. The head of police saw him and said nothing; looking haggard, he went past him to the concierge's desk. Bora assumed he came to consult Maelzer, and prepared himself to wait longer; after overhearing Caruso ask for the Minister of Interior instead, he knew that the Italian police would fill in the names missing from Kappler's death list.

Maelzer came out of the dining room and was very brief and businesslike, as if yesterday's anger had not spilled out into today. He looked well rested. He told Bora that in case the field marshal inquired, he was to report that all had been taken care of. By noon all major selections would have been made.

Bora asked who would materially execute the order. Maelzer said he would know by noon, which to Bora meant there was uncertainty whether the army, the SS or the Fascists would carry out the sentence. Who was to be included in the list? Maelzer spoke fast. Criminals, partisans and Jews, three hundred and thirty of them.

Bora was glumly returning to his battered car when the thought first came to him that Guidi might be among those arrested at Via Rasella. Any anger he'd felt for police apathy during the attack left him. His foreboding grew worse after he was unable to phone anyone in authority at Regina Coeli. Bora *had* to talk to Kappler now, but all the while the dark inside him widened at tremendous speed.

Francesca ate breakfast in bed, nursed by Signora Carmela. She was hungry, and when she finished, she asked for more. Signora Carmela said there were only dry beans and a small piece of bread in the house, because the inspector had not come home or sent the groceries.

"Well, I'm hungry," Francesca snapped back. "Why don't you send the professor to buy something at the store? I pay the rent, and board goes with the room. If you and your husband don't want to go out, then ask for something next door."

Signora Carmela would not argue. It was cherry-lipped Pompilia who gave her a generous piece of nearly fresh bread and a small hunk of cheese, with ill-concealed satisfaction at being asked. From the threshold she watched the old woman trip back to her door. "Aren't the lovebirds up to doing their own shopping?" she called after her.

"I'm sure I don't know what you mean," Signora Carmela said.

Francesca was on the telephone when she came back in, and quickly lowered the receiver.

"I feel much better," she said, in a pacifying tone.

Signora Carmela placed bread and cheese on a plate, and this on the kitchen table.

At Via Tasso the atmosphere was feverish. It didn't take much observation to notice that several of the officers had worked through the night. Kappler had had time to shave but was filmy-eyed, going in and out of doors; Sutor wore dirty-blond stubble on his face, and was gulping coffee in thirsty draughts. "Hey, here's Bora," he announced to someone in the office behind him, who turned out to be Captain Priebke. "Bora, have you brought some names?"

"No. I've come to talk to Colonel Kappler."

"What about? We're busy as hell."

"I suspect an Italian police official was detained by mistake at Via Rasella."

"Who?"

"Sandro Guidi."

"The horse-face of the Reiner case? What the hell would he be doing at Via Rasella?"

Bora ignored the question. "If I'm right, it's obviously a mistake. Please check your list of detainees."

Sutor's face darkened. "What are you up to really, Bora? Who sends you?"

"I'm here on my own. I *worked* with the man, remember?"

"We don't have a general list of detainees." Bora knew Sutor was lying, but there was nothing he could do about it. "You'll have to go to Regina Coeli and see if he's in the slammer there. We've got other things to worry about."

Priebke peered out of the office with half of his face smothered in shaving cream.

"Yes, why don't you go to Regina Coeli, Bora?"

The jail lay across the city, on the other bank of the Tiber. There was heightened activity here as well, especially in the German-controlled Third Wing. Bora had to wait before someone finally came to talk to him. They had no idea who might be in the batch of two hundred and more brought to the temporary detention camp at the Ministry of Interior, nor if any had been transferred here. No one was allowed to see the prisoners. He'd have to ask the SS at Via Tasso.

"I come from there. All I want is to get the man out of jail if he happens to have been brought in by mistake."

While he was again kept waiting, Bora looked at his watch. It was nine forty-five when a lieutenant emerged from a doorway to inform him sharply that they knew nothing of a man called Guidi. He left. In the bleak corridor of the ground floor he was again hounded by an angst-filled foreboding, which he still did not want to name. And though he knew Sciaba was here, he refused to worry about him right now, because he remembered Kappler's promise to transfer him to the Italian Wing at the end of March. And it wasn't yet the end of March.

Outside the jail he stopped by the bridge, collecting his mind. He watched the river coil crazy eddies around the piers, carrying spring mud and bits of young leaves from the rains in the hills. Anxiety was becoming physical, a hyper-vigilant pessimism Bora had never known to be wrong. From below, a fresh, bitter odor of water wafted up the bridge's arches, where swallows dived to gather bits for their nests.

At this time Kappler was again meeting with Caruso. And still there weren't enough names on the list.

Back at Via Tasso, Bora stopped Sutor in the hallway. "They told me Guidi's been arrested," he lied. "Give me the papers to get him out."

Sutor did not get impatient at first. He went to his desk and picked up the list of hostages to be shot in the afternoon. He scanned it and held up a page for Bora to see. "You're too late."

Bora read and his mouth went dry. "You can't be serious, Captain." He had a hard time controlling his voice. "I have word from General Maelzer that only proven criminals would be included."

"Caruso recommended the name. It's all legal, Bora."

"The hell it is!" Bora knew he was raising his voice and did it all the same, forgetful of the people around the office. "You must remove this name from the list, do you understand me?"

"Get a hold of yourself."

"Take his name off the list *right now*!"

Sutor struck a threatening pose, coming chest-to-chest with Bora. "We've been working at this for twelve straight hours – what's with you, are you fucking crazy or queer for this Guidi?"

"Remove the name, Sutor!"

Sutor took his breath. "Only if you put your name down in place of his."

They came dangerously close to blows. Bora left the building in a rage, a frantic grind of thoughts milling through his mind:

appealing to Maelzer, the embassy or the Vatican. Calling Wolff directly… As if any of those actions would work. Under the incurious eyes of the SS men at the door he steadied himself and entered his car. He put a cigarette in his mouth. Without lighting it he drove off to St John Lateran Square, and took the road that led out of Rome.

Francesca had washed her hair in the sink. Seated on the rim of the bathtub she began to dry it with a towel. Even without a full-length mirror she knew she was growing big quickly. None of her dresses fastened any more. Thank God there were only eight weeks to go. Yesterday's close call had for once frightened her, but she was all right today. No one had been caught. No names given. Talking to Rau's contact this morning, she'd understood from their agreed-upon code that he was fine too, and out of Rome by now. Whether he would return or not depended on how things developed. The morning newspapers carried no news about the attack, nor did the radio. It meant the Germans were confused, and in disagreement as to what to do next.

She weighed the possibility that Guidi might be involved in the investigation of the attack, but it was unlikely. He'd probably left Rome instead, having finally decided what side he was on. After she finished blotting her hair she left the bathroom. "I'm going for a walk," she announced to the Maiulis from the door of her room. "It's nice and sunny out."

All Bora knew was that Field Marshal Kesselring was still at the Anzio front or returning from it, possibly by way of the once flourishing, quaint villages of the Alban Hills. It was a desperate proposition to reach him in the battle zone, but he decided to make straight for Genzano, which at a distance of thirty-five miles was the farthest of the hill towns, and would allow him to trace his way back through others if he missed him there.

The countryside was at the time of year when every hour makes a difference in color and measure of green. Almond trees bloomed white along the slopes and craggy spurs of ancient lava flows, and at any other time Bora would love the sight. None of it interested him now. When an American reconnaissance plane hovered alongside him on the state route, he ignored it. For a time the plane followed his car at no more than fifty feet of altitude, then peeled off and was gone.

The volcanoes blistering the countryside south-west of the city had long been extinct and filled with water, which made them into round, deep-rimmed lakes with the clarity of mirrors. Their sides were hairy and thick with an uninterrupted coating of woods, and only recently bombs had scarred them bare here and there. Making for their green humps, Bora drove past countless antique and new ruins, minding none. It was nearly eleven o'clock. In little over four hours the executions would take place.

Genzano huddled on the outer rim of the smaller of the two craters, bristling with vineyards; Bora speeded up the road that led to its venerable center, with his eyes now and then on the hazy view of the city like a shore of endless pebbles below him, until the curve took it from sight. The houses were pale orange and yellow at the sides of the street. A timelessness of sorts seemed to hang about even though the rumble from the front was continuous, and the smoke rising from it could be seen down the plain toward the sea, less than fifteen miles away. There was an army patrol in the square and Bora stopped by them.

They listened to him at attention. They had just escorted the field marshal to town; he was having lunch at the Stella d'Italia restaurant. Bora followed with his eyes where the soldiers pointed, and went to park by the entrance. Army cars lining the square alerted him of a conference taking place inside. He prepared himself to wait for the others to leave. Reaching for a cigarette, he found that he'd never lit nor removed the one in his mouth since leaving Rome.

Bora's secretary had a run in her stockings, which Colonel Dollmann marked as a discordant note in her otherwise perfect army outfit. "Where is the major?" He looked away from the run when she turned around from the file cabinet.

"He left at 0700 hours and has not returned since," she said.

"Has he called?"

"Yes, just now."

"Where from? I need to meet with him."

"Genzano."

Dollmann decided to show no surprise, although he asked, "What in Heaven's name is he doing there?"

Bora watched the field marshal spine the fish in his plate, the tines of his fork heedfully dividing the fragile, waxy flesh, white with a brownish shade; the spine appeared neatly, daintily shaped, nearly transparent, easily surrendering the meat around it until it lay exposed. Kesselring picked up the wedge of lemon and squeezed it over it with even pressure of thumb and forefinger. Caught by sunlight, a spray crowned the slice as juice trickled on the dish. He mopped his fingers on the napkin and began to eat. Bora looked away.

"Truly, Martin, you know better than that."

"No, *Herr General Feldmarschall*, I don't. I don't. I need a note from you within the next few minutes, or Guidi is dead. I would not have come here had I known better."

Kesselring looked up from the dish. They were outside on a vine-covered balcony that overlooked the lake, and there weren't enough new leaves on the trellis to shield the sun entirely; the red branches did most of the covering. "None of us is clean in this business. Did you not order reprisals during your stint in Russia?"

"Against guerrilla forces, yes."

"And what's 'guerrilla forces' to you? Do they speak Russian, do they wear *valenki* boots? I don't see why you're choosing to become involved in this. If it's friendship you're thinking of, there's no such thing in war. There's camaraderie, not friendship – and for an Italian, after what they've done to us! Awful things have happened before. What's different this time?"

"*Herr General Feldmarschall*," Bora said dryly, "they will start shooting in less than three hours. If you think an innocent man is worth saving, I beg you to give me a signed message for Kappler."

"This Guidi, he's not Jewish, is he?"

"No, he's not Jewish."

"You *know* that."

"Yes, I know that. He's not Jewish."

"Because if he were Jewish, you understand —"

"For God's sake, *Herr General Feldmarschall*, I'd ask you if he were Jewish, don't you see?"

Kesselring took another bite, then let go of his fork, watching him. Bora kept self-control with an obvious effort; still he held his stare, and his lips were unmoved.

Kesselring had his big bony laugh. "We go back forty years, your stepfather and I. Best commander I ever had. You're like him, but even more unorthodox. You're courting trouble." With the napkin he wiped his mouth from side to side. Moderately he drank some white wine from his glass. He poured some for Bora, who did not even acknowledge the gesture. Finally he stood up with his burly frame. "I will call Colonel Kappler and speak to him in person. Wait here."

While he was gone inside the restaurant, Bora fidgeted. In the incongruous peace of the view, his heartbeat pounded at the sides of his neck, and the explosions from the front seemed never to end. He understood all too well that Kesselring did not wish to apply his signature to a written order.

The field marshal was back eventually. "Kappler is not in. I left a message with his adjutant. Everything is fine. Guidi's name will be pulled from the list and he will remain at Regina Coeli until you pick him up."

Bora thanked him. Sweat gathered on his face at the release of tension. In less than an hour he'd be out of Via Tasso on his way to the jail – and that would be before two o'clock.

Kesselring sat again. "It's all right, Martin. Now let me eat in peace."

Francesca had lunch at her mother's.

"What are you going to do with the baby?" her mother asked, taking her long hair in hand and sweeping it behind her back. She was still young, narrow-hipped, large of breasts, with a hungry mouth and fingertips stained by tobacco. Francesca remembered seldom seeing her in other than a robe; in the summer sometimes she was naked. They knew one another's bodies very well.

"Do you have stretch marks?" her mother asked when her first question was not answered.

"Some."

"I can't understand why. I got none with you."

"I'm going to have it at the Raimondis'," Francesca answered to the first question. "You know her, she paints watercolors. He's a physician, and they have no children. She's been sketching me every month and tells me how *beautiful* my belly looks. She bought me three new dresses."

Her mother half-closed her eyes, with her hand on a pack of German cigarettes across the table. "I kept you."

Francesca shrugged, with a little smile. "The man who rents with me – we've gotten together a couple of times. He feels so guilty about it, he asked me to marry him."

"What did you tell him?"

"I laughed in his face, Ma. He's a policeman. What would I want to marry him for?"

"There's something to be said for those who offer."

Francesca went to the long mirror on the door to look at herself sideways. "We'll see if he asks again."

*

A look at the still-distant southern periphery showed Bora that the roadside airport ahead was being strafed. He took the first right turn with the intention of reaching Rome by a parallel route, only to find that the Centocelle Field was under attack, too. So it was by circuitous country lanes that he finally came to Via Tasso at five past two. SS men would not let him through the door. Judging by the number of vehicles jamming the street, Maelzer had decided to charge Kappler with responsibility for the execution. Bora decided he'd try Regina Coeli again and physically get Guidi out of there.

Dollmann was waiting for him by the car.

"I don't know why you insist, Major; all decisions have been taken. Kappler went to Maelzer's at noon. Mackensen refused to give men from the army, so Kappler took it upon himself. Caruso was supposed to complete the list by one p.m., but didn't. Kappler is on edge, and it's just as well that you didn't get to meet him. There's nothing we can do to stop it now."

As briefly as possible Bora explained to him the situation. Dollmann set his face in a hard manner. "My poor man, by this time they're dragging everyone out of the jails to be shot. If Kesselring didn't sign a piece of paper, you have nothing."

Bora refused to panic. "Will you come with me to Regina Coeli?"

"No. I'm going to meet Wolff at Viterbo."

Bora drove off. At the head of Via Nazionale he discovered he was out of fuel. He lost twenty-five minutes waiting for a can of petrol to be brought down from one of the dumps. The soldier told him, "You've got a leak in your tank, Major. One of the bullets must have damaged it the other day. You'll be dry again if it doesn't get patched."

Bora told him to work at it, and with pain worsening in his arm he walked up the street to the Ministry of Colonies, where he placed a phone call to his secretary and asked for another car to be sent down immediately. Fifteen more minutes passed before a camouflaged BMW arrived. Bora took his maps, the extra petrol tank and continued toward the river.

It was some time past three when he crossed over, only to find that the trucks until this morning crowding the jail's courtyard were gone. He went in. The Third Wing had been nearly emptied. He worked his way to the Italian Wing. Guidi was not there. Neither was Sciaba. And now the memory of General Foa gave him a shock in the blood, because he knew he'd be first on Kappler's list.

For some minutes Bora sat slumped at the wheel of the car. In the sunshine, the warm light of day created red swirls before his eyes. He had stomach cramps. He'd eaten nothing since the negligible lunch of yesterday noon and felt light-headed. The pain in his arm was at one point so sharp, he winced on the seat and had to grab his forearm. All the same he had to think, quickly.

Where? Where in Rome would over three hundred men be brought for execution? No, not in Rome. Out of Rome, obviously. But where? To one of the barracks, no doubt. There were tens of them, all around the perimeter of the city, forts and fields and proving grounds. Which one might be chosen from this side of town? He thought at once of the barracks at the northern edge of Rome, past the Vatican, a long row that formed a virtual military citadel. Forte Bravetta was where executions by the Italian Army took place, way out on the Aurelia. And there was the old army shooting range in the northern bend of the Tiber.

He roused himself and walked out of the car to ask the Italian policemen at the entrance of the jail in which direction the trucks had left. They told him they had crossed the bridge, which Bora could not understand. "You mean they went toward the center of Rome?"

They didn't know. The trucks had gone across the Tiber and taken the river road that followed it.

"North or south?"

"South."

Back in the car, Bora studied a map of the city and its environs to make sense of the directions. It had to be out of Rome. Three hundred and twenty bodies are difficult to dispose of, and somehow he could not envision trucks returning to town with such grisly cargo for the Romans to see. True, he'd gone through Russian villages where the SS had solved the problem by having the victims dig their own mass graves. There was no time today, unless the graves had been already mechanically dug by engineers. Where, the question was, and how far?

It had to be Forte Bravetta, the military compound due west of where he stood now. Resistance leaders had been executed there in the past week. It stood in an open, desolate stretch beyond the church of Madonna del Riposo, where nothing but blackened stumps of medieval towers and deep ditches marked the way. The truck drivers might have chosen to get there by the level ground of Viale del Re, crossing the Tiber again, two bridges down. He took the road skirting the park-like hills behind Regina Coeli, hoping to overtake the convoy.

He did not, and there were no trucks at the Bravetta compound. The Italian officer on duty was courteous to him, but no help at all. Bora felt he could shout with disappointment. All day, despite his rushing from place to place, he had kept the goal before himself with some measure of confidence that he would achieve it. Now for the first time he felt that he would not: that it was over, that it was past four twenty and Guidi was dead. Great discouragement took him. He was hungry and in pain. Hunger especially infuriated him, a base animal reaction when everything else was more important than that. He was tempted to drive straight to his office and hole himself in it, thinking of nothing any more.

The Italian officer watched him with sympathy from a few steps away. He said, "Major, I won't ask what you're looking for, but whatever it is, give it up. There's nothing you can do."

Bora felt a new spurt of obstinacy. "How long does it take to execute three hundred people?"

The officer's blue eyes blinked. "Are you telling me or are you asking me?"

"I'm asking your opinion."

"It depends. With a machine gun it takes five minutes. But if it's a regular military execution, why, it'd take hours."

"How many hours?"

"Four or five at least."

Bora entered the car and started the engine. "Thank you. Now I must try to believe that."

Francesca laid the new dresses on her bed. She liked best the dark blue one with a white trim at the neck and sleeves, too elegant to wear with cotton stockings.

It made her nervous to have heard no news on a German reprisal, especially when whispers of the attack had begun to circulate. She wondered whether she could safely go back to work in the morning. Out of a drawer she took the silk stockings Guidi had given her and rested them by the dress, judging them a perfect match.

In the parlor the Maiulis were talking to neighbors who had come to listen to the radio. Above all other voices, Pompilia Marasca's could be heard asking why the inspector had not been home in two days. Signora Carmela replied something about engaging the help of St Anthony and St Jude, who had "never been known to fail." Silence was made when the professor turned the radio on for the five o'clock news.

Twenty minutes later Martin Bora had driven back to Regina Coeli, where he once more considered his options. There were six roads out of Rome by which the trucks might have traveled south; he had no idea of the final destination, but knowing the actual way out of the walls was a first step.

Having heard from the policemen how the prisoners had been bound in groups of three, hands tied behind their back, he asked for a pocket knife. The request caused some curiosity, but a switchblade was produced. Bora drove to the place where Via Portuense left the walls, and inquired of a shopkeeper about a convoy, to no avail. At five thirty he tried the same with a woman sewing on her Via della Magliana doorstep. At five forty he was on Via Ostiense, where he began growing unnerved at the lack of information. The Ardeatine Gate came five minutes after that. A beggar told him that no army vehicles had gone by since the morning, and even then, it was just a single car. Bora tore himself from there and reached St Sebastian's Gate just after six o'clock.

The sun was going down and the enclosed, ominous body of the Roman gate stood over him with its two round towers cramped in by walls. Bora took a disheartened look at the centuries-old outline of St Michael engraved inside the archway to guard it from foreign invasion. Across the street a shoemaker was getting ready to close his shop. He said that, yes, trucks had been passing by all day, the last few of them not long ago.

Bora felt as one who has been doused with icy water. Drowsiness and pain were gone from him in a brief surge of nervous energy, forgetful that it had been nearly three hours since the executions had started. The reality of it hit him only after he went past the gate in the orange sunset that drew shroud-like, immensely long shadows from the walls flanking the Appian Way.

If he let go of tension for a moment, dangerous weariness came on him, a desperate need to sleep after thirty-six hours of waking. It was by inertia that he functioned now, because hope could not possibly attach itself to such slim possibility as Guidi's survival until this time.

He grew so dazed at one point that his car went off the road and into the grassy verge, where he steered away barely in time to avoid crashing against the wall. There was a fountain a few steps ahead, just a metal pipe spouting water into a mossy basin. Bora walked to it and put his head under the cold flow.

Less than a mile from the city wall was a fork in the road. A wild, romantic place he knew well, with fig trees peering from fenced yards and the baroque facade of a chapel by the curve. Here at *Quo Vadis* the fleeing Peter encountered Christ and turned back to Rome in shame, having asked the question that became the name of the chapel, "Whereto Goest Thou?"

There was no one in sight he could ask for advice, and Bora had no time to look for anyone. He bore left and continued until the road divided again. He ignored the lane descending into a field. He'd passed the entrance of one catacomb, and already the side road leading to the Cemetery of Praetextatus came up. This entire area was honeycombed with underground passages used as Jewish and Christian burials in Roman times. Tunnels extended for prodigious distances beneath the surface, intersecting at angles on several levels of resilient but easily cut volcanic stone. Bora traveled on a crust under which thousands were buried.

It was too coincidental for him not to draw the grim parallel. He soon dismissed it because of the repercussions such violation would have in the Vatican: yet everything else about the idea made sense, when the catacombs themselves had been dug in abandoned stone quarries. The grim image of a natural grave spurred Bora to press on, to Praetextatus' burial ground. He'd ask at St Sebastian's, where Via delle Sette Chiese merged close by.

The door to the ancient basilica was not locked. Inside, the darkness within was nearly complete, though it was one of those clear, sweet springtime evenings laced with sparrows and scent of blooming grasses.

Hearing the sound of army boots, a man kneeling in the front pew got up and made a sideways motion to slide away. Bora told him to stop. It was a small priest with a suffering face, a bird's neck swimming in his collar. Bora dragged him toward the faint light of the doorway. He spoke to him curtly, barely in control of his words: it was now seven o'clock.

"I don't know," the priest moaned. "I don't know who you are."

It was abject, complete fear, Bora understood, but had no time to examine or allay. He dug into his shirt collar and held out a medal by its ribbon. "Look, the scapular medal. I'm Catholic. I must know if German trucks have gone by."

"I have seen none."

Bora took a deep breath. Good. Good. It meant the execution place lay somewhere between here and the walls. "Are there any quarries or sandpits nearby?"

The priest rolled his eyes. "Quarries? Yes. No one has used them in a long time, though."

"*Where?*"

The directions included country paths and backtracking at right angles toward the ledge of a small river due north. "Don't go into the valley. Keep to the ledge."

Bora ran to the car. In the waning light things were seen and unseen, their contours blurred. He drove on, remembering to swerve toward the ledge only after he had nearly come to the river. No signs of trucks. Darkness below. He rolled down the window. No sounds.

Again the need to let go and close his eyes came. He was in the middle of nowhere and it was dark. It was late. The dead were all around, old and new, but he could not see them. He felt an unbearable nearness and yet a sense of being utterly lost. Why had he been allowed to come so far and fail? A taut braid seemed to be unraveling inside him. It would fast become frayed unless he held to it somehow, in some other way. He mechanically began to say the old Latin words as if it'd make a difference, arms folded on the wheel and his head on them. Broken thoughts, old Latin words, over and over, to keep the braid inside from growing slack. *Illuminare his, qui in tenebris et in umbra mortis sedent* —

Then he heard the sound. Eyes wide open in the dark, he sat up. It was the muted, distant sound of gunfire coming at intervals as if from a distance, or an enclosed place. The car faced south, and the reports came from the west, past the wide band of catacombs along the Appian Way.

Bora jerked the car into reverse, backing through the countryside onto the road. He rejoined it near Via delle Sette Chiese, which he found blocked by the SS where it crossed the Ardeatine. His mind was working now in reckless but logical patterns. He turned around and careered toward Rome nearly two miles in order to enter the Ardeatine from its north end, although there would be troops there, too. Soon he could see the slits in the blackened front lights of trucks entering the road from the opposite direction. Gaining speed, he caught up with them as they went through the roadblock, where no one stopped him. They were engineers' trucks, and even so Bora refused to let his heart sink.

The convoy pulled into a depressed space right of the road, where a ledge concealed pits or caves. The shots came from there. At the glare of lanterns Bora distinguished twenty or so men huddled by the entrance to the caves. They neither moved nor spoke, while the guards watching them were as loud as drunks. They took notice of him, but did not stop him from approaching. In a yellow shaft of light Bora saw Captain Sutor walk out with two soldiers, and at the same time, from his tall figure and sloping shoulders, he recognized Guidi in the group of prisoners.

The rest was like a fast-paced dream. Bora ordered the closest SS to free the tall man, receiving a stuporous look in response. Guidi might have heard, but did not react at all. When Bora yanked him from the group, he also jogged the two men bound to him back to back. Relief and frustration ran so high in him, Bora could no longer manage them. With the switchblade he hacked at the rope, careless of wrists and hands. After the rope gave way Guidi still did not move. Bora pulled him to himself, and Guidi, whose feet were bound, fell on his knees. Exasperated, Bora threw the switchblade at him. "Here! Run to my car when you're done!"

"Not without the others —"

"*Fuck, Guidi*! Get to the car!"

Guidi's companions were desperately trying to hopscotch away when the guards began to make hazy sense of things and fired at them. The men fell, and the whole group of prisoners was frantic now. Sutor turned on them, shouting. Then he saw Bora and flew at him.

"Are you out of your mind?" he howled. "What do you think you're doing?

Bora's gun swung up from the holster. "I'm carrying out Kesselring's orders. Try to stop me."

Guidi was staggering in a daze when Bora came running, jostled him forward and at the inertia of his response put the gun to his head and forced him to race to the car. Still Guidi absurdly resisted entering it, but Bora's toughness was like metal under the uniform. By brutal kicks he drove the prisoner in at last, knees crashing against him until he was inside and the door locked.

When Bora went to open his door Sutor's face floated out of the dark into the shaft of light behind him, a disembodied mask of strain. He was trying to maintain some check on himself, but his mouth twitched hard. Bora entered the car and gave gas to the running engine. As he backed up to regain the road, Sutor spoke over a small burst of gunfire from the caves.

"You think you got something, Bora. Do you hear those shots? They just put two bullets through your General Foa's skull."

The car roared out of the gravel-strewn space. Its tires spun and flung rocks around as the guards herded the last prisoners back toward the cave with the butts of rifles, Sutor at the lead, blaspheming and throwing punches into them.

They had come several miles through roads unknown to Guidi before Bora drove off the pavement and braked on a rise in the land. He turned the motor off.

Sweat drenched his armpits and stomach; his face was bathed in it. He let go of the wheel and rested his shoulders against the seat, too tense to shiver, the whole of him keyed hard for the fight and unable to relax. He glanced over to Guidi, slumped on the seat by him.

Dark and complete silence, though Guidi was breathing – he could hear that. The front lay silent Anzio's way, but a reflection from burning fires was a mockery of dawn. Cool night air trickled from the window. Young trees with new leaves made soft sounds as of paper.

Bora feared letting go. He sat up because he feared letting go and growing weak thereby. An extreme need to weep mounted in him, which he held down by anger but not very well. He swallowed his need to weep, feeling as if someone had flayed him open and exposed the raw vulnerability beneath, his intimate self turned inside out like a jumble of guts for people to see. Had Guidi said something at least, he needed to hear talk. But Guidi was still and silent.

Around the car, above it, the night wove on looms of silence and untenable emptiness. Bora looked up at the cruel star-pricked sky without turning his head, and the effort of rolling his eyes to one side sent shooting sparks of pain into his temples. He could not let go.

Men's life was nothing, nothing. At any time the stars could crush them from their pointed and multiform distance, a cascade of worlds against their weakness. It was only anger that kept grief at bay, but the emptiness was untenable. The silence, absolute. Bora looked in disgust at the pitiful tangle of his soul. It was like bloody offal and deserving mercy only in the measure he could give mercy to any human being for failing himself and others. He deserved nothing if he let go.

And yet, one by one, by physical process, the knots of his tension began to fray. One, then another and another, and he was terrified to come unstrung when the work was not yet done.

When he tried to fight it he began to ache from within his contracted shell, a deep mortal ache and strain of all his muscles, as if his body were a wound crying for him. Bora did not let go.

Neither would he drive back to Rome. He went to Donna Maria's country house, sitting by itself on a hillside. He parked in the yard. Through the dark soft night he walked to the house, opened the door.

Guidi did not move until Bora swung the car door wide and said, "No one will look for you here. The bedrooms are upstairs. Go to sleep. I'll come tomorrow as I can."

At the Flora only some of the offices were manned. Dollmann's message on his desk was over nine hours old. Bora called Soratte and spoke to Westphal, who said, "Get a hold of Dollmann at once."

As Bora sat down to dial the colonel's number, Dollmann called from the Excelsior.

"Bora, thank God you're back. Get here immediately. No, I can't tell you. I'll meet you upstairs."

Like a machine, Bora got up. He had no idea of how he looked until he stepped by a mirror in the lobby of the hotel and saw his face. Even then, he merely took care to tuck the scapular under his tunic and to straighten his ribbons on his way to the elevator.

Dollmann greeted him outside of the banquet hall. "Wait in the next room. Kappler is here, and so is Wolff. I will keep you informed. You must call the field marshal as soon as this is through, and before the conference breaks. If you think what you witnessed is bad, wait until this is done with."

In a daze Bora watched the colonel re-enter the room. He was too tired to stand, but did not dare sit down lest he fall asleep. So he walked the floor back and forth, the line of marble tiles waving before his eyes as he did. He was too numb to ache by now.

It was eleven before Dollmann came out. Bora had crawled to an armchair and was trying to steady his hand enough to drink coffee without spilling it on himself.

"Bad news," the colonel said. "We're still discussing the

situation, but it seems as though the consensus is to deport all Roman males. Envision that."

Bora was appalled, but things were entirely out of proportion in his mind, and he found nothing to say. Two more hours passed, which he could not recall as anything but a blur, though he managed to stay awake. He even stood up at Dollmann's next appearance.

"It's coming soon now, Bora. We're approaching a decision. Himmler will be called next. At my message you must rush out of here."

Bora said he would. Less than twenty minutes later Dollmann came out in a hurry. Bora was sitting by a small table with his head on the folded arms. A fourth cup of coffee sat by, untouched. Gently Dollmann shook him with the news.

"The last trip for today, Major. Then you can go to bed."

It was past three when Bora walked into his room at the Hotel d'Italia and stumbled across his bed. It had been forty-six hours since he had last slept in it.

Two hours later, when the alarm went off, Bora cried tears of exhaustion as he struggled up, because he did not want to face the day. In the shower he turned the water on and – having found it warm – he let it grow warmer, then hot, and stood under it in a cloud of vapor, scalding his neck and shoulders until they painfully turned red. Then he wore the dress uniform required for the SS funeral and went to work.

6

When he drove to the service, an SS lieutenant tried to prevent him from dismounting. Bora pushed him aside with the door and the lieutenant pinned him against the side of the car.

"You shouldn't be showing your face here after yesterday!" He was a very young and angry man, red-eyed with crying or fatigue or both, and the only way Bora knew he had not been one of the executioners was that his breath didn't smell of alcohol.

"Do me the favor," Bora elbowed him to step onto the sidewalk. Being held back by the sleeve infuriated him. He pushed back the SS and found himself grabbed again. Sutor watched from the church steps. Relatives of the dead soldiers, flown in from the Tyrol, were looking on also. Bora shouldered the lieutenant hard, and couldn't have kept from creating an incident had Dollmann not appeared with his sarcastic face like a keel pointed to the disturbance.

"Ah, Bora," he said from the steps, raising a glove in hand. "Are you coming in?"

Grudgingly the lieutenant stepped back. Bora joined the colonel, who preceded him inside.

"I'm starting to think you lost your paw by getting too close to the lard jar, Major, like the cat in the Italian proverb."

"If that's the case, you know it is human lard this cat has gotten too close to."

"Sh, sh. Don't you become impertinent. I have my troubles as it is. You look awful."

"Colonel, you have no idea."

"I heard Kappler's report. It's best left alone. Where did you take Guidi?"

Bora told him. Dollmann nodded. "Stay in Rome. I'll go fetch him. After all, we met at the party, so he shouldn't be alarmed by the uniform."

During the service Bora wished he could crumple somewhere out of sheer emotional weariness. He stood apart from the SS, who formed a hurt and bloodshot-eyed cluster of their own. It was impossible to let his guard down when he expected to be provoked again at the end of the ceremony. His grief was of compounded losses, personal and shared. All pains and deaths were mirrors of it; there was no end to them. The thought of mangled bodies in the coffins, the thought of how the butchered piles in the caves must look now was overwhelming. In the presence of those who had done the killing, a chill went through him as of his own death.

But outside there was no incident. The SS merely went their way, and he to his office.

Back from Soratte, Westphal dismissed him early. Bora drove to his hotel, where he slept until eight in the evening. At this time he brushed his teeth, shaved, put on a fresh uniform and went downstairs to get drunk.

As for Guidi, he arrived at his doorstep on foot, since Dollmann had discreetly left him at the corner. As chance would have it, no one was in the apartment. Guidi walked to his room and lay in bed. Without thinking, his mind a forced blank, as though a piece had been taken out of it in self-defense: the hours elapsed between his arrest and the moment he had come to in Bora's car, parked in the dark stillness of the death-bearing night.

He slept for hours, as he had done in the country villa to which Bora had driven him. Only in the middle of the night did he awaken, still numb enough not to feel hunger, or thirst, or other physiological stimuli, his whole system jealously shut down. In the obscure shapelessness of the room, what he'd replied to Dollmann's warning floated back to him, but recalled as if someone else had acted the part. "Do you expect me not to talk?" The SS colonel had not flinched. "I expect you to pay your debt to the living. The dead don't give a damn about you or me or what's been done." Then Guidi slept again.

In the morning, news of his return traveled fast. Within moments there were tenants at all doors, a crowd in the Maiu-lis' parlor that risked toppling the saints from under their glass domes. Questions poured like water from a faucet, and in the flow Guidi said nothing other than he had been detained by mistake after the *accident* they had all heard about. Everyone wanted to congratulate him. Only Francesca, out with friends, was not there. Words jumbled on words. "They say the Pope asked the SS not to do it," and, "The doorkeeper thinks her cousin was killed with them." Pompilia Marasca came insufferably close, breast thrust under his nose. "Have you heard what happened to other prisoners? The Germans took them and tied them inside a Roman tomb and buried them alive, hundreds of them!"

Guidi tried to swallow, and could not. He flung his arms to get free of her and the other well-wishers and went coughing out of the parlor as one about to smother. After hacking and spitting in the handkerchief by his bed he was again able to breathe, but did not rejoin the company. He found a cowardly comfort in staring at the mirror until his face became a blur: the face nondescript, featureless, of one who – of hundreds – had been chosen to live.

26 MARCH 1944

When Bora began to sit up in bed, the room reeled upside down around him. The corners formed a see-saw where the light from the window was blinding, even though it was early in the morning. He lay back on his elbows, trying to steady his vision if not the rest of the world.

It was his room, at least, whatever had happened meanwhile. The last thing he remembered was ordering English gin, and plenty of it. He sat up finally, though he had to shield his eyes from the brightness of the room. Perceptions bobbed up to the surface like buoys that have been forcibly kept below, popping out and floating. He remembered nothing, really.

It was not his habit sleeping naked, but he was. And there was perfume in the room, in the pillow. A nauseous head-splitting pain laid him flat on his back again. Cheap perfume. And something on the mattress pricked his shoulder blade. He held up a woman's hairpin. His eyes opened wide and he looked at the ceiling swing back and forth for a while. He didn't have the slightest idea of whom he had brought to bed last night. For once he had not kept wise control. For the third time he hoisted himself on his elbows. Looking around he saw there was no evidence of his using a prophylactic, and he thought he must have really been drunk, then. He reached into the drawer at the right of the bed where was a sealed packet of them – as if he couldn't tell already by the state of the bed that he had used none.

It was one thing sitting at the edge of the bed with his feet on the floor, and another getting up from that position to reach the bathroom door. The doors were no steadier than the walls. Bora managed to lean over the bathtub and pour a bath. There was water, and it was hot. He sat in it to soak. He knew he'd start worrying as soon as his head cleared enough to remind him that this was no place and no time to have intercourse without protection.

Cardinal Hohmann was livid and looked dead with his eyes closed, unwilling to listen to what Bora told him. Never had such as this been done. Never. In the shadow of Peter's and Paul's grave, no less. He was dismissed. Dismissed, dismissed. There was no message for General Westphal, and he was dismissed.

Bora, still nursing his hangover, was not about to be dismissed. "May I point out to Your Eminence that seven Italian civilians were killed along with our soldiers, some of them children? One boy was cut in half by the explosion."

"Do not sicken me, Major. As if you cared. This is how you observe your open city status."

"It doesn't mean we're to be bowled down without redress, Your Eminence."

"Ten to one? You call it *redress*?" Hohmann's eyes opened behind the spectacles, and it was as if sharp bits of metal were boring holes out from his devastated old face.

"All we want is for *L'Osservatore* to present a balanced statement toward the army."

Hohmann closed his eyes again. The splendid sunshine only carved hollows in his countenance this morning. "Dollmann has already been here to ask."

"Dollmann is SS. It's because the army wishes to distance itself from what has happened that we must have assurance there will be no overt criticism of us in your press. Hard feelings breed unadvisable actions, and these breed hard measures."

"None of your sophistry, Major Bora. Come out with it – what do you offer in exchange?"

"We will pull some troops out by Wednesday," Bora said through his teeth.

"What kind of troops – the non-essentials?"

"Everybody is essential now."

"How many?" Bora presented a typewritten piece of paper and Hohmann read. "So, do you also get involved in blackmail these days, Major Bora?"

"We must do what we must do, both of us. Do I have Your Eminence's word?"

Disgustedly Hohmann set the paper on his lap. "All you have is a heartsick old German's word. It is disgraceful for you to be here, and for me to listen to you. I hoped better of my students." When Bora clicked his heels, Hohmann sighed deeply from his sparrow-like chest. "Tell me, what was your dissertation, in the end?"

"*Latin Averroism and the Inquisition.*"

"And your position on the non-eternity of the world?"

"I agree with Aquinas, Your Eminence – *Sola fide tenetur.*"

"It isn't all we manage to hold on to by faith alone, Major." Hohmann waved him away. "You disappoint me more than I can tell."

Bora left through the ornate door, without looking back.

Crossing the waiting room of the cardinal's residence, flooded by the brilliant Roman morning, with a swell of the heart he recognized Mrs Murphy standing there. She was dressed in black, and Bora caught himself impractically hoping she might have somehow become a widow meanwhile; but she was simply in the required attire for a papal reception. She saw him and nodded in reply to his salute. Bora was still turned toward her as he stepped past the threshold. Here he ran down a group of Japanese nuns waiting to see Hohmann, to whom he profusely apologized though they did not understand a word he said.

27 MARCH 1944

Guidi returned to work on Monday to find that three of his men had been arrested by the German Army. "Do you mean the SS?" he questioned Danza. "No, army. Major Bora led them." Instantly on the phone, Guidi reached Bora. Any expression of gratitude was so buried in him by disgust and hatred that all he did say pertained to his men's release.

Bora's coldness, in return, was like well water. "On the day of the attack, gunfire came from your police station. My car was struck by it."

"The men were confused, like everyone else."

Bora said something in German to someone, curtly. Then, "I spit on your men. It's you I must know about."

"What do you want me to say?" Guidi chewed on bitterness. "I would not intentionally fire on you, Major. Now let my men go."

"Let them go? They're on their way to Germany." And Bora put the receiver down.

28 MARCH 1944

As Guidi prepared to leave for work on Tuesday, Francesca asked him, "Where have you really been?"

She had taken the excuse of a sunny morning to wait for him just outside the door. In the awkwardness of her figure she resembled a beautiful boy to whom a strange load is tied. Guidi wished to feel less for her, because she felt nothing for him, and he knew. But she was asking him, her face keen and undeceived. And since Guidi said nothing, she invited him to walk, and down toward Piazza Verdi, where Guidi would board the tram, they went slowly. "I just found out from friends. How did you get away?"

"I can't tell you."

She took his left wrist in hand. "They cut you loose or did you cut yourself loose?"

Guidi pulled the cuff of his shirt back over the gash Bora had caused in severing the rope. "No thanks to any of yours. As far as I can tell they managed not only to kill some forty people, but got nearly ten times as many butchered as a result."

"You're wrong. You're dead wrong. It shows you understand nothing about fighting the Germans. How do you know what works and what doesn't?" When a man crossed their path from the other direction they both went quiet, and Francesca turned around to see if he was looking at them. "What works is killing *more* Germans, not less."

"Then I hope next time whoever is responsible will show his face afterwards to get shot."

"What for? As if the Germans would be satisfied with one or two people!"

Guidi had no more desire to lie than he did to explain the confusion of feelings inside him. "Look, I've been in your room while you were out. I found close to eighteen thousand lire in it, and I must know where they come from and what you plan to do with them. The neighbors are talking: all we need is a false step and the Maiulis might end up dead for it."

They were in the square now, and the sun-filled facade of the Mint shone like the backdrop of a gigantic theater. Francesca stopped, hands on her belly. "You, or I, or the Maiulis, mean nothing compared to what's at stake. I told you before, either you turn me in, or you shut up about it. As for you, how do I know the Germans didn't plant you among the prisoners to make them talk?"

"Don't speak nonsense." Guidi felt bile in his throat at the thought of Caruso, who had sent him a typed card of congratulations for escaping *a most unfortunate mishap, of which we have been officiously informed by the Germanic Ally.*

"You can always turn me in to your crippled German friend. The extra weight would help me hang, wouldn't it?" Francesca spoke in a low, taunting voice, and but for the ugly bulge between them, she'd never been so beautiful.

"Stop it, Francesca."

"Well, you can't have it both ways. Now that you say you know about me, you're either a part of it, or you've got to turn us in."

Guidi's words came out of him unrehearsed. "I'll have it neither way. I'm moving out."

"Good. I have someone who's looking for a place to stay. I can tell him there's an opening. Frankly things are going to run much better without you in the house. Go ahead, pack. Let me know when you're done so I can call my friend."

Guidi felt foolish. He had never had the intention to move. Now less than ever.

Francesca was still looking at him. "I don't know what you want from me. Rau doesn't come any more. I quit going out at night. You wanted to make love – we made love."

"You did none of those things for me. They were expedient."

She started walking back, one fatigued step after the other. "Right now everything is."

31 MARCH 1944

The hospital on Via di Priscilla, near Piazza Vescovio, was where many of the injured SS were recuperating from their wounds. Bora went there on Friday and asked to see a physician.

"You're aware, Major, that the incubation period is at least seven days."

"I know, I know. It happened a week ago."

"Do you have any symptoms?"

"No, but I hear it can be asymptomatic."

"We'll have an answer on the culture in ten days, but need to follow up with serological work. It takes five weeks for positive serology." The physician had been setting things ready, and now pressed with his forefinger on the hollow of Bora's arm to choose a vein to drive a needle into. Blood frothed black in the shaft. "It would help if you tracked the woman down."

"She could be a Hottentot for all I know. I was dead drunk."

"Not so drunk that you couldn't perform."

Bora looked up spitefully from the syringe. "*That* hasn't happened to me yet."

In front of the hospital he was stopped by Dollmann, who was coming with the German Consul to visit the casualties, and urged the diplomat to go ahead of him. "Have you heard the latest from Kappler, Bora?"

"The last I heard was that such a stench came from the caves, they had to pile loads of garbage in front of them to disguise it. As if you could mask the smell of death."

"And now he's going to tell the Roman press 'what really happened'."

"It's somewhat late for any mitigating statement, isn't it?"

"It makes no difference. The *King of Rome* wills it. What is it, Bora? You look a bit low. Is everything all right?"

"I had some difficult dealings with the Vatican."

"*You* have! How do you think I fared, this past week? It was hellish. They kept insisting that I publish the names of the hostages shot last Thursday. I understand how anxious the relatives of anyone who's in jail must be, but I couldn't accede, Bora. Even the Pope asked, and I had to tell him no. I'm asking *you* to join me on Monday in giving a tour of Rome to the foreign press. Charm is the name of the game, and incidentally all we have to give. If you take the Spaniards, I'll take the Swiss."

"What is to be shown to them?"

"The city, of course, and some of the suburbs."

Bora caught Dollmann's evasiveness. "What if the Spaniards ask to see the Appian Way?"

"Take them quickly to the monument of Caecilia Metella and back. But make sure the smell doesn't get as far as that."

2 APRIL 1944

On Palm Sunday, summer saving time was introduced, which meant Bora continued to get up and leave work at dusk. On Maundy Thursday, he wore civilian clothes to accompany Donna Maria to the Sepulchers of St Martin-in-the-Mounts, also known as Little St Martin's.

"Do you think it'd embarrass me to be seen with a man in a German uniform?" she teased as he helped her up the ramp of the church.

"I'd rather not chance the trouble, Donna Maria."

"And is that why you don't come to visit often at all?"

"Yes."

"Then come to visit my cats. They miss you." She stopped to take her breath while he opened the door of the church for her. "These stories of people being killed in caves, Martin – they're stories, aren't they?"

"I'm afraid they're true."

"For the love of God. Have you done any of it?"

The scent of incense from within was sickening. Bora said, "No, Donna Maria."

7 APRIL 1944

At two o'clock on Friday morning, when the telephone rang in his hotel room, at first Bora thought his alarm clock had gone off three hours early. He groped for the receiver. "Dollmann here, Major," he heard. "Steady yourself."

The Americans have come. In a split second Bora was sure of it, and the schedule of the next hour was mentally laid out before him. "I'm steady," he said.

"Cardinal Hohmann has been found murdered. Come down at once." An address in the center of Rome followed, which Bora heard through his astonishment as from a hollow, fearful distance.

Via della Pilotta was an old street behind the Trevi Fountain, perpendicular to the axis of the monument; low archways crowned its length, seemingly buttressing the sides of it. Bora was not familiar with the place, and identified the doorway only by the presence of Dollmann's car and a police van. The stairs inside were dark. Bora had to grope his way to the landing, where Dollmann waited for him in the ribbon of light from the flat's accosted door.

"It's a bad affair, Major. Go to the bedroom."

Bora went past him to enter, and at once the stench of blood washed over him. A glance into the bedroom sufficed him, before the flash from a police camera made it into a blind space of muffled sounds. When Dollmann followed, the policemen were insisting that nothing be moved, but Bora was covering the cardinal's body with a robe he'd grabbed at the foot of the bed.

"Please don't touch the woman, Major," the policemen warned.

"Do as they say, Bora," Dollmann added. "You see how bad it is." Across the bed, the SS faced him, given away – even as Bora was – by his pallor. Together, they walked back to the landing, where they stood and lit cigarettes. "What are we going to do? This is a bad mess to cover," Dollmann muttered. "The *scandal.* And on Good Friday of all days."

It had taken this long for Bora to succeed in saying anything. "Who is she?" he asked.

Dollmann groaned. "One of the Fonsecas. A fine woman, I thought… What an ugly business this is. Of Borromeo we knew, but who'd have thought it of our own Hohmann?"

"I don't believe it."

"Now, Bora. It's only because he was your teacher. The evidence is there."

To Bora the smell of blood gave a kind of fever, and out of that discomfort, felt so many times before, he wanted to know, "How did you find out about it?"

"Entirely by accident. I was to meet the cardinal at Babington's yesterday afternoon to discuss the Easter concert. When he did not appear, I thought it strange, as he's the soul of punctuality. I sought him in the usual places, with no luck. Well, I thought, could he have taken sick? No one was at his residence, by which I assumed his secretary had already gone home, as indeed he had, in order not to violate the five o'clock curfew." Dollmann glanced back toward the crack in the door, from which the muffled voices of the policemen came. "The appointment at

Babington's was at four forty-five – I was to drive the cardinal home afterwards – but by the time I did the telephone rounds and tracked down his secretary, it was nine o'clock. The fellow told me Hohmann had gone to a one o'clock appointment with Baroness Fonseca, location undisclosed."

"How so?" Bora interrupted.

"Just so, and it wasn't the first time that Hohmann didn't say where he was meeting her. Not seeing him return to his residence, the secretary resolved that the cardinal had come directly to Babington's. I disabused him of that opinion, demanded to be given the Fonseca address and telephone number, and called this place. I received a busy signal, and after several attempts over an hour and half, I suspected the phone was off the hook, which incidentally it was. So – you know me, I like to find out what goes on – eventually I decided to come here in person. This I really did not expect."

Having finished his cigarette, Bora held the stub between his fingers as if wondering what to do with it. "How long do you think they have been dead?"

"The police say six to seven hours, and the phone had been off the hook at least since nine thirty, when I first tried to call. As far as I can tell, she shot him and then herself. And as far as what they were doing, there can be no doubt in anybody's mind."

"Oh, for the mercy of God. It's entirely out of character, Colonel!"

"How would you know? Do you *know*?" Dollmann was placing another cigarette in his mouth. "We're all moral icebergs – tips showing, and that's all."

"I don't believe it of Cardinal Hohmann."

Inside, the policemen had nearly finished their preliminary work. Newly arrived medics were with difficulty bringing stretchers up the narrow stairs. Against Dollmann's advice, Bora told them to wait below, and walked back into the Fonseca doorway. For a time, he spoke to the policemen – a uniformed man who was checking the bathroom for clues, carefully stepping over a scattering of minute glass splinters, and a plain-clothes man with the camera – and it was in the middle of the conversation that the SS reluctantly joined them.

The uniformed officer was saying, "There's no question that blood flow and the pattern of stains indicate it happened right here on the bed, and that the old priest," (was he being coy, as the scarlet robe lay visibly on the rug at the side of the bed, or had he decided not to draw conclusions from that?) "... well, the old priest was *with* her when it happened." A slender man with a thoughtful face and a Lombard accent, he looked around the room for a time, then added, "If a note is found we might learn of a motive. My experience is that with crimes of passion, though, everything can happen unexpectedly and with little or no premeditation. The pistol is a 1915 army Beretta, such as officers carried in the Great War. Tracing it to either one of the victims would help."

Averting his eyes from the nakedness the officer had uncovered again, Bora said. "You had better communicate at once with Assistant Secretary of State Montini," and to Dollmann, in German, "What will be the official version?"

The colonel looked as though he'd taken ill-tasting medicine. "They'll likely claim illness or derangement, and won't broadcast it until after Easter, if they can manage it. It'd be an even more grievous scandal if it came out now, as she was the darling of charity circles. The question is, if the lay press learns of it, there'll be no stopping the mudslide."

Sternly the Germans watched the policeman call the Vatican, and vaguely mention a dreadful accident to a prelate. "Quit mulling about this," Dollmann told Bora afterwards, easing him ahead of himself out of the bedroom door. "It's what it looks like, so reconcile yourself with it." On the landing, out of his breast pocket, he took an envelope which he passed on to his colleague. "She did write a suicide note, clear as the light of day. It was on the bed table when I arrived here. I took it upon myself to remove it before the police joined me, whatever good it'll do. I'm giving it to you only so that you won't be tempted to look into some alternative explanation that sadly isn't there."

Bora would not look at the note before getting back to his hotel. Aghast as he was at the events of the night, the contents made things worse.

My beloved sister, Cardinal Hohmann and I will have gone to our judgment by the time you receive this. Know that I was the material executor of this act, but that – terrible as it might seem – it is still less than the shame before God and man of our months of secretly sinning together.

Pray for us,

Your sister Marina.

It was merciful that now, at four o'clock in the morning, there was just about enough time for Bora to wash thoroughly, change uniform, and go directly to work.

After the morning briefing, General Westphal made a guarded attempt at minimizing matters.

"Well, well," he replied to Bora's news from his stance by the window, "the sad truth of things. What a way to be rid of our difficult contact with the Vatican. Borromeo must feel he's gone up a notch." Below, workers were setting up stands for the Easter concert to be held in front of headquarters, *a gift to the Roman people.* "And how are the Fascists coming along with the interrogation of the Nazarene College students?"

Frowning, Bora gathered the general's mail. The sight of the bodies on the bed – even after all the death he'd witnessed – had made him physically ill, and he was running a fever because of it. Thinking of his angry last words to Hohmann, he said distractedly, "Kappler has them now."

"Poor Kappler, it seems no one appreciates his tour de force at the caves. Even teenagers have the gumption to criticize him in class." Westphal turned, as if the thought had some humor in it for him. "It's good that the deportation of Roman males fell through – he'd have every housewife in town flying at him with rolling pin in hand."

Bora had started opening envelopes and cut himself with the penknife. Westphal watched him take a handkerchief out and laboriously try to dab his palm. "You know, Bora, I'm getting worried about you. What does Chekhov say about men without women – that they turn clumsy?"

"He says they turn stupid."

"That, you're not. But you wouldn't get so emotionally involved in things if you had something else going – even old Hohmann got himself some. No? Well, disbelieve it all you want, he had a lover and she blew his head off in bed. Oh, *never mind* the blood drops on the floor, that's what we have maids for."

8 APRIL 1944

On Saturday, Cardinal Borromeo agreed to meet Bora after the yearly baptism of converts in St John Lateran.

"If you're coming to mourn Cardinal Hohmann, I hope you will not expect me to say anything but *parce sepulto.*"

"He was not one to need forgiveness," Bora said testily. "No, sir, I came to confirm that the removal of troops I negotiated with the cardinal is completed."

Borromeo looked a bit annoyed. "So, you don't want to talk about Hohmann? I'm surprised. Conceited though the poor man was, he had good words for you now and then." Bora was really so grieved – and Borromeo could see it – it was cruel of him to speak as he did. He sipped from his demitasse as an anteater from the termite mound, with dainty draughts. "I know you've come to speak about him. Sit down, peace of angels. I can't understand why laymen think they have to speak in riddles to us – I can speak straight." After finishing the coffee, he balanced the cup in the hollow of its saucer, his eyes on Bora's bandaged hand. "To say that I'm sorry he died – that's immaterial now, isn't it? We're all just passing through, and all that. I regret the way he went, which reflects badly on all of us. But then we all have our failings. How weak the flesh is. It is a strange physiological fact how man's flesh gets weaker and weaker from the midriff down."

Bora, who had read and reread Marina Fonseca's suicide note, looking uselessly for hidden messages that might give him a clue as to its veracity, was now dismally convinced it meant just what it said. Still, he kept his cool at Borromeo's words. "It's interesting that you accept uncritically that Cardinal Hohmann did in fact die as we are told."

"Why, don't you? Heaven forbid that I should be curious about such unsavory details, but I saw the police report. It is *graphic*. You probably could add to that, as you were among the first on the scene."

"I hope you're being so negative because you're distraught at the loss, Cardinal Borromeo. Surely you had the opportunity to appreciate how good he was."

"Oh, I did. I did. The question is, how much did *you* appreciate him?"

Even in his grief, Bora was suddenly wary of Borromeo's words. Hohmann's political outspokenness had relegated him to the Vatican no differently than his own had landed him on Westphal's staff. How much was known here, he did not know. Borromeo watched him squirm, and then said, "Time will come for both of us to express our appreciation, each in our own way." It was a quizzical statement, but Borromeo would add no commentary. "Anyway, you should know that Cardinal Hohmann was close to Marina Fonseca – charitable enterprises, of course. They were often seen together, lately more so than ever."

Despite all evidence, Bora was tempted to leave in outrage. "He was nearly eighty. How much of an intimate relation could he possibly maintain?"

"Ha! You're naive for a soldier, and a doctor of philosophy." Unexpectedly the cardinal laughed. "Speaking of lighter and better things, our dear Mrs Murphy tells me she saw you the other day."

Bora felt instantly removed from the strain of the moment. An ineffably gratifying, wholly physical reaction made him bristle at the mention of her name, hearing that she had spoken of him to the cardinal. He was careful to say nothing, but Borromeo would not let him get away with silence. He rang a bell, and the ubiquitous little cleric appeared on the threshold with a second tray of espresso. "Her husband will return to Rome this afternoon, and Nora – she's well educated, you know, and lived in Florence as a child – will have to curtail her volunteer work. Young Murphy is to drive his father from the station."

"*Drive* him?" Bora had no choice but to speak up. "She can't be old enough to have a grown son."

"Mrs Murphy married a widower. He's quite old enough to have grown offspring – and not to wish for new ones." Borromeo sipped from the second cup not differently from before, extracting the drink by silent suction. "It grieves her, I think. She *loves* children." He stared at Bora, amiably. "But we all have our crosses to bear, eh?"

That afternoon, Dollmann called Bora at the office.

"Have you read today's *Unione*, Major?"

"I don't patronize communist newspapers, Colonel Dollmann."

"You ought to read this one. Your beloved teacher is plastered all over the first page, along with an exposé of the last century of Vatican malfeasances… Are you there, Bora?"

"I'm here."

"I was speechless myself, at first. Tried to find out who leaked the information to a clandestine rag, to no avail. Whoever did it, the cat's out of the bag now – not even the Pope will be able to drive it back in without scratching himself. I heard on the

206

news that Marina's sister refuses to comment on the news, and well she may."

The scandal was enormous. Although the official press refrained from picking up the story without substantiation, by Easter Sunday it was everywhere. Bora met Dollmann at the concert and asked him not to bring up the subject today. Dollmann agreeably nodded, and handed him the issue of *Unione.*

10 APRIL 1944

On Easter Monday, when traditionally Romans went "out of the gates" for the first picnic of the year, all principal highways had been made off limits to civilian traffic by German authorities. So people munched their modest lunches on balconies and on the benches of what city gardens had not yet been requisitioned as dumps for materiel. Even so, in the movie district of Cinecittà – where according to Westphal most of Bora's colleagues had their lovers – three German soldiers were killed. Bora was sent to investigate and make recommendations.

He found Kappler already there. Gamely Bora greeted him, and agreed that deportation of the men in the district may be the only answer. "But make sure you put them to work. It's no advantage to keep them clogging the jails."

"Except that it takes manpower to watch them on work detail."

"Why don't you just go ahead and tell them to shoot on sight?"

Kappler's lips nearly disappeared. "I'm so disappointed in you, Bora."

"Frankly, Colonel, it's mutual. I thought yours would work better under pressure."

"It was bad for my men to see you come the way you did. It's unforgivable. Now I cannot trust you anymore."

"It can't be helped."

*

From Cinecittà, though it was to say the least a circuitous way back to the office, Bora drove to the Cassia. There, before the modern, pine-surrounded house with a locked garden gate, he rang the bell and gave the maid his calling card, on which he had scribbled as further identification, *One of His Eminence's former students.*

Within minutes the maid was back without the card, but to report that Baroness Gemma Fonseca declined to meet with anyone at present. Bora had no choice but to accept the refusal, and the only consolation he granted himself was to drive back slowly along the meandering northern course of the Tiber.

The silt-yellow water ran among green and blooming fields, courted by swallows. Warm, sensual comfort was in the air, which he bodily craved, so much so that he stopped the car before reaching Ponte Salario and sat outside, breathing the clean springtime wind. And he felt – no, he *knew* – that things would be so much better if he were allowed to fall in love with Mrs Murphy.

After work, unwilling to see the usual faces at his hotel just yet, he stopped by Donna Maria's. The old lady spoke up in dialect, "*Martì, me se vojono magnà i gatti,*" with concern in her voice. "I can't let them out, poor creatures, because they'll make stew out of them. Yesterday I lost Pallino."

Bora bent to caress one of Donna Maria's three survivors. Through the years, the cats had been a permanent fixture, the old ones being replaced by the new, until this was entirely a second generation.

"Pallino trusted everybody," she said, "that's the problem. I should have taught him better." Between them, on a low table, lay a folded copy of *L'Osservatore*, bearing the first official news of Hohmann's death. It was a well-written but late and useless attempt to curb the scandal, which Bora had read and now moodily glanced at again. "We aren't spared anything, are we?" she added, setting aside the tatting pillow.

"I don't believe it. I don't."

The old lady clasped her hands. "That's what everybody thought back in '89, when that other disaster happened near Vienna. I mean, when the Crown Prince and the little Jewish girl were found dead at Mayerling. What a shock that was! Just like now. We'd all been in love with Rudolf at one time or another – oh, he was *beautiful*, and married to that staid young goose Stephanie. All we girls thought it terribly romantic to be found dead with the Crown Prince."

Bora sat facing Donna Maria, at once favored with a cat on his lap. "Was it in fact suicide, as they say?"

"I'm afraid so, though all the paperwork was destroyed and – you might know this – all those involved in the investigation sworn to silence. There were rumors, of course, that the Imperial Secret Service had done Rudolf in for his pro-Hungarian stance, and it didn't help the thing that he had syphilis and could have no more heirs."

Bora swallowed. "I see." The cat in his lap smelled the bandage on his hand, and nuzzled it. "Donna Maria, did you know Marina Fonseca?"

"By sight. She was so much younger than I – forty, I think. No, I didn't know her, other than she spent as much on clothes as she did on charity. I believe you were introduced to her family once, but were a child, and would not remember what she looked like."

Bora didn't say how he had seen her last, hair matted with pasty blood against the twisted sheets, when the police wouldn't let him draw her knees together at least. "Why would anyone want to do as they did?"

"Oh, well… If you must justify it to yourself, Martin, you must also put yourself in her place. A cardinal of the Church is a prince all the same. Dying with him might have held the same horrible fascination it had for us court girls back then."

"I don't want to justify it to myself, Donna Maria. I refuse it."

"That's just what you do, isn't it?" She retrieved the tatting pillow, resuming her agile play of ivory bobbins on it. "You don't mourn for things and people, and ought to."

"There's no time."

"One of these days time will be made whether you like it or not."

Bora stood. "Donna Maria, I must go."

"No, you mustn't. You can spend the night here, and you know it. Your room is always ready. This is your house."

But Bora did go. In the morning, as soon as he reached the office, he heard from Dollmann over the phone that Pasquino, one of the three *talking statues* of Rome, had been found with an anonymous message around its stubby neck for all to read.

> *Ai tempi bboni der gran Papa Sisto*
> *er cardinale fu l'arma de Cristo:*
> *mo' stemo a vede 'na cosa assai barbina,*
> *ar cardinale je piace la Marina.*

"What does it mean?" Westphal asked him a few minutes later.

"It's a distasteful pun on Baroness Fonseca's first name, which is the same as 'Navy'. It says that while in the old days the cardinals were the army of Christ, now they prefer his Navy."

"It's a capital joke, Bora. Write it down for me, I want to circulate it. So, what else is new about old Hohmann?"

"The Vatican forbids an autopsy."

"What about the Fonseca woman?"

"It depends on her family, but if the Vatican has a say in it, I wouldn't expect miracles. A plain post-mortem is the best we'll get. As Colonel Dollmann puts it, they did have bullet holes in their heads, and her fingerprints are on the weapon. The handgun belonged to her late husband, a collector of side arms and great hunter. They say she was a remarkable shot herself."

210

Good-humoredly Westphal nodded. "If only the Reiner girl had been a champion diver, you'd have your answer for that one, too."

At dinner that evening, Francesca, who was gone from the house as long as ten hours a day, announced she would no longer work until after the birth of her child. "I got some money from home, so I don't have to keep standing behind the counter with this weight on my feet."

Guidi had nothing to say to her. In the two weeks since he'd returned to work, he had gathered as much additional information on her as he'd been able. The child was her employer's, as it seemed. She had seen him off and on for three months, and when he'd offered to marry her, she'd turned him down and moved to Via Paganini. As Danza had reported months ago, nothing political had emerged, but Guidi knew by now how selective or blind the eye was that Roman police turned to violation of the curfew, illegal gatherings and the like. Francesca was *involved*, impossible to say to what extent. The danger came from the SS and from fanatics like Caruso.

In those two weeks Bora had not been in touch, though only the bloody climb of Via Rasella separated his hotel from Guidi's office. Guidi had made no effort to see him either, even though, now that the evidence found in 7B was back in his hands, he'd had it examined and should share the findings with him.

Dinner had been scanty, and Guidi left the table hungry. Francesca went to her room, where he knew she hoarded dry biscuits. In her condition, and with bread rations down to one hundred grams per day, he could not bring himself to making an issue of it. As for the Maiulis, they lived on little, and slept off their appetite by going to bed early.

After the house was dark, Guidi walked to the phone and dialed Bora's number at the Hotel d'Italia. Bora simply said, "Come."

They met in Bora's room, the first time they had faced each other since that terrible Thursday, and no word was made of it. The German said, "Have a seat." His wife's photograph was still on the table, with the pilot's snapshot tucked in one corner. Otherwise, the bed was made; no clothes or personal objects lay in sight. Guidi had the impression that Bora lived here ready to leave at any time.

"Major, the ashes found in 7B match those found in the Reiner bedroom. They come from onion-skin or writing paper of similar consistency. No, not ledger paper. The rest – fibers from a woolen blanket, a candy wrapper, fruit peels and the apple core – merely point to someone's presence in the apartment. But the ashes draw a possible connection."

Bora concealed his surprise, if he felt any. Fully dressed despite the late hour, he hadn't as much as removed his belt and holster. Either that, or he'd worn them again for Guidi's coming. He asked, standing at the foot of the bed, "What about the shoe imprint in the ashes?"

"From what I saw at the shoe store, it's consistent with a rubber sole. The wrapper is from an Italian nougat. There's a strong possibility the murderer hid unseen in the apartment, and perhaps even stalked Magda from there. No special locks had been placed on the door, so…"

"I went back to 7B," Bora said. "Even though I had the key, I tried to open with a penknife, to see if it could be done. I failed, but in the process I noticed stearin inside the lock."

"Someone had an extra key made from the mold?"

"It appears so. But whether or not the squatter in 7B was the killer, he knew how not to leave significant traces. Even the toilet seemed unused at a first exam."

The debt to the living. Guidi minded Dollmann's words, and yet all he could feel were the bruises of Bora's punches and kicks while being forced into the car. Odd, how bits of memory were coming back from that night. The hours previous to that were still a merciful blur in Guidi's recollection. "Did you find anything else?"

"This." On the palm of Bora's hand, a small object came into view. "It was lodged between the tuck and dust flaps of one of the storage boxes. It looks like a button from a shirt cuff."

Guidi snatched the button. "Let me see." He studied it under the light from the table lamp before closing his fingers firmly around it. "It isn't a man's button, Major. It comes from Magda Reiner's dress."

Once more Bora guarded his surprise, but not so well. "Wasn't she wearing a nightgown and a robe when she died?"

"She came home in a brown dress, and there's a missing button from that very dress. It means — " Guidi had to check his excitement. He needed a cigarette, rummaged uselessly for tobacco and paper in his pocket, and already Bora had tossed a pack of Chesterfields on the table.

"It means that she was in 7B with the killer."

"Maybe." Having found matches in his pocket, Guidi lit a cigarette. "For now, it means she was in 7B that night, possibly between the time Captain Sutor drove her home and the time she fell to her death. What was she doing there? Had she heard noises from a vacant apartment, and gone to check on things? Unlikely that a woman alone would do that. And – if she did – was she let in, or did she have the key? Whatever happened in 7B, she survived it long enough to change into her bed clothes." Guidi savored the good tobacco. *Would I keep the picture of the woman who left me?* he thought. *Why does he? Either he's still in love with her, or he wants to keep away from someone else.* "Surely Merlo had no reason to be in 7B, nor did Captain Sutor – her lovers she would likely receive in her apartment."

"What about the ashes? Was someone burning papers in her bedroom or in the vacant apartment?"

"Well, somehow they migrated from one place to the next. Light as they are, they'd easily attach themselves to clothing or hair. The residue in 7B, at any rate, is more noticeable than in the bedroom. So, in the forty-five minutes between her return home and her death, Magda Reiner was in a place to which she theoretically had no access – 7B – possibly met someone there, went back to her room and prepared for bed. Next, she was dropping four floors down to the sidewalk."

"*He* was the one she was afraid of."

"Likely, and someone she would not or could not speak about with her co-workers. We assume she'd met him before he killed her, but that's not necessarily true."

"Shirker, partisan, German deserter, escaped prisoner, spy. For whom do you vote? It has to be one of those. And was it Sutor she argued with before her death, or the mysterious tenant?"

Even as the thought *Antonio Rau speaks German* went through him, Guidi blurted out, "If I have to vote, it's either a deserter or a spy. What's the name of the man who went missing in Greece?"

"Potwen, Wilfred. I can't see how he could have gotten here, but there's plenty I can't see at this moment." Thinking of Hohmann, of Gemma Fonseca's refusal to see him, Bora started to unbuckle his belt, which – made heavy by the pistol holder – came undone quickly. He placed it across the back of a chair. "Have you noticed how in the file I retrieved from Caruso's office there is no mention of a search previous to ours?"

"Yes, but he might have *failed* to record it. I wouldn't draw any conclusions from that."

"He might have said the truth about not having access to the Reiner apartment. We know he got Merlo's old glasses from Sciaba's store."

"If you mean that Captain Sutor is a more likely candidate for a preventive search, I agree. He might have removed items of clothing or such from her closet. It doesn't seem as though anyone will be able to get out of him whether he did it, or why, and Sutor has other means at his disposal to get rid of people."

It was the first oblique reference to the caves between them. Bora's hint at relaxation – the removal of his pistol – was at once belied by his posture, and the phone ringing at that moment was a relief to both men. Bora eagerly picked up the receiver and listened to whatever was being said to him. "I have to go," he said then, without explanation. Belt and pistol were taken up again.

Guidi readied to leave also. "Can we get together tomorrow? I'll be going through Magda's personal items again."

"I don't know. Try me at the office."

They came out of the hotel together. Across the street, a full moon lit the powerful intricacy of the gate shielding the Barberini Garden. Guidi, who had been lined up with the others against it, under SS guard, had to look away. He saw Bora glancing down the darkness of Via Rasella as he unlocked his car. Between those two landmarks, in that stretch of irrelevant pavement, any hope of friendship had been killed also.

"It's been nearly three weeks," Guidi said.

Bora made no comment. But he did turn to Guidi, sketched in the dreary light from above. Much as he longed to ask for advice regarding Hohmann's death, the time was not right.

"It was Caruso who put your name on the list, not the SS."

14 APRIL 1944

On a splendid spring mid-morning, Field Marshal Kesselring went to visit the Pope, with Westphal and Bora in tow. It was an extraordinary concession for military men, albeit in civilian clothes, to be allowed in the Vatican. On another occasion Bora would have felt privileged, but he'd been at Campoleone until the night before, a ghastly trip through the reality of no-man's-land. His left arm ached badly, stabbing pains radiating from the mutilation up to his shoulder. He was nervous about that afternoon's serological test, and perfunctorily going through the motions until the moment he was introduced to Patrick Atwater Murphy.

The diplomat was an energetic man of Borromeo's age, with a florid complexion and bright eyes. He laughed too easily, in Bora's reckoning, but so did most Americans he knew.

"That's an interesting name. Bora – a direct relation to Luther's wife?"

"We don't stress the likelihood."

"So, of all names, your parents called you Martin, eh?"

Bora looked Murphy in the eye, feeling his own youth and loneliness as an injustice in the face of this man's glib ease. *He lies in bed with her and doesn't want her children. What a waste.* "Only because I was born on Martinmas."

They engaged in as pleasant a brief chatter as the occasion permitted, with Murphy commenting in his Boston drawl on his return to the boredom of a city where "every public *pahk* is an excuse for heathen rubble", and what they called a "swell steak" tried a man's healthy appetite. "Thank God 'Cahdinal' Borromeo is such a good sport and tourist guide. If it weren't for him, my wife'd be dragging me from cultural pillar to operatic post. So, anyway. What do *you* do in real life, Major Martin Bora?"

How much we have in common, she and I. Coolly, Bora said, "I don't go posting religious theses on cathedral doors."

At the hospital, Bora did not expect to meet Treib, the weary-faced army surgeon from Aprilia, who – having recognized him from his office – came to greet him in the hallway.

"So," he said, "you made it back in one piece, Major. Yes, we retreated from there too, surviving POWs and all. It's good to be in a place where I can have enough cotton to make tampons out of. See *this?*" He acknowledged a bullet scar on his hand. "They almost took me and two medics prisoner near Albano."

"You don't say. Who was it?"

"Partisans, I suppose – no uniforms anyhow. We got away by the skin of our teeth, and two lightly wounded Americans managed to scramble off with them. How's your leg?"

"Fine. I'm here for a different reason." Bora kept straight-faced. "I need a Wassermann test."

Treib looked at him in the same manner. "Was the first blood work negative?"

"Yes."

"Well, let's go."

Afterwards the surgeon brought the results to the waiting room, where Bora had been sitting and pacing around for an hour. "Congratulations. The Wassermann is also negative. We'll repeat it in two weeks to make damn sure. It seems you haven't gotten anything else, either. Very lucky, the women are ridden. May I remind you to use caution if you frequent prostitutes?"

"I don't," Bora said dryly.

Treib's bleary eyes traveled to Bora's wedding ring. "Well, who was she?"

"Probably a whore from the hotel. If I haven't paid her she'll show up, and I'll know. It was the night after the *trouble* at the caves, I wasn't thinking. And I'm no longer married," Bora felt he should add. "But I do want to be able to reproduce in the near future."

"Would you care to take a look at some infected blood?"

"No, thank you."

"It's really interesting how the little devils whip around."

"I get your point, Captain."

217

7

"I felt I should apologize for refusing to see you. The last few days have been very difficult, and I am still trying to shield our mother from hearing what happened to Marina."

Gemma Fonseca resembled her sister in age and looks. Fair, gray-eyed. The quiet elegance of her house – a deco interior of lacquered smooth lines – was much like her person, but there was a lack of sparkle in both, and a nun-like severity to the turn of her face as she invited him to enter. "I should have known from the note on your card that you might have good intentions. How may I assist you?"

Bora removed his cap, which the maid came to take with a curtsey. He related his distress at the events, though it was such a resplendent Sunday morning, everything inside and outside of him demanded happier things. "My respect for the cardinal brings me here," he concluded. "You could say he was my spiritual father, so it's particularly painful for me to face his death, and your sister's."

Framed by the clean angles of the parlor's door, for a time she looked at him, as if wondering how much she could share with him. On her cheeks, a delicate, nearly fragile skin stretched taut over the bones, and her wrists were also thin, blue-veined. The left eye was slightly off, looking outwardly only enough as to make her stare oddly fixed, as that of an icon. Her figure seemed strung up by some force of will or pride. "I appreciate your condolences. Marina and I were very close."

Her tension was such that Bora found himself hoping she would take a seat and relax. "Lack of a thorough post-mortem will not make things easier," he said cautiously, going through his own process of assessment. Gemma Fonseca was visibly tempted to take a seat, but did not.

"Why so?"

"Because its absence will clinch the apparent motive for the deaths."

Instantly, she gained a desperate, nearly wild look on her unadorned face. Her hand sought the sofa, and on a corner of it she sat, only the rigidity of her shoulders maintaining a semblance of control. She began to weep without lowering her head, hands knotted in her lap.

"I so much hoped you would say that, Major. I am so grateful you said it."

If nuns cry, they cry like her. Like a sky that rains and cleanses itself. Bora sat facing her. He was not embarrassed by her reaction because it had no anger and no noise. "My expectation is that you might offer me clues contrary to what seems, and I do not believe is."

"I don't know that I can. Until today I have been putting the authorities off, but I will have to answer their questions sooner or later."

Bora had the suicide note in his pocket, but said nothing about it, rather, "I wonder if you could favor me with a sample of your sister's handwriting."

Whatever she thought of the request, without questioning it she reached for a sleek silver box on the tea table, and from it handed a pale blue envelope to Bora. "This had been mailed Friday morning, and arrived the morning after Marina died."

It was the same fine cotton fiber stationery of the suicide note, and – even after a cursory examination of the contents, a thoughtful, innocuous family letter – undoubtedly written by the same hand. Whether Bora's profound disappointment was apparent or not, Gemma Fonseca finally prompted him. "Will you tell me the reason for your request, Major?"

"By your leave, not now." The tall capitals, rounded loops, the slight downward slant of the lines were familiar to him, as he'd learned from brooding over the note in days past. Nonetheless, Bora asked, " May I keep it?"

"If you wish. You see there's no reference to a crisis of any kind. Although we never lived more than fifty miles apart from each other, Marina and I exchanged letters every week. It was a habit we picked up as adolescents and kept ever since, even during her marriage."

Dollmann is right, and so Borromeo. I should reconcile myself to it. Bora sat, looking beyond Gemma's mournful figure, toward a gleaming doorway of aluminum and glass. "Did you keep all the letters?"

"I did, Major. But in anticipation of the police's securing them, I have already disposed of several, for no other reason than they are private and were never meant for eyes other than my own. You might as well know this."

Bora did not often feel defeated. At this moment, though, it was as if everyone in this sordid affair – Hohmann, Borromeo, the sisters – had betrayed him, and nothing and no one could be trusted. Gemma Fonseca might have read through his disgust this time.

"I was tempted to destroy all, much as I treasure them. Had I not received your visit today, I probably would have."

Yes, and no one would have been the wiser for it. Bora spoke automatically now, only because he'd after all come here on an errand. "Should you wish to find out more about me, my references are Cardinal Giovanni Borromeo, Ambassador Weizsäcker and Countess Maria Ascanio, who knows me best of all." It was his turn to set limits to the meeting, and he stood to indicate that he was ready to go.

Gemma Fonseca extended her had toward him from where

she sat, a small gesture of controlled despair, which came in no way close to touching him. "Please, Major. Do not go in haste. Let me tell you how good Marina really was."

17 APRIL 1944

On Monday, the working-class Quadraro district, which Bora and Westphal had crossed in January on their way to the coast, sat under a cloudy sky. In the unseasonable warmth, the Fascist militiamen sweated in their black cheviot shirts. The SS had already changed into summer uniforms, but perspired even more. It took them hours to round up seven hundred and fifty men in reprisal for the death of two militiamen. A red-faced Sutor confronted a crowd of loud women, many holding small children in their arms. Their bawling recriminations no doubt annoyed him, but Bora knew that seeing his Mercedes parked a few steps away had to be the greatest irritant. So he stood by with an unlit cigarette in his mouth, monitoring the progress of the operation for General Westphal.

That evening, though he'd heard about the deportation, Guidi did not raise the issue with Bora. It was best to say nothing, especially since Antonio Rau had mysteriously resurfaced for his Latin lessons, and Francesca's pregnancy was in the late stages. As for himself, he'd never even brought up with the Maiulis his intention to leave the apartment.

Just before sundown they met in Bora's car, parked in the green darkness of the Villa Umberto gardens. A waning moon sailed over the heads of the trees with a sheen of silver, and through the open window the scent of flowers came from the old beds of irises and roses. As darkness increased, even under the tree cover the blush of the embattled western sky flared bright at times. A low *voom-voom-voom* accompanied the brightness.

Bora was in pain, which was less apparent from his stiffness than from the attempt he made to counter it. He said, "I have

221

arranged for you to interview a second embassy employee who knew Magda Reiner. Hannah Kund is her name, now serving in Milan. Not a close friend, but she does speak serviceable Italian. She'd been gone from Rome since her furlough before Christmas, and it was a shock for her to hear of her colleague's end. I took the liberty of showing her the personal items still in her bedroom, and she was particularly surprised that Magda Reiner's keys are missing."

"Why would she particularly notice that detail?"

"That's what I asked, Guidi. The Reiner girl had a silver key chain she made much of, a Greek meander motif her fiancé had sent her from Athens. Apparently she kept all her room keys on it. Now, although she had some clearance at the embassy, she was by no means privy to sensitive material —"

"*That we know of,*" Guidi intervened.

"True. But she would not carry around keys to relevant offices on her key chain."

"So, the killer locked her doors to fake a suicide and took the keys."

"He might have also wanted to delay the entrance of the authorities. And of course, the apartment was searched before we arrived. They could have taken the keys then."

Guidi felt vindicated. "My point exactly, Major. Caruso and Sutor, in one way or another, had access to her place, and so probably Merlo. Surely the killer did. As for Magda's button – and Magda herself – she ended up in 7B. Was she forced in there? Not likely, since she somehow returned to her apartment and got ready for bed. But she did lose the button, the front, top button of her dress. Was there a struggle in 7B?"

"That, or sexual intercourse." Bora said the words, recalling with acute melancholy the handful of torn silk at his wife's feet, the last time he'd made love hoping she still cared. "Whoever was in 7B could have followed her afterwards."

"Whoever was in 7B was *hiding*, Major. Spy, deserter, whatever. The question is, was Magda hiding him? Was it she who made a copy of the key to the vacant apartment?" And because Bora sighed, Guidi said, "I can see it troubles you."

"The death of an embassy employee? It *should* trouble me." But tonight it was the thought of Dikta, and pain, that troubled Bora most of all. "Well," he spoke up, "let us say it was Magda Reiner who made a copy of the key to the vacant apartment, for whatever reason. Let us say she met someone there. Whoever it was, she did not wish to receive him in her room – for his sake, or her own."

"Or both. Concealing a deserter, unless your policies have changed, carries the penalty of death."

Again Bora sighed. The surgeon in Verona had warned him that pain would return. Aspirins and other painkillers no longer worked, but he had been resisting the temptation to ask for morphine so far. Fleeting and weary, the want came at times to have his whole arm taken off, and the pain with it.

"I'll check with the locksmiths in the area," Guidi added.

"Fine. I can confirm that she first met Merlo and Sutor at the same party celebrating the March on Rome, on 28 October 1943. Fräulein Kund reports her friend 'couldn't choose between the two, but seemed afraid of one in particular.' No word about which one. There had been this young Emilio, and also a no-better-identified Willi."

"As in Wilfred?"

"We don't know. I plan to phone the Reiner family again." Bora took his cap off to rest his neck against the seat, letting his shoulders slouch. Brighter flares blanched the sky, and the low *voom-voom-voom* intensified then. It was as good a time as any to bring up what else troubled him. "By the way, Guidi, what do you know about the Hohmann-Fonseca case?"

"I know it happened." Guidi had not expected Bora's mention of the murder. He'd heard about it, but it was both out of his district and perhaps of his league, given the rank of the victims. "Why, did you know either of them?"

Except for what Gemma had said about destroying some

of the letters, Bora decided to report all he knew, aware that Guidi would have access to all the police had gathered to date. "I'm asking the favor of a professional consultation on a matter of handwriting," he concluded. "I disbelieve the facts because of my affection for the dead. I realize that everything else, including this, points to a murder-suicide."

As daylight had nearly gone, Guidi took out his flashlight to glance at the envelope addressed to Gemma Fonseca and read the note inside it.

"Here is another letter from her," Bora said, "written one day earlier."

Once more Guidi read. "It's the same hand," he remarked then. "The suicide note is less steady, but given the circumstances, it is to be expected. You realize you're to turn this evidence in, Major Bora."

Bora did not reply, slowly massaging his neck. "Marina Fonseca had dismissed the household staff for the day," he volunteered. "And as for the cardinal's secretary, he's a young Austrian Jesuit, unlikely to question anything or anybody connected to the cardinal. He's in shock at Santo Spirito even as we speak. The handgun, which Baron Caggiano used in the Great War, had been taken from a cache of antique weapons in the Fonseca's principal residence at Sant'Onofrio."

"Clearly the baroness had not abided by the rules."

By closing his eyes, Bora was more keenly aware of his pain, the scent of blooming shrubs, and the distant battle. "Of turning in usable weapons? No. But unless she'd kept the pistol handy for the last several months, I also wonder how she fetched it from a remote villa in the environs, served neither by tramway nor public cars. I assure you, it's remote. All roads at Sant'Onofrio lead to the mental hospital, and her place overlooking the Valle di Rimessola was made unreachable by bombs during the winter."

"Didn't the cardinal have his own transportation and chauffeur?"

"He did. But on that day he asked to be driven to the Pantheon Square well ahead of the one o'clock Fonseca appointment. From here we lose his traces until the time of his death."

Guidi gave back the envelopes. "The household staff might be worth talking to again, on the side. What about the bodies? You must have had a chance to observe some details."

"Other than the obvious wounds? You perceive it was a challenge for me even to look at them."

Only because you knew one of them, Guidi couldn't help thinking. "Were there noticeable bruises, abrasions? Signs of a struggle?"

"Nothing I could see without moving the bodies."

"Was there sperm?"

Bora felt a rise of nausea – it was the physical pain, most likely – and managed to keep it down. "I don't know. There was such a mess of blood in the sheets. What puzzles me is why the cardinal would set up an afternoon appointment he didn't intend to keep."

"Perhaps he forgot about it. Or couldn't keep it." *Voom-voom-voom.* In the dusk, the sky beyond the trees flared and grew dim. Guidi said, turned to the window, "They must be grinding Aprilia to dust."

"They must."

Still, how sweet the evening air was. Guidi fished into his pocket for cigarette paper, then for tobacco. Slowly. "Major, how could you *stand* what happened at the caves?"

"I had no choice in the matter."

"That's what you say, but for three weeks I've been asking myself why you did what you did for me. You were under no obligation."

No reaction came from Bora. Only after Guidi had finished rolling himself a cigarette did he break his silence. Reluctantly, as it seemed.

"In Russia, when my brother's plane crashed near our camp, my men did not know who he was from his documents. We have different surnames. It took the discovery by Sergeant Nagel of the photo of Peter and myself in the flight log for them to know. Even before my regimental staff knew, it was the non-coms who came and stood there and offered me their regrets."

"I'm sorry, Major."

"Ah, Guidi... I did so well, as expected of a man who leads a regiment. I told them I valued their sentiments, thanked them and dismissed them. Inside my tent the radio was on and I sat by it. That's all. But you could have shot me and I don't think a drop of blood would have spilled out of me. I was as dead as a man can get without dying. Could I keep him from being killed? Yes, I could have talked him out of volunteering for Russia, but I encouraged him instead. I was guilty. I stayed guilty and know I am guilty, and that's why I could not let you die at the caves. Your life had nothing to do with it." He flicked his lighter and lit the cigarette in Guidi's mouth. "Here, you see? My brother's lighter."

"You could not have prevented your brother's death."

"I only told you so you know what was on my mind in March."

Guidi accepted Bora's refusal of gratitude because it dispensed him from having to feel any. And he dreaded the idea, but the great difference between Bora and himself was how much suffering each of them had seen so far. Not even his agonizing closeness to execution equated the sum of risks and choices and losses Bora had faced. It dismayed Guidi that he might *have* to suffer in order to gain punctilious mastery of himself: Bora was bound in it but as wounds are in their dressings, ready to bleed if these are removed. It was fitting, Guidi thought, that Bora should be outwardly scarred, because he was no less so inside.

When Bora entered his hotel room later that night, he felt a peculiar sense of intrusion that had nothing to do with house-keeping, his change laid out, or fresh towels in the bathroom. *No,* he thought. *Someone has been here, looked things over and left.*

Still, he kept nothing of value in the drawers, and nobody steals books. He checked wardrobe, bed stand, medicine cabinet, and as he did so the feeling dissolved, exorcized by his touch until things were familiar again. *Perhaps not. Everything is here.* He struggled to remove his boots, but the rest of the uniform came off quickly. He readied a shirt for the morning by hooking the link on the right cuff.

18 APRIL 1944

Traveling with Dollmann was new to Bora, who had many times driven to Soratte in a different car from General Westphal's, but never with an SS.

The mountains growing in size before them had rounded slopes like tired waves of limestone, purple in color; when the car speeded along maple-flanked stretches, green shadows trembled on the windshield. Small farmhouses, islands in a sea of vineyards, seemed friendly, but Bora looked at them knowing it was in such places that guerrilla activity was planned, and from them that it was carried out. An old want to fight took him – the *want* he had told Guidi about, which was nearly as good as love. The carefully weighed risk, and freedom to take it.

"Do you know what *Edom* means?"

Dollmann's question took him aback. "No."

"It's Hebrew, and stands for 'Rome' in apocalyptic texts. You should know these things."

"Should I?"

"There's been a marked increase in the forced exodus from Edom in the past two weeks, which is about as long as our Hohmann has been dead."

Bora let some saliva gather in his mouth before swallowing. He was tempted to ask the question, but wouldn't in the presence of the colonel's Italian driver. Dollmann understood and said, "Feel free to speak. He's a good boy."

They say Dollmann fucks his chauffeur. Bora thought of the gossip, trying not to look at the young man in the front seat.

227

"Well, Colonel, how active was Cardinal Hohmann in opposing Kappler's *relocation* plans?"

"Plenty." Dollmann seemed amused by Bora's intent listening. "In his own intellectual way he was an old ass, Hohmann was. For one thing, either he cared for one or he didn't. You, he liked, which didn't keep him from giving you the runaround more than once. He didn't like me – which is all right, and reciprocated. He had been an early supporter of National Socialism, which says much for you as his student, but then you were young and no doubt soaked in the maudlin revanchism and anti-Bolshevism of our blessed 1930s. The Spanish Civil War didn't cure you, but cured *him*. It wasn't your old philosophy teacher you confronted these past months. It was an embittered elder whose nationalism tottered under the agony of choices. He wasn't as unscrupulous as Borromeo, bless his heart, who's a man for the times – he was *making amends,* something neither you nor I have to do or wish to do. Am I correct?"

"On which or how many counts?"

Dollmann simpered. "I know your kind, Bora. You don't fool me. Politics to you is a cloak for bare militarism, which is as ideologically unsound as I can think of. Kappler suspects it, and Sutor smells it, but I *know.* Still, you watch yourself by being good at what you do."

Bora kept absolute control over the muscles of his face and neck, mostly not to give Dollmann the satisfaction of thinking he had unsteadied him. "I'm a captive audience, Colonel – we have an hour to go."

"Oh, I said all I'm going to say about it. Preaching isn't in my line."

In the following minutes, ostensibly spent by Dollmann reading a Roman reportage on *Signal,* Bora fidgeted. Hohmann had been active in some risky humanitarian concern – he suspected which one – and this concern had been thrown in disarray by his death. It was like fishing with wet wool. The clue had been given, but was flimsy and treacherous, and the forces at play immensely stronger than its unraveled length. "Are you warning me or informing me, Colonel Dollmann?" he asked when he saw that the SS kept silent.

"*La sto aiutando*," Dollmann told him in Italian, without lifting his eyes from the magazine. But "help" was not exactly in Dollmann's line either.

At Soratte it became apparent that the field marshal was setting plans for an orderly retreat from Rome in the near future. The 10th Army and 14th Corps were at their extreme point, and the line drawn across Italy too long to man. The French were an unexpected element of worry, and there was talk of a new American landing, even closer to Rome. It was so dismal, Bora caught a flicker of despairing hilarity in Dollmann's eye, which he shared in a nervous way.

"May does it, gentlemen," Kesselring was saying, his big bulldog face low on the maps lining the table. "The not-so-merry month of May only leaves us a chance to save face. When the 'Spring Battle' is through we'll all have learned our propaganda lesson, not to mock the enemy for being slow. We should have told them to take their time instead of taunting them. On a daily basis, Dollmann, keep the spirits up in your social rounds in Rome and you, too, Martin. Having our face bloodied doesn't mean we lose aplomb."

"What about Rome, *Herr General Feldmarschall?*"

Kesselring knew Bora had asked the question. His eyes remained on the net of lakes and rivers spider-webbing the site of the city. "The time Rome'd buy for us, we'd lose before History."

Kesselring and his commanders were still conferring when Bora and Dollmann left the room and walked outside.

"Well, Bora, how much worse can it get?"

"We could commit excesses, Colonel. I've seen Sutor round up the people at Quadraro. How is it we always end up being uncivilized?"

Dollmann laughed. "What do you mean, 'end up'? We *are* uncivilized." The season was still cold at this altitude, and the

229

noon-time air sunny and bracing. The SS pointed out to Bora some of the trails hidden in the mountainous surroundings in the facetious manner of a merry tourist guide. "From here, unbeknownst to you, you can afford a full view of the hollows wherein at least two communist partisan bands prosper. Now then, don't be depressed, Major. And in reference to our chat in the car, keep it in mind. Even better, let me quote the Good Book." Dollmann tossed at him the bundle of soft woolen clues. "*That thou doest, do quickly.*"

"I don't appreciate the simile."

"Well, Kappler makes a blasphemous enough Christ, does he not?"

Bora unexpectedly smiled at Dollmann, without friendliness. "I do believe you are acting the tempter, Colonel Dollmann, but I don't care to jump from this or any other tower."

Dollmann answered the smile testily. "You're already in mid-air, Major Bora. All you can do is fall well."

That evening, Donna Maria looked at him over her spectacles. On her invitation, he'd taken off his tunic and now stood in the collarless white shirt, priestly in appearance but for the gray braces crossing it. "What's wrong, Martin?"

"Nothing's wrong, Donna Maria."

"You can't stay put and it's unlike you." Bora sat down. "Now your mind's aimless."

He wouldn't tell, nor would he answer a direct question. Donna Maria seemed to see through him all the same. There went her scrutiny again, which made him feel like sand eroding. He sat under it no differently than on the day he had come to tell her his wife had left him.

"Tomorrow they're burying Marina Fonseca."

"Well, it's time they did, don't you think?"

"Once she's in the vault, there'll be no telling how they really died."

Donna Maria frowned. "You should put that ugly story out

of your head, Martin. It's done, and that's how it happened. Let the old man lie in peace, if that's how he lies. Leave it alone, Martin."

"I can't."

How could he tell her he was physically afraid? Not since many months had he been so afraid. *Things, matters* were looming again. His senses were mercilessly keen. Like months and months ago, he'd have to revert to a stage of elementary denial, and head straight for danger.

She motioned with her head to the growing length of lace like a delicate, intricate tongue hanging from her tatting pillow. "That's lace for a wedding dress, Martin. I wouldn't be straining my eyesight on it if I didn't think you had enough sense to live to get yourself married again. Whatever it is, leave it alone."

"Donna Maria, I can't."

"Then I hope you know what you're doing."

Bora listened to the tinkle of knick-knacks on the massive buffet, thinking that, like the little warnings coming to him, it was caused by a much larger rumble. He could not take heed anymore than he had two years ago in Russia, or in Poland. He watched Donna Maria with an odd sense of comfort. She was safe, yet not maternal – there was no taboo to her. He could tell her what he didn't tell his parents, as he had in no way referred to Dikta's leaving him in his recent letters to them, to ensure they would not, either. But Donna Maria – he was comfortable with her like with a wise old lover. And so grateful for the emotional shelter she provided him, the quirky need to confess an ancient sin came to his lips, as if owning it would somehow ward off evil to come.

"Donna Maria, do you remember when I was a boy, the day I came home so late? I was not locked in the museum as I told you. I went to see Anna Fougez at the Jovinelli. And before that I'd been with your friend, Ara Vallesanta. I should have told you then, but I was ashamed – I did make love to her that afternoon at The Seagull."

Donna Maria giggled, bent on her pattern of pins. "Why did you think I suggested you go to the country with her? If you had to learn, I wanted you to learn from the best. She was good, wasn't she?"

"You knew!"

"I couldn't very well let you try your luck in Rome by yourself at less than sixteen. Of course I knew. What else was there to do? Your mother had begged me not to assign you a worldly *uncle*, as we always did with our boys in Rome. As for your stepfather, he wasn't the kind who would have a man's talk with you on anything else but horses and artillery guns."

"It weighed on me these many years, Donna Maria."

She sought his hand across the tea table, and he offered it.

"I'd do the same now if I thought you wanted it, but you're like me – always looking for more than a lover. It's hard, Martin. Hard and lonely. So I watch you, and work at your next wife's dress."

Back at the Hotel d'Italia, the dining room was half-empty. When Bora entered, one of Sutor's women – Sissi or Missy, with the sequined ribbon in her hair – recognized him from the party at Dollmann's, and promptly made for his table.

"Well, if it isn't the major who learned tricks in Spain. May I join you, Major?" When Bora said nothing, but gestured to the chair facing him, she sat down. "They say that all German women must leave Rome by the end of the month. It's because the Americans are coming, right?"

"You seem to know more than I do."

"Well, I wish you and I would *get our heads together* before then."

Bora snickered, because she was good-looking and silly. "I'm afraid it's impossible."

"Why? Is there somebody else?"

"There's some*thing* else." For a foolish moment Bora was tempted to tell her that it wasn't until 30 April that his final Wassermann test would run. But he caught himself, since Sutor would hear of it then. A waiter came to ask whether the lady would stay for dinner, and readily she said she would.

Unimpressed, the waiter turned to Bora, who managed not to compromise himself, saying, "If she wishes."

"So," she took up, "why did you say you were staying at the Flora?" Her disillusioned, young mouth smiled widely. "No, come to think of it, don't answer that one. Tell me, are you going out again tonight?"

"No, I'm going to bed."

"It's a good place to go." She said little during dinner, ate with enviable appetite and then asked for a cigarette. Butter and lipstick left a ring around it with her first draught, as they had on the rim of her glass. Bora looked at her uncritically, as one observes a strange carnivorous plant.

"So, Major, will you give a working girl a chance?"

"No." He moved the chair back to stretch his legs without meeting hers. "I hate to say this, but I really don't like being solicited."

"Well, that's flattering. It's not what you told Captain Sutor."

"I like to be wanted, which is very different. You don't want me, Miss."

"How do you know?"

"I hope I can tell want when I see it."

She had taken her compact case out, and – peering into the square little mirror – was applying heavy strokes of lipstick on her lower lip. "That's funny, because you look to me like the kind who falls for a woman who doesn't even know he exists."

Bora followed the motion of her hand on the upper lip and the grimaces she made in the process. Yes. That was true enough. And what would Mrs Murphy say?

19 APRIL 1944

On Wednesday afternoon, Westphal gave him leave to attend Marina's burial, a strictly private matter to which Bora had however been invited by Gemma Fonseca.

The area of the cemetery where the family vault lay bore signs of hasty repairs to monuments and intricate crosses. In the devastation, wreaths of palm leaves and fresh flowers seemed to mourn the loss of monumental art no less than that of human life. Only Gemma was present with her mother, a decrepit figure in a wheelchair, wrapped in mourning like a winter night.

After the ceremony, Gemma handed Bora a manila envelope. "I wanted to give you these also. I thought of them after you left the other day."

Bora looked inside, where several postcards from Marina were gathered.

She lowered the veil in front of her face. "Those, the police – who took the letters – had no interest in. You will find the messages altogether of a trite nature, I fear, but they are other samples of her handwriting."

It was Dollmann's chauffeur who'd driven the women here. Bora accompanied Gemma to the car, where he made sure her mother was comfortably returned to her seat, and then asked for a few minutes more. From the *Verano* gate they walked back, only far enough inside the cemetery to be safe from prying eyes, before Bora showed the suicide note. He was ready for the reaction that must necessarily follow, but not for the words she pronounced, still weeping.

"Marina wrote this with her right hand – why?"

"I don't know what you mean."

"She was left-handed. Ambidextrous, actually, but never used her slower right hand for correspondence. Never with me, certainly."

Seated behind the wheel of his car, afterwards Bora compared all the samples he had. The unsteadiness Guidi had remarked upon, and ascribed to the writer's state of mind, could well be explained by Gemma's comment. He tried to contact the inspector upon his return to the office, but heard he was off to Tor di Nona after a gang of tire thieves, and not expected back for the day.

Indeed, it was past nine in the evening before they spoke by phone, as Guidi had stopped by the office on his way back from the periphery and found Bora's message. Having heard what the German had to say, he interjected, "The fact remains that the victim's sister recognizes the handwriting. You *assume* there might have been coercion of some kind."

"Or that by writing in a fashion unusual for her – but not detectable by others, since most people are right-handed – she sent, as it were, a distress message. Any news about the post-mortems?"

Guidi was tired and silently yawned into the mouthpiece. "I have hers, which was given to me by colleagues as a courtesy. The Vatican had its own medical staff draft the one for the cardinal, and they hold on to it. No, Major Bora, I can't. I'm stretching the rules as it is, and I had to insist with my counterpart to get it, as his office had been rifled overnight and he was not in a generous mood. Either I bring it over to your hotel, or you stop by to look at it."

Bora showed up at the police command within ten minutes. Marina Fonseca's death, he read, had been caused by a self-inflicted gunshot in the right temple – crushing of both bone tables, destruction of brain tissue, massive hemorrhage, et cetera. Noticeable mydriasis. No other signs of violence on the body. Small discolorations present in the hollow of her right arm, such as are caused by a hypodermic needle. Bora reread the sentence and then asked Guidi if he could make a phone call.

At the other end of the line Gemma Fonseca was defensive, not just surprised. "Didn't I mention it to you? Marina was a diabetic. She controlled her disease by self-administering intravenous insulin three times a day. It was thanks to our good relations with the Vatican that she could continue the cure, scarce as medicines are these days."

"I see. Do you happen to know the individual dosage?"

"To the best of my recollection, it was twenty-five units. Whatever do you ask for, Major? She was scrupulous about her diet and medication, and never came even close to neurasthenia or any other of the mental disturbances hypoglycemics are accused of. Please tell me what this is about."

"I was hoping it might help me figure things out, that's all. Thank you. I may have more questions when we meet next."

Guidi had watched him, standing by with his hat on in the attitude of one ready to go home. It peeved him that Bora always looked energetic, and his latest investigative tangent on an open and shut case frankly annoyed him. Without a word he retrieved the medical report from the desk where Bora had laid it, and turned the goose-necked lamp off. Bora took the hint, and headed for the door.

"Am I mistaken, Guidi, or isn't your heart in this?"

Politely the inspector let Bora out before switching the overhead light off. "My heart has nothing to do with it, Major."

21 APRIL 1944

Hannah Kund came to the police station first thing Friday morning. Guidi judged her somewhat masculine, with her blond cropped hair and flat shoes, blouse and necktie. Had he not known she was not the girl who'd been reassigned on account of the "lesbian" kiss, he'd have drawn conclusions from her appearance. She answered every question without hesitation, adding nothing unless specifically prompted to do so. Magda was a good girl, just a little mixed up. What did that mean? Well, she liked men and they sometimes took advantage of her. What kind of advantage? At least one of them had roughed her up. How so? Slapped her around, bruised her neck... Patiently, Guidi reconstructed Hannah's version of Magda Reiner's life in Rome.

She regularly sent gifts (Lenci dolls: she was a regular at La Casa dei Bambini) to her little niece in Germany, accompanying them with cards reading, "Love from your Auntie." Clearly her daughter, now eight years old. Drinking was a "bit of a problem", in Hannah's words, from which Guidi inferred Magda Reiner might have lost control at parties. Her career as an embassy secretary might have ended soon, even without her death. Names of boyfriends? Some of them she spoke of, some of them she kept quiet. The names he heard, Guidi knew already, none of them better identifiable or traceable to the scene on the fateful night. Merlo and Sutor had met once in the lobby of her apartment building, as she returned to it with Hannah. Sutor had made a scene the following day and called her a slut. An Italian Air Force pilot had seduced her in the back seat of a car just three days before her death. All in all, though, it seemed she'd never gotten over the loss of her fiancé in Greece.

Hannah Kund sat upright in front of Guidi's desk, her blond-lashed eyes unwavering.

"Magda used to say that a past lover sounds always so much better than the present one," was the first phrase she'd volunteered.

"Did you know if she'd recently had a new set of keys made?"

"Why, yes. That's another reason why I noticed her key chain was missing. She'd asked me to go make a copy of the key to her apartment, because hers had broken in the lock."

Guidi was careful to keep his excitement down. "Did she give you the pieces of the old key?"

"No. She'd made a stearin mold of the keyhole."

"And when was this?"

Hannah Kund peered into a small book, apparently last year's agenda. "The first of November."

"Anything else you can tell me about Magda Reiner?"

"It's not really relevant, I don't think, but she hoarded food. She bought all she could and took it home. What kind? Canned food, mostly, and sweets. She loved those nougat sweets – Moretto, I believe they're called."

Guidi did not recall seeing large quantities of food in Magda's apartment, and made a note of it, though in these days of scarcity it might have been a temptation impossible to resist for those who had searched the place first. The wrapper in 7B, however, was from a Moretto.

23 APRIL 1944

On Sunday General Westphal was at Soratte, and so Dollmann. In the morning Bora went to Via Giulia seeking a meeting with Cardinal Borromeo, who – suspecting he was after Hohmann's post-mortem, or some related document – pretended not to be in. As he was scheduled to meet his commander in the evening to go over the developments around the Alban Hills, Bora could not insist. Back at the office, he sat by the phone waiting for last-minute updates from the front. At six he left for his overnight stay in the mountains, but was flying back before long with a sensitive message for General Maelzer. Maelzer, typically, ordered him to hand-deliver the answer. Bora had only the time to stop by his room for a new container of aspirin on his way to the airport.

As he was leaving the lobby of the Excelsior the lights went off, and when he arrived at the Hotel d'Italia, the power had not been restored. The whole building was dark. Candles flickered at the bar and on tables, where people spoke in hushed tones. Bora found his way up three ramps of stairs with the help of a flashlight, which he had to put away to place the key in the lock with his right hand.

Later, he couldn't remember whether he had expected it or not, but, two steps into the room, there was a rustle of clothes on both sides of him and at once his arms were jerked into immobility. Pain raced up his left shoulder. A handgun sought his head and came to lodge under his chin, hard against the floor of his mouth. *Two, three men. The pistol is not army.* Bora fought but could not get himself loose, nor could he lower his head, and the front of his body was open to blows. He tried to throw himself down, and the gun was cocked. Bora heard the click in his head.

No words being spoken, still the men were close enough for Bora to smell tobacco and stop struggling, anxious to recognize by smell and contact who it might be, and whether the men wore uniforms (they didn't). The momentary relaxation caused the grip to relent enough for him to turn halfway and drive his knee up the groin of one of those holding him, hear him yelp, and his right arm was free but already they were landing powerful short blows on him. Pain infuriated him and he thrashed around enough for them to try to grasp his hair, but it was too closely cropped, so they held him by the neck then, twisting his right arm behind his back and upwards, until the spasm in it made him rigid and stock-still.

Bora had no doubt they'd break his arm. His muscles trembled in opposition to the jerking motion upwards. It was as if an electric current shot through his shoulder, creating sparkling chains of light before his eyes. He twisted in pain and the gun was frantically driven back against his head. Agony in his elbow made him stiffen with heart in mouth for the splintering of the bone. He tried to close his right hand in a fist and couldn't, no more than it'd be possible for him to keep from crying out any moment.

Something seemed to roll out under his feet just then. Visible as a pale swath on the floor, light from the hallway lamps glared, spreading under the door. Pressure on his arm fell and Bora unadvisedly swung it around to hit the man with the gun, offering himself to be brought down by a crashing blow in the back of the ear. He never lost consciousness, though he had a nosebleed and was too dazed to follow the men out. Back on his feet, he staggered to the bathroom to turn on the water in the sink. He soaked a towel and wiped his face looking away from the mirror, trembling with the release of tension, or mounting anger. The water reddened in the basin when he squeezed the cloth. He had to stand there to stanch the flow, which wasn't much but kept coming. He ached all over, but other than that he was unhurt.

The room was in chaos. He could see reflected in the mirror how drawers had been rummaged through, emptied and their contents dumped on the floor, the wardrobe ransacked. His army trunk pulled out from under the bed and overturned, books, papers, photographs and letters spread around it. Even the bed had been searched. Angrily Bora watched the reflected chaos in the room swing away as he opened the mirror cabinet and reached for the painkiller. He was out of Cibalgina, so he gulped three aspirins, straightened his uniform out, and drove back to the airport.

In the morning, a call from Via Tasso awaited. Bora returned immediately after entering his office at nine o'clock. When Sutor rudely asked why he had not been in earlier, he protested, "I want you to know I haven't even gone to my hotel room to shave yet."

There was a pause on Sutor's part. "How so?"

"I just returned from Soratte. I spent the night there."

The line seemed to go dead on the other side. Bora was curious. He felt his temples begin to pound under the skin, and with the quickened heartbeat the bruise behind the ear hurt. The sense of danger peaked in him for the first time since last night. In spite of it, his voice stayed calm, even indifferent. "Well, how may I be of assistance?"

"When did you leave for Soratte?" Sutor asked instead.

"At 1800 last night. I told you, I spent the night there."

"You're lying."

Every word counts. I can't make a mistake. "Why should I lie, Captain?"

"Let me ask General Westphal about it."

"The general is on the line with Berlin. Of course if the matter is urgent, I will alert him at once." Bora took the short breath of one preparing to lift a weight or sustain a physical blow. "I don't understand your apparent insistence on my being in Rome last night, Captain Sutor. I don't recall any function I should have attended."

Sutor hung up, never having given the reason for his call.

According to his instructions, Bora's hotel room had not been touched. When he returned to it that evening, in a cool mind he separated the clothes that needed washing or ironing; the rest he replaced in drawers and wardrobe. Books and magazines found their way back onto shelf and bedstand, small objects – cufflinks, medals – were gathered again in their boxes. He wanted to know what was missing. Thoroughly he went through the papers tossed out of the trunk, dividing them into piles: photographs, sheet music, manuals, sketches.

It was obvious that his address book was no longer in the bed-stand drawer (the prophylactics were still there), but he hoped it had been thrown somewhere in the scattering. It had not. He went as far as emptying the drawers again to make sure, looked behind the radiator, the bed, in the bathroom – nothing. To make things worse, the power failed again. He sat in the dark, chewing on the powerless need to make somebody physically pay for it.

26 APRIL 1944

There was a tender spring rain outside when Bora and Guidi met at the police station over the noon hour on Wednesday. The roofs shone like mirrors under the veil of water, and on the west side of the room the windows were tearful.

Bora made such a valiant show of ease, he was sure Guidi was taken in. After listening to the inspector's report on his interview with Hannah Kund, he made a note of the date and place where the new key had been made. Then he said, "Well, I have news, too. You'll never imagine who came to see me at the office this morning. His gummy head polished like sealskin, it was Merlo himself. Officially, it was to invite General Westphal to a performance of *I Pescatori di Perle*, but I knew what it was about. I let him talk. He knows his opera, I can tell you that. He never recognized me from the Pirandello play, but has heard from someone within the Rome police that Pietro Caruso is after him. Knows I'm your counterpart in the investigation, knows about *you*. Clearly Caruso has his enemies, and this is really amusing, because now it's all up in the air."

Guidi grumbled. "It's hardly amusing at all, Major. What did you tell him?"

"Ah, that's the *good* part. I don't often relish my position as an aide, but the perception of power that comes with it is exhilarating. I told him that I – I left you out of it, since you haven't any power – had proof he was at the scene of Magda Reiner's death. I told him he's suspected of having pushed her out her bedroom window, adding that his rough treatment of prostitutes is also common knowledge."

You haven't any power. Guidi didn't think for a moment that Bora was protecting him and was offended.

Bora ignored him, smiling, with his shoulders to the window. Ominous as it was for him that the intruders in his room might be after the suicide note and had to content themselves with his address book, he maintained a demeanor so congenial as to sound convincing to his own ears. "He was taken aback, Guidi. Had no idea Caruso is trying to pin murder on him. Claims he'd been adamant about Party accounts at the National Confederation of Fascist Unions and has made enemies. He assumed they'd try to turn the tables on him in matters of money, but not this. Describes himself as a good husband who would never want this to reach his wife's ears. 'She must be deaf, then,' I told him. Guidi, I was enjoying myself. When it was over – and it took him the better part of two hours to spill it out – I felt so ambivalent about him, I'm telling you now that he might be the killer after all. According to him, Magda Reiner threw herself at him at the 30 October party, besieged him with phone calls until he would agree to a rendezvous. Wore no undergarments on that occasion and nature took its course. No woman had ever done that for him, and he was understandably flattered. *Loved* her, he says, like a high-school student."

"What utter nonsense, Major!"

"I'm not done. As Fräulein Kund told you, one afternoon he ran into Sutor in the lobby of the Reiner apartment, and did not buy the tale Magda told him – that Sutor was there for Hannah Kund. Had a militiaman spy on Sutor's movements after hours and was aware he visited her. Says he never heard of Emilio or Willi, but by the third week in December, his love had turned to hatred, like Othello's for Desdemona – his own words."

"But of course, he swears he didn't kill her."

"Quite the opposite, he won't swear either way." Bora glanced down in the street, still speaking in a good-natured voice. "You can be sure I pressured him, but he's quite more defiant than I'd have given him credit for. Challenged me to prove he killed her. Didn't threaten me, because he knows better. As for you, Guidi, after I told him you would not blindly accept Caruso's indictment of him, Merlo said he expects you to do your duty as an honest functionary. And added *you*'ll never be able to prove he did it."

"That remains to be seen. What about the glasses?"

"As poor Sciaba said, he'd returned them to the store. Claims that the case – which is interesting – disappeared from his office at the beginning of February, and that he doesn't know how either object ended up in her apartment."

"Naturally he'd claim *that*. And does he admit to having seen the body?"

"He does."

Guidi clammed up. It vexed him that Caruso had given him to believe Merlo was too powerful to be trifled with, and had thrown his own weight around when the provincial policeman had not toed the line. What Bora said was true, he had no power. But it remained to be seen whether he couldn't prove Merlo's guilt.

"I tried to reach the Reiner elders," Bora tried to mollify him. "No success thus far, as their house was bombed and they moved in with friends. As soon as they're tracked down, however, I'll ask more questions about our Greek-Front Wilfred, the 1936 affair and any present liaisons the girl might have gotten into. Unless of course she fell in love with a partisan in hiding, and we're back to square one."

Guidi did not notice how punctilious Bora's pretense of levity was. His mind went back to Antonio Rau, whose movements in Rome before his coming to Via Paganini for Latin lessons were shadowy. He was not especially tall, but would the clothes Magda had bought fit him otherwise?

27 APRIL 1944

Cardinal Borromeo distanced himself from people by refusing audiences and making them sit through long waiting periods indoors, and by other but no less successful methods out of doors. This time he gave an appointment to Bora at the Ara Coeli shrine by the Capitol Hill. There was a measure of malice in it, since Bora's leg injury made the vertiginous climb of one hundred and twenty-two steps a reminder of a bodily as well as moral need for humility. Borromeo watched him, standing on the slab of an ancient scholar who had mortified himself by choosing burial in a much-trafficked threshold. "You're not panting," was the first thing he said.

"I hope not, Cardinal. Give me six months and I'll be running the distance up."

"In six months you won't be in Rome."

"'Man proposes and God disposes,' Cardinal. Miracles happen."

"Do you really believe that?" Borromeo preceded him into the church, cool in comparison with the dazzling warmth of its threshold. "In miracles, I mean."

"Well, they're a tenet of the Church."

"So's the Virgin Birth, and you and I know it's physically nonsense."

"I won't discuss theology with my betters."

"But you discussed philosophy with Hohmann."

"I know philosophy."

Dressed in a plain black cassock, Borromeo seemed very long, a string bean of a man. Negligently he kneeled facing the main altar and signed himself before taking a place in the first pew. From a rich leather folder he extracted a coverless journal, which Bora recognized with a start to be in Hohmann's handwriting. "I believe this is what you were after when you came the other day, and I wouldn't see you." He allowed Bora to follow a paragraph or two with his eyes, then replaced the journal in the folder. "If it is, here is how things stand. Number one, I will not give it to you. Hohmann's secretary, who is not as dull as he seems, took it home when the cardinal failed to stop by his residence after meeting Marina Fonseca, as perhaps he'd been instructed to do in such cases. It is now in Vatican hands, never to emerge again if we can help it. Number two, this encounter will have never taken place. You must deny it if need be even in the confessional."

Bora lifted his eyes to the opulent ceiling of gilded wood and stuccoes, as if to find inspiration there. "Why would the cardinal's journal be of such interest to me?"

"My dear Major, I am a bit older and worldlier than you are, with all that my little kingdom is not of this earth. I keep myself informed. Hohmann kept a journal at the university. You have *friends* in common – you are his spiritual heir. There is no reason to keep from you what he initiated. What he initiated, you must continue."

"And what would that be, Cardinal?"

With a condescending smile Borromeo laid the folder in his lap and rested his hands on it. "Now, then, Major, do not ask the obvious."

Bora felt exposed, just one step below vulnerability. "Why don't you give the charge to Colonel Dollmann?"

"Because he has a hard time keeping things to himself. Besides, you are Hohmann's great admirer, he who defends his honor in death. What is it, Major Bora, are you getting cold feet as the Americans draw near?"

"It isn't the Americans who worry me."

"I see." Borromeo studied him. "Since surely you agonized over it, be informed that Hohmann was asexual like an old capon, and Marina Fonseca the frustrated widow of an impenitent sinner, a typical case of *vagina dentata*. I was her confessor, you can take my word for it. Now, what are your conditions to continue Hohmann's work? I am ready to negotiate."

At this point of his bachelorhood, even a *vagina dentata* sounded fleetingly attractive. Sullenly Bora held his hand out. "Two. The first is, let me have the journal."

"Sorry, I don't intend to let anyone have it. I'm already bending the law in the Jesuit style. It's written in Italian, as you see, and be content that it refers not so cryptically to individuals identified as *Vento, Bennato* and *Pontica*."

What learned but hopelessly transparent covers for *Bora*, *Eugene* Dollmann, and *Marina* Fonseca. It seemed to Bora that danger had entered the holy space and crammed it full of shadows. He'd run away if he could, wanting none of this. So he said, "I will do nothing before being granted to read this text at leisure. Nothing. Not even show an interest." And when Borromeo, after a dry silence, seemed to waver, he prompted him, "When and where? I'll give you my second condition then."

The cardinal stood to leave, without bothering to cross himself before the main altar this time. "Tomorrow evening at the infirmary of Santo Spirito. At seven o'clock. You'll be interested to know that Mrs Murphy volunteers there," he added with a smile entirely out of place. "It will give you a chance to practice your excellent English."

Once at the foot of the stairway, Bora was about to enter his car when he recognized Dollmann at one of the tables of a café across the street. The colonel lifted a cup of espresso in a toast. "This city is getting smaller and smaller, Bora! Fancy seeing you here. Are you skipping lunch for church these days?"

8

28 APRIL 1944

The evening sky was turning above the tangles of wisterias, filling the Roman gardens with deeply scented grape-like clusters. The heavy perfume, breathed elsewhere, brought to mind days and images of other days, words heard and said to others, a different world of which Bora no longer was a part, because that world had altogether gone.

At the Santo Spirito infirmary, Borromeo was nowhere to be found, likely to avoid hearing Bora's second condition. A plump nun handed him a sealed envelope. In it, an unsigned and typewritten message read, *Ask for Mrs Murphy. She knows nothing, but has the folder for you.*

Not knowing what to think of the arrangement, but less disappointed now by the cardinal's absence, he did ask for her, and was waiting in the hallway when a young woman's voice reached him from a double door. "You realize you shouldn't be here in uniform."

Bora recognized the singing American speech and turned on his heel. Mrs Murphy stood a few steps away, holding a tray of bloodstained bandages.

"You're right," he admitted. "I'm sorry – I come directly from work."

Had she been less beautiful. Unhappily Bora looked at her, and she at him.

"What are you doing here, Major Bora?"

"I'm here at Cardinal Borromeo's prompting."

"Very well." She handed the tray to a gliding little nun, stepped into a doorway for a moment, and came out of it with a sealed manila envelope, which she stretched to him without coming close. "As I understand, you are to return this within three hours at the latest. You may sit in there. And please have Sister inform me when you're done."

Bora struggled to remove his eyes from her. "Thank you."

"Good night, Major."

Bora stepped toward the small room, but halted on the threshold to watch her as she walked down the hallway, away from him. Under the electric light she was ruddy-haired and very different from Dikta, who was fair and good-looking as mares are good-looking, strong and tall. Mrs Murphy was not frail but smaller, daintily made – she had nice hips, fine ankles, an adorable curve of the spine onto the small of her back. Bora felt lonely for his wife's want of him and wished there were someone with the same want.

The reading took two hours, at the end of which the web had so closely been woven around him, even the instinct to escape he had felt at Ara Coeli was impossible to heed. Aside from mentioning frequent meetings with *Pontica*, whom Bora understood to mean Marina Fonseca, Hohmann – who had not seen fit to speak openly to him in life – was compromising him in death: and not so indirectly, laying out unfinished plans that begged to be taken up.

He was aching and in a despondent frame of mind when he returned to the hotel. Had Dollmann not waved at him, he'd have ignored his presence at the bar. But now he had to join the colonel, though he politely refused to drink a sambuca – he detested the drink's soapy taste and its turning milky when water was added.

"We didn't have a chance to speak after you left church yesterday." Dollmann spoke over his drink. With a finger he was drawing slow circles on the rim of the glass, in a gesture Bora had seen women make, and which in women he had always found attractive. Not here and now. He ordered mineral water and gave up thinking of a way to take aspirin without Dollmann inquiring about it. So he placed the medicine bottle in plain sight on the counter, deftly unscrewed its cap, let three tablets roll out and put them in his mouth, all with his right hand, taking a sip of water after them.

"I'm glad you don't toss your head back when you drink," the colonel only observed. "Some people do. I find it doltish."

Nothing ever happened by chance with Dollmann, this much he knew. Nothing he said was accidental. When their elbows nearly touched, Bora avoided the contact. He felt very insecure near the SS. There were sexual reasons for it as well as political ones, and knowing how well informed Dollmann was, how much he had to do with all that went on, he kept aloof – not hostile, but watchful. Only when the colonel said, "It was fortunate you had nothing compromising in your address book," temper got in the way of prudence.

"Was anyone expecting there should be? I'm a creed-bound officer."

Dollmann shook his head. He lay the address book on the counter, and because Bora did not motion toward it, he pushed it over to him. "Be quick and copy the addresses you most care about. It has to go back. I warned you."

"You warned me about my diary. As for whatever else they might have been looking for, it's where it won't be found."

Even after the sambuca was gone, its soapy, pungent aroma stayed in the glass. It was a tiny glass and Dollmann poured himself another dose. "Bora, what does it take to seduce you? Most men like being seduced, even on a national scale."

"Kappler tried it before you, Colonel."

"Do you presume to compare my reasons to Kappler's?"

"No, but seduction is what it is."

"Let me give it to you straight, then – unless something is done to restore the fabric broken by Hohmann's unfortunate death, there will be disaster coming to the Vatican, the Lateran, St Paul's and everywhere else Jews are hidden."

"Well, you're Himmler's friend."

Dollmann made a significative gesture by joining his wrists, fists closed. "You may have one hand, but it's free."

And this was no spiderweb that he might hope to tear. Bora felt as though a wild animal inside him were trying to sniff the trap, going in circles to recognize the smell of the hunter. He resisted Dollmann even to the extent of avoiding his glance, though he was not one to be spoken to without facing his questioner.

Leaning with his elbows on the counter, the colonel spoke nearly into his ear. "Have you not put your career and your life at risk for Guidi, who is nothing to you, just like your wife was nothing to you? Are you not sticking your neck out for a dead priest? It's time you joined your own."

"No one is *my own* that I can tell."

"Except for me."

Bora heard the sentence slide into him, and was hurt by it in an unexpected, personal way. "Then prove it to me – you know as well as I do who is behind the cardinal's death. What will you do about it?"

Dollmann laughed a low gurgling laugh. "That's not a good move, Bora. Take the pawn back and place it somewhere else – I won't penalize you for it." Then he was silent for a time, during which tension strained between them. People came and went to and from the counter, and to them they must have seemed only officers drinking after hours. But in the end Dollmann turned Bora around, grimly. "Listen to me. I speak to you from your shadow side – not quite your dark side, but the one that receives less light. I come closer to what you are seeking than any surrogate brother. Guidi is not your counterpart – I am. He is weak because he does not dare and is without passion, and so he cannot and will not be your friend. His heart is dull. But you and I, we are two of an intellectual kind, we play the game well. We have played it since we met, and we could as easily as not have been enemies, but had too much in common. We have a kinship, and I claim it."

"And what will come of it?"

Dollmann forced the address book into Bora's hand, and Bora saw there was a piece of paper in the middle of it. He pulled it with thumb and forefinger, carefully. He unfolded it and recognized it as an SS list of families due for arrest in the morning. By their surnames he knew they were Jews. "This is a restricted document!"

"It is."

Bora swallowed. "What do you expect me to do, sleep over the knowledge of it?"

"No. I plan to make you uncomfortable."

How well the trap worked. Bora was close enough to smell the steel of its hinge. He said, staring the SS in the face, "Colonel Dollmann, it may have been different for you, but in the past five years I tried to look at this ordeal as having the only redeeming quality of every war – that all issues are clear-cut in it, all allegiances beyond question. I had my doubts and God knows I dealt with them as best I could, but the awful moral choice won't go away. I don't need you coming here to remind me we're all hanging from its noose."

"Nicely put. Would you care for a sambuca now?"

"God, no."

Dollmann placed the piece of paper in Bora's pocket. With his back turned, while the major scribbled a few addresses on his calendar, she said, "There's *Tosca* with Maria Caniglia coming up at the opera. Will you join me?"

Bora gave back his address book, coldly. "Who is singing Cavaradossi?"

"Gigli, who else."

"I'll come."

On Saturday morning, Bora's secretary put away bundles of papers in the drawers of her desk, cleared her few things and asked General Westphal whether she could leave now.

"Don't you want to wait until the major comes back from Soratte? It'll be less than an hour now."

She said she didn't. Westphal felt sorry for her, but let her go.

Professor Maiuli told Antonio Rau that he believed no progress had been made during the weeks of Latin lessons. At this speed, they'd still be at the second declension by *Ferragosto*. He had to apply himself, what the devil. It was almost like stealing, to take money for lessons that did not seem to penetrate, as he said, "past the auricular pavilion". Rau apologized and promised to do better: it was a privilege coming here in any case, even if just to listen to one who knew Latin better than an ancient Roman. Besides, there might be a chance to intensify his study. With his mother who had been ill, and relatives come to crowd their house after the raid on Via Nomentana, he wondered whether he could impose himself for a couple of weeks. He was ready to pay a hundred lire per day and he'd be content to sleep on the sofa in the parlor.

Signora Carmela, who'd been listening, said that of course it was up to the professor, but she thought it would be more equitable to calculate a monthly rate and divide it in half. Rau acted insulted. It was out of the question.

"Do I really look like I can't afford it? Besides, I don't know how long I need to stay. Could be less than two weeks, but it could be more. It all depends on my relatives, you see, whether they find other accommodations or not. I have permission to relocate from the authorities." If they didn't mind, Rau added, he'd bring along three or four suitcases from his parents. They contained nothing breakable and would fit under any bed.

The perspective of fourteen hundred lire spoke black-market

meat and cheese to the conservative Maiulis. And everything about the agreement told them not to inform Guidi for now.

30 APRIL 1944

At eight o'clock in the morning, on a Sunday when the Piazza Vescovio hospital was unusually quiet, Captain Treib told him, "You're back in business. Your last Wassermann test is OK."

That he should say so made Bora smile, not only because of what it meant, but for the informal concession to American talk. "Let's go to my office," Treib was adding now. "There's something else I want to discuss with you." And once seated behind the metal desk, he came to the point. "How often are you in pain? Every day?"

It'd be no use hiding things from him. "Nearly every day," Bora said.

"It's not going to get better, you ought to know. I'm sure they told you up north, and they might even have tried to fix things. You'll have to have it opened again."

For a moment it was like sitting in front of the Italian surgeon, five months earlier. Bora lit himself a cigarette. "I can't afford time in a hospital."

"The question is, can you afford being ill on the job?" Treib kept calm watery eyes on him, leaning with his chair against the drab gray wall of the room. "When this is over you're going back to your regiment, I'm sure – I've seen you under the bombs at Aprilia. The diplomatic interlude has been for recuperation." He lowered his eyes from Bora's stare. "So, what's the story of this pain? Are you one of those whom luck made feel immortal?"

Bora smirked. "Two years in Russia, including being caught by, and escaping from the Red Army, with hardly a scratch. It was difficult to accept that the same invulnerable body should be injured on a useless Italian country road."

"And now?"

"Now I ask myself whether a man in pain acts as he would in normal circumstances, or reacts to his own suffering, projecting it. Is well-being a prerequisite to restraint?" Bora half-smiled. "I maintain balance, but at what cost, I don't know. My wife tells me I'm stoic. I'm not. I just put things off. I refuse them. If I say there's no pain, by God, there's no pain."

"But there is."

"There is. And it's true that what I want is field duty. That's where life is real."

"Only because the opposite is so real." Treib lifted his own hand, scarred by the partisan bullet near Albano. "As I found out two months ago."

Glad to change subject, Bora stalled the talk of surgery. "So, what about the prisoners who got away when you were waylaid?"

"Well, they got away. They were two of the wounded we originally caught at Salerno, one of them for the second time."

"Wounded twice?"

"No. Captured twice." Treib's smile did not relieve the weariness of his eyes. "But he managed to escape twice, so we're even. Even with a bullet in his thigh, he jumped like a rabbit over a maze of hedges and was gone."

"You do run when they're after you." And he was thinking of Stalingrad, of his own close escape, but said nothing more about it. Spain, Poland, the Ukraine – years of chasing and being chased. Putting out the cigarette after an extended last draft, he asked, "Off the top of your head, what can you tell me about diabetic coma?"

Treib acted as if he didn't know Bora was stalling. "Do you mean diabetic or hypoglycemic coma? There's a difference."

"I wouldn't know."

"Well, the second turns up when blood sugar falls below 0.7, with the appearance of the first symptoms – weakness, sweating, nervousness, mydriasis or dilated pupils. By the time you get to 0.3, you get loss of consciousness and coma. The first is occasioned by insufficient insulin. Some of the signs include dry skin, typical acetonic breath, contracted pupils. Untreated – and sometimes even treated – they both lead to death. Come, Bora, what will it be? I'm willing to work on your arm and put you out in two days. You won't be able to wear the prosthesis at once, but you'll be on your way to feeling better."

"If I get a weekend off, you can have me. So, if you administer insulin in excess, you could induce a hypoglycemic coma?"

"You could. Regarding surgery, take a few days off – it's all lost anyway, can't you see?"

"No." It was the last thing Bora wanted to hear and he cut the surgeon short. "Not up north. There's a year's worth of fighting in the mountainside."

"Well, all right, a year's worth, maybe. Do you want to go through it on morphine?"

Bora looked away. This, too, he'd heard before.

Capturing the moment, Treib set the chair straight. He looked at his calendar. "I'll meet you here Saturday after next at five o'clock. Eat nothing that day. Bring a change and your shaving kit. And a book to read, maybe."

"I want to be out within twenty-four hours."

"I'll kick you out as soon as I'm sure you won't have a secondary hemorrhage."

1 MAY 1944

By Monday, fires could be seen burning from the high points of the city in the not-so-distant hills, down the plain to Velletri and even in the east toward Tivoli. From the relative quiet of Mount Soratte, Kesselring listened to Bora enumerating the historical treasures of the small towns north of Rome, saying now and then, "I'll do what I can," or, "This is the last war when art or archictecture or anything of that sort will be spared." They were at the end of a briefing and the field marshal was indulgent toward his insistence on details. "You give me all these annoying reminders, Martin, while I have such comparatively good news for you. Effective this month anti-partisan guerrilla activity in Italy will fall under my command, and under the control of army officers in the field. It's true that we'll still be a hybrid – my head and the Supreme SS Chief's on one neck – but partisan reconnaissance will be up to those as yourself."

"What about Rome?"

"It's still up to Kappler's men in Rome."

Guidi found it contemptible that the Romans were ecstatic at General Maelzer's late distribution of staple foods. Hammering of air raids all around the city gave the spring day an echo of storms to come. The only piece of good luck he could think of had come in unlikely form: the visit of a militiaman, who reported having been in the neighborhood when "the German girl had been killed". It was the first direct reference to murder Guidi had heard from a witness of sorts. And though he had no doubt that this was the very man Merlo had sent spying on Captain Sutor, potentially conclusive information had come from the meeting.

Sitting with his back to the window (he didn't care to see the walls of the houses across the street, scarred by bullets after the bomb had exploded nearly six weeks before), he reread his notes. Sutor had in fact accompanied Magda Reiner home, but had not left at once. He'd spent at least fifteen minutes inside, and then emerged again at about seven fifteen or seven twenty. Magda was with him and they were apparently arguing. Sutor had entered his car, and sat in it while she presumably returned to her apartment. But then Sutor had gone back inside. *And he'd stayed inside.* In the commotion that followed in the street after the death, the militiaman could not tell when the SS had left the apartment building. But he was sure he'd been inside when Magda met her end.

Guidi was tempted to call Bora, but thought better of it. Why give him one more chance to take over and twist things his way? *No, this piece of information is mine. I am the policeman. This goes neither to Caruso nor to Bora.*

That evening he was looking forward to a bit of self-congratulation in the borrowed peace of Via Paganini when he met the sight of Antonio Rau, ensconced in the Maiulis' parlor. Rau showed himself curt, even rude. When Guidi tried to convince him to walk outside and discuss matters at once, he refused. "What's there to discuss? I pay the rent same as you do."

Dinner was richer than usual but dismal in mood. The Maiulis munched their food like unobtrusive mice, linking eyes with one another. Francesca and Rau chatted in forced tones of levity, and when Rau came up with some Latin ditty to rouse the professor from his sulks, Guidi had had enough. He left the table and went into his room.

Face up on the bed, he looked at the humidity stain on the ceiling, one of which he had for the past four months identified as a frog-like creature, tongue extended. So, that's how it was. This was the *friend* Francesca had been trying to accommodate, and Rau's coming posed an even more immediate threat to the household. Surely the SS kept an eye on the whereabouts of their translators. His absences from the city and now his move to another address might be noticed; however, he'd obtained permission to relocate. The little he had eaten came bitterly to Guidi's throat as he thought of being dragged into this game when he'd been the one the Germans had nearly killed at the caves. But Francesca was right. It had come after all to choosing allegiances.

The frog-like stain on the ceiling seemed to swing as he moved his head on the pillow. Rau had avoided him tonight, but would have to face him tomorrow. Sure. And then? The one who was caught was Sandro Guidi, who could neither tell nor turn in, nor yet be silent. He stood from his bed after a while, walked to the dining room and announced he would be moving out by the end of the month.

*

Dr Mannucci, staying late at his pharmacy as usual, went to close both doors after Bora asked the question. "I thought you had come a long way from your command just to buy Cibalgina," he commented. And then, reverting to the question at hand, he added, "You could find out about the prescription through the Brothers of Charity – they run the pharmacy at the Vatican. I wager the lady acquired her medicine there, as insulin is hard to come by. Sagone brand, isn't it?"

"I don't know."

"It has to be. Belfanti, Erba and the others vanished from the shelves months ago."

"For all of my acquaintances at the Vatican," (Bora shamelessly made use of Montini's and Borromeo's names) "I doubt the good Brothers would tell me whether her prescription had in fact run out. You would have much more clout under the circumstances."

Mannucci removed his fat cat from the counter, saying, "Down, Salolo, down," and shook his head when Bora tried to pay for the painkiller. "I promise nothing, Major. Give me a couple of days before you call again, and I'll see what can be done."

Bora did not have to wait so long, however. On Friday afternoon, the pharmacist telephoned with the news. It had taken some doing, but Brother Michele had relented enough to indicate that the Fonseca prescription had only been recently renewed. Alone in his office, Bora saw the piece of the puzzle fall into the pattern with such neatness as to give him a chill.

At last it all made sense. The fragments of glass vials in Marina's bathroom, pointed out to him by the Lombard policeman, who'd commented under his breath, "I wonder what these are about, there's no container and no syringe anywhere." The injection marks in Marina's arm. Her dilated pupils.

Bora said, "I'm in your debt, Dr Mannucci." And, to the gruff "Not at all" from the other side, he continued, "But I insist. So much so that I allow myself a small piece of advice. Remind your in-laws, *if* you have any, and *if* they reside at Largo

Trionfale, to take good care during these difficult times. The army is less inquisitive than others about hidden firearms, but we do have our curiosity."

9 MAY 1944

On the same day that Sebastopol fell to the Russians, a dinner party was organized for General Wolff. Bora was required to attend for Westphal, a minority of one at a table of SS. No one spoke to him and he spoke to no one. Dollmann glanced his way from Wolff's table, and after the dinner advised, "Have our dear Westphal send you to the Vatican with some excuse tomorrow. Wolff has a private audience with the Pope, and there'll be politicking going on."

Bora had slept poorly and was in a touchy mood. Just before dawn he'd dreamed that his room had been emptied, his uniform searched and his diary stolen from him. But it was his room at Lago, months ago, his winter uniform from the Russian days, and the diary had nothing but Dollmann's name written in it. He was about to say no to the proposal. Still, this might be a chance to approach Borromeo privately about Cardinal Hohmann, and he sought permission to go.

True to his habits, he never followed the same route twice, and instructed his driver to pick him up at headquarters over the lunch hour on the following day, and take him to the Vatican by way of Corso Italia, Via Salaria, Via Paganini, Via Aldovrandi, Viale Mazzini and Viale Angelico.

10 MAY 1944

The shot had not been heard from the apartment, partly because Signora Carmela had the radio on. Guidi happened to be home between trips to Tor di Nona, where an investigation of black-market activities was as lost a cause as he could think of.

Neither the shot was heard, nor the skid of the Mercedes' tires on the pavement and its braking after jumping the curb at the elbow of Via Paganini. What followed was a racket in the stairwell, and soon a frantic hammering at the door. Guidi heeded it at once. Antonio Rau stormed in, jostled him past the threshold and bolted the length of the hallway into the bathroom, and out of its window to the back. Less than ten seconds later, a German soldier with sub-machine gun followed, crashing through the same route and out of the window.

Signora Carmela was not so petrified that she could not stand up and scream. Out of the kitchen there came the professor in his shirtsleeves, and already – magnified and made harsher by echoes in the stairwell – Guidi recognized Bora's angry voice, ordering a group of heavily armed soldiers to enter one of the apartments.

He couldn't help crying out, "What on earth is going on, Major Bora? What is this?"

Bora did not look back – he was at the foot of the stairs and incited the soldiers to rush up. "Stay out of my way, Guidi!" Neither Guidi nor anyone else did otherwise when the major himself barged into the Maiulis' house. Without asking he looked around for the telephone and spoke a few sentences into the mouthpiece. From the stairs there came the sharp cries of Pompilia Marasca, whom the Germans must be bodily hauling out of her apartment.

"But what's the reason?" Guidi asked with such anguish in his voice that Bora did answer.

"Get the rest of the tenants out into the street if you want to be useful. They shot at my car just outside – I got a window's worth of glass in my goddamn lap before the man ran into this building."

Guidi blanched at the thought of Antonio Rau. The Maiulis were brought out to join Pompilia, who protested enough for one of the burly young soldiers to have to hold her, breasts bumping on him as he did. Pistol in hand, Bora climbed to the second floor, followed by Guidi who tried to talk sense to him, knowing it was no use. "Wouldn't we have heard the shot, had it come —"

"Shut up."

The obligatory list of tenants tacked by the door was snatched by the soldiers. One by one, people were pushed and goaded and shouldered out of their rooms, and in a few minutes the field-gray bustle of more soldiers poured in from the street and began searching the apartments. Guidi feared what could be found in Francesca's room. Helplessly he stared at the soldiers awakening a storm of tinkles from the glass domes in the parlor, invading kitchen and bedrooms. From the Maiulis' room came an excited call that caused one of the soldiers to race up the stairs for Bora. Two suitcases were produced in the parlor and opened on the floor for the major to see. There were old suits packed tight in them, but Guidi understood by the way the Germans handled the clothes and smelled them that grease stains gave away weapons that had until recently been hidden in them.

Bora would hear nothing more. He had the Maiulis brought back in. Signora Carmela seemed not to understand the connection between the suitcases and immediate danger, but the professor did. He bridged a sheepish, desperate look at Guidi. He told Bora that he gave his word of honor he had been unaware of the cache, but was ready to answer for it as head of the household. Bora silenced him. "You bet you are." He turned to Guidi. "Who else lives here? You and who else? Your girlfriend? Who else?"

"A man by the name of Rau, a student of mine," Maiuli interjected.

"I'm not talking to you. Guidi, who else lives here?"

"That's all, Major."

"Where's the woman?"

"Out, but let's not be absurd, she's nine months' pregnant. What could you want with her?"

Bora left the parlor and Guidi after him. Francesca's room was being searched by soldiers: not until thoroughly going through it did they enter the bathroom, where Bora ordered them to search everywhere, even inside the water tank high above the toilet. It paid off. Wrapped in a watertight envelope, there was a handgun hidden in it.

"We had better find this Rau or your girlfriend goes in, pregnant or not."

All the adult males were made to file out into the narrow street, including students, the old piano player and the professor. As for Pompilia, the soldiers hauled her into the truck with repressed grins after she let her skirt fly over her knees and the girdle snaps showed on her thighs.

Guidi stood on the doorstep, apart from the others. Bora's Mercedes had come to a halt across the street, in the recessed space of the building facing it. It seemed impossible that whatever had blasted the large hole in the side window could have missed him. The driver was sweeping glass out of the back seat. How had the attackers not seen the army truck following the staff car? Likely the larger vehicle had slowed down to negotiate around the curve where a series of private garages reduced the pavement. In any case, hands crossed behind the nape of his neck, Antonio Rau was being led back from Via Bellini by two soldiers.

When Bora stormed into the Mercedes' front passenger seat and slammed the door shut, Guidi came to bang on it. "Am I not under arrest like everybody else?" he yelled.

The German lowered the window only enough for his voice to come across with immense contempt. "You *wouldn't dare* shoot at me."

In the desolation of the house, women congregated to the Maiulis' parlor to lament, unaware that weapons had been found there. When numbly Signora Carmela informed them,

Guidi had to step in to keep them from clawing at her. They appealed to him: he was police, wasn't there anything he could do? Guidi felt he could do nothing until Bora's anger boiled down. But Bora's anger was likely to boil *over* after learning that Rau was a translator for the German occupation forces.

Francesca came back at about five o'clock. From the state of the house it was clear what had happened. She went from room to room, finally standing by her own door with a pale look of anxiety. There Guidi joined her. She spoke to him in a low, quick voice, "It's not my fault if the idiot got himself caught, is it? Now I've got to worry about myself, if he talks."

In her rifled parlor, Signora Carmela wept. "How could Antonio do this to us, Francesca? It must have been his relatives who put the guns in the suitcases... But how did one get inside the toilet?"

"Stop crying," Francesca said irritably, "it's no use whatever." And, to Guidi, "How is it that you're still here? Did the Germans decide you're no threat?"

Guidi let her show concern in her own way by righting pictures and replacing the glass domes on the saints. Her coolness before danger impressed him. "Do you want me to drive you somewhere?" he suggested.

"No." She sat in the professor's armchair, which brought a renewed flow of tears to Signora Carmela's eyes. Only after the old lady went to cry herself to sleep could they talk freely. Francesca smiled an enigmatic smile. "What's there to do? If the Germans come for me, I can hardly start running. It isn't as if they don't shoot pregnant women."

"Maiuli won't last a week if they get him to clear rubble or drag bodies out of it."

"They could have said no to Antonio when he suggested bringing the suitcases along. You can't be responsible for people's stupidity."

"But what if Antonio talks?"

"It'd be a mess. He knows lots. The SS will want him for sure – why, they *know* him."

"And what will happen to you then?"

"If I'm lucky they'll kill him before he talks."

"Jesus, Francesca, that's no answer!"

Francesca had that strange, queerly relaxed smile again. "If you're afraid for me you're wasting your time. Whatever happens, happens." Hands hugging the bulge of her body rising from the groin, she looked over to him from the armchair. "It's getting low. In a couple of weeks it'll be out, and then we can make love again."

Guidi stepped back, heavy-hearted at her words and for having given her reason to pronounce them. He had neither desires nor impulses at this point, and everything he felt was packed in a sadness of things to come.

11 MAY 1944

Bora was alone in the office when news came of the massive attack on the Gustav Line. He was instantly in a cold sweat. This was the final battle Kesselring had forecast, and had begun with the simultaneous firing of more than one thousand big guns, from Cassino to the sea. What a time for Westphal to be on leave, along with several of the army chiefs. He put out of his mind the fact that he had just lost Rau to the SS, and began his rounds of calls to the field marshal and to Maelzer's office. He also had to find a way to trace General Westphal.

Suddenly it was a matter of days. Three weeks, two weeks, maybe less. He functioned by methodical routine, concentrating on one thing at a time, and if events did not lose magnitude, they came into focus and perspective. In fact, it would only take three days for the Allies to billow over the Line. In the evening he flew to Soratte, where he learned that as soon as the stronghold at Cassino fell, withdrawal would follow to the immediate periphery of Rome. Bora had to walk out of the conference room to collect himself. Westphal, just arrived, exchanged a grim look with him, and for the first time he seemed to be very close to nervous collapse.

Back to Rome on the following day, Bora found that after a counter-attack German resistance had broken around the hard-held heights facing the valley opposite Cassino, and the Moroccan troops were streaming through. When Sutor laconically called him to communicate that Antonio Rau had forced the guards to kill him before anything could be extracted from him, it came as an anticlimax. Bora actually began to laugh over the telephone.

Guidi debated all day Friday whether he should swallow his pride and approach Bora about the professor, whom he'd seen carting dirt at one of the bends of the Tiber with a handkerchief bound on his bald head to shield it from the sun. A German soldier who looked no older than sixteen sat on an empty oil drum a few steps away, careless about the speed of the operation. Still, it was hard labor for one who had never lifted anything heavier than a book.

Despite encouraging news from the "free" radio stations, Signora Carmela had slipped into a state of mute apathy and had to be all but spoon-fed. She spoke of the professor as if he had died already, and had hung a black ribbon on the front door. At dinner time Francesca received a phone call from a woman who did not identify herself, but only said, "The wine has turned."

From her reaction Guidi knew it was serious. "Is it good or bad?"

"Good," Francesca said in a trembling voice. "Antonio died without telling on us."

On Saturday two more mountains along the Gustav Line fell to the enemy after less than four hours of fierce fighting. Mount Majo went over to the French at three o'clock.

At five o'clock Treib called from the hospital to remind Bora of his appointment. It was Westphal who took the line, and told Bora in a rough way, "Get your ass over there. You're not going to save the front by being here rather than where you're scheduled to be."

Guidi was relieved to hear that Bora was not available, because he could tell himself he had given it a try. From the non-committal orderly who took the line at headquarters, he received an unasked-for piece of information. "The major left the following message for you, Inspector. *I have news worth reporting. Contact Captain Hanno Treib at the Piazza Vescovio hospital if I am not back in touch by Monday.*"

14 MAY 1944

"Well, there's the curious cat, minus the paw he left in the lard."

Turning his head on the pillow renewed the agony down Bora's sutured left arm. "Come in, Colonel Dollmann."

Dollmann stood by the hospital bed. "Why didn't you tell me you were having surgery? I looked for you everywhere. Here's a book of poetry for you." He sat, with a sweep of eyes at Bora's figure under the light quilt.

"Thank you. If the stitches hold well, I'll be out tonight or tomorrow morning at the latest. Would you please tell General Westphal?"

"Westphal is at Soratte. He sends word for you to take it easy."

"I'll be out in the morning at the latest."

Dollmann let his attention wander to the heavy bandage at the end of Bora's arm, supported by a folded towel so that the wrist lay slightly above the level of the elbow. The arm was strong, blond-haired, fatless. Bora closed his eyes so as not to watch Dollmann watching him.

"How's the front?"

"We're losing ground fast. St Maria Infante is next. The men are working miracles, but miracles don't cut it any more." Dollmann stood up. He went to close the door and walked back to the bed. "God willing, the field marshal will convince the Führer not to torch Rome."

Bora opened his eyes. "Is it being contemplated?"

"At this point, very much so. Look here, Bora – I only have a few minutes, and came to do more than inquire about your health. I hate to do it this way, but you're immobilized enough and low enough to have to listen." Dollmann leaned closer with his torso at an angle, like an anxious priest listening to confession rather than one about to reveal any truth. "I know more than you think about everything. I know what Borromeo is putting you up to, without realizing or caring about the risks it entails. I know about Poland, about Lago. Deny nothing, I *know*."

Bora felt a surge of nausea. Only having already vomited everything, even saliva, curbed it a little. "I wish you'd let me be, Colonel."

"Far from it. Whatever you suspect might have happened to Hohmann, I beg of you, let it go in view of what I have to say. It's because of my knowledge of you and your visit to Foa that I approach you, and expect you to listen as closely as you ever did to anything in your life. It's the last act of importance you will carry out in Rome, since we are defeated in every other sense. Bora, an informer has been turning Jews in to Kappler for several weeks. Gets paid for it. Hundreds of people – no, do *not* interrupt – hundreds of people who could have survived this time have been hand-delivered for deportation. What that means, God forgive us, we both know. Hohmann managed to counteract the operation to an extent, but now he's gone. He would expect you to pick up where he left off."

"Colonel, Cardinal Borromeo has already —"

"I am not speaking of humanitarian intervention, Bora. Understand me. And answer nothing unless you're ready to do something about it."

Dollmann did not let go of Bora's eyes, and Bora kept track of Dollmann's features closely. He had to steady his breathing. Deep raw pain traveled from the reopened wound and freshly severed nerves, a debilitating bloody pain. Death, as on the noon hour at Ara Coeli, passed between them quickly, like the shadow of a cloud before the sun lessens the light of day. A transitory darkness which both sensed, and virile grief, different in Dollmann than in him, but no less manly. Bora's need to rebel gave in to that grief. He made a motion with his head, not quite a nod. "I understand. How can it be done?"

Dollmann's forehead was sweaty, a reaction that seemed not to belong to such a controlled, sarcastic face. He impulsively reached his hand to Bora's knee. "Thank God, Bora. Thank God. This is what I came for. Enough for now; details will follow." He pulled back on the chair, letting go of Bora's leg with a slow withdrawal of his hand. "Before I leave, tell me if there's anything I can do for you."

Bora was anxious to be left alone, and to put out of his mind what had been said until now. "Yes," he replied. "There is. Do all you can to find me a copy of this." He passed a handwritten note to the SS. "No, I have no idea where there might be one, but I need it most urgently. And I will need the name and phone number of the records section chief at the Servigliano transit camp."

Dollmann nodded, already on his feet. "Should I let Guidi know you're here?"

"No."

"Very well." From the foot of the bed where he'd laid it, the colonel moved the book he had brought closer to Bora. "The poems are by that charming American Fascist, Ezra Pound. Do read 'The Garret' after I leave. I… Yes, well, Bora, we'll be in touch."

Bora swallowed, a motion that sent blind bursts of pain up and down his arm. He watched Dollmann reach the door without turning back, and walk away. His arm seemed to yearn for a mouth to cry with, and he was reminded of the old stoic saying, "But the parts which are beset by pain, allow them, if they can, to give their opinion about it." His body wanted to shout. He struggled with its need for a time, breathing hard. His soul wanted to shout also, because of what Dollmann had told him.

The book of poetry under his right hand was slim, a fine edition. He fingered its spine, opened it and leafed through it without large movements, until 'The Garret' came before his eyes. It was a short poem that ended, *Nor has life in it aught better / Than this hour of clear coolness, / The hour of waking together.*

How well Dollmann understood him. It was like everything else with him: the seduction he gave in to was inside him as want already, and it only needed a little chafing to arouse it. There had never been a rape of his mind. On the frontispiece, in black ink, the colonel had penned in lieu of a signed dedication the embittered pun *Roma Kaputt Mundi.*

Francesca soon grew weary of Signora Carmela's dejection, and besides, she wanted a warm meal. "You'll have to get out of this mood," she told her impatiently. "You're lucky he's still in Rome. If you were less useless you'd go and bring him something to eat instead of squatting here doing nothing."

"I can't go out alone to the other side of town…"

"You'll have to if you want to see him." And because the old woman seemed not to respond more than by shrugs, Francesca sought to distract her. "Come on, I'll let you feel the baby move."

Signora Carmela had never thought of the possibility. "Feel the baby move?"

Hesitatingly she drew close to Francesca, whose light dress draped the front of her body so that the out-turned navel was perceivable under the cloth. Signora Carmela would not touch her on her own, so she guided her hand to the flesh. "Wait. There it goes."

Signora Carmela was stunned. Again and again she reached for her belly throughout the morning, curious as a child. "Does it hurt? It must hurt. Does it hurt?"

"It doesn't hurt. Why don't you make some soup? The baby would like that."

On Monday, Bora felt at his lowest physical ebb since coming to Rome. He had hoped to be out by noon but began hemorrhaging at five in the morning. After a brief struggle to stop the blood flow, Treib would not hear about his leaving. "If you stay very still and do as you're told, I might let you out by Wednesday. If anyone calls for you, I'll tell them to come back then."

So Bora lay flat, grimly conserving energy. He let the nurses wash, shave, feed him, check his temperature, blood pressure, inject him, ask him if he wanted anything for the pain. Only to this he said no, because he wished to keep his head clear. He tried to sleep instead, and drifted in and out of strange images. Behind the door of the room was a calendar print of the she-wolf (a gas company used it as an advertising device), and with that before him he fell asleep.

In his dream, the Bronze Wolf came to crouch on the bed, but not as a watchdog: as an animal bent on keeping him from ever getting up, ever getting out. The price to be let go was, he knew, his right hand and he said, "I can't, I can't – what would I be able to do then?" Then it was Mrs Murphy who was sitting at his side, and she kissed him and was so good to him, he thought he could not possibly love anyone else. Dollmann walked in the dream next, in a bizarre white summer uniform, looking like a prim Navy commander. He asked Mrs Murphy to leave, and told him, "You can't have her until you do what you must do," and then he saw that both his hands were gone, and the she-wolf sat by the door with his medals in her mouth.

Pompilia Marasca returned on Monday afternoon, to a reception of anxious faces from doors and landings. She looked no worse for her arrest, and even wore a pair of new stockings, with seams marking her strong calves. She walked to her door without paying attention to looks and comments. Only when one of the second-floor tenants asked her how it had gone, she looked up with the gathered brow of a martyr, a sign that she was ready to be interrogated on her ordeal. It turned out that she had been brought to the Mantellate female prison and kept there overnight, with all kinds of horrors going through her mind. She had been asked questions and then released.

"Have you seen the professor?" Signora Carmela asked from her door.

"Not since they divided men and women, and I was the only woman. They brought them to work." Pompilia glanced at another inquirer, her cherry lips pursing. "Me? They wouldn't make *me* work. I'm all nerves. They could tell that."

"So," a third questioner pitched in, "Where have you been since they let you out?"

She would not answer. "I need to rest." She tossed her head in a motion of long-suffering determination and disappeared into her apartment. But to those who were persistent enough to find out, it appeared that – in a tucked-away little day hotel near the Termini Station – to the great satisfaction of her late captors, Pompilia had done some hard labor in her own way.

17 MAY 1944

When Bora left the hospital on Wednesday morning, Guidi sat by the entrance. He explained he'd called on Monday as per their agreement, and Captain Treib had told him to return today. Seeing Bora's arm in a sling and without prosthesis, he said nothing and Bora volunteered nothing about his health.

"I'm glad you're here, Guidi," was his greeting, as though they hadn't left one another a week earlier in the worst way possible. "I managed to telephone Magda Reiner's parents before being admitted."

In the same tone, Guidi replied, "I assumed that's what your message meant. Did you find out anything of use?"

A row of uncomfortable chairs lined the anteroom's wall, and Bora used one of them to lay his briefcase flat and open it. "The little girl's father was an American."

"I don't see how it helps us."

"It doesn't." Bora took out a large book from the briefcase. "Courtesy of Colonel Dollmann. The man in question was an obstacle-race finalist. She named her daughter after him."

"Well, that's good. I still don't see…"

After showing Guidi the title – *Die Olympischen Spiele, 1936* – Bora opened the book to the illustrated pages covering the 110-meters obstacle race. "Here. Please look. The gold medalist, and holder of the new world record, was Forrest Towns, USA, with 14.2 seconds. Another American, Pollard, won the bronze medal with 14.4 seconds. After the Canadian O'Connor, who came in sixth, was a third American, William Bader. Magda's parents never knew his last name, as she kept mum about it; but the little girl was baptized Wilhelmina."

"Well, Major – William is not a rare first name, is it?"

"No. And Willi, as mentioned in Magda's letters, is a German endearment for Wilhelm or even Wilfred, not a nickname for William. I just thought it was *interesting*. Her parents told me the athlete was from St Louis, a city in Missouri."

Guidi had so many worries – about Francesca, about the aftermath of Rau's killing, about Caruso's hatred for him – Bora's eleventh-hour interest in Magda's love life was infuriating to him. "So now we know who the child's father is, Major," he said under his breath. "Is this what you called me here for?"

"In days to come I hope to know more than that." Quickly Bora replaced the book in his briefcase, and with it in hand preceded Guidi out of the hospital. "I also wanted you to do this for me." He handed a scribbled list to the inspector. "We need to get all the details possible on what was dumped in the garbage in Magda Reiner's neighborhood on the night she died. Surely with the open market nearby, the garbage men go through the bins."

Guidi put the list in his pocket without reading it. "I imagine you have no interest in hearing what *I* might have found out in the past few days." In the sunny springtime air, he felt alive and rebellious, and just about as sick of Rome as he was sick of the war, Bora, the Germans and the Americans, too, who might be good at winning Olympic medals but didn't seem capable of breaking through Nazi defenses.

Bora tossed the briefcase in the back of his Mercedes, waiting by the curb. "But I do. I am most curious, and frankly, without your standing up to Caruso, I might have been tempted to throw *Ras* Merlo to his compatriots. Please tell me, but not here. I abhor talking in the street."

They drove in the Mercedes (the side window was still without glass) back to the city center. Bora felt a deep dislike for the encroachment of modern housing on the once suburban villas. Guidi kept his counsel until they reached Latour's at Via Cola di Rienzo, since it was clear Bora craved coffee and would have it in the best place available. Facing the major over a steaming demitasse, and resolute not to inform him that Sutor had been inside at the time of the murder, he announced, "It wasn't Magda who went shopping for clothes. The description fits Hannah Kund."

Bora looked genuinely interested. "It may be because Hannah spoke Italian and Magda didn't."

"In any case, she certainly did not volunteer that piece of information when I spoke to her. Also, the neighbors noticed that Magda often stopped by the market bins on her way to work and dumped garbage from a paper bag. People notice these things, in times of scarcity, as she seemed to go through more cans than you'd expect one person to consume. And I am ahead of you as regards any evidence thrown out on the night of her death."

"Excellent. Is there a blanket on your list?"

"A German army blanket, which a garbage collector took for himself – yes, it's in my office now. The man reported finding in the same bin a stack of German military magazines, some of them ripped crosswise, apparently to make them into toilet paper – these, too, he brought home. I showed him a few recent issues I'd gotten my hands on, and as far as I can judge he recognized the headings of *Signal, Adler* and *Wehrmacht.*"

Here Guidi stared at Bora, who only said, "Well, at least they planned to send all branches of the service down the drain. What else?"

"A sealed bottle of mineral water, three unopened cans of meat, a can opener and a pair of fancy women's underpants. The magazines are long gone, and also the bottle and the cans. Can opener and underpants are in my office with the blanket. All of it was stuffed in a pillowcase."

Bora made no attempt to conceal his elation. "Well, that's outstanding. What about the key chain?"

Guidi shook his head. "It was probably disposed of elsewhere, or taken along."

"Well, it's still good. But why did it take you so long to get this information?"

"The garbage collector assigned to Magda's neighborhood had been 'borrowed' by your colleagues to clear rubble from the air raids until a week ago. He grudgingly gave up the loot, especially the underpants, which he'd made a present of to some girl."

Bora had finished his coffee. He took out a cigarette pack and offered one to Guidi; after a moment of hesitation, he put the pack away without taking one for himself. "I'd be obliged to you if you had the material delivered to my office," he said. "Much as I dislike the idea, the underwear will fall into my bailiwick, as I'll have to confront Merlo and Sutor with it. We will be in touch by phone in the next few days."

*

By evening Bora was at Mount Soratte. Hours earlier the field marshal had sent out orders to abandon Cassino. Early on Thursday he visited the troops at Valmontone, on the directly threatened Highway 6. He was weak and in severe pain, but the events were too enormous to dwell on it. On his return to headquarters he reported to Westphal, who looked exhausted, and left work at about eight – in time to join Colonel Dollmann for dinner and the long drive back to Soratte.

As they traveled along under the cover of night, the conversation circled around the desperate situation of the troops at Fondi, but it was mostly because neither one of them wanted to be the first to resume the conversation initiated at the hospital.

"Borromeo told me you managed to meet with him briefly yesterday," Dollmann said when talk of endangered defenses was exhausted. "What is new?"

"With him, the riots around most every Vatican soup kitchen."

"And with you?"

Bora had agreed to drive the first half of the trip over, and though he knew the road well, he kept absolute attention on the pavement unrolling before them from the dark. "I told him I think I know what happened to Cardinal Hohmann and Marina Fonseca." Dollmann's silence he expected, so he added, "For whatever it's worth, I told him in confession."

"Well, I'm not privy to the disburdening of your eternal soul. Where's the suicide note? Hand it back."

"That is in the care of His Holiness himself. As for my hypothesis, Colonel, you might as well hear it. If we both know, after the end of the war one of us can inform Gemma Fonseca."

Dollmann groaned from the darkness where he sat. "This is most annoying. Why don't you tell Guidi?"

"Because he's had his troubles from certain quarters already. I dropped the subject with him when I realized where it was going. For now it's nothing but a hypothesis, as I said, but a more plausible one than the Mayerling scenario prepared for us. What would you say, Colonel, if I told you that Baroness

Fonseca, having met the cardinal at a politically friendly home somewhere near the Pantheon between one and three p.m. on 7 April, had to return home to self-administer the second insulin dose of the day?"

"I'd say nothing."

"Well, what if I added that the cardinal, having ample time to return to his residence and get ready for the four forty-five meeting with you, accompanied her there, as the lady sometimes grew unsteady just before her treatment?"

"I don't follow you."

"You will if I add that persons unknown, concealed in Marina Fonseca's city flat and armed with a Beretta removed from her all but inaccessible villa at Sant'Onofrio, and loaded for the occasion, surprised the couple as they entered."

"You are being *fantastic*," Dollmann commented.

"Am I? I daresay, Colonel Dollmann, that a sickly woman and an octogenarian make fairly easy prey. I submit to you that she was forced to compose the 'suicide' note, but that – even in her extremity of illness and terror – she had enough spirit to embed in it a message of distress by using her right hand to write it. And I don't think it an abuse of your patience adding that they then injected Marina Fonseca with a massive dose of insulin, causing a nearly immediate collapse. They undressed her and placed her on the bed. With a frail old man like the cardinal, God knows; an insignificant but well-placed blow could bring him down. Afterwards, it was just a matter of securing her fingerprints on the handgun, arranging the distasteful scene, and staging the murder-suicide with the selfsame gun."

"That's even more fantastic, Bora."

"Less fantastic than it is for an adulterous couple to leave front and bedroom door unlocked in wartime, or for a diabetic to use up at one sitting the doses expected to last her well past the holiday, and leave the empty vials but not the syringe for the police to find. And certainly less fantastic than the sudden murderous craze of a long-standing member of the Tertiary Order."

Bora added nothing else, and Dollmann was as silent as a grave for the following ten miles or so. Even then, he only said, "You have everything but the murderers."

It was Bora's turn to keep his counsel as the glum periphery sank further and further behind them. The lonely fork in the road by the olive groves of Fiano dimly came up before he spoke again.

"I told you, I have those, too. But – like the policeman whose office was rifled even as my room was – I am not so deluded as to go after them now."

As for Sandro Guidi, he did not regret having given a thirty-day notice on his rent. Thanks to Danza he'd already secured new accommodations on Via Matilde di Canossa, off Via Tiburtina, where he'd soon move his few belongings. Truly, he was anxious to go.

Getting up on Friday, through the half-open door, he could see Francesca massaging her legs on the bed, stretching to reach for them as she sat up with a face of discomfort. These days she was sweaty, often nauseous, not bothering to change from her nightgown.

"Need anything?" he asked as he went by, and she gave him a look of disgust. "Close the damn windows in your room, will you? I can smell the stinking asphalt and it makes me want to puke." And it was true, she vomited often, and every half-hour she headed for the bathroom with a waddling walk he couldn't reconcile to the boyish thinness of a few months ago. Dr Raimondi, whose wife had volunteered to adopt her child, had invited her to stay with them until the delivery, but Francesca made it clear she had no intention of being cooped up anywhere until the time came. So she spent her days reading magazines between the bedroom and the toilet, shrugging off Signora Carmela's lamentations about the professor. To Guidi she had little to say, but then he acted as if leaving in less than a week's time meant nothing to him.

Driving to work on a morning that looked like enamel, Guidi simply wanted to extricate himself from the situation. As for the Reiner case, blanket, can opener and underwear had been duly delivered, but Bora had neither called back nor showed up.

20 MAY 1944

Dollmann and Bora were less than half an hour from Soratte when the colonel, who had taken the wheel, silently handed him a folder from the leather case at his side. Bora rested it on his knees to open it. In the delicate light of early morning, as they steadily climbed toward the redoubt, the informer's nameless photograph and one typewritten page of details already seemed like an obituary. He'd nearly forgotten about this. "As promised," Dollmann reminded him, observing Bora's response to the material through the corner of his eye. "Return it as soon as you're well acquainted with it, no later than on our way back." All he could see was a setting of the jaw under Bora's skin.

"Is this all we know, Colonel?"

"It's all you need to know."

"How dependable is the informer's routine?"

"Very. Never missed a date so far."

"So the next trip is on the twenty-first."

"Sunday, correct."

Bora spoke heedfully, keeping his eyes on the folder. "I will be there."

"How do you plan to do it?"

"I'll use my side arm from twenty feet away, no more."

"It's risky."

"Everything is risky if it's not done well. This will be done well."

Seeing a column of armored cars approaching in the rear-view mirror, Dollmann pulled to the grassy side of the road to let them pass, and spoke over the idling of the engine. "What if something goes wrong? You know I cannot help you then."

"Like all seducers, you're not expected to be there if there's hell to pay."

"We're both doing it to spite Kappler, I think."

"Not I."

Dollmann flicked some ashes from his cigarette off the dashboard with a finicky sweep of his gloved fingers. "How do you know I will not turn you in afterwards?"

"I don't. It's likely that I don't care. We all go to bed with our conscience and must face it in the morning. I haven't been to Stalingrad to break down and worry about Kappler."

The armored cars went by, so dusty as to be soon indistinguishable from the hillside as they rumbled on. Dollmann lowered his eyes, rubbing his fingers to dust the cigarette ash off them. "What would Wolff think? I have pangs of remorse about him."

"It was Wolff who to please the Pope released Vassalli from jail, with all that he's a socialist and a Resistance leader. It seems to me we make our own laws as we go along."

Dollmann put the car in gear and started on the road again, and Bora squared an amused look at him. "I will not turn *you* in, no matter what."

They did not come back to Rome until the morning of Sunday, the 23rd, when Gaeta had already fallen to the American troops and the Aquino airfield had been taken – and lost – by the British. Bora skipped lunch to telephone *Ras* Merlo at the detached office of the National Confederation of Fascist Professional and Artistic Unions.

Merlo recognized him at once. A confused background noise might have meant he'd gone to close the door, and he followed his greeting with an anxious, "So, Major, have you caught Magda's killer?"

"I am trying to." And though Bora knew he should have added some form of deferential address, he didn't. "There's a delicate question I must ask, regarding the matter at hand. No, unfortunately I have no time to meet you in person; the telephone must do." As he spoke with the receiver cradled between neck and shoulder, Bora undid the brown paper package containing the objects Guidi had recovered from the garbage collector. Setting aside the can opener, he fingered the folded army blanket. "No doubt," he said, "you perceive the importance of your sincerity in answering me."

"Well, of course I do!" Merlo sounded uneasy at the other end of the line. "What is the question?"

"Did you give the following gift to Signorina Reiner..." Inside the blanket, Bora had found the pair of women's underwear. Unwilling to touch them, he stared at them as he gave a description. "Silk briefs, off-white, with a double row of gray lace..." but then he had to handle them to look if there was a label. "No label. They were made to measure, as it seems."

A dead silence followed on Merlo's part. Bora kept his eyes on the delicate cloth, meticulously stitched, and as extraneous to the severe top of his desk as he could think of. He had, in truth, a great desire to pass his fingers over the silk, to feel the finely knotted grain of the lace, but it was neither the time nor the place. He was about to insist on an answer when an irate question from Merlo came hissed in return. "Where did you find them? I demand to know."

Perhaps because he was aroused, Bora's irritation followed. "You're hardly in the position to demand anything, Secretary General. Did you buy this undergarment or not?"

Merlo snorted into the phone, impatiently. "And what if I did? It's not a crime to give a gift."

"That's true. Did you?"

"Yes. I had a set of them made for her after she'd chosen the silk on Via Tritone, at ISIA. This – *that* pair – she was wearing on the day she died. We... well, suffice it to say I know she was wearing them, Major. And this outrage had better lead somewhere."

Magda Reiner was not wearing them under her nightgown when she died. "It will," Bora said, and put the phone down.

A few streets away, Francesca told Signora Carmela she did not feel well.

Guidi was returning from buying the Sunday edition of the newspaper when to his surprise it was Pompilia who rushed out of the Maiulis' apartment. "Have you got your car out there, Inspector?"

"Yes, why?"

"You've got to take Signorina Lippi to the doctor, quick. Her sac has broken already!"

"What sac?" Guidi reached for the keys in his pocket.

"Never mind, just get the car to the door!"

"Where's Signora Carmela?"

"In the parlor, praying to St Jude, the goose. *Will you get the car?*"

Francesca was doubled on the edge of the bed in her room. Pompilia hovered in front of her, and all Guidi could really take in was that the bed was soaked with liquid, and the floor, too, but there was no blood. Francesca fought back help with one hand, and rocked back and forth without straightening up, letting out throaty cries in between the words she moaned: "I'm dying... I'm dying... I'm dying..."

"You're not dying." Pompilia raked back the hair from Francesca's face as she leaned forward. "You're just paying back the fun you had." And to Guidi, who stood, seemingly incapable of getting started. "Grab a quilt and help me take her outside."

It was difficult to sustain Francesca, who had to be all but dragged through the hallway and past the parlor where Signora

Carmela covered her ears with her hands. It was even more difficult to pass through the front door, so Guidi went first, sideways, then Francesca, knees bent, her great body rubbing against the stationary leaf, and finally Pompilia. The neighbors were strung along the ramp of stairs, and their presence only elicited a more clamorous display from Francesca. *She is doing it on purpose,* Guidi thought stolidly. *It's just like her. Or else she's really in pain.*

"How long do I have to take her there?"

"You'll get there all right – just don't stop on the way."

They placed Francesca on the front seat, and covered her with the quilt. She was sweaty and red-faced with strain, but the neighbor said, "As long as she moans like that you're fine. If she starts holding her breath in to push, you'd better step on it."

The Square of St John Lateran was divided into light and shadow by the great masses of the basilica and its annexes. Hopeful pigeons speckled the sky over it in search of food. Two German soldiers sat on a green wooden bench, young and lost in their oversized, faded field-gray uniforms. An old priest, looking like a black mushroom under his wide-brimmed hat, climbed the steps to the church. Enormous apostles perched in two rows as frozen suicides on the edge of the awesome facade, at the sides of a titanic cross-bearing Christ.

Bora had left his car at the corner of Via Emanuele Filiberto and walked into the blue shadow projected by the Lateran Palace to wait. He was efficiently not thinking of things at hand. He enjoyed the morning, the city. He felt a brimming love for the city today, a juvenile irresponsible romantic love for it. There was the narrow entrance to Via Tasso, cut through the block of buildings fencing the northern side of the square. An army truck was parked at the beginning of Via Merulana. The few soldiers in it were invisible to him. He walked out of the shade after checking his watch. His arm ached deeply in the sling, but differently from before – the ache was fresh and crude, bearable. And the holster of his gun was unlatched already.

Guidi welcomed the emptiness of the wartime Sunday streets as he raced through them, a white handkerchief secured between the glass and the upper edge of the window to mark an emergency. He'd studied the itinerary, just in case, and confidently drove toward Via Morgagni.

Francesca did not answer his attempts to distract her. Her face was contracted and she let those deep moans out, grabbing at her body. "Hurry up," was all she said to him in a husky voice. "It's killing me, hurry up —" and then she'd cry out and start moaning again.

They'd come halfway down Viale Liegi before Guidi saw the German roadblock ahead, barring the crossroads of Via Tagliamento and Viale della Regina. There was nothing to do but stop and frantically reach for his papers to show to the soldiers. But the soldiers did not want to see papers: they were here to keep all traffic from Viale della Regina. Guidi left the car and showed his police identification, which did not impress them. *Polizei*, it was all very well. But even the police couldn't go through,

"I have a woman in labor in the car!"

At his gesticulations the Germans grew wary and lowered the guns from their shoulders. One of them shoved Guidi toward the car and Guidi answered in kind. The muzzle of the gun found the pit of his stomach, and then an army lieutenant came from across the street to see what was going on. Guidi tried to explain. The lieutenant understood and spoke back in heavily accented Tyrol Italian. "These are all excuses – we've seen plenty of women pregnant with pillows. Go back, go back."

"Will you take a look at her?"

"No, go back."

"If you don't let me through she'll have the child right here!"

An acute cry from Francesca drew Guidi back to the car, and the lieutenant too, but warily. She cried out, "Ooooh, it's coming, it's coming..." and the German was less rigid, but still unconvinced. Then she did the unthinkable, lifting up her nightgown and exposing the dome of her belly. The German turned crimson.

"I'm sorry..." he stammered. "Get going, then, get going!" And to the soldiers, "*Nur heran!*" to make them get out of the way.

It was under the unlikely escort of a German army motorcycle that Guidi drove Francesca to the Raimondis' home. Things moved quickly upon their arrival. The doctor and his wife helped Francesca in, to a room already prepared for her. "Is it almost time?" Guidi anxiously asked.

"Not quite."

"But she said..."

"She said you had to get out of the jam with the Germans. She's definitely in labor, but it's going to be a few hours yet."

Guidi couldn't help thinking that Clara Lisi, in Verona, might be going through the same ordeal now, bearing her executed lover's child. Another criminal case, another disappointment in finding out what the truth was. How foolishly close he'd been to falling in love then, too. "Should I wait?" he asked Dr Raimondi.

"No reason for you to stay. She's in good hands. We'll call when the birth occurs."

Eugene Dollmann sprang to his feet when Bora walked into the lonely back room of the Birreria Albrecht on Via Crispi, so calm in appearance that the colonel thought him successful.

"The routine has been broken," Bora said. "The informer did not show up. I waited close to one hour and I had to move eventually. Are you sure Kappler is not on to this?"

"I'm sure of it. I can't understand what happened."

Bora would not take a seat. "I'm due at Soratte all day tomorrow," he said. "Unless there are unforeseen developments, I will be at St John's again next Sunday."

Letting him into her venerable parlor, Countess Ascanio said he looked pale. Bora was in fact starting to let go of the tension accumulated while waiting in the square, and felt numb. He undid his tunic without removing it. Seated in his favorite chair, he let the cats come to rub against his boots and seek his lap. On her invitation, he kept some of his clothes here, and now, without giving her time to ask questions, he said, "Please help me change, Donna Maria. I'm in haste, and will need help with my shirt and tie."

And he was in civilian clothes when Mrs Murphy saw him at the Santo Spirito infirmary at half past four on Sunday. He wondered whether she spent any time with her husband. She knew he'd asked to see Cardinal Borromeo, but still, she walked out of a doorway to ask, "Whom are you waiting for?" Bora stood up to answer her, and she listened, with that open way of looking at him, saying, "When was your arm worked on? You shouldn't be up running errands."

"It doesn't really matter, does it?"

"No, except that it fits your government-sponsored childish hero routine."

Bora would have grown irritable had anyone else spoken the words. "It has more to do with work than heroism," he grinned back.

"As you wish. The cardinal will be here momentarily – you'll have to wait."

"I'll wait."

Slim and secure in her springtime frock – how well Bora knew that beautiful women are secure with men who like them – Mrs Murphy leaned against the frame of the door. "We have Gaeta, have you heard?"

"I heard."

"How long before Rome's turn comes?"

His security, too, rose a little. "I wouldn't know. So far the speed from the shore has been about 0.3 miles a day. The Melfa River is at least four times the distance from Anzio. Could be a year and a half."

She smiled and drew back from the doorway. "You don't lie well in English."

"I lie even worse in German."

"I'll tell the cardinal you're here."

Guidi picked up the phone when the call came. It was some time after six o'clock, and he had spent the past seven hours in the parlor, which at last Signora Carmela had deserted to try the saints in her bedroom. "Francesca had the baby ten minutes ago," the delighted voice of Signora Raimondi came. "It's a beautiful boy, at least four kilos. She's fine, fine. Everything is fine. If you forgive me, I have to go help my husband. Good night."

9

22 MAY 1944

On Monday, the success of the French advance was a blow even for the hard-bitten Kesselring. No overt dismay was spoken as long as all the officers were together. In private Westphal said, "Bora, it's a disaster. We can't hold water with a sieve. As soon as you return to Rome, start implementing the first stages of detachment. Run to Frascati then – see for yourself what the latest news is. Cisterna especially, see what's happening there. They'll try to join in the Reclamation Land. Call from Frascati. After that, stay in Rome until I get back."

Bora landed at the beleaguered Centocelle strip after a rocky flight. There had been a storm on the way, and enemy fire had reached the flimsy single-engine machine, so that they had for the last ten minutes or so barely limped above green, fat fields, skimming trees and losing power.

"How soon do you need a ride back?" the pilot merrily asked him as he left the plane. "I'll need a while to patch this up."

"Not tonight, thank you," Bora was glad to answer.

Although the rain had not reached the city, a dark wall of clouds to the east created a citadel of shifting battlements. The scent of moisture rode the wind, and jasmine bushes in bloom at the edge of the field saturated it. A strong breeze blew by the time Bora arrived to headquarters to start the orderly motions of retreat again, four months from the day he had last done so.

It rained large star-shaped drops on the sidewalk two hours later. With a whipping sound they came down as though individually directed to earth, and once more the scent from visible and invisible gardens rode the air. Bora believed he had trained himself into near-perfect control, but the odor of the earth receiving the rain was strangely arousing to him. He wondered whether he had wasted his nights in Rome, now that he had to leave it and did not want to. He must quit thinking of Mrs Murphy, and find someone else. Find someone else. Whatever days were left – find someone else, and not go away from Rome without at least once making love as he needed to do, long and slow and hard and no apologies for it, no drinking, no worry of disease.

"Where to, Major?" the army driver asked, standing at attention.

"Frascati."

It was a formidable storm that hit Rome, charged with electricity, running bizarre St Elmo's fires on telephone wires and tall churches. A yellow sky fringed the steel-dark clouds where the storm had passed already. Whites gleamed phosphorescent, reds stood out bloody; colors were muted, soured. It seemed to Bora to be leaving behind a city smoldering under a biblical pall of smoke. When it started to rain he could no longer see behind or ahead, but from the side window the immediately engulfed ditches ran high, turbulent and muddy.

In his mind, Bora kept rehearsing yesterday's conversation with Borromeo, who'd agreed to meet him at the infirmary as a matter of privacy, or else – why was he thinking this? – to encourage him to see Mrs Murphy. As his second condition, he'd asked Borromeo precise questions of the "did you or did you not?" type, and the cardinal would not admit to anything directly. *But indirectly*, Bora thought, *I learned he's contrite about it – as contrite as Borromeo will get about anything, and I'll get him to give me details later on. Claims we should have known it was going on, that it is part of the Church's humanitarian mission, though helping those in need is apparently construed as including royalists as well as partisans, enemy soldiers and double-dealers. He admits sometimes "errors are made" – I never get used to it, how the clergy speaks of errors as though they arose on their own, through no one's fault. Worse, he admits to losing control of things, occasionally, to the extent of not knowing what happens after the succor is rendered. That could mean many things, including what I think happened. Christ, I only hope the Church will be as forthcoming when we need a helping hand.*

24 MAY 1944

At ten minutes before six on Wednesday morning, Bora stepped into his office and turned on the light. The telephone rang almost immediately. He lifted the receiver and listened to the report of heavy bombardment to the west. "When did it begin?"

The voice seemed to come from another world. "Five minutes ago."

Bora made a note of the hour – five forty-five a.m. – and asked other routine questions. "Call me back when it's over," he concluded. He had spoken to Westphal on another line when the call from the outskirts of Anzio came back: they had just stopped now. Bora looked at his watch. Forty-five minutes. Not unusual, yet he was uneasy. "How strong was it?"

"Very strong, a hell of fire and smoke. Can't see a thing past it."

Bora wandered with his eyes on the map. No matter what they told him, his attention kept returning to Cisterna, set in a hub of roads, with a spidery route to Valmontone across the saddle of the Lepini Mountains. Cisterna lay only eight miles from Frascati, guarding the lakes in the Alban Hills. Bora stood by his desk as he waited to speak to Westphal again, with concerns too vague to put in army terms. How could he say that in two weeks they'd be routed north of Rome because of what happened now? What he reported was factual and constrained, though the mood must have been conveyed, as Westphal paused before remarking, "Let us hope it's not as bad as that."

On Wednesday, too, Guidi moved out of the apartment on Via Paganini. Signora Carmela did nothing to detain him, and even helped him pack. "I'll tell Francesca you said goodbye."

"Yes, please. You should have enough groceries until she comes back tomorrow. Meanwhile I'll do what I can to obtain the professor's release. I saw him this morning and he told me he's doing fine – has made some friends in the work crew. He thinks he's found an ancient coin while digging on the riverbank. Don't worry about him."

Suitcases at his feet, Guidi decided to call Bora's office before leaving. From Pompilia's apartment there came music – 'Signorine Grandi Firme' – and the stomp of dancing feet. For a creature all nerves she seemed to be able to entertain two and three men at a time, mostly naive teenagers she managed to meet who knew how, and where. Their immature laughter came too, in raucous waves.

He had to hold the line several minutes before the major came to the receiver. Gruffly he identified himself. "Bora here." Then, to Guidi's direct answer, "Yes, I did," he replied, "Merlo admitted the underwear was his gift to the girl, and said she was wearing it on that day when they met for a quickie in the afternoon. Since she had none on when she died, it stands to reason that the killer threw the briefs into the trash with the rest of the objects found there."

From Bora's grumpiness, Guidi suspected how desperate the military situation was. But they had to make the best of the few times they could discuss matters, so he thought out loud. "Well, we assume the blanket and the other objects belong to the mysterious tenant, and that she had provided them to him. We assume he killed her, for whatever reason. Why would he go through the trouble of disposing of the stuff, when escaping must have been more urgent?"

Bora was quiet for a few seconds, during which shuffling of papers was heard. Then he said, "More urgent, maybe, but not necessarily more expedient. He *had* a safe hiding place, after all. In the confusion that followed the murder, there was probably enough time for him to lock her doors, take the keys, grab all the evidence he could from 7B, dispose of it in the bins down the street and escape. Your police reports state that it was eight o'clock before they arrived on the premises, and one more hour passed before the Security Service showed up."

Here was the moment, Guidi thought, to throw his own wrench in the works. "Except for Captain Sutor, who was reportedly still in the building when Magda died."

Bora's silence was complete this time. Even the papers were still at his end of the line.

"I am not going to ask how you know," he started again, with an undefinable edge in his voice, "as you must have your sources. But answer me this – do you think he killed her?"

"First answer *me* this, Major – would you prosecute if I said, 'Yes'?"

"I would."

Guidi had no doubt Bora would. "Well, the answer is that I don't know yet." He reported quickly on Sutor's movements, as observed by the militiaman Merlo had sent after him. "It was a German who was overheard arguing with Magda shortly before her death, Major, and a German blanket and German newspapers that were disposed of. And whoever was concealed by Magda may be the innocent bystander to another liaison, and to murder."

"Maybe. I am starting to develop my own credible theory, but don't have time to expound it now. If that's all for the moment, Inspector, I must go back to my work."

Guidi cleared his throat. "Actually, since we're on the line, let me ask you for the release of Professor Maiuli. Will you do what you can to —"

"I'll do nothing whatsoever."

"Consider the benefits of an act of forbearance at this time."

"This time? This time is like any other time. Don't annoy me, Guidi."

Guidi spat the words out. "Forgive me for insisting, but I doubt things are as usual."

Bora slammed the phone down.

Unwilling to accept the refusal, Guidi tried the number again. It was busy at first, and then someone answered in bad Italian that the major was out of the office. The inspector thought it an excuse, but Bora had left for Cisterna, now directly threatened by American troops.

From her balcony at Via Monserrato, Donna Maria watched the evolutions of airplanes directly overhead, swift fighters circling and plunging in combat with one another. When cockpits or wings caught the sunshine, a glint like lightning came from them, and then they were high and small and dark again. From his car Bora watched them too, on Route 7, barely past Ponte Lungo. Unlike Donna Maria, through his binoculars he knew it was German airplanes that went down in graceful extended arcs. They fell on the side of the green hillocks to the east, or toward the cream-colored scar of the limestone quarries Tivoli way.

By the following day, the Americans attacked Cisterna. The army rendezvous happened in the reclamation land near Latina, which meant there was little to be hoped for now. Westphal collapsed during a briefing and was hospitalized for exhaustion, so Bora took his place at Frascati, where he spent all day with Field Marshal Kesselring.

Francesca returned home on Thursday morning, alone, as if nothing had happened. Her figure was once more slim under her clothes, though breast and belly had not resumed their shape. She let herself in and went straight to Guidi's empty room. "Can I have it?" she called out to Signora Carmela. "I like the bed better."

"Where is the baby?"

"With my mother," she lied.

Signora Carmela seemed to shrink under her hump. "You're not bringing the baby here?"

"Not for now. If you don't mind, I'm going to move this saint's picture – it gives me the creeps."

"St Gennaro? The creeps? Why, he's the most powerful saint in the book! Easily offended, too. You shouldn't move him, it's bad luck."

Francesca had already reached for the frame and pulled it down. "Here." She presented it to Signora Carmela, "You can have him in your room, so you get the good luck, eh?"

"I already have St Lucia and St Carlo, and they don't get along with Gennaro."

"He'll have to find a home inside the wardrobe, then, because I don't want him."

"The Blessed Yellow Face isn't going to like it."

"He'll get used to it. What's there to eat?" She followed the resigned Signora Carmela to the kitchen. "Any phone calls for me while I was gone?"

"Only one, from your mother, about an hour ago. She wanted to know if you had a boy or a girl, and how you were doing."

Francesca grinned, with both hands gathering her hair behind her back. "She must have called right before I got there with the baby."

As for Guidi, he liked his place at Via Matilde di Canossa. He had a flat of three rooms, up two ramps of stairs from the street, in a neighborhood of Regime-built workers' tenements – *case popolari* – that until recently had been all open fields and isolated small villas. Across the Via Tiburtina, the wall of the Verano Cemetery curved, besieged from all sides by tenements and modern houses, some of them bearing the signs of nearly a year of air raids.

He had his own radio now. In the evening he listened to Radio Bari and the BBC broadcasts after hearing the national station of Radio Roma, in order to have a more likely view of the events. Cassino, Fondi, Terracina were in the hands of the Allies. Nothing remained of the Fascist airport at Guidonia. Explosions had continued all day, closer and more readily traceable to the lake region of the Alban Hills, where fighting was reported heavy.

He had no reason to wonder, but he did ask himself what Bora felt on these days made to sharpen a man's resistance if he's winning, and wear it down if he's losing. Likely arrogance and generosity battled in him, with his inability to let go. They had come close to being friends only because Bora had wanted it, tyrannically. Though it never entered his mind that the German's unexpected lack of insistence about the Hohmann-Fonseca case might be meant to protect him, Guidi grew melancholy at the notion of Bora's offer of friendship. Not being able to dislike him was even worse than despising him.

The telephone was on the next landing, one floor down. Thursday evening, Guidi called Signora Carmela and ended up speaking to Francesca. She told him the professor had just been released, and then asked for a ride to Piazza Ungheria in the morning. "Must go back to work, don't you know?"

By habit, though it was an inconvenience, Guidi said yes.

At two o'clock that night, he was awakened by a terrific explosion, enough to rock the house like an earthquake wave. Not an airplane bomb, unless just one had been dropped. The Germans were probably blowing up ammunition dumps and military facilities on their way out. He listened for more noises and when nothing came over the rumble of cannonade he had grown used to, he went back to sleep.

Bora had been the one to bring orders to destroy the dump. He stayed with the engineers to watch the results, and thought the rage of fire racked by repeated bursts was beautiful in the darkness. Surely more impressive than the blowing up of the two city airports hours earlier. No one would take off from them any more. Roads cut, bridges collapsed, railroads knotted in bundles and torn: his Stalingrad nausea was creeping up, but slowly. They were starting to kill this city, and he could not bear the thought of it, yet he carried the orders to do it in his briefcase.

Air raids hammered the outskirts of Rome on the morning of the 26th; the air was convulsed with them, and still here and there, in the gardens and open spaces, dynamite wrecked what the Germans could not carry along. Bora was in the hard-held town of Valmontone when Tivoli's dumps were hit by enemy bombers, and though the mountainous spur of Palestrina separated his position from the limestone ledge of Tivoli the noise was overpowering. Twenty miles across the valley, Cisterna had fallen to the enemy.

When he returned to Rome, there was an odd activity in the city. German diplomats and journalists had already cleared most hotels. Fascist officials with wives and lovers and suitcases filled with money had vanished overnight while the lesser ranks stayed, grim and black-shirted, to take what came. Army trucks drove north. Tanks slowly ground north. Mounted artillery guns wheeled north. Columns of wearily marching men streamed as gray ribbons to the north, flanked by officers ghostly with dust and dry blood. The people in the streets – refugees, bombed-out families, partisans, priests, false priests, whores – were angry. The whores practiced English in paper-bound, dog-eared booklets. "*Cum on, Johnnee. Johnnee, want to mek lov? I gotta seester, Johnnee, litta seester.*"

His office was all but empty. He stepped into it to take down the watercolors of Rome from the walls. He took his diary from the safe and placed all in his briefcase. From it, he took out a P38 – not his own, another army pistol he'd carried around since Russia, taken from a Soviet prisoner who no doubt had taken it from a German soldier. He'd tried it out at Valmontone, and now laboriously cleaned it, as it would come in handy before he'd dispose of it. Although his appointment with Treib was not for two days yet, he had already removed the sling and was using his left arm. It didn't hurt much.

Having left the Flora, he ordered his driver to take him to the center of town. On the way he did not look at the lines of dark-faced civilians, or at the army vehicles slowly negotiating the narrow streets in a direction opposite from his. At the Spanish Steps he got down to buy flowers from a gray-haired vendor squatting by a wealth of fragrant bouquets. Leaving his car at the foot of the Capitol Hill, with an armful of lilac and mimosa he climbed the long steps to the square, where the cobblestone, weblike corolla of the pavement surrounded the empty pedestal of Marcus Aurelius' monument.

Inside the locked museum, Bora knew full well the tense Wolf bared her teeth from above the sandbags, as if victorious over what they meant. Ears erect, she watched among the frescoes that had struck him so deeply when he had first returned to Rome. They told the story of the defense of the Capitol from barbarian invasion, and much as Bora had wanted to see himself on the side of the Romans, it was all too clear that he belonged to the *other* side.

Around the pedestal, senseless without its imperial rider and casting a long shadow, he walked to the central double ramp of stairs of the Capitol itself. There within her niche, flanked by recumbent statues of hoary river gods, the statue of Rome as Minerva sat enthroned above and behind the empty stone basin of the river's fountain. Clad in porphyry, armed, holding the globe of the world, as the ancient Latin verse said, in her extended left hand. *Roma caput mundi.* Bora felt a renewed envy of the culture she represented. And shame for his own, regret and guilt. Carefully, he laid the flowers on the edge of the fountain, stood at attention to salute, and left.

In his office, Eugene Dollmann was like an island of spruce indifference in the turmoil. He was supervising the packing of several sealed bottles of a very dark, nearly black wine. *Il Messaggero*'s pages were torn and crumpled by the orderly to separate the bottles during shipping. "That way I'll also catch up with the news," he joked. "Best-kept secret in the region, this Cesanese wine – thick and full and mild, but it does trick you – a great wine for merriment. Stains as deep as elderberry. And say, Bora, I'm shopping around for a gift to give General Wolff. Something artistic but not heavy. What do you suggest?"

Bora was grateful for that lightness in the face of frenzy. "If he likes oils, a Coleman is a good choice. If he'd rather watercolors, I'd go with Roesler Franz."

"Will you come with me to Via del Babuino tomorrow? I was thinking of Perera or one of the other shops."

"Save time, Colonel." Bora opened his briefcase. "Here are my watercolors by Franz – give them to the general."

"Are you sure you want to part with them?"

"Yes. I've spoken to the field marshal, and I'm going back to field duty as soon as we leave the city. I won't need Roesler Franz where I go."

"Did you get regiment command?"

Bora nodded. "I meet the men at Lake Bolsena."

Having packed the wine, the orderly left the room. "What about Sunday?" Dollmann earnestly asked.

"I'll carry on as planned."

"Do you want me there?"

"It's not necessary. I confronted all the anxiety I'll ever confront, and worked it out to the details. From Aristotle's *Ethics* to Marcus Aurelius' *Meditations*, in a big circle I came back to my hometown Leibniz and his simple advice, 'It must be done: it will be done.' The point I had most trouble with was not owning to it if it comes to that – I'm a poor liar."

Dollmann looked mildly alarmed. "You have no choice. Think of it – you'd ruin the operation. Westphal would be embarrassed, myself probably implicated, your family disgraced, let alone what would happen to you."

"Well, I've gone through all that, and I'm fine."

*

As for Donna Maria, she was not deceived by self-control. She kept wary eyes on him that evening, afraid by what he chose not to tell her. "Martin, we've known one another twenty-three years, and you've been to me the son I never had – please don't frighten me. What is it you'll do tomorrow?"

Bora shook his head, but more to forbid himself to speak than to refuse her. "I cannot tell you, Donna Maria. If all goes well I'll see you tomorrow night."

Her shoulders sank. "You frighten me. This has nothing to do with the war, does it?"

"Everything has to do with it. I can't get away from it."

"You can stay here and not do it."

"I can't. Please go to Mass for me in the morning."

Bora stayed at her house until very late. And little by little, absent-mindedly at first, he began telling her about Russia, about his brother's death, about Stalingrad. The terrible stories found a way out of him like the telling of a dream, and because the crimes were not his, he could not free himself by speaking of them, a witness chained to the sight of them forever.

Oh, what he had seen, what he had seen and carried inside these years, the gaping long holes of the East with victims ready to fall in them, the burned-out churches and villages where as from a defiling incestuous meal the stench rose of seared human flesh. Blue flies clustering over dead bodies, over countless dead bodies that lay tainting the spring and infecting the summer air. Only wintertime starkly sealed the corpses in their own frozen blood, as in crackling cloaks of eternity. How he had without guilt, yet guilt-ridden, followed in the wake of the SS through *Judenfrei* regions where for weeks blood had rotted in the swollen cadavers. One would turn them over and the nauseating odor of rotted blood would follow the jellied black ooze from mouths and noses, which the first time staggered him nearly to unconsciousness.

He spoke to her unrelieved by the ordeal, incapable of

damming the words until all was said. And he wouldn't allow her to touch him afterwards, and would not touch her.

"Go to Mass for me tomorrow morning, Donna Maria."

It was past one o'clock when he returned to the hotel. He began to undress, but did not go to bed. He felt the warmth of the season on his torso, under his armpits, a gentle moisture such as from embracing someone closely, and God knows he was alone. Along with the loneliness before one's death, he thought, there's only the loneliness of one about to kill.

Seated on the bed of the impersonal rented room, he removed the barrel from his Russia pistol and secured it to his own side arm. Disassembling the gun with one hand was a chore, but he had practiced it often enough to be proficient at it, pieces coming apart and then together again. He timed the interval between extracting the P38 from the holster and aiming it, squeezing the trigger and putting it away. Replacing the clip, too, which he had to do holding the weapon against his chest with his left wrist. He did this for nearly an hour. And though he had been target shooting at least once a week since coming to Rome, still he held the empty gun at eye level and exercised the steadiness of his arm. Were the telephone to ring now, he'd be wrenched out of concentration like a limb torn from a tree. His mind clicked not differently from the hours spent in the car after his wife left him, a purely mechanical function of nerve centers. One thought to the next, like an electric clock linking seconds into minutes with a red thin hand. He removed the scapular medal from around his neck and put it away. Over the flat of his briefcase he wrote two letters, sealed them and placed them in the inner pocket of the tunic he would wear in the morning.

The gifts to the dignity of man are desperate and expensive beyond reckoning.

On Sunday morning, Treib glanced at the envelopes on his desk, looked up at Bora and down again. He could see one of them was addressed to General Westphal, and the other to Erwin Franz and Nina Bora von Sickingen, presumably his parents. A well-used, cloth-covered, strongly bound diary followed. "What is it? Are you going back to the Russian front?" And because Bora – who came from tossing his Russia pistol into the Aniene from Ponte Salario – amicably shook his head, Treib continued, "I didn't think so. How long do you want me to hang on to these?"

"Until we move out of Rome. The diary I'll come for tomorrow."

"And if you don't?"

"My parents can have it, then."

It was all they said about it. Treib placed the objects in his drawer and locked it.

In his apartment at Via Matilde di Canossa, Guidi looked forward to the day off. At noon he'd go for a bite, take a walk perhaps and return home to lounge. He planned to catch up on reading and correspondence, waiting like everybody else for the Americans to come. Things were changing, imperceptibly. Though he'd neither spoken directly, nor seen Caruso since their scene in March, rumors were that the head of police was apprehensive about a German retreat. He'd likely leave with them, though the Germans despised him and some – like Bora – made their antipathy obvious and obnoxious.

Owing to damage to the aqueducts, there was no water in the apartment, but Guidi didn't need to shave today, or cook for himself; he had enough in a pail to flush the toilet and brush his teeth. Stretched on his bed, he unfolded a newspaper and began to read.

*

At that time Bora was driving away from Piazza Vescovio, bound for St John Lateran's.

From his room by the Spanish Steps, Eugene Dollmann glanced at the elaborate column sustaining a statue of the Immaculate Conception, ninety years old this year. Like a vase surmounted by a crown and a cross, the strange baroque bell tower of St Andrew-in-the-Groves rose above the roofs down the way. He was nervous for having to trust someone else to achieve an end, and genuinely concerned for Bora. Love of intrigue had as much to do with all this as his sense of justice. In the past two weeks he had more than once been tempted to cancel the plan, but once he'd agreed within his own mind to act, Bora never went back on his decision. To those he had merely added external confirmation. So Dollmann stayed in his room, pacing the floor for a while and returning to the window, where fat spring clouds sailed, laden ships behind the serpent-conquering Madonna.

Bora passed St Mary Major, at the other end of Via Merulana from the Lateran.

Donna Maria fed her cats, with an ear to the cannonade awakening the porcelains on the shelves. Martin must have stopped by very early this morning to leave a bouquet of flowers on her doorstep; no note was with them. The maid walked in to ask, "Is the major coming to dinner tonight?"

Donna Maria distractedly petted her oldest cat, a mangy black male with a white spot on his neck like a Roman collar, familiarly known as Monsignore. "I hope so," she said. "I hope he comes."

Bora entered the square from Via Merulana and parked his car.

The day was a clear May Sunday of blue shadows; deep and less deep they drew themselves inside the arches of the Pope's loggia and under buildings, alongside the obelisk in the square behind the basilica. Young priests flagged their skirts in and out of the Lateran Palace. Across from it stood the old

Hospital of St John, at the entrance of which Bora parked his car facing Via San Giovanni.

The great Renaissance facades hemmed the wide, irregular space in bricks and stone, ornate moldings. It was on this piazza that for a thousand years the popes had looked from their apartments, jubilees had been declared, rebels and assassins executed. Bora left the ignition key in the lock and got out of the car.

He scanned the population of the square. Two soldiers sat on the railing around the red granite obelisk brought from Thebes centuries before. Across the pavement a woman pushed a baby carriage in the direction of the baptistry, toward Via Amba Aradam. Back to the square, a young private was taking photos of the ten-arched loggia, while a group of priests with leather portfolios flitted around the side of the Lateran and entered it. It all reminded him of the early German days in Rome, when there was time for tourism and taking snapshots.

As Bora stood by his car, an old couple left the hospital behind him – a gray-faced man accompanied by his wife, both very slowly bound to catch the tramway or bus at the other side of the palace, by the green facing the basilica. Next to his car there was an ambulance with no one in it.

At the entrance of Via Tasso, two blocks away from where Bora was, two SS men stood guard at the corner. They were now following with their eyes a flock of gaily dressed young women near the gate of the Scala Santa.

Bora glanced at the watch on his right wrist. It indicated fifteen minutes to eleven. At eleven once a month the informer had regularly come to rendezvous with a Gestapo plain-clothes man to exchange the list for money. He could not see the plain-clothes man, who was perhaps standing back in Via Tasso or its parallel, Via Boiardo.

Bora felt the benign warmth of the sun on his shoulders. He had thought things over very carefully, and at this point everything had been weighed in his mind. All doubts on one side, all certainties on the other, and by far certainties outweighed doubts. The only real question was from which of the seven streets leading to the square the informer would arrive – his ability to act depended on this. An arrival from the Scala Santa would make the shooting impossible under the eyes of the SS. Worse if the meeting happened near Via Boiardo. He was hoping the informer would approach from Via Merulana or Via San Giovanni, preferably the latter.

Meanwhile he took minute note of everything: smells, colors, sounds, dimensions. It was as if his eye were a precise mechanical or camera eye, lying about nothing yet feeling nothing either. The sky, with swallows. The echoes of the nearing front. A window among the many of the Lateran Palace was open. The church loomed, a gigantic wreck landed from a planet of autocratic antiquity.

The young soldier with the camera climbed the steps of the loggia and entered the shade to take a photo of the square. The woman pushing the baby carriage had nearly reached the corner of the baptistry, but stopped to pick up the child and pacify it. Bora waited for eleven o'clock. The calm in him had risen to brimming point. Could one be too calm? Such security, such security.

The SS lit cigarettes and sat on the hood of their car. From the open green before the basilica two Luftwaffe men were approaching, recognizable in their smoky gray uniforms. Resting every five steps, the elderly couple passed before the obelisk. At ten to eleven, a warning of anxiety tried to rise in him like a discordant note – the informer would not come, or would escape him. He had waited uselessly last Sunday. Bora took a deep breath and held it to steady himself. The soldiers by the obelisk left their perch for the stairs of the loggia. The Luftwaffe men were a sergeant and a private – they too had cameras. The private's head was bandaged under the field cap.

Sunday was good, actually. Neither Kappler nor Sutor would be at Via Tasso. Likely the officer on duty would not know him.

A bus stopped at the mouth of Via Amba Aradam, but no one alighted from it. It started again and crossed the square, turning wide around the obelisk. The old woman waved at it. The bus did not stop and continued down toward the green, past the powerful flank of the palace. The Air Force private took a snapshot of the sergeant posing before the obelisk.

Five to eleven. Bora's heart took in a long draught of blood. The informer was coming from Via San Giovanni. He recognized the features from the photo Dollmann had showed him, and forgot everything else – SS, plain-clothes man, witnesses. Unemotionally he watched from his place by the car, hand crossing before his body to unlatch the holster. He would let his target walk into the square and past Via Merulana, but not reach Via Boiardo.

The young soldier kept taking photos. The woman with the carriage had turned the corner and soon would be gone down Via Amba Aradam. It was just past five before eleven. The SS chatted with each other.

The informer's steps were neither rushed nor slow, as if the way were familiar and followed by rote, with a careless attitude of business at hand. The thought suddenly came to Bora that it was like the unobtrusive and deadly entrance of a virus into the system, coming in with the unspoken power to kill. Soon the target would be within range. Thirty-five steps away, thirty-four, thirty-three. Thirty. Twenty-five.

Bora took the Walther out of the holster and gripped it firmly. The Luftwaffe men struck a conversation with the soldier carrying a camera. A priest strolled out of the palace, nose in a newspaper.

Bora stretched his arm until eye and gunsight came in line, and the informer's head in it. There were no thoughts in his mind at this point. He fired one shot.

The target fell, suddenly crumpled like an animal that is given a killing blow. Bora replaced the Walther in its sheath, latched it. It took him four seconds. People turned, wondering what had happened and whether the report had come from the square at all. The SS had not yet taken notice. Bora walked toward the body, one step after the other on the sun-soft asphalt. It took ten seconds to cover twenty steps. The young soldier had let the camera dangle around his neck from its strap.

Others began to drift in this direction, none yet too close. The Luftwaffe sergeant took his pistol out. Bora looked down. The woman had been hit in the temple, and was dead. Her eyes were open wide. Blood snaked quickly down to her ear, her neck, the white-trimmed blue dress until it reached the pavement. Bora leaned to take a piece of paper from her hand, and already there was a noise from the mouth of Via Tasso, where the SS had been alerted by the gunshot. Bora placed the paper in his left cuff but did not move. After sending his companion for help, one of the SS was running in his direction.

Less than twenty seconds had passed from the shooting. From Via Boiardo the plain-clothes man rushed to where Bora stood. Ignoring him, he searched the body: hands, pockets, straw bag, bra, garters.

Coldly Bora asked, "*La conosce?*" playing into his pretense of civilian identity.

The Gestapo lifted a congested face to him. "Have you seen anybody shoot?"

Bora merely repeated the question in German. "Do you know her?" and whatever retort the man had in mind, he recognized the crimson stripes on Bora's breeches, and kept it to himself.

The SS were back in force, corralling people to the center of the Piazza. The young lieutenant who had argued with Bora at the funeral led them. Shouting in their coarse way they spread to guard the entrances to the square.

Bora stood with immense self-control. The SS had begun ordering all soldiers present to take their guns out, and felt the barrels for temperature, smelled them for exploded powder. Bora watched them. The ranting young lieutenant tramped up to him. "What about your gun? Get your gun out, Bora!"

"I'll do nothing of the kind."

"*Get your gun out!*"

Bora set his face hard. "Don't you come near," he spelled out, and there was such threat in his voice that the young lieutenant was for a moment cowed and then tried to draw closer.

Dollmann's voice came like cool water from behind. "It will not be necessary, Lieutenant. The major was with me."

Bora turned. The colonel was a step away, white-faced and elegant and calm. Wherever he had come from, soon they were side by side.

"But, Colonel," the lieutenant protested, "I must —"

"Are you putting my word in doubt? Go check the houses around. We may still be in the gunsight of a killer."

The words galvanized the lieutenant into commanding his soldiers to scatter into the surrounding blocks. Dollmann looked at Bora, who breathed slowly, very deeply. "Get rid of the list. You can give it to me."

Bora did not glance his way, but relaxed visibly. Two soldiers were lifting the body of the woman, and only blood stayed in her place. A physician had emerged from the hospital, but the SS would not let him past them to examine her. People were starting to flock around the spot. The young soldier took a photo of the men removing the body, and an SS snatched the camera from him and opened it to expose the film, which made Dollmann smile.

"They stay stupid, don't they."

Bora finally looked over. "I'm taking the list to the Vatican, Colonel. Thank you."

"No one leaves the square!"

The lieutenant was having his vendetta. All present, including Dollmann and Bora, had to wait until Sutor arrived, since Kappler was with a woman friend somewhere and couldn't be traced. Sutor didn't drive until eleven-twenty, by which time Dollmann played an irate scene with him.

"I had an appointment with the vice consul ten minutes ago,

and because of this idiocy I am made to appear tardy, Sutor! I hope you have a better reason than the death of some Italian slut to keep me here!"

"*Herr Standartenführer*, the embassy is just a block away – I see no reason for you to grow so irate. The men did as they were ordered."

"You haven't heard the last of it, be sure."

Sutor was angry. He scented trickery. Turning in a rage to Bora, he demanded, "And you, Major? What were you doing here?"

"I was actually coming to discuss Antonio Rau's interrogation with you."

"On Sunday?"

"How am I supposed to know you wouldn't be there? I often work on Sunday."

Sutor boiled inside. For a crazy second he was tempted to seize both men and take Bora in, but was afraid of what Wolff or Kesselring might do. Too furious to speak, he choked in gall as he let both of them go.

Dollmann traveled in Bora's car past Via Tasso to the nearby Villa Wolkonsky, where he alighted. Bora turned left, and by way of Via Manzoni crossed Rome in a zigzag to the Tiber bank near Ponte Vittorio, where he stopped to toss the clip and used barrel in the water. Back in the car he replaced the original barrel on his P38, gave it a good general cleaning and placed a fresh clip in it.

The appointment was at the Vatican Museum, where Borromeo was nowhere to be found. It was the Secretary of State, Cardinal Montini, who received the list, and glanced at it with a pained expression on his hawk-like face. With his back to the window of the small room, Bora observed him silently read the names of Jews sheltered by religious institutions and of Jews living under assumed identities, with addresses and hiding places. He said, "Your Eminence, I wish to confess the killing of the woman who carried the list."

"I'll send in a priest." Montini began to leave the room.

Bora prevented him by stepping to the door. "I wish for you to hear it."

Newspaper folded under his arm, Guidi walked down the street from his apartment to a nameless trattoria, popular with railway employees and government workers. He sat just inside the doorway, where the warmth of the sidewalk drifted in, a pleasant rush now and then to ruffle the hem of the tablecloth. On the opposite sidewalk, in front of one of the many soup kitchens organized by the Vatican, a barely moving queue of refugees and idlers wormed to it from around the block. The doors had just opened at twelve.

The waiter had gotten to know him in the past two days. "Inspector," he winked as he brought a small carafe of wine, "the Americans are four days out."

"Is that a fact."

A motion of the head to the back room might equally indicate a radio hidden in it or someone come from the Alban Hills with the intelligence. "They saw them."

Guidi did not comment. He hoped it were true, for the city's sake. For the Maiulis' sake. For the sake of Francesca and those like her. He was halfway through a dish of pasta when the waiter tapped his shoulder discreetly, to make him look out of the door. German army trucks went by, their tarpaulins lowered in the back, either empty or carrying loads they did not want the Romans to see. The people in the soup line lifted hateful faces but gave no voice to their exasperation. A column of ambulances followed, battered, mud-caked, windows spattered gray. Blood dripped from them as from butcher carts. Guidi remembered the meat truck he had sat in on his way to the caves, and how it smelled of animal death in the nostrils of those about to be killed.

"See what I mean?" the waiter insisted. But when a German staff car stopped by and a girl-faced junior officer came to ask for a drink, he obligingly produced a pitcher of water and a glass. Guidi watched through half-closed lids from his chair, noticing how the inside of the soldier's mouth seemed pink and raw in the chalky mask of his face.

Afterwards the waiter, towel in the crook of his arm, leaned with a smirk against the door frame as the staff car started again and continued north. "I keep a gallon of water for the Germans, I do – special for them. In a gallon I put a glass of piss. Not enough for them to notice, but I do get a laugh when I see 'em drink it. They're too bushed to notice. And if they say anything, I tell 'em Rome is famous for its stink water, that the popes paid a fortune to drink it and pass stones." A sudden doubt went through him. "Inspector, do you think a glass of piss is enough to hurt 'em?"

"Probably not."

In his lonely office, Bora took a sip of water and put the glass down. He had difficulty swallowing, as if his throat were somehow locked, stopped, and liquids struggled going down as breath coming up. The undoing of tension was always painful in excess of tension itself. He had been tense until all fibers in his body hung wired for action. And what shamed him most, what seemed unbearable at this hour was how he had been tempted to shoot the SS lieutenant who insisted to see his weapon. That was the reason for carrying an extra clip – not to conceal use of his gun, but to kill other Germans if it came to it. The admission of it brought a wave of blood to his face. It seemed to crest in him as though blood could crest in a human body, veins being but channels for it to tide occasionally in passion or regret.

All parts of him were undoing tension gradually and with pain. Thighs, upper arms, the muscle bands on his chest, the shield of his stomach. To the acute soreness of his left arm he did not even pay attention. He could not confront the possibility of chronic pain resuming in it. He moved the glass of water away from himself, wishing for numbness; but anxiety mounted within, for blood to carry and make him blush and grow pale. Like debris all aches and pains, losses, departures, estrangements, defeats rode the wave of his blood. The faces of death witnessed and caused, and yet to witness and cause: the deaths ahead, including his own.

He was grateful to have orders to travel to Valmontone, north of which the sole delivery route for the nearly encircled 10th Army clawed the mountainside.

"The world's currency is ingratitude." In their parlor, Professor Maiuli shared with his wife a rare moment of bitterness. "My dear, I had taught Antonio Rau nearly up to the fourth declension, wherein I planned to include the five exceptions of *assentior, experior, metior, ordior* and *orior*. I had finally driven into him the inchoative reflective verbs – except for two of them – and what did he do but betray our trust? I could forgive him for contributing to my arrest, but he nearly caused Francesca's, who is a strange girl but undeserving of political suspicion."

Signora Carmela adjusted a crocheted doily behind his head. "They say he died."

"Do they now?"

"Francesca heard it some place."

"And where is she today? I thought she'd be back for lunch."

"I thought so, too. I'm keeping a dish warm for her." Signora Carmela let go of a moaning sigh. "Things aren't the same without Inspector Guidi, who was the only dependable tenant. He never did say why he was leaving, except that it had nothing to do with our treatment of him."

"Well, let's hope she stays at least."

Guidi paid the bill, then returned to the table to finish a half glass of wine. Meanwhile, *Osservatore Romano* at hand, a priest entered in a black flutter. The waiter obviously knew him well. "Don Vincenzo, good day. The usual?"

"The usual."

Guidi gulped the wine. As he stepped out of the trattoria he overheard him tell the waiter in a low voice that the Germans had just killed a woman in St John's Square.

"So what's new, Don Vincenzo?" The waiter philosophically took the report.

28 MAY 1944, AFTERNOON

The shelling at Valmontone was deafening. Some of the hits came across the plain from the American positions at Artena, on its limestone rib balanced between deep waterless ravines, only three miles from the Valmontone train station.

Bora covered his right ear to capture, mostly by lip reading, what the 65th Division officers were telling him. High above them the Collegiate Church, exposed as a sprout in the heart of the bean-shaped town, braved shells and puffs of smoke. Down here rubble of bomb-shattered houses created some shelter, but pieces fell from it, tiles, beams, entire inner walls, some of them seemingly held up only by wallpaper.

Only after several failed attempts and interruptions was Bora able to get the line with Kesselring, who was at Frascati. The only receptacle the Signal Corps had found to set up the telephone in was a latrine in the back of a grocery store, now used to house the wounded and the dead. Bora yelled in the telephone, standing before a urinal brimming with stale, bloody waste. There was no water in the pipes, and with good reason, since there were no pipes left outside the room. Artillery fire battered some place nearby, so close that the inner wall of the latrine shook and lost sheets of plaster, baring the bricks. While Bora talked a captain came in and, careful not to step into the yellow pool on the tiles, undid his fly to relieve himself. Bora turned halfway from him, still shouting into the mouthpiece. When he finally walked back into the store, paratroopers from the 29th Armored Grenadiers, blanched with agony and blood loss, were being hauled in on improvised stretchers, some of them simple unhinged doors.

The nearly thirty miles back to Rome were not advisably traveled until after darkness set in. So Bora waited for the explosions to bloom in the darkness. Long and bright were the intervals of magnesium flares. Shells traced through the night like fantastic meteors, fireworks, Roman candles, like a fearsome hell mouth opened south and west to expose the devilry below. He boarded his car at nine o'clock. The two miles to nearby Labico would be the most dangerous, with all that the hills hugged it tight to form a deep gap. It entered his mind as he started off that the SS might be waiting for him in Rome.

It took him an hour to come in sight of Porta Maggiore, the aqueduct marble gate into which Highway 6 entered the city. Rome seemed abandoned. As a revenant, the events of the morning flowed in from the streets he traveled: worse, he felt compelled to go through St John's Square, though it lay outside his route. He drove slowly across it, was twice stopped by German patrols on his way into and out of it. Someone had placed a sprig of flowers where the woman had fallen.

Guidi had no curiosity about the identity of the woman shot by the Germans until later on Sunday evening, when he called his office and inquired. They had no information on her, other than it seemed to be a freak accident. There was no description, and it was unclear who had fired the shot, or why.

At Via Paganini Signora Carmela heated the dish she had kept for Francesca and served it to her husband. "She'll have to be satisfied with a sandwich if she comes now," was her comment. "I try to take care of her but she's a hard one to care for." She lovingly watched the professor bite into the supper. "Eat, eat – you need to regain your strength after all you've been through."

*

Bora was used to the heterogeneous population of the hotel, which he mindlessly surveyed upon entering the sunken lobby. There were always the same people at the bar, or lounging on easy chairs waiting to go upstairs. Barely disguised prostitution went on, and all pretenses of seemliness meant nothing once one heard what was being said between the officers and the women.

He was about to cross the lobby to start up the stairs when he recognized Mrs Murphy waiting in a small armchair with a controlled face of anxiety, hands in her lap. Her being here threw him entirely. He hoped for a moment, for a moment… When she caught sight of him and came to her feet, he joined her at once. "Mrs Murphy, has anything happened?"

She seemed grateful he chose not to misunderstand her reason for being here.

"Major, I have a favor to ask. I went to your command hours ago, but was told by the orderly you were not expected any more tonight, and then I remembered how Cardinal Borromeo mentioned you stay here."

Yes? Why would he? Why would he tell her?

"This is terribly awkward, really. It's wrong for me to be here."

"No, no, please. Tell me, how may I be of assistance?"

She tried to keep some hold on her anxiety, her lovely face only half-raised to him. "You see, I'm not even sure I can get out now. I've been here two hours. It's after curfew. It'd be terrible if I couldn't…"

Her distress made him feel a surge of tenderness, an eager need to protect her and please her. "Don't worry, I'll escort you out. It's best if we don't meet here, in any case."

By the sidewalk outside were Bora's and Mrs Murphy's cars. "We could go somewhere else." Bora hesitated. "I'm not sure where. I wasn't expecting…"

"It will not take long."

"Let's go to my office."

Once they arrived at his office, her composure rebuilt itself, while Bora went through an insecure mental list of his likely needing to shave, shine his boots, et cetera.

"I hope you understand this visit must remain private, Major. I do not wish for His Holiness to hear that I have come to plead with someone in your position. As a lay person, it is altogether my initiative."

Bora couldn't help asking, "Does your husband know you're here?"

"I wish to embarrass him even less."

Now that she had removed her lacy gloves, her hands bloomed like lilies from the cuffs of her jacket. Bora looked at her hands, at the wedding ring on her finger. Self-consciously with his thumb he circled the useless gold band on his own right hand. "I understand."

"I was hoping to meet you in person because we had occasion to speak in days past."

Bora invited her to sit. She did, and he took his place behind the desk. He'd have liked for her to see the office with the watercolors of Rome on the walls, less naked than it was. The half-filled glass of water on his desk reminded him of the anguish of a few hours ago. The shot fired this morning had not yet died in his ears – not even the wild shelling at Valmontone had covered it. But he was calm. He was in control. Only her scrutiny weakened him. He moved the glass further away from himself.

Mrs Murphy kept thoughtful eyes on him. Hatless, her head was perfectly wrought against the white walls, young and graceful, her consciousness of his observation of her only revealed by the firmness of her voice. "I recall your mention of it, Major Bora, and offer you a chance to prove how much you care for children. There is – you must know – an American Red Cross shipment of powdered milk which your army halted and has been holding in a warehouse for three weeks. You don't need it, or don't need it as much as the Roman children do. I have come to ask that you release the shipment to the Vatican, which can best distribute it."

Bora didn't know of any such shipment. He glanced at her, taking a notebook out of his drawer. "Is that what you do, work with children?"

"And with mothers. I volunteer in the obstetrical ward." She paused, as if briefly forgetting the business at hand. "This morning I helped coach my first birth."

He felt a man's clumsiness at her words. "It must be – of course I know nothing about it – but it must be hard. For the mother, and for the person who assists her."

"I think it's beautiful."

Bora looked away with sudden shyness. He felt vulnerable, because she could read through him and was silently doing it even now. He had no desire to escape: he only wished she'd read him truly. If only he could say to her… Her scrubbed, delicate but healthy face threw him into a turmoil of confusion. With aimless resentment, he felt his married life had been a waste. "Why are you staring at me?" he said in the end, grieved by his mutilation enough without her calm study of him from where she sat.

"I'm waiting for you to make up your mind. I wish to know if you will help me or not."

"You ought to know that you honor me by asking."

She dodged his words. "I'm afraid I'm just being pragmatic. Your emotions are rather transparent, Major."

"Not to me."

"Well, I am not mercenary, but must act as I think right for those under my care." She sat upright, her shoulders straight under the light blue cloth of the jacket, as unwilling to show weakness as he was. "I trust you will not exact prices I can't pay."

"My emotions are not very transparent if you think I will."

"I don't think you will. I think you *might*."

Bora sighed. He felt weary, drained of combativeness. His mind was clear, but his feelings ran muddled. He ached emotionally. He simply wanted her to like him. "I will do what I can."

"What does it mean?"

"I will obtain the powdered milk for you."

"When?"

"Tomorrow."

"Do you have the authority?"

"I have the authority." He drew back on the chair and faced her intensely, not as one who wants to intimidate. Rather, as one who lets the sight hurt *him*, deliberately. And he knew she could see the longing in him, a physical and intellectual hunger for his counterpart, and stern unwillingness to ask for it.

Mrs Murphy held his stare. He was what women call handsome, even striking: that he was honorable troubled her, because she still did not like him. But she felt she understood him. This, she did not show. What she let transpire was a hint of vexed concern, sharp like a blade kept half-hidden but capable of cutting. "Thank you. What do you ask in exchange?"

"Nothing."

"Nothing?"

"Here." He handed her a paper he had been scribbling on. "This is a safe-conduct for you to drive home."

When she rose from the chair, the gloves she'd placed on her lap slipped to the floor from it, like lacy birds. Falling like a condescending, unthinking part of her – the glimpse made him ache as if he had seen an intimate part of her revealed and untouchable. Before he could reach for them she'd rescued them at her feet and the image was gone. Across the surface of the desk, Mrs Murphy extended her hand to him and he did not take it, but lowered his head in a stolid, repressed military salute. She left the room.

He sat at his desk for some time after her departure. Not to relax, because the opposite was happening. He felt a dangerous need to give in. Worse, a lowered threshold of tolerance, reached and passed already. He regretted letting her go without at least exacting from her the toll of accepting his reasons. Couldn't she tell? And if she could tell, why did she not say, "I cannot, but I understand"?

Holding the line was no longer enough. He had run on borrowed time and borrowed calm for a full year, putting up a nearly infrangible front of self-control and even cheerfulness, and he saw now that not having taken time to confront crises only multiplied their weight. For the past year he had functioned at an increasing pace but only by inertia, as though speed were gained down the emotional incline he was traveling. Tonight he could no longer hold the line. Her coming had somehow torn resolve from him. The fabric inside was beginning to rend, fraying the weave. What was wrong with him? He could not think. Nothing he thought would not hurt. Tonight not one care allowed itself to be stashed away. From the inner shelves of his orderly mind things were falling of their own accord, and refused to be put back. He let them come down, unwilling to scramble them into their holes.

He drove through the sad streets of Rome to get away from himself, nearly to the Vatican and back toward – but not to – St John's Square. He drove circuitously, and finally to Via Monserrato, where he was tossed by an inexorable feeling of being lost and without reprieve. Donna Maria's old doorway was like a shore to him.

She kept entirely quiet even after Bora walked into her music room. She had been horribly anxious for him, and now that he was here she sensed that although he was physically unhurt something was very wrong. But she knew men, and how they do not want to be asked as they first come in, so she sat with her bobbin lace at hand, following the pattern drawn by pins on the cushion, deftly criss-crossing the ivory pieces.

Bora had taken his cap off and unbuckled his holster belt, tossed the weight of leather and metal on the armchair, was undoing his collar. She could follow his movements without lifting her eyes, by the rustle of cloth when he removed his tunic and threw it on the back of the same armchair. It slipped off from it with a soft sleek sound of lining. The car keys were coming out of the breeches' pocket. His boots silently crossed the carpet as he walked over to the piano to lay the keys on it.

She could hear him heave and looked up at last. Bora stood in the middle of the room, lips tight, blinking hard to keep control but fast losing it. She felt him break down inside, piecemeal, so quickly that no wilful opposition to it could avail. A long time she had been waiting for this, unsure that she wanted to witness it. The lace-making pillow left her lap for the basket alongside her, because a woman's knees are where sometimes men are brought by great anguish and grief. Still she did not look at him, out of pity mostly. How long since a man had come to her to cry.

10

Sandro Guidi realized that if the Germans were involved in the killing at St John Lateran's, no photos of the victim would be forthcoming. What summary information about the incident available at the police station on Monday was useless, and he'd put her out of his mind when Danza came in to hand him a leaflet claiming the dead woman's affiliation to a resistance group. On a hunch – he was not yet worried, just uneasy – Guidi called the Maiulis to ask for Francesca. The maid answered that the couple was out, and as far as she knew, Signorina Lippi was at work.

At lunch he drove to the address Francesca had given him as her mother's. When he rang, a middle-aged woman came leerily to open.

Before long, they were sitting across from one another. She kept her hand on a pack of cigarettes, so that Guidi wouldn't see they were a German brand – but he had already. In the small kitchen, a sword of sunshine created dancing reflections on the tiled wall. She yawned. There were deep circles under her eyes, but her eyes were beautiful. The beauty of her face was different from Francesca's: there was a disillusioned, yet less harsh cast on it, as though life had dealt differently with her, or she had reacted differently to it. She was wearing a house robe and the generosity of her body showed, but neither nor was Guidi was concerned about it.

The deep cleavage of her breasts was simply there, like the light on the wall.

"Is she in trouble?"

Guidi shook his head. "Not with us, anyway," meaning the police. "I'm a co-tenant." By professional habit Guidi took note of, but did not judge the undone bed, clothes on the floor, twisted newspapers used to start the fire in the cooking stove, cigarette butts overflowing from the ashtray and from cups and saucers, no two the same.

In a way she was more beautiful than Francesca. The hands were the same, slim and long, with fingers that seemed four-jointed in their length. She pushed back the hair from her face as Francesca did. "I don't know where she is. She seldom comes here. I know she had the baby a week ago. Sorry I can't help you."

"Has she mentioned she might leave Rome?"

"Not that I know of. But she's done this before." She hungered for a cigarette, obviously, and was trying to find a way to reach for the pack without exposing it. She finally drew it closer to her by backing it up slowly in her hand while she talked, and next the stubby cigarette was in her mouth. Guidi took his matches out and lit it for her. "I've been trying to get in touch with her. I drove by her workplace and found it closed for good."

"So are most stores, until the Americans come."

Guidi kept his mouth closed. Since yesterday, he had run in circles without facing the possibilities. He was afraid of viewing the body of the dead woman at the morgue. So he sought Francesca elsewhere. Her mother's face grew pinched when she took a drag. Smoke from the cigarette was blue, but that which exhaled from her mouth was slightly yellowed. It came to Guidi that perhaps Francesca had mentioned his relationship to her, and tensely he wondered what she thought about it.

"Look." She glanced at a cheap little watch on her wrist. "I don't mean to send you away, but I've got a painter coming. He'll be here in minutes, and if you don't mind…"

A painter. Sure. Guidi stood up, and she didn't. He left, careful not to stumble on the worn steps that led outside. At the bottom of the stairs, the sidewalk shone like an explosion of light.

Bora's first care that morning was to ensure that the Red Cross shipment was delivered to the Vatican. The second was to follow up, at last, on what had happened to Antonio Rau in Via Tasso. Sutor answered the call and at once launched into an invective against Rome, the Resistance, and how there just wasn't enough time to haul the bastards in. "That double-crossing son of a bitch Rau was just one. If the army had done its duty in the field there wouldn't be so many alive and in hiding."

Bora sensed Sutor's anger, but still said, "Had you not shot Foa, you might have a voice of sanity in this mess. You could have shot somebody else other than Foa."

"Yes, we should have shot *you*."

"I hope you're speaking in jest, Captain, and even then I'm not amused."

"Just wait until you remove those stripes from your breeches…"

Bora laughed into the telephone. "You're so used to threatening, I think at times you forget to whom you're speaking."

All of Sutor's repressed bitterness surfaced, so that his voice grew shrill as it did. "I'm speaking to a meddlesome English half-breed whose ass we should have broken long ago, but will soon."

"Well," Bora said acidly, "we will see about that."

"Yes, we'll see about that. This isn't Verona, you know. You keep on that path and you'll end up in the German People's Court!"

Kappler picked up the line then. Bora couldn't tell whether he'd stood by or just walked into Sutor's office. His tone was collected. "You do irritate my officers badly, Major Bora."

"Only because I refuse to be bullied, Colonel."

"You have your flaws. Overbearing cuts it in the field, but won't do with brother officers."

"Are you talking about me or Captain Sutor?"

"A bit of both. But in a pinch I know where my loyalties lie."

"Well, tell the captain I don't like being threatened. I will not stand for it."

"There's much you don't stand for, Major Bora."

Dr Raimondi was friendly and brief when Guidi called his office. "We haven't seen Francesca since last Friday, Inspector. Would you tell her, when you see her, that the baptism will be on 4 June, at St Francesca Romana's? We'd love to have her there. You, too, if you wish to come."

Guidi swallowed. *They must think I'm the father.*

That evening, at the military hospital, Treib returned the diary with the same lack of comment shown upon receipt of it. His tolerant face resembled dough under the feeble overhead light. "Do you still want me to hang on to the letters?"

"Yes, please."

"You trust me because I'm a physician."

"No. I trust you because you were in Russia, as I was."

Treib made a grimace of agreement. "Very well. And how is your arm? Let me take a look at it." He went through the observations of the case, and then, helping Bora to put his tunic back on, said "So, have you found a clean piece of ass in the past month?"

Bora, who was thinking of Mrs Murphy, was startled. "No."

"Time is getting short if you want to do it in Rome. Truth be told, I'd be too tired to make love even if the chance came. How does the song go? '*Maschine kaputt...*' You're probably one of those whom strenuous activity arouses."

The surgeon needed a ride, and gladly Bora drove him to his flat a few streets away. Treib stumbled out onto the sidewalk. "I'd invite you over for a drink, but I'm too tired."

"Good night."

"Good night." With sudden concern, Treib leaned in, through the side window. "What will you do now? Where are you going?"

"Not to the hotel. If I go back now, I'll bed a whore."

"Watch it, friend. It's not worth it."

Bora nodded and drove away.

For reasons so obscure he couldn't bring himself to look at them, Guidi left his apartment late that same evening and returned to his office on Via Del Boccaccio. There he parked the car and walked up the sad climb of Via Rasella to the opposite end, Via Quattro Fontane. A stenciled quarter moon allowed him to judge that Bora's Mercedes was not by the curb, but he paced the length of the street to make sure. PAI guards and German soldiers stopped him, in both cases satisfied with his papers. Nowhere was Bora's license plate – WH 1377445 – to be seen. He had not yet come to the hotel. Guidi stood by the corner, waiting and wondering what he waited for, other than for Bora to arrive and walk out of the car. He had nothing to tell him. Why should he wait for Bora? His mouth felt bitter.

It was Bora, somehow. It was Bora's fault. Guidi stood there with a lunatic, befuddled want to hurt him, this obstacle to his hate for the Germans. It was all because of what Bora had done, whatever he had done. Whatever. He was angry with him, resentful of the offer of friendship and – tonight – angry enough to hurt him.

Scattered echoes from the Anzio front seemed palpable, as if sounds and lights flashing could be reached for and somehow held in hand. Guidi waited, his soul numb and motionless like a hub in the reel of his thoughts.

The telephone rang in the dark. How Dollmann found him at Donna Maria's was a mystery. His voice came over the wires, unmistakable in the prudence of his approach.

"Are you alone, Bora?"

"Why, yes."

"I just wanted to make sure I didn't interrupt anything. Knowing your interest in anti-partisan warfare, I wanted to pass on the following item to you. Leaflets were printed overnight and circulated by a group that calls itself *Unione e Libertà*. I quote, 'Once more the hideous game of barbarism has been played out in our city. On the twenty-eighth of the current month a woman comrade was without provocation gunned down by a German assassin in the Lateran Square. We who knew her hold firm the belief that love of freedom will not be extinguished with her death. Meanwhile we call on the Roman people to rise against murder and abuse,' et cetera. I thought you'd be interested in knowing. It's amazing where one has to find good news any more. Have you had dinner yet?"

Bora glanced at the fluorescent dial of his watch. "It's nearly midnight!"

"No matter, I know a place where we can still dine."

Two cars had arrived since Guidi's coming, neither of them disgorging Bora onto the sidewalk. Guidi leaned against the wall and wondered whether he'd be here at all, had he heard from Francesca tonight. Facing him, the hefty garden gate of the Barberini Palace reminded him of the awful Thursday in March. Any closeness to Bora had ended that day, in spite of the fact that he'd survived. The others had died. Being here with his anger was part of reclaiming his place with the others. The creeping of the stars above seemed to come through an effort of the celestial vault, marred by the glare of war at the horizon.

What did 'hurting Bora' mean? How do you hurt a soldier? The only way, of course – Guidi shifted his weight on his feet, back and forth. Bora was sometimes unaware. He might be, coming back to the hotel. Slowly, slowly, the stars crept above, seeking the eaves of the roofs to disappear. It surely could be done, if someone had shot a woman at midday in the public square and got away. Guidi needed to be here with his anger and fear and grief. He needed to believe that a massacre and the outrage of barely living through it brought him here, not something else.

No chink of light, nor outside activity revealed that the restaurant was open. Dollmann must have called in advance, because there was a waiter standing at the door to let them in. A few privileged guests sat at the tables, some of them well-dressed women. Dollmann watched Bora watch the women, and daintily picked up the napkin from the glass where it sat, spreading it on his knees. "I have my problems, too," he ambiguously confided. "No intellectual should be burdened by the misery of our lapsed state, but here we are. You should have made provisions for – shall we say – your human frailty." And because Bora testily avoided an answer, Dollmann answered, "Your flaw is that you need friends. You should settle for lovers, relatives and colleagues. Your quest is useless."

Bora sighed. "You surmise that lovers, relatives and colleagues cannot be friends."

"Correct. Even I am not your friend. Only your ally."

"Well, I have had friends, Colonel."

"Ha. And what happened to them?"

"Some died."

"And the rest?"

"We're no longer friends."

Dollmann smiled a clever smile. "Cigarette?"

"No, thank you. I quit about ten days ago."

The menu came, they chose food and wine, and then the SS said, "You quit, why?"

Bora relaxed eventually, seemingly amused at his own words. "I'm cleansing myself for the pan like a snail. I should probably eat sawdust, too."

"You're superstitious!"

"And scared." Bora poured wine into Dollmann's glass and his own. "I like to call it concern, but it's fear. I haven't had the full benefit of it in a while – it feels cozy to get it again. My best risk-taking comes from it."

Guidi closed his eyes so as not to see who came out of the car that had just pulled in by the curb. Then he looked, and it wasn't Bora. He stepped back behind the corner. His mouth was dry.

He had to leave. As suddenly and erratically as he had come, he had to leave now. Bora would not return tonight. And if he did return, he didn't want to be here waiting. The stars ran between roofs when he hastened back to his car, where he sat as if hiding from them.

There were many reasons for him to stay, yet one among them chased him from here. It was true: his anger had started on that day in late March, but when his own men had fired at Bora from the windows of the police command, he had not stopped them.

How could he stay? Out of guilt, out of that guilt, he was not ready to kill.

Hours later, on the bleakest spring morning he'd seen, Guidi walked out of the morgue with a loud hum in his ears. His hands shook so badly, he could not search his pocket for the car keys, and he had to sit down in the hallway to regain control.

It was no comfort that he had lied to himself from the start about her death. For two days, he had said no. Now he felt as if part of him were sick and rotting, and although it was not love – it might never have been – he felt he should cry. His face twisted, but the tears did not come.

"Does she have relatives?" the morgue attendant asked. "Somebody has to bury her. I read the leaflet and the papers, and I don't want no problems with the Germans. If there are relatives, you tell 'em to bury her."

Guidi said he'd take care of things. How his hands shook. Looking at them made him aware of this weakness that he loathed about himself. His anger was tainted by it, and produced only a stunted, malicious want to find and destroy the man who had killed her: but out of revenge, spite, something less noble and fierce than hatred. If he could only steady his hands.

From the morgue he drove to St John of the Hollyhocks, a church with three altars and six famous burials, near Ponte Sisto, because its parish priest had been in the square when Francesca had been killed.

The priest, who needed a shave and a bath, shrugged at the questions. "It's not like I really saw anything, Inspector. Just the body after it had already fallen. So did everybody else in the square. There were two men standing by her, and soon there were several, some in uniform, some not. All Germans. They might have shot her from a window. I didn't see her get shot."

"She was shot at fairly close range, and from the square."

"Well, the SS asked every soldier to take out his gun, so they must have been satisfied none of them had fired."

"Are you trying to defend the Germans?"

The priest shrugged again. "I'm simply telling you what I saw. If you want to put words in my mouth, it's your words, not mine. I felt badly when they didn't let me come near to say a prayer over her, but now that we read she was a communist – well, it'd have been a wasted prayer. This is all I saw, and you can stay here all day; there's nothing I can add. No, I didn't pay attention to the uniforms. They're all SS to me. Why don't you ask the orderlies at the San Giovanni Hospital? Maybe they paid attention."

Guidi did. In the square, had he wanted to look for it, no sign remained of where Francesca had been killed, and under an immense blue sky, German patrols stood at all street corners. In a quiet room of the hospital he met the orderly, a white-capped fellow with a brutal face, whose split eyebrows suggested he probably boxed in his spare time. Unlike the priest, he told Guidi he'd seen it all. "All, I've seen. Just ask me."

"Where were you when the shot was fired?"

"I was wheeling a patient out of surgery."

"So you were not at the window."

"No, but I ran to it right away. There was a German standing by the body."

"In uniform?"

"Sure. How else would I know he was a German?"

"What was he doing? Did you see his face?"

"No, he had his back to me. He was just standing there. Tall man, an officer. Then a civilian came and they talked to each other. The civilian started going through the woman's clothing, looking for documents, maybe. Then other Germans came and there was some kind of argument going on."

Guidi was disappointed. "But you didn't see anyone with gun in hand."

"No. By this time the Germans started aiming their rifles at the windows, so I backed up and tried to look through the slats of the shutters. There wasn't much else to see, though. They were all gone in half an hour's time."

"In conclusion, you did not see the murder."

"No, but..."

"You did not see the murder," Guidi repeated in disgust, and walked away.

In his office, Bora had just heard the latest alarming news from Velletri and Valmontone, the last obstacles on the Allies' way to Rome. Time was pitilessly short. For days he had been trying to reach by telephone the transit prison camp at Servigliano, to no avail. Now, with the Reiner folder open in front of him, he tried – and failed – again.

That Captain Sutor should show up unannounced at his doorstep did not surprise him. He'd dreaded it. Still, calmly putting down the receiver, he said, "I was not expecting you, Captain. I'm due out, so can we meet sometime tomorrow?"

"Not likely. I'm here to discuss the incident on Sunday."

"I see." Bora unlatched his holster, ignoring Sutor's startled reaction. "Would you like to examine my side arm?"

"After giving you ample time to clean it? No."

"It's a serious statement you're making, captain. I hope you can corroborate it."

Sutor looked around, again self-assured. "Actually, the woman's death is secondary. What I want to know is who else was in the square. Priests, housewives and privates can get away with telling me they didn't see anything. But you're not one not to pay attention."

"There are times when I am distracted."

"Colonel Dollmann was there with you."

Bora closed the Reiner folder and put it in his briefcase. "Well, have you asked him?"

"Some things I cannot do. We understand you were the first to come by the body."

"That's true." Having locked the briefcase, Bora stood. "But altogether it's curious that you care. She was a partisan. A communist. Whoever got rid of her did us all a favor."

Sutor's face was unmoved, like a tracking dog's. "Who shot her, Bora?"

"I do not know."

"The shot came from an army P38."

Bora came around his desk, leisurely. "Pity. There are thousands of those around."

"Who shot her?"

"I don't know. And I resent being cornered this way."

"Come, Major, don't lie to me. Who shot the woman?"

Aware he could not yet safely leave, Bora faced the SS. "I told you, I don't know."

"Somebody shot her. You were there. Either you saw it or you did it. If you didn't do it, you're protecting someone."

For an instant, the anxiety of his dream-state flight from a flesh-eating animal risked to undo him. Still, Bora moderately reached for the briefcase, and took a step toward the door as if his patience were being tried by a rude guest. "Captain Sutor, I greatly resent your words, your tone and your intrusion. This concern with the death of an enemy of the Reich is suspicious to me, and I intend to bring it up with General Wolff. I want to hear what unrevealed interest the SS and Gestapo had in this woman, and why one of yours searched her body before my eyes."

"That's none of your business." Sutor tried to keep the pressure on, but was not as forward. It was like a narrow breach of energy into which Bora slipped and found his way.

"Am I to understand that your command might have done business with the member of a communist group, possibly the same that caused the massacre at Via Rasella?"

Sutor's thick neck turned red, as if someone were choking him. "You're speaking nonsense to protect yourself."

Bora said, "Get out!"

"You think you're clever, and so does Colonel Kappler, but it's not going to work —"

"Get out!"

"*I will not get out!*"

"Then I will." Bora walked past him, and across the threshold. "Search my office while you're at it. See what else you can find."

Signora Carmela didn't understand why Guidi had asked to speak privately to her husband. She sat in the kitchen waiting, until the men joined her there.

"There is bad news," the professor told her then in a forcible monotone. "Francesca has been killed."

The old woman heard him very clearly, but turned to Guidi all the same. "Inspector, what is he saying? I don't understand."

"It's true. The Germans killed her. She is the one we read about in the newspapers."

"My God!" Signora Carmela cried out. "Oh, my God, my God!" Her husband tried to reach for her but she eluded him, fleeing to her room and what saints she kept there. "Oh my God, the poor child! Oh my God, my God!"

Maiuli seemed unable to lower his arm, still poised to catch his wife. When he did, he had tears in his eyes. "Was her death hard?"

"No." Guidi had to unlock his jaw to speak intelligibly. "A clean shot through the head. She died instantly. Probably never knew what happened."

"But why would anyone…?"

"It appears she was involved in politics more than you or your wife realize, Professor. I'm going into her room to remove anything that might be dangerous for you."

"She… Do what you must, Inspector. She slept in your room, lately."

Guidi chased all nostalgia in order to function. The trained policeman in him searched the room, the *other* Guidi being kept out of the way. Quickly enough, he found some money rolled tightly at the bottom of the dresser, about six thousand lire. There was an empty envelope with her name on the table, no return address. Magazines, paperback mysteries, her old shoes. A small bottle of cologne. Her cotton dresses. The silk stockings he'd given her, carefully folded.

Professor Maiuli stood by the door with the look of a beaten dog. "Inspector, tell me the truth – did you know about her activities?"

Guidi did not turn around. He was holding up the mattress with one hand, rummaging under it with the other. "Yes, I knew."

"You could have told me, at least."

"You would not have been able to lie when the Germans came."

"Maybe not, but it'd have been with some sense of honor that I'd have let myself be arrested then."

"It makes no damned difference now."

Maiuli chewed on his dentures like a calf on cuds. "And the German officer who had me hauled in, he was the same man who came to talk to you at night. He knows you well. The reason why you didn't try to talk him out of arresting the rest of us, who had nothing to do with politics, was to protect Francesca. I understand. But you didn't have to act behind my back."

Guidi let go of the mattress, tossing up the quilts with both hands. His anger at her death was starting to peak. His motions were disorderly, pretexts to move his body around to discharge energy. Having found nothing else, he stormed past Maiuli and across the hallway to Francesca's old room.

Maiuli did not follow him. "I'm glad you no longer live with us."

The furniture in the other room was empty. Still Guidi searched corners and crannies the Germans would surely rifle. He even picked up a folded piece of paper stuffed under the lame leg of the writing table. It was blank. Some phone numbers scribbled on a pad he crumpled and drove into his pockets. There were sketches of nudes and faces on top of the tall wardrobe, which he took down and lay on the bed – no date on them later than 1943. Reaching over his head Guidi felt behind the molded rim crowning the wardrobe, and at last his fingers met with paper. Standing on a chair, he discovered several carbon copies stuck tightly between the molding and the top of the wardrobe. He pulled them out and chose one of the sheets at random.

What he read were the names Bora and Montini had read, but neither of them had reacted as Guidi did. For a moment his sight went dim, because this was an inconceivable, frightening second death of Francesca in him. In a feverish sequence he read names of unknown people, names he had vaguely heard, entire families locked in the brevity of the typewritten space condemning them. He was unable to remove his eyes from the name of Francesca's mother, neatly printed beside her address on the riverfront.

Their ears were no longer paying attention to the shooting. With the tense mask of his face drawn over the skull, Kesselring looked aged in excess of his years, and only the jutting double row of his teeth gave him an appearance of aggressiveness. "Why didn't you tell me you're having trouble with Via Tasso, Martin?"

"The field marshal has other things to worry about."

"I thought it'd had all been resolved after March." A shell came whistling by, and promptly both men ducked. The trench was built into a natural escarpment, edged with belabored shrubs and skinny trees. American troops could be seen now and then to the south-west, glimpses of dull cloth at which sharpshooters aimed.

When Bora looked, the shell had lifted much dirt, raining back mostly on the American side. Compared to the last one, the aim had been adjusted: a little more fine-tuning and they'd be bursting on this side of the escarpment. German artillery fire whirred overhead, aimed at British positions. He knew what the odds looked like on the map. The next shell fell much closer, fifty yards away. Someone was making mistakes on the German side, too. An 88 came down far too short and burst into a thicket where the soldiers had spent the night; trees splintered in all directions and branches went flying like javelins and arrows, along with clumps of dirt and roots.

Kesselring was steadily walking the line of the trench, his big head sunken into his shoulders. "We'll have to withdraw." He chewed on disappointment. "Or by this afternoon all we'll have on both sides will be meat in the dirt. How's morale?"

"The men don't want us to quit Rome."

"I can't blame them, but we will quit it. Take me back to Frascati."

When they had driven a stretch toward the rise of the town, amid gray puffs of explosions flitting before the sun, Kesselring said, "Martin, I want you to apologize to Kappler and Sutor both."

Bora, who was concentrating on driving, felt his hair stand on hand. "*Herr General Feldmarschall*, I have just requested the opposite!"

"That's precisely why you will express your regrets to them."

"But the honor of the army... It's unheard of! Put yourself in my place, *Herr General Feldmarschall.*"

"If I were in your place I would apologize."

Bora saw well how it was. "With all respect, Colonel Dollmann had no right to inform you."

"Bigger fish have been speared for less. As you know, tomorrow night there's a party at the Flora, and it is proper you should apologize then."

"In public?"

"It won't kill you."

Bora was so angry, he nearly went off the road. "*Herr General Fieldmarschall*, I'd rather you directly reprimanded me."

Kesselring grunted. "I don't want to reprimand you. I want you to apologize to Kappler and his adjutant. I expect to hear from Dollmann that it has been done. Be stark sober when you do it, and make sure you do it with the decorum befitting your post and your family."

In her small kitchen, Francesca's mother wept. Hands knotted under her chin, she wept big tears and Guidi felt powerless to console her. He was full of loathing, and of course must warn her of danger without telling her how he knew. What he should do with the money found in Francesca's room had been unclear to him until now, though he'd taken it along. Now he slipped it out of his pocket, still tied with a rubber band, and placed it on the table.

"Six thousand lire," he said, and though it was hardly believable, he added, "from Francesca's savings."

To the south the Germans must be blowing up another bridge or ammunition dump. The windowpanes shook hard. She made a humming sound as she wept, neither moving nor looking at the money.

"The child will be christened on Sunday, in case you wanted to see him. And in case you wanted, you know, to dress her and —"

"No."

"They'll bury her in the morning."

She looked at him despairingly. "I don't want to touch her. Don't ask. I can't touch her, I can't go see her. Here, take the money, give her a good burial."

Guidi stared at the stained tablecloth. "It's not necessary. It's taken care of. You don't have to worry about that."

When she reached for his hand he did not expect it, was startled by the contact and drew back, but she held him. Her hand was cold, wet with tears. "But you – are you sad about it?"

"I'm numb. I don't know what I am."

Though he returned to Rome late in the evening, Bora received a call from Cardinal Borromeo, who sounded worried and wanted him to stop by his residence before leaving the office for the night. At his arrival – they met privately in a small studio hung with tapestries – the prelate showed himself even more agitated than over the telephone. It seemed that Kappler had warned the Vatican to surrender partisans and defectors hiding in the Lateran Palace.

"You also hide enemy soldiers, Cardinal. But I'm in no position to intercede with the Gestapo or the SS."

"That's what Dollmann told me, and he is an SS! Who is to speak for us?"

"If the Holy See didn't have a guilty conscience, you wouldn't mind Kappler's intrusion. I feel no differently from the way he does on this one. The men you conceal are the same who shoot my men in the field – there can be no commerce between us on the abetting of enemies. I tried to do what I could for others," he would not use the word *Jews*, "but if I had the authority, I'd go through your labyrinthine rooms looking for partisans myself."

"So we're to be trespassed against!"

"You haven't been trespassed against yet, unless you count that stupid Caruso's raid on St Paul's. The fact that Kappler gives you fair warning surprises me. I wouldn't."

"Well, and you tell me this even as His Holiness expresses paternal feelings toward you."

"I'm in debt to His Holiness. I should try to kill informers more often."

Distractedly Borromeo paced the small room back and forth, three long strides each way. "That shipment of Red Cross milk – I saw your signature on the papers. How did you think of it?"

"I'd rather not say."

The cardinal stopped with a half-turn that made his gown flash red. "I hear the officers' luggage has been packed out of hotel rooms."

Bora didn't look at him. It was the reason why he had come back from the front, to gather his things from the hotel and Donna Maria's, and to say farewell to Treib, who was likely to leave early with the less gravely wounded. Of course, there was still the call to Servigliano, and wrapping up the Reiner case with Guidi as much as he could.

Borromeo was staring at him. "Tell me at least this, Major – do you believe Kappler will have time to raid the Lateran?"

"Well, it *is* across the square from Via Tasso. He could be there in three minutes."

"I am speaking of psychological time."

Bora kept his cool. "If I say yes, you might try to remove those you are hiding, and if I say no, you will surmise that we are abandoning Rome. I refuse both alternatives. Forgive me, Cardinal, but I won't answer you."

"Hohmann taught you well." Borromeo opened the door for him.

From Via Giulia, a long, dark distance separated Bora from Piazza Vescovio. He drove there nonetheless, past the long solitude of Villa Ada, facing the serpentine course of the Aniene. The hospital was dismal at night. Its halls looked longer, like guts full of waste. More acutely the stench of disinfectant rose from the floor and breathed from the walls. Bora shivered while passing between the rows of metal beds. From the indistinct darkness of their blankets one of the men breathed hard and loud as from a split throat, and another one whimpered. And there was in the shadow a double line of trembling, swallowing, or staring upward waiting for death.

Treib sat by himself in his office, slumped on a cot. He made a jerky gesture with his head at Bora's coming and wearily waved for him to come closer. He said nothing, his head lolling as if too heavy for his neck when he tried to sit up. He looked exhausted.

"I won't stay long, Treib. I only stopped because I thought you'd be leaving by now."

"Who's leaving? The transportable wounded have already gone off this morning."

"And what are you doing here?"

"I stay with the rest. There are twenty-five thousand German wounded in Rome. If I don't stay, I won't be able to sleep at night for the rest of the war." The muscles of his cheeks tried to pull the sides of his mouth into a grin. "I stay for the same reason you go."

Bora shook his hand. "Take care of yourself."

"Oh, I will. All I have to do is surrender." Treib pointed at a gray residue in a small steel basin. "That's what remains of your two letters. I'm glad there was no need to send them."

It was just past nine in the evening when Bora returned to his office at the Flora, and – after making sure his diary was still in the safe – sat at his desk. For a few minutes he simply sat there, with his eyes closed, trying to empty his mind of the jumble of sounds and images jarring inside him, until the silence of the room felt like an ocean that would mercifully drown him. Then once more, with little hope of succeeding, he went through the motions of telephoning the transit camp at Servigliano, whose contact number Dollmann had obligingly provided while he was in the hospital, days ago. Unexpectedly, this time he was able to get through.

The records section chief listened without interrupting. He'd likely expected Westphal's aide to berate him for the escape of detainees after the night-time bombing of three weeks earlier, and when no reprimand came forth, he was more than willing to answer questions.

"Yes, Major," he said after a long interval likely employed shuffling papers, which had made Bora fear the line would fall again. "He had been originally brought in on 17 September from the Salerno Beachhead. Within days succeeded in slipping away from the Italians, who as you're aware ran the camp until early October. Most of the escapees were caught by us, but he managed to stay at large until late in February of this year. I remember the circumstances, because he led us on a wild goose chase, and it was at the same time we received the prisoners from Malta and Tripoli. Where had he been meanwhile? The interrogators didn't get a straight answer out of him, but he was well-fed and wearing civilian clothes. Surely he was not hiding in the woods, as he claimed, or mooching off some dirt-poor farmer. He'd been wounded in the thigh, also, an injury which had been professionally attended to. My opinion is that he stayed in town somewhere, maybe Ascoli Piceno, maybe further south, hoping to rejoin his own. Only by accident did a militiaman guarding the Ascoli bus station become suspicious, and when it was clear that the man couldn't speak the language and tried to get away, he shot him. The bullet took out his right ear lobe. Even so the

Italians had to race after him, because he bolted. Only blood loss got him down."

Bora had not hoped for this to happen, really. He was astonished that he had guessed right, by the pertinent information, and by the speed with which his energy peaked, as if the day hadn't been as hard as it had been. He sat up in the chair, barely guarding his enthusiasm, taking quick notes. "You said 'maybe further south'. What makes you think so?"

"His forged papers were too well prepared. I'm thinking Pescara, or even Rome."

Still scribbling, Bora wanted to whoop. "Did you keep the clothes he was wearing at his capture in February?"

The records section chief sounded puzzled. "Why, yes, Major Bora. As by routine."

"Do you have access to them? Fine. Before we close, I will ask a couple of questions about his clothing and shoes, and for a description of his leg wound. No, no. Just humor me. Meanwhile, I want you to keep him in isolation and watch him closely until I can send for him."

"*Send* for him? I don't understand."

"Sergeant First Class William Bader, US Army, is wanted for the murder of Magda Reiner, a German national, secretary at our embassy here in Rome."

No sooner had Bora put down the receiver than he dialed Guidi's number. It was nearly ten o' clock, but this could not wait. The phone rang for a long time, then the sleepy voice of a toothless old man answered; it had to be the professor, Bora thought, and asked for Guidi.

"The inspector doesn't live here any more," the sleepy voice said. "He moved out, and didn't leave an address or a phone number."

Bora realized now that he hadn't spoken to Guidi in a week, that he'd made himself scarce for a variety of reasons, and it must have come across as though he'd dropped the ball on the Reiner case. Now that he had something to say – that he had all but solved the crime, and needed to talk over the details, he'd have to wait until the morning to talk to Guidi. The morning? No, he was to join Kesselring in the morning. Tomorrow night, maybe, if a shell didn't take his head off or the Americans didn't break through.

Well, there was no helping it. Once more Bora walked into the dark street and into his car, with the dance of artillery fire flashing like pale northern lights overhead.

Half an hour later, Donna Maria looked on when he silently packed his few things and set them by the door.

"I'll be back to see you, but these have to go tonight." He stepped into the parlor and lightly touched the photo of himself and his brother, linking arms somewhere in Russia. "You had better put this away, too."

She did not want to cry, and angrily waved her hand at him.

31 MAY 1944

Bora spent Wednesday at Frascati, and was grudgingly back in the evening for Dollmann to come as a witness during the reception at the Flora. Having shipped out their luggage, both men were in undress uniform. Neither of them brought up the apology at first, but Dollmann lightly gossiped about the officers who would attend the party. "As for you, you nearly ruined what you had so nicely held together, just because you got angry at Sutor. At least you should have had the sense to remonstrate with Kappler, not to a private's son, an upstart idiot who already didn't like you."

Against his will, Bora took the punishment. "Kappler will know I do not mean it."

Kappler actually said, while Sutor gloated and made the rounds of the hall cracking jokes and drinking to the humiliation of the army, "You're more sinister than you let on, Bora. If this was your idea, you're genial. If not, you have a clever advisor."

Bora had enough to do trying to keep his temper down. He managed one of the most hard-fought smiles of his career, so as to hide a murderous want to get even. "An apology was called for," he said, meaning it literally.

1 JUNE 1944

There was a soft pink haze at the horizon, where chubby clouds grew bright at the lower hems. Even the battering of artillery sounded new at the start of the day.

Field Marshal Kesselring snapped the new epaulets on Bora's shoulders. "Well, Martin, let's hope the war lasts only long enough for you to make full grade. I was quite older than you when I made lieutenant colonel. But, boy, those were other days." He grimaced with his big teeth, like a bulldog. "I, too, used to look so spruce in the morning when I was thirty, and an adjutant in the Bavarian Foot Artillery." They shook hands. "I'm asking again for permission to abandon Rome without a fight," he added. "We'll know by tomorrow."

It was all there was to the ceremony. Temporarily quartered in and around a chapel in the Frascati countryside, paratroopers took up their positions for the day. On a kitchen table found God knows where, Kesselring consulted muddy commanders over maps and typewritten sheets. Bora was familiar with that fiction of control on paper, the last step before giving up.

Danza was not one to pry – he'd figured out what the story was between the inspector and the dead girl, and kept his mouth shut – but this morning he asked him, standing at attention before Guidi's desk, what he would do when the Americans came.

Guidi was surprised at first, though it was clear that everyone was thinking the same thing, and it just came down to who would raise the argument first. Toeing the line, because one never knew, he said, "Danza, governments change, but the police remains the police. I've been thinking of possibilities." He couldn't tell Danza that in the last twenty-four hours he had toyed with the idea of joining the Resistance, and promptly shelved it. He had no desire to fight anything. The last six months had upended his life, and it was enough.

"I have been thinking of possibilities, too," Danza replied, understanding there would be no confidence-sharing.

Guidi nodded. He was a good fellow, Danza, and coura-geous, too. As for him, it was as with most things; even the urge to seek vengeance had been short-lived. He saw things from such a balanced equipoise, he grew bored with himself, but did not get hurt.

At mid-morning, there was a call from Caruso. The tone was so accommodating, Guidi was at once suspicious. "So, Guidi, how have things gone with you?" It was hardly the cir-cumstantial greeting one replies to, so Guidi was quiet while for the next five minutes Caruso complimented him on suc-cessfully closing a diminutive, irrelevant case of profiteering at Tor di Nona. "Your good work makes me forget our spat." The chief of police laughed a narrow laugh. "Let bygones be bygones, eh?"

Still Guidi listened.

"By the way, since you are working with the Germans on the Reiner case, especially with this major, what's his name…"

"Bora."

"Bora, yes. I thought it had something to do with winter weather. The north wind, hee, hee…" The laugh was so narrow, he must be barely opening his mouth, Guidi thought. "Do you see him frequently, yes?"

That's what it was about. 'Guidi kept non-committal, "I have barely seen him since the end of March."

"But you're on good terms."

Guidi was thinking of Bora racing up the Via Paganini

stairwell with his armed men. "We're not friends, if that's what you mean."

"I think you're quite mistaken in that, Guidi. He's been… Why, he's even given me some hard times on account of you."

"I didn't ask him."

"Well, I know he's still in Rome, so I am asking you to contact him."

Not ordering, *asking*. Guidi sneered into the mouthpiece, noiselessly. "Surely the chief of police would have easier access to him than I." He took his little vendetta.

"Except that Bora and I have had our differences – professional things. Set up an appointment with him for me."

"Yes, Dr Caruso."

"The sooner the better."

"Very well. And since we're here, allow me to remind you that the investigation regarding the Reiner case will continue, *even as the situation changes.*"

Caruso's lack of immediate reaction could have many reasons. "That may be," he said afterwards, "that may be. But whom will you work with? *Ras* Merlo hasn't been seen in over two weeks, and for all we know he may no longer be with us."

Guidi clenched his teeth. "He's not the only suspect, Dr Caruso. And what makes you think anything happened to him?"

"Dead or alive, Merlo disappeared. You have no other accused on hand. Your phantom tenant is nowhere to be found. With victim, accused and witnesses gone, *even as the situation changes* you haven't much of a case, do you? I'm telling you so that you won't waste your energy."

Dollmann hardly made a secret of the fact that he was saying his goodbyes. Of his many acquaintances in Rome, he got to see most on 1 June. When someone mentioned to him that Frosinone had fallen to the 8th Army, he remarked, "I can't think of nicer people it could fall to," and, "Have you been to Frosinone? It's a dreadful little place."

At his exit from the Excelsior, where he'd had lunch with General Maelzer, he found Kappler waiting for him by his car. "We need to talk, Colonel Dollmann."

"Why not?"

"It's about Bora. We'll have to do something about him."

"Do you think so?" Dollmann circled his thumbs, leaning on the shiny side of his car to keep his chauffeur from Kappler's stare. "You're probably right. Officers like him confuse the troops by seeking alternative allegiances to those set by the Party."

"That's not what I mean." Kappler set his skinny jaw forward. "He killed the woman in the square, I'm convinced of it. I can't believe he dared, and no one actually saw him open fire. Not even you, although you were behind him."

Dollmann did not lose control over one muscle of his face. "Of course we know how keenly he pursued partisans elsewhere. All *he* knew is that she was involved in partisan activities."

"Maybe." Kappler looked up at the beautiful June sky. "He's not the kind you can intimidate."

"Do you speak from experience?"

"He's not the kind you can intimidate, let's leave it at that." There was a short break in Kappler's train of thought, reflected by a pause. "Naturally I won't touch him if you tell me not to touch him."

Dollmann removed a speck of dust from his sleeve. "I'm not telling you anything."

That evening, crabby in his armchair, Caruso frowned with displeasure. "Damn that German, it's the third time you've tried – is he ever in?"

"It's hard to say. He may just refuse to come to the phone." Guidi looked around, hands behind his back. He could smell haste in the air. It showed in Caruso's insistence and his furtive glances at the watch, which conveniently he'd slipped from his wrist and placed where he could read it through the corner of his eye.

"It's nearly eight o'clock, Dr Caruso." He pretended not to notice his attention to the dial. "If you do not wish me to leave a message at Colonel Bora's office, and there's no word that he will be available later tonight..."

"You can't leave, if that's what you're thinking of. Stay right where you are, and in half an hour we'll try again. Now call his hotel room. We haven't checked there in forty-five minutes."

"May I at least call my office and check on things?"

"*After* you call the hotel."

Bora was not at the hotel, but Danza, who picked up the phone at the police station, said that Colonel Bora had left a message during the afternoon. "Said it's urgent, Inspector. Said to be at the office tomorrow afternoon between two and three, as he's calling you there."

"All right, I'll be there."

But Guidi didn't tell Caruso that Bora would seek him on the following day.

11

2 JUNE 1944

Early on Friday Dollmann traveled to Frascati despite the artillery battle and the clogged roadways, like nightmarish general maneuvers gone awry. The space between Rome and the Alban Hills was an extended battleground through which he meandered to Kesselring's headquarters. The first sign of Bora's imminent return to the field, in his fashion-conscious eye, was that he had cropped his hair in excess of neatness, until the nape of his neck was shaven clean. He was in fatigues, and as on the first time Dollmann had seen him, the pleasurable impression of toughness flushed him a little.

"Happy name day," Bora said.

"To me and the Pope, thank you. How goes it?"

Bora shook his head. Kesselring had just written off the string of mountain towns between Frosinone and hard-held Lanuvio. Valmontone was practically lost. They met the field marshal, who after a polite exchange of greetings added, "When you go from here, Dollmann, take Colonel Bora along. He has his orders. Leave the city as graciously as you can."

The SS simpered. "There's a Verdi opera tomorrow evening."

"Good, let's have a memorandum about it. All of you will attend, including General Maelzer."

"It's *Un Ballo in Maschera,*" Dollmann added, without adding he'd leave Rome in the morning. "The idea of a political plot during a masked ball is too coincidental to take it with a straight face, but we'll act our parts well."

Afterwards, as they drove back, Dollmann said, "It's been fun. When all is said and done, what fun it's been. There never was a city like Rome, and the chance to operate in it... Ah, it's been fun."

Bora was too tightly hemmed in by melancholy to see what fun it might have been. His regret for leaving Rome outweighed everything else.

"Now be good and continue your irreplaceable service as soldier, Bora. It will see you through political hardships, were you to incur any. The game's entirely unfair, but play it to the best of your ability. For a shrewd player, the best move is always his next. You can't win by checkmate, but how well you can hold your own. Until the board is tilted."

"That, you know, I'd never do."

"Oh, the angel of God will tilt it, even as he'll unhinge the axis of the world at the end of days. Allow me to wax poetic and convey to you that all that remains in conclusion is Love."

Bora was taken aback by the words, but rallied quickly. "Given or received?"

"Given, of course. That which we receive is soon digested. That which we proffer – my dear Bora, you're the one who should understand that – is what keeps us going."

Bora was silent for a time. He was thinking of Mrs Murphy and feeling rather sorry for himself. "Regret is all I can feel right now. It taints everything."

'Why? Your love for others stays."

"Do they want it?"

"They want it." Dollmann looked out of the car to the confusion of vehicles and retreating men. "Do you remember when we stopped by the Bronze Wolf, and you put your hand into her mouth? It was symbolic, and I thought of that gesture for a long time. There's a self-destructive streak in you, your former wife is right. It must be checked. With some luck, it will be checked." He made a little waving motion of dismissal with his hand. "What we did, God is going to count in our favor."

"I hope so."

Dollmann pondered a good long while before speaking his next words. He blurted them out while they were halted and his chauffeur waited outside for a disabled tank to be removed from the road. "You're worse off than you think, Bora. The apology only bought some time. The best thing for you is that the Americans are at the gates and Kappler is dismantling his apparatus, not building it – the Gestapo can produce a file on you in twenty-four hours."

Bora rolled down his window – the car was stifling, both men perspired heavily – and then opened the door altogether, placing one foot out of the car. "Well, those for whom we did what we did can recite the *kaddish* on my grave."

"Don't say such things, not even in fun!"

"I'm not saying them in fun, Colonel."

At two o'clock, Bora telephoned Guidi, and for a couple of minutes related the conversation with the Servigliano records section chief. When Guidi tried to say something, he charged, "Don't interrupt me. I haven't much time and must make it all clear. It is *not* speculation! It's all logical, and we should have thought about it from the start. Whom could Magda Reiner be hiding? An enemy of some kind. A partisan? Unlikely, as he could hardly operate out of a German-owned building. A shirker, then? She spoke no Italian, so it made sense it might be a German deserter."

"So, you found the boyfriend from the Greek Front…"

"No, I didn't. And of course it needn't even be a German, but *someone who spoke German*. I thought about that late neighbor of yours, Antonio Rau, but the Gestapo says he'd been nowhere near that side of Rome. So, I thought, could it be an enemy soldier? How likely is it that an Allied soldier would speak German? I set this aside, as all I had was possibly the

German nickname 'Willi'. But then I began thinking of that William Bader who placed fifth in the obstacle race at the Berlin Olympics, the father of Magda's child."

"Which is why you showed me the book in the lobby of the Piazza Vescovio hospital. I thought you suspected Wilfred Potwen."

"I did until then. But at the hospital the surgeon told me of a wounded American prisoner of war who'd escaped near Albano after a spectacular race leaping across fences despite his impaired leg. The surgeon mentioned a detail that intrigued me: this was the man's second time in imprisonment. He'd already escaped the Servigliano camp and headed south in October of last year, and had just been nabbed trying to sneak out of Rome."

Guidi saw no logical connection whatever, and was keeping his peace only because Bora was not one to have the phone clicked down on him. He said, moderately, "There must be hundreds of Allied prisoners in and out of custody, Colonel."

"Yes. Precisely. It took me forever to get hold of the records section chief at Servigliano, and frankly I had little hope they'd recaptured the man. I was merely expecting to hear confirmation that he'd been there in September, whoever he was. But recapture him they did. The partisan unit that freed him in the Albano countryside headed north to Ascoli Piceno, where William Bader, with new, well-forged papers, was caught for the third time, after a second bounding race."

"But so far you've only placed Bader in Rome."

"His clothes and his shoes place him in Magda Reiner's care, and in 7B besides. He was wearing the rubber-soled shoes she'd gotten Hannah to buy for him at Calzaturificio Torino, and – though they were worse for wear – the clothes from Vernati's."

Guidi had gone from disinterest to keen attention, and satisfaction for his part in the case was only curbed by prudence.

"But how likely is it that she would run into her old flame in a city as large as Rome by accident?"

"Well, Guidi, clearly she ran into him. I am revealing no state secret if I tell you that the Underground or the Church, or both, have operated in favor of all kinds of people, even to the extent of pairing them up with people they'd known in the past. I have confirmation of this particular case from an excellent source." Bora meant Borromeo, whom he'd practically forced to cough up the information. "And you have yourself attended one of our infamous parties, where everything and everybody come together."

"So, this Bader had found his way to Rome from Servigliano, hoping maybe to join the Allied forces coming up the peninsula. Good enough. Having met Magda, she volunteered, or agreed, or was forced to hide him in a place both reasonably secure and close by, just doors down from her own apartment." Guidi did not add the obvious, that Bader was waiting for the Americans to reach Rome. "But wouldn't she be afraid that someone else from the embassy would go into 7B and discover her lover?"

"It's likely that she knew when supplies were to be picked up from storage. Still, it was a dangerous game and she must have been in great fear of being discovered. One of the ways in which she hoped to cover up her clandestine activity was to 'pick up' not one, but two men from our side – Merlo and Sutor."

"Which is why she started dating them shortly after the 30 October party. Bader must have just arrived at her doorstep about then."

"Precisely, Guidi. So, throughout November and most of December she was running the razor's edge of working at the embassy, dating two rivals and hiding the father of her child, now an enemy and fugitive. She might or might not have considered the possibility that Merlo and Sutor would grow jealous of each other. The fact remains that by 9 January all

351

German civilian employees were ordered to leave Rome. This protocol was undoubtedly known to embassy personnel by the end of December."

"So she told Bader that he had to pack."

"Possibly. Or else things had gotten untenable between them. No doubt he knew she was carrying on with two other men, and whether or not it was to protect him, he might have – let us say – resented it. She hoarded food for him, bought him clothes, had a copy made of the key to his hideout – might have had a hand in securing false papers for him. But he had to stay locked up while her lovers came to visit overnight." Bora spoke in German to someone in the office, and then took up again in Italian. "Now, what do you say to this reconstruction of events. When Sutor took her home from the holiday party on the night of her death, he tried to convince her to let him stay. They argued over it and he left in a rage, under the watchful eye of the militiaman Merlo had set after him. He *did not*, as the militiaman was instructed by Merlo to tell you, stay in the building. Had he done so, and I hate to admit it, Magda Reiner might be alive today."

"But if Sutor had left, what about the witness who overheard Magda arguing in German in her apartment?"

"Well, remember Bader was from St Louis, which has a large German immigrant colony. Magda's parents knew little about the athlete she romanced in '36, but they did tell me he spoke German. He *is* the 'Willi' Hannah Kund spoke of. I believe that after Sutor left, she went into 7B and confronted Bader, probably to tell him or remind him he had to pack soon. In addition, God knows, he might have been in a jealous rage. They probably scuffled in the place, or made love, or both – think of the missing underwear – and she lost a button from her dress. I think she, or the Vatican, had gotten him a new set of forged papers, and he burned it to force her to let him stay. This would account for the ashes, which migrated from 7B, likely on his clothes and under his shoes, when he followed her to her apartment. Here she changed for bed, but they ended up arguing again and were overheard – *speaking German*. She might have threatened him, and I suggest he struck her and decided to push her out of the window, as a flight of four storeys would undoubtedly conceal any blows to her face or head and dispose of the danger she now posed."

"But in the confusion after her fall, with Merlo in the whereabouts, neighbors and then the police gathering, would Bader be able to get away?"

"Why not? The light was off in her room, according to reports – indeed, with all that the window was wide open, it took PAI some time to figure out from what apartment on what floor she'd fallen. Remember, the killer locked her bedroom and front door. As we posited earlier, he took her key chain (that, we may never find), went back to 7B to dispose of his bedding and a few other objects in one of Magda's pillowcases, and slipped away in the dark. I'd like to say we made escape from Rome close to impossible, but you and I both know how much actually goes on at night."

"Why do you say that?"

"No particular reason. But it's true, isn't it?" Bora took a breath. "It irks me to think of it, but Bader nearly managed to get out of Rome, though it took him some doing. He was caught without papers on Via Portuense late in January, and only because he was shot in the leg. After ending up in the field hospital at Aprilia, once again he gave us the slip near Albano on 15 February. He got new papers along the way, probably from the Roman underground that set him free. What irks me most is that he was in the field hospital when I visited it, and that I might have even helped him out of the accursed rubble. Anyhow, although the forced evacuation of the hospital after the bombing bought him a couple of weeks on the lam, he's back in our hands now, and I promise you he'll stay there and face trial." This time Guidi could hear the smirk in Bora's voice. "I am thrilled more than I can say."

As this was obviously the sole reason for his call, Bora put down the phone, without giving Guidi a chance to mention Caruso's request for a meeting. And there was no telling what Caruso would say to the possibility of exonerating *Ras* Merlo from the charge of murder.

That evening Cardinal Borromeo was having dinner, and listened to the radio while he did so. Unceremoniously for his station, he asked Bora to sit at the other end of his long refectory table. "A bit of tongue, Colonel Bora?"

"No, thank you. I am on my way to Countess Ascanio's, but had to stop by. Cardinal, are you going to the opera tomorrow?"

"I never miss the season's opening. I have seats with the diplomatic corps. Why?"

"Excellent. Thank you. I need to see you there."

Borromeo made a very strange face. "Colonel, you do not plan to…"

Bora understood, and blushed violently. "It's best if you do not offend me by saying it, Cardinal."

Another slice of tongue was transferred by the manicured hand of the prelate to his plate. "I'm relieved. About-faces greatly trouble me. But you are meeting me now, so it must be for someone else that you wish to see me."

"Yes."

"For the *sake* of someone else?"

"You could say so."

"I'll be there. Now, don't run off. Stay seated, and give yourself ten minutes to think whether you really want to *meet me* at the Opera House."

Bora would not argue. He sat back, resting his shoulders against the padded back of the chair. The music was very well known to him – Schubert's unfinished Sonata in C major. He had played it beautifully once. Not just as an accomplished interpreter, but with beauty. With beauty. How does one draw such beauty back into oneself? He had unwisely used his time in Rome, and as such he must be chased from it. The love proffered, Dollmann was right: it was the love *not* given that haunted him tonight. Across the tureens and cruets of the narrow table he looked at Borromeo, who remorselessly broke Church discipline by eating meat on Friday.

"I'll see you tomorrow night after the end of the opera, Cardinal."

Donna Maria had not really spoken to Bora since Sunday night. They'd been avoiding each other in the strange little ways people who are close elude real contact, through courteous superficiality. Tonight Bora found her in the dark parlor with the window open, a distant glare of fires visible over the crest of the roofs.

He undid his belt and laid down his gun. Like a lover he put his arms around her from behind, holding her. She rested her head against him. "Martin, it's burning in the hills." She stared out. "Look out there, look – what's down that way?"

Bora looked where the sky tongued red, higher at times than others. "Either Castel Gandolfo or Albano." And he felt her ache in the security of his hold, knowing it was not to last.

"Martin, when will you…?"

"Soon enough, Donna Maria."

She tried hard not to cry at the words. She freed herself and went to sit on her sewing chair, still facing the window. Bora sat at her feet.

"Why don't you go to The Seagull? You can stay there, just stay there until the Americans arrive, and then it's going to be all right. No one need know. You can make your war end there."

He stroked her knees. "Now, now, are you really telling me this, Donna Maria?"

She pulled a handkerchief from her cuff and blew her nose into it. "No, I'm not. I'm being a foolish old goose. But what else can women do to keep their men except weep?"

"I don't think Dikta ever wept."

"She didn't keep you, either." It was the opposite, but Bora kept silent. Donna Maria dabbed her eyes. "I know what you're thinking, Martin. The truth is that until *you* let go, she's still inside and won't let others in."

He didn't want to talk about it. Pulling away, he tried to remove himself from her mind reaching out. "It's not easy any more."

"Why, what's the matter? How are things different?" Against his will, she took his left wrist and placed it on her knees. "How are things different?"

"You're holding the difference, Donna Maria."

Her grasp around his wrist was unanticipated, hard, to the edge of pain. "Am I? Is *this* the difference? You are perfect *now*."

The words raced at him. They opened an unexpected chasm, the caving in of a crust of pretense, under which his disbelief and need for the words were ravenous. "How can you say that? If ever there was hope for some perfection before…"

"That's where you're wrong. Perfection is sometimes achieved by subtraction, not addition. You're perfect now, or you never understood perfection. A hand was well worth the prize of it." She placed his right hand on his own wounded arm. "You had better listen to me, Martin Bora – *this is perfection*."

That night, when he arrived home after the lonely drive to the Tiburtino district, Guidi found two men waiting at the top of the stairs. Dim light rained on them from the bulb hanging above, like yellow dust. Hand on the rail, without stopping he slowed down his climb.

"Inspector Guidi, we're Francesca's friends."

Silently Guidi stepped up, took the key from his pocket. The men stood aside to let him pass, waiting until he opened and nodded his head toward the inside of his apartment. But they let him walk in first. By the bulges in their coats Guidi knew they were heavily armed. "To the kitchen," he said. Here, he pulled a couple of chairs away from the table and the men sat down, wide-kneed as swaggering farm boys, hands spread on their thighs.

Guidi stood before them, and because they looked the room over for exits, he casually removed the pistol from the holster under his arm. "I'm listening."

No other explanations were given or asked. The younger of the two, so dark as to seem blue-haired, with a narrow and obstinate forehead, said, "Francesca talked about you."

"And said…?"

"That you could be counted on in an emergency."

Guidi said neither yes nor no. "What else did she tell you?"

"That you're familiar with a German aide."

So, it was all coming to a head, somehow. Guidi remained tense, even if no warning had been spoken and the men seemed altogether deferential. They were idealists, whom Francesca's death filled with honest and daring rage. Ignorant, no doubt, of the source of the money that floated from her to their cause. Guidi had the impression that, had they known, they might have killed Francesca themselves. He said slowly, "It's true, I know Colonel Bora. Now I'm familiar with you, too."

The blue-haired youth clicked his tongue to dismiss the similarity. "You just met us. But the German – we know who he is. He fought the partisans up north. We tried to get him last month and another comrade paid with his life for it."

"Rau?"

"You know how it went. This Bora, he hasn't returned to his hotel in days. Where is he?"

Guidi's attention ran from one man to the other – the older one was partly bald, pale, with deeply set, passionate eyes. Yes, that was true, Rau had paid with his life for it. And whoever had killed Francesca could have had reasons he, Guidi, could not and would not tell her two companions. Perhaps to protect Francesca's memory, perhaps not to soil these men's grief. Making them wait for an answer, Guidi knew he was facing the foot soldiers, those who risked their skin without fuss.

Those who did not indulge in double-dealing and could not be negotiated with or mollified. Finally, he said, "I have no idea of where he is." And, "Why don't you go after those who killed her like a dog?"

"If we knew who it was, we'd do it, make no mistake about it. So, about Bora – will he try to see you before he leaves Rome?"

"Your guess is as good as mine."

"We can't get close to him at the Flora, Inspector. You, he met where you lived before, and elsewhere. We're not asking what you did or said when you met, but now is the time to do your part."

Guidi was tired. The words didn't disturb him; he had thought of them before. "What are you asking me to do?"

"Bring the German to us."

3 JUNE 1944

The voice that answered the phone was deep, and well known. "Bora here."

Guidi had nearly lost hope of reaching him this morning. For a moment he seemed to forget what the call was about. Uneasily he presented Caruso's plight to Bora, who listened.

"If the chief of police wanted to contact me, he should have done so personally. I have no time to see him today. Tomorrow morning, perhaps."

"At what time?"

"Nine o'clock sharp. If he's even two minutes late, the meeting is off."

"I'll tell him." Neither man lowered the receiver, waiting for the other to add something.

Caruso swept the phone from Guidi's hand and slammed it down. "Tomorrow morning?" He had an exasperated air about him and nearly as much arrogance as he'd shown Guidi before. "What does he think I am, a subordinate who is shelved until he *has time* to deal with me? You should have insisted on a meeting today, this evening at the latest!"

Guidi kept his peace. He knew Caruso had packed overnight and was ready to go.

"Does this Kraut think I'll go begging?" he was spouting off. "Does he think he can instruct me on punctuality? There's still hierarchy in the German Army – he cannot do as he pleases!"

"It's hard to tell at this point what the German can and cannot, or would not, do."

"He's trying to save himself, that's what it is!" Wide-eyed with panic, Caruso paced the room. "He's planning to sneak out of Rome and will not show up at all in the morning, making me waste time." He stopped short of admitting he, too, was racing north, but it hardly needed spelling out. "The Germans are leaving like rats. Day and night, getting out. Whom does Bora think he's fooling? But I'll show *him*. I'll go at once to his command and *demand* to be received. I'll show him whose guests he and his are."

Bora was so amused by Caruso's presence at headquarters, his anger was lessened by it.

He came to meet him downstairs, in the lobby where he waited in a fury.

"I thought our appointment was for tomorrow morning."

Caruso grew apoplectic at the words. "It's hardly at a lieutenant colonel's convenience that a general meets!"

"If the general is asking for a favor, he may wish to forego rank protocol."

"I only expect what is *due* to me."

"German escort out of Rome?"

Clearly Caruso did not expect to have the initiative taken from him. He mouthed like a fish pulled out of the bowl, searching for words. "My long collaboration with German authorities demands that I be ensured a safe passage to rejoin our forces in the north."

Bora stared at him with a face in which Caruso read neither empathy nor involvement. A hard-eyed face whereby he knew the Germans would leave him behind and to himself, to be torn by the mob if need be as had been done elsewhere. Had Bora at least said something in the way of a refusal, he could argued argued the point, but Bora said nothing.

"Look here, Colonel," he insisted. "You owe it to me!"

"We owe you nothing."

Caruso seemed about to choke on saliva and spite. "I have... *How can you?* I have made it possible for the Germans to rule this city!"

"We didn't need you to rule."

"I..." As hopelessness yawned before him, words poured out of Caruso unrehearsed and fervid with reproach, tragic in their sincerity. "I have... Do you mean to say... After I prostituted my office to your authorities..."

"That's your problem. Don't come to us with scruples."

"But I demand that you provide me with an escort! I demand, I *command* you to do so!"

"I am not at your orders."

Caruso looked like one whom the measure of betrayal is engulfing. "You ungrateful whoresons!" he cried out in agony. "You goddamned filthy whoresons, you tricked me! I gave you all I had and you took advantage of me and now you think you can throw me away! But I won't let you! I'll go straight to Maelzer; I'll show you who is in control!"

The shouting attracted soldiers to the lobby, but Bora dismissed them with a gesture.

"The door is there and Via Veneto is outside the door, Dr Caruso. Would you care for a glass of water before you go?"

Guidi hadn't had time to finish saying what he wanted when Caruso had snatched the telephone from him. After returning to his office he dialed Bora's number again, and Bora answered, unruffled even after meeting Caruso. "What is it, Guidi?"

"Colonel, I couldn't get the head of police even remotely interested in the resolution of the Reiner case. I expect you'll take care of prosecuting it."

"You bet I will."

"Also, I was thinking that we haven't met in over two weeks, and maybe we should." Guidi regretted the word. *Should? Is "should" the right word? Why will he think I said "should"?*

Bora did not answer.

"I was thinking about noon. How's noon for you?"

Bora stayed quiet. Whether he suspected something, or was taken aback by the invitation, he kept an obstinate silence that made things more difficult. Guidi was glad Danza was out of the office, as Danza was one to see through people. He continued, "We could meet at Villa Umberto. What about Goethe's monument? We could meet there. It will be a matter of minutes." Despite himself, he swallowed hard. "I do have to talk to you." The only sign that Bora remained at the other end of the line was that the receiver had not been clicked down. "What do you say?"

"I'll be there."

At eleven, Kappler had just taken leave from General Maelzer when he met Bora coming up the stairs at the Excelsior, bound to report to the general about the Reiner case. They exchanged a salute. Bora had already gone several steps when the SS addressed him. He turned to where Kappler stood relaxed, hip against the banister.

"Bora, just out of curiosity – what did your father die of?"

"Cancer."

"What kind of cancer?"

"Throat."

"Did he suffer very much?"

Bora was carrying his leather briefcase, which now he placed at his feet to appear calmer and less in haste than he was. "I don't know, I was just born. I expect he did."

Kappler nodded. "Do you ever worry you might get the same?"

"Sometimes."

"And are you afraid of pain, Colonel Bora?"

"Yes."

"It's good that you are, you know." Kappler brought the flat of his hand to the visor of his cap. "Have a good trip north, Bora."

Back from the Excelsior, Bora made an unplanned stop by his office before driving to Villa Umberto, across the street.

"Colonel, there's a message from one Inspector Guidi for you," an orderly informed him as he walked in. "He says he can't make the appointment."

"Did he say why?"

"No, sir."

Guidi arrived alone at Goethe's monument, and sat by it for half an hour before the blue-haired young man idly strolled by and asked for a light. When Guidi held out a match for him, he said, "It looks like our friend isn't coming," and took a drag of smoke.

Guidi blew on the match. The pompous marble group, with the poet standing on a fat, elaborate capital like on a wedding cake, was blinding in the midday sun. "It seems so."

"Why did you tell us he was?"

"Because he was."

"Well, make another appointment with him." Guidi's lack of reaction made the young man intolerant. "You know, you're a policeman already, a servant of the Regime. You'll look an awful lot like a collaborator if you don't do something *right now* about having dealt with the Germans on a regular basis."

Guidi gave him a void look. He had been rolling himself a cigarette, and he now ran the along edge of paper with the tip of his tongue to moisten it. One hand on his hip, Goethe seemed about to take flight from his crowded monument. "We've all played into the Germans' hands one way or another. Where were *you* on 23 March?"

"This is June, Inspector. Let March sit where it is." The man watched Guidi leave the bench, hands in his pocket. "Where are you going?"

"To lunch."

"We'll be in touch later today."

Guidi shrugged.

That afternoon, Bora was driving down Via San Francesco, but even in the car he was aware of the change, not knowing what it was. He rolled down his window and listened. Got out of the car. Against the mirror brightness of the sky, the heads of the pines at the edge of the park rounded dark above him. For the first time in months he heard the wind rustle through them. The sound of the wind whispering in the branches over the silence. He held his breath, listening to the lack of noise. Suddenly the whole city, the whole world had fallen asleep, and enchantment would hold it now for a hundred years in stillness. He could all but hear his own heartbeat. The small creakings of the car that cooled off after stopping. The crinkle of a piece of paper that came wind-tossed over the pavement. And the tidewater sound of the pines over him.

Guidi was eating at his trattoria without hunger. Across the floor, with plates of pasta balanced in his hands, the waiter stopped in mid-stride. His face looked stunned, as if he'd been hit and wondered where the blow came from. Guidi put down his fork and raised his eyes to the door. Silence was a visitor. It came in and people looked at it and were amazed, and didn't know how to greet it, or what to do with it.

Signora Carmela perceived the cessation of noise, that was all. The glass domes in her parlor ceased tinkling, and, suddenly taciturn, the saints stood beneath them.

The shelves in Donna Maria's parlor also grew quiet. She set the lace pillow aside and went to open the window. The street was mute. Swallows cut through it as scissors through cloth. From one of the roses Martin Bora had given her the petals fell, and even the falling of petals on the table had a soft sound of its own in the great silence.

Cardinal Borromeo was saying Mass alone, and stopped. With his face to the altar he listened, so unmoving that the candle flames before him became vertical and long in the twilight of the chapel.

The woman with the cherry lips let go of the skirt she had been zipping on her fleshy side.

At the hospital, Treib sat up in his chair, eyes on the wall clock.

Maelzer poured himself a glass of Frascati wine and gulped it all.

Bora realized how much he had missed silence, and welcomed it no matter what it meant. The living and the dead, he felt, could now rest within themselves. Jails and barracks and graves would feed on silence, and hope for peace. His last orders in Rome entailed the destruction of barracks, depots and dumps, but not until tomorrow. He was grateful, ever so grateful he did not have to break the silence today.

When Guidi returned to the office, Danza, who was a model of timeliness, was not there. On his desk, just outside the inspector's door, his uniform was neatly folded, cap and pistol holder laid above the rest. No pistol in the holder. On a sheet of notebook paper, in pencil, the words, *It is more honorable now to be a partisan than a policeman.* And several banknotes were clipped to the paper, so that it couldn't be said he'd made off with state property without paying.

Nothing in some time had seemed as bizarre as the opening of the opera season Saturday night. Bora sensed great relaxation in the air, even humor. The theater blazed with elegance of dresses and uniforms, beautiful women and decorated men. The Fascists had nearly all gone, but Germans filled the audience. Rumors were that troops had taken position south of the city, but the exodus of entire units continued in the dark outside.

Having arrived with Donna Maria, whom he had after much insistence convinced to come, Bora saw among others General Maelzer accompanied by two women, and Kappler with his lover, a discreet Dutch girl Dollmann had heartlessly bad-talked to him. Without much hope he looked around to catch a glimpse of Mrs Murphy. She'd mentioned studying Italian as a child in Florence. Did she truly like opera? Were all the diplomats still around? Borromeo's box, which Donna Maria pointed out to him, was still empty when she and Bora took place in their box opposite to it. By a stir of clothing in the semi-darkness, after the lights went down, he perceived that he'd come, not alone, just as the curtain rose.

At the intermission he was about to ask the old lady to join him in the foyer. He did turn, and that was all he did. Across the theater, in a lilac gown that enclosed her like a flower, Mrs Murphy sat in Borromeo's box.

Donna Maria, sunken in her seat like a black satin turtle, noticed his stare. "I don't want to go downstairs," she said, peering at the box through her opera glasses. "You go."

Bora paid no attention. He disappointedly watched the cardinal's box fill with visitors, and did not move.

"Well, Martin, weren't you to meet the cardinal?"

"Not with other people there, Donna Maria."

"If I wanted to talk to somebody, a mob wouldn't keep me from doing it."

Bora faced her frankly. "It's propriety, not shyness."

She sat in her jet-embroidered satin with a scowl. When she shook her head, the diamonds at her ears flashed their diminutive lightning. "Martin, pay attention to the opera. You might learn something from the love story in it."

At the second intermission she caught Borromeo's eye and signified she wanted to meet him in the foyer, to which she descended, leaning heavily on Bora's arm. Immediately cornered by General Maelzer, Bora had to shoulder his way among epaulets and bare backs to the other side of the hall in order to approach Mrs Murphy before the start of the third act. She saw him coming and did not move from where she stood. "I can hardly believe you are still all here," she coolly interjected. "The silence of the guns is ominous."

"I am so glad to see you, Ma'am."

As once before, she smiled at the British formality of his address. "Thank you." At her side was stationed a tall adolescent, whose face was ridden with acne and incipient fuzz. "May I introduce my stepson Patrick Junior? Patrick, this is Lieutenant Colonel Bora." Bora nodded his head, ignoring him entirely. "Patrick will be entering Columbia in the fall."

An impatient glance was all Bora could volunteer in the way of acknowledgment. He understood the meaning of the boy's presence, but was so desperately pressed for time, he rejected it. With a slight bow of his head, he said, "Mrs Murphy, I ask you the kindness of allowing me to speak to you privately after the performance."

"For what reason?"

He found himself justified in lightly touching her elbow to guide her aside. "There's a favor I must beg of you."

"Is it in return to yours? I should have known."

Her face, her eyes. I must remember them, must remember the way her lips move, the cast of her face when she looks away. The color and scent, her small perfection. "Please give me a few moments after the opera, Mrs Murphy."

"If you insist."

The third act went by, with Donna Maria quite sure Bora had heard none of it. He slipped so quickly out of the box afterwards, she decided to wave to Cardinal Borromeo for him to accompany her below. Soon she saw how Bora, having succeeded in dodging Maelzer, other uniforms and the pimple-faced boy, was now talking to the woman in the lilac gown.

"I wasn't hoping to see you here, Mrs Murphy, so I planned to give this to Cardinal Borromeo." Unobtrusively, he placed a small envelope into her hand.

"Is it for the cardinal, or for me?"

"It's for you." She began to open it, and he prevented her. "I'd rather if you didn't. I'd like to talk to you for a minute. There'll be time enough to read that."

Mrs Murphy slipped the envelope into a round, beaded purse. "I cannot imagine —"

"I believe you can." Bora had such a cowardly desire to hold her, he had to force himself from doing it. "Mrs Murphy, I am —"

"Leaving? That's quite obvious."

"It's not what I meant."

"Well, it's very contrived for all of you to be here."

Bora disregarded what she said, was not listening at all. "It's been very important for me to make your acquaintance. I have been *really* thinking about you a great deal."

"How so?"

"With respect. Oh, with much respect."

"You flatter me."

"If circumstances allowed, I would show my respect for you."

She looked behind him, clearly made uncomfortable by his words, but unwilling to concede she was. When she returned her eyes to him, her gracious calm was regained. "I appreciate your intent. Circumstances do not allow. Now, what is the favor you ask of me?"

"Not to throw my note away."

"I don't even know what it contains!"

"Please do not throw it away."

She could have looked away from him now, but did not. "It's a silly request."

"Not to me. Promise me you won't." Bora heard the testy earnestness of his own words, but lack of time made him discard diplomacy for any method that would convince her.

"Very well, I promise."

"Thank you." He'd have kissed her hand hadn't Maelzer stepped between them with a champagne glass in each hand, jostling them apart from one another. And already the pock-marked young Patrick rejoined her, with the bored look of one who wants to leave. "Goodbye, Mrs Murphy."

"Take care of yourself, Colonel Bora."

Grasping her cane, at the same moment Donna Maria told Borromeo, "Nino, you haven't changed in forty years. You're still as devious as in the old days."

"Alas, Donna Maria, you would know. It's hard to go straight in this profession."

"And on top of it all you're blasphemous! You never did take your calling seriously."

Borromeo smirked. "How can I help it? I was in love with you even as a young priest."

"Liar. It's true that you were in love, but not with me."

"There's no pretending with you, is there?"

"Well, it makes no difference, but that's why I'd never use you as a confessor. Now tell me, what will happen to my godchild? I've seen tonight what you've been up to."

"He's in the hands of God, like the rest of us. And so is she."

Donna Maria tapped him with the knob of her cane. What a bad priest you are – *the hands of God*! God ought to squash you between them like a fly."

Guidi's apartment felt hollow like a seashell, in the silence of the outside. It made thinking too easy. The noise of war had for weeks been used by all of them as an excuse not to think deeply. All unconfessed truths surfaced now, guilts and regrets and what gutless ambiguity had first made him invite Bora to an ambush and then give him a way out of it. In the face of Danza's quiet decision, he was ashamed of both actions.

It was common knowledge that German officers attended the opera tonight, but unlikely for an accident to happen in the heavily patrolled surroundings of the theater. He fully expected the young men from *Unione e Libertà* to bound up the stairs to his door any time, vengeful in their ignorance of Francesca's dark side. He had no answer ready for them. He'd say what he'd say, whatever came to his mind.

Donna Maria had already left with Bora when Mrs Murphy opened the envelope. Smoothly Cardinal Borromeo approached her. "Good news?"

She looked up from the note in disbelief. "Your Eminence, the man is out of his mind!"

Borromeo smiled. "Whether he's out of it or not, he certainly has much on it. Well, don't worry. Only about ten per cent of them will make it past the first miles out of Rome."

"And I promised not to throw it away!"

Borromeo, notwithstanding his abominable English, was nevertheless dying of curiosity to read the note. "You could give it to the Holy Church for safe keeping, thereby observing the promise without having to keep it around."

"It's a rather private note, Your Eminence."

"Oh. You are an innocent recipient of it, I hope?"

"No, because I haven't discouraged him enough."

The cardinal raised his eyebrows philosophically. "You can no more keep a man from falling in love than from getting himself killed for some empty cause. Give it a little more time, and Bora might succeed in both." He craned his neck, and Mrs Murphy hesitatingly showed him the note.

My dear Mrs Murphy,

I realize it sounds highly presumptuous from a man who has no control over his destiny, but some certainties must be spoken despite the oddity of circumstances. For two months now I have been telling myself that, no matter what awaits either one of us in the near future, in five years' time it will be my honor to marry you. Despite all that cries out the opposite, please believe

I know this in my soul. And if my soul should be wrong, then be so good as to think sometimes of this German, whom I do so wish for you not to despise.

Borromeo made an effort not to smirk at the signature. How truly German Bora was, who should identify himself to his beloved as "Yours respectfully". He held his hand out, but Mrs Murphy quietly replaced the note in the envelope, and this inside her little purse.

The dark, younger man was alone. He came close to midnight – a rap on Guidi's door, a grating of fingers rather than a strike of knuckles. "You shouldn't leave the door open," he said, warily walking in.

Guidi, who had been reading *L'Inafferrabile*, put it down. "It could only be you, the Germans or the Americans. The way I see it, there's little I can do to prevent any of you from getting in."

The young man sat astride a chair. "We got the German aide," he announced, eyes leveled at him. "He's dead."

Guidi's heart felt as if a hand were squeezing it, an unexpected, icy and cruel grasp. "Imagine that." Words came out of him like drops. "Imagine that. And you didn't even need my help to do it."

"Well, we thought you'd want to know. We must have shot him ten times at least."

The icy hand stayed around his heart, much to Guidi's surprise. And the drops of his words fought to trickle out. "It's the only way to make sure."

With a flourish, the young man whipped his gun out and cocked it. "He begged us not to, but we kept shooting."

"He *begged* you?" Not Bora. Not Bora. Guidi suddenly saw through the lie, and even though the gun was pointed at him, he felt like laughing in relief, and anger for feeling relieved. "I bet you finished him up with a hole through the head."

"Right through the head, yes."

370

"*Why are you telling him this nonsense?*"

Guidi did not move, though the cocked gun dangerously swayed when the young man turned to the door, where his older companion stood. "I just wanted to see —"

"What's there to see, you jackass? And why didn't you lock the door? Never mind him, Inspector, we wouldn't be here if we'd gotten the son of a bitch. He was at the opera, all right, but we couldn't get close. Looks like they'll pull out tomorrow, so we need you to get him here – not at the park, *here*. Once we're done, you don't even have to worry about the body. The Germans are running to save their skin." Sheepishly the younger man left the chair, and the balding partisan turned it around to sit in it. "So, what time can you get him here?"

Guidi picked up his paperback again. "I won't get him here."

"What do you mean?"

"If you want him, you'll have to get him yourselves. He's neither immortal nor invulnerable – you find him and you kill him." He ignored the men's incredulous faces, the fierce anger of the younger one. "I had my chance to kill him and didn't. As for your pointing your guns at me, it can't be worse than the Germans did to me in March. After waiting hours for death at the caves, I think I can stand under your guns until you fire."

4 JUNE 1944

Most officers had left before dawn. Bora found Donna Maria ready to see him off. She looked older and frailer but was entirely dressed, down to her jewelry, even though it was five in the morning. "I'm going to work, Donna Maria."

"And away."

"Yes."

She kept up her image of control. Impatiently tapping her cane on the floor, she demanded his embrace and then pushed him back. From the top of the piano she took a flat, soft bundle of fine wrapping paper, bound by a ribbon. "Your next wife's wedding lace. Take it along."

Bora smiled at her hopefulness. "I may not be able to keep it safely in the next few weeks. Won't you keep it for me?"

"No. This is the last visit we'll have with each other, Martin. Every time I knew I'd see you again, but not after this time. And I want to give you the lace with my hands. Put it in your briefcase. Let me see you do it."

Bora did so, with care. "Donna Maria, you'll live to be a hundred."

"I hope not."

Guidi sat by the window and rolled himself a morning cigarette. Swallows criss-crossed the space in front of the window, calling to one another with shrill cries. He'd already gone down the flight of stairs to the telephone, but the line was dead. Anyway, what could he tell Bora, short of informing him the partisans would wait for him here? He couldn't think of a practical way to keep him away if he ever planned to come. To distract himself, he tried to turn the radio on. There was no power. No tramways would function, no lights would go on. And the silence continued.

When he left home to buy the Sunday edition, Guidi found that none had been published. Stray groups of Germans were still shuffling past, dazed and hollow-eyed; those crowded in the back of trucks slept on one another despite the uneven ride on cobblestones. The last of the Fascist leaders rolled on, their faces hidden by spread magazines as they read yesterday's news to hide themselves from the people. A few militia privates who tried to hitch rides were knocked about by cars and trucks, and the Germans woke up then and struck them with the butts of their rifles to keep them down.

The Lesson for the day read, "The just man, though he die early, shall be at rest."

Bora came out from early Mass at St Catherine's, down the street from Donna Maria's. He walked to his car and drove to the Excelsior, where he sat about half an hour with commanders of the Corps of Engineers. Then he took from the Hotel d'Italia what remained of his few things, leaving only a razor on the side of the sink. By old war superstition, he'd learned always to leave one small object behind, as his security for coming back.

The hotel lobby was empty. While he had a cup of coffee, an SS man came looking for a colleague. Bora knew him from Kappler's office, and asked him how things were. He heard that Kappler had left Rome at eight o'clock.

The SS looked unnerved. "There's terrible strafing on the way, Colonel. Airplanes swooping down from all sides – we might as well have been killed fighting in the street. Goodbye, Colonel."

From the sidewalk, as he returned home from the newsstand, Guidi recognized *Ras* Merlo only by his shiny pomaded head. In hastily thrown together civilian clothes, he was stepping across the street with a small suitcase, likely bound for the Tiburtina train station. What better place to hide from his own, principally Caruso, than this peripheral working-class district? He must be trying his luck out of the city now. Guidi was about to call out to him to stop a moment. He'd introduce himself and – mostly to spite Caruso – tell him that Magda's death had been solved. As if this were the right moment to talk of German lovers.

All the while Merlo kept going toward Via della Lega Lombarda, taking quick short steps like a toy that has been wound, a scene of haste as grotesque and surreal as the Pirandello play now so long ago. Even when a confusion of loud voices was heard behind the street corner, he did not relent his march, but, white-faced, he made straight for it.

Mobs of exasperated people roamed the streets looking for swift vengeance, Guidi knew well enough. "Merlo!" he shouted. "Here, Merlo!" He was unable to make him stop, though his eyes darted toward the sidewalk where Guidi stood waving to him "Into the doorway, quick!"

Merlo continued to walk mechanically. "I'm an honest man!" he shouted back. "I've done nothing wrong, the people know I've done nothing wrong!"

"*Come into the doorway!*"

Guidi had no time to insist. A screaming crowd came from around the corner, men in shirtsleeves and hatless women. It would have parted and streamed past Merlo, too, had one of the women not recognized him. Promptly the mob surged and tightened around him like a knot.

"*Fascista, Fascista!*"

Merlo's voice was only heard once, crying out that he had never stolen from the people. His suitcase, snatched from him and held aloft, traveled over the crowd from hand to hand.

"*Fascista!*"

Punches and kicks were flying already. Appalled, Guidi ran upstairs to fetch his pistol. When he opened the window to look again, he saw how tearing and throwing blows, men and women exorcized the suffering of months, and by their motions Guidi knew the man in the middle had fallen and was now being trampled.

It took all of five minutes, after which the third shot Guidi fired in the air was finally heard. The undulating mob drew away from Merlo and looked down at him, half-naked and bloodied, his face smashed into an unrecognizable pulp. Next, they went for his suitcase, which was forced open with a renewed frenzy in search of money and stolen goods.

There was only underwear in it.

The engineer yelled, "She sure went down beautifully!" meaning the Macao Barracks by the university.

Bora had a list, from which he scratched another line. The telephone office at the Ministry of Communications had gone first, followed by dumps and fuel depots; next would come

374

train stations, radio stations, the block-long Fiat Works. "Try to avoid the houses around," he said.

"We'll do the best we can."

Before noon Bora reported to Maelzer with the Reiner dossier, to be forwarded to the German ambassador.

"Fine, fine." Maelzer put the folder on a chair, shook his hand, gave him a sealed bottle of vodka and left Rome.

The trattoria had been badly shaken by the explosions of the barracks nearby. Curtain rods had fallen from the windows, and two panes had been blown right off the sashes. Stacks of dishes had cascaded onto the floor and Guidi had to stumble past them to sit down at his usual place. Lunch was served in pots and pans. But the waiter had a sparkle in his eye. "The English are in Rome already!"

Guidi, who'd done all he could to get the sight of Merlo's mauled body out of his mind, finally succeeded in doing so. "No-o!" he said, making an incredulous face.

"I'm telling you they're at Porta Maggiore, or just outside. Look – meat!" The waiter placed a pan under his nose. "I bought it from the Germans this morning, and ten minutes later they were *giving* it away. Flour, sugar, canned pork – I couldn't haul all of it!"

Bora had a glass of water for lunch. It was all he could hold down. He hadn't been so nauseous since Stalingrad, but that's how it was. He continued going down the list, and looking at the map of Rome on his knees he realized he had long ago stopped viewing it as the old exquisite organism it was. Today it only looked like a combination of checkpoints to destroy.

Back in his apartment, Guidi sat on his bed and then lay on it and fell asleep. For all he knew, the partisans were watching his house, and there was nothing he could do about it. He couldn't reach Bora and warn him – hell, Bora was probably long out of Rome. So he slept.

When he awoke, the clock marked five in the afternoon. No more explosions. Silence once more. He went to the window. The streets were empty. The Germans had left. And the Americans – the Americans must be entering from the south. The electricity was still off.

Bora left headquarters for the last time at six o'clock in the evening. He checked the amount of fuel in his car. With a letter from Maelzer to hand-deliver to the Secretary of State, he drove to St Peter's. The square was empty. No German guards cordoning it off as in months past. He walked the interminable, echoing corridors behind a swift, young Irish priest who kept his hands clenched against his chest like a maiden.

For about an hour Bora sat with Cardinal Montini, answering his many questions. At the end of the meeting, he was given a cased rosary "from His Holiness". It was the third or fourth he had received since coming to Rome, but politely he thanked the Secretary and put it in his briefcase. The orderly mound of other such cases, he perceived, awaited the first Americans who should walk in here hours from now.

At nine o'clock there was some shooting near St Mary Major, apparently an engagement between the last of the Germans and soldiers of the 5th Army, then no more sounds. Guidi blew out the candle and sat waiting in the dark, not knowing for what.

At ten o'clock suddenly the power came back on. His radio began to blare some happy music and the light flashed bright. By habit, Guidi hastened to the window to close it, but saw that all lights at all windows were on too, none shielded, none covered. They were only windows, but seemed an unbearable blaze of splendor coming through the night. Scampering was heard below, running in the street. Faint voices of rejoicing traveled from all corners of the city, a long way off.

The knock on the door he had expected all day. He went to open, fully ready to confront the partisans, but it was Martin Bora.

He nearly jumped back in surprise. Bora did not convey the image of being in haste, though he must be. Guidi was too astonished to say anything. He waved an invitation to come in. Whether Bora understood it might be so that a German would not be seen at his doorstep, he gave no impression of minding it. "I have come to say goodbye,' he said.

Finally Guidi got his wits together. "What are you still doing here at this hour? Everyone has gone. The Americans are already at the outskirts..."

"They're in the city," Bora mildly corrected him. "I know. But this is the earliest I could find a moment to stop by."

Guidi forgot about the partisans. He stared at Bora with a crazy need to weep. "I'm glad you came."

Bora said he was glad he did.

"Do you have transportation?"

"Oh, yes."

"Is there... anything you need?"

Bora laughed a little. "No, I'm traveling light. It's the safest way to do it."

From his gear Guidi surmised he wasn't simply going north. It was in battle array that Bora left Rome, likely to set up resistance along the way at a railroad bridge or bend in the road, or village perched on the mountainside. "I don't expect us to meet again," Bora continued with a lightness of sorts. It was unlike him to lack intensity, unless he was by force keeping himself from it. "So I had to stop." He stretched his hand out, and Guidi hesitated before taking it, for a moment thinking they should be embracing instead. But Bora was not a man to embrace another. He stood looking straight at him, hand vigorously clasped around his. "Goodbye, Guidi. Be well."

Guidi watched Bora turn to the door. Then his sickly unwillingness to be hurt angered him into what he said next. "There's something you must hear," he said when Bora was already past the threshold and bound for the first step. "I will be joining the Resistance even as you leave the city."

Bora halted on the step without turning. He simply nodded and continued down. His quick pace went down the stairs, and shortly his car drove off the curb into the night.

At Porta Pia the cheering was wild as the American convoy traveled along Corso Italia toward the abandoned German headquarters, looming on the curve that bent deeply in the direction of Via Veneto. Mrs Murphy sat up in bed, wide-awake at the sound of voices under the windows. Her husband stood at the windowsill in his pajamas, talking in English to someone below. "Welcome to Rome, boys!" he was saying, and she began to laugh and cry.

Guidi sat with his door still open, as when Bora had walked away. When the two men bounded upstairs, he had been waiting for them.

"He's been here, hasn't he?"

"You shouldn't have left your lookout to celebrate. Yes, he's been here."

"Which way did he go?" Even the older, wiser partisan was high-strung, hopeful and keen like a hunter who found the trail.

"North."

"Well, of course, north! Don't you play stupid, Inspector – which road did he take?"

"The Cassia."

"Did he tell you that? How do we know it's true?"

Guidi believed it to be true. "If you catch up with him," he said, "you'll know."

A long way from the Cassia, near Ponte Salario where one could see the moonlit shaft of an ancient watchtower and little else, Bora walked from his car to the wayside inn. "Colonel," his driver asked, "is this a good moment to stop?"

"Yes, it is."

The innkeeper remembered Bora from a couple of lunches with Dollmann, but tonight he was beside himself at the sight of German uniforms. His wife could be heard crying in the bedroom when he looked down from a narrow balcony above the door. "What's that? Who's this? Oh, it's you, sir! Go with God, go with God, don't get us involved now that the Americans are so close!"

Bora began to laugh despite himself, and it was strange to be laughing in the full light of the moon on a night like this. "All I want is for you to set dinner for however many you can serve, and I want to pay in advance."

"*Dinner!* Are you joking? You have the Allies behind you!"

"Come get the money, man, and tell me how many you can serve. I don't care to shout from here."

The innkeeper came downstairs, but only cracked his door. "Eighty, maybe a hundred."

"A company, that's perfect. Here, pay yourself."

The man felt the money Bora drove into his hands. "It's too much!"

"Throw in some extra wine."

"You don't have that many men with you…" The innkeeper peered out.

"It's not for my men."

"But then —"

"If the Americans ask, tell them it's compliments of the German Army. They've done well."

Ahead on the Salaria, explosions went off, and airplanes were heard coming low. The innkeeper all but closed the door. "When do you want the dinner prepared?"

"Right away. And keep your lights on."

Guidi left his apartment for Porta Maggiore, where American jeeps were already parked. Young soldiers hustled about, groups of people clapped from the sidewalks, waving handkerchiefs at the glare of headlights. A bare-headed, bespectacled officer asked him something in English, and Guidi shook his head. "*Habla español?*" the American tried.

"*No, parlo italiano.*"

"*Pero usted entiende?*"

"*Un poco.*"

The officer wanted to know how far it was to St Peter's, and which way to get there. He took out a map and showed it to Guidi under a flashlight. Halfway through his halting explanation Guidi caught himself sobbing. The American saw the little drops on the paper and was embarrassed. He turned the flashlight off. "It's okay," he said after some time, taking Guidi's arm in the dark. "It's okay. I understand."

The bridge to be held was two miles ahead, and the strafing had been heavy, but for now silence and darkness were remade. Bora's Mercedes had blown two tires. The driver was working at it by the side of the road. A slope rose on the right, hemmed with summer grass, gorse and quaking brome. From the moonlit fields there came a scent of poppies growing in the wheat. Marshes lay to the left of the road toward the river, and out of the boggy soil stumpy trees rose, where small owls asked their question, *kee-hooo?* Further up began the olive trees. Bora walked away from the car and into the field.

An ancient ruined sepulcher stood receded from the road, or was it one of those old shrines with naive prayers to the saints? Bora sat on a low wall. An opaque near-summer sky hung overhead, and there was a summer temperature already, but caressing, comfortable. The city lay behind, and ahead lay an unlimited darkness of villages perched on rock walls, narrow defiles strangled by vegetation, river valleys, steep mountain passes. The fugue of nature, high and low, plains and ranges, slow rivers, foggy expanses, all the way back north, as though one were barred from here, condemned not to stay. As though this were an Eden, and he with his were banished for the sin of arrogance.

He harbored regret, not anger but regret, deep sadness. Looking at the stars, he found the constellations so different from the night in late March when he had driven off from the caves with Guidi. That was a springtime dark sky with stars like pins holding it up. This sky was lighter and as though sagging, with stars caught in it like in a dragnet. No comparison at all. Sadness, that was it. An undefinable sense of belonging here and wanting to stay behind. But Time caught up with all of them, through the cannonade, and the importance of this act of departing. Everything shrank into a capsule enabling him to see past, present and future in neat order, without anger and without anguish.

The dark entrance of the brick structure was visible to him in the shade of the moon. Where windows had been, empty orbits opened. It was pitch dark inside, probably too overgrown with nettles, used as a latrine maybe, and then at sunup green flies would go in and out of it. Or else the grave would remain empty, as a barren womb.

Bora's desire to see the ruins up close was checked at once. There was no time, no time, time was a luxury again, and he couldn't see ahead of himself any more, destiny-wise. Wife, family, his city, destruction, the end of the war, like a jumble of cold winter mornings and coming to grips with life. Another life, maybe, other family, children – too far ahead to see, when Death may be waiting anywhere for him, and acceptance of it did not make it less frightening, so that was not the solution either. Accepting Death won't make it walk off nor give you respite because you acknowledge it. He knew, he accepted that, and wondered whether it was possible to have a vision of the future and this to be a lie – physical destruction bound to happen shortly, even tonight.

So he felt a little sadness for himself, too, as a finished vulnerable being; not anger, but sadness. Flashes rose and a low, renewed echo of gunfire rumbled now and then from the left, behind and ahead. New worlds were forged out of that convulsion in the land. *Yet these horizons must be dark again some day, and tranquil, with girls looking at them at night from their balconies, thinking back of us then, long gone, long gone, many of us long dead. And pulsating flickers may go off now and then in those dark horizons, but mean nothing...*

Well, he was alive. Alive and well, and getting out of Rome. And he'd solved not one, but two cases. The little sadness inside was tempered by that satisfaction, even as political risk was postponed. That, too, was a success.

The soldier stood by him at attention. "Car's ready, Colonel, sir."

Guidi, along with most Romans, never went to bed that night. Daylight found him wandering with people he didn't know toward St Peter's Square, where the Pope was to come out to bless the crowd. American soldiers in rose-strewn jeeps rode tossing sweets on the sidewalks, where women and children scrambled for them. Cigarettes were pressed into his hands by smiling men in dust-colored uniforms and he grew tired of saying, "No, no, thank you," and began accepting them.

"If you don't want 'em, I'll take 'em." A young boy trailed him, with a petulant beggarly way which made Guidi feel ashamed.

"And what are you going to do with them? You're too young to smoke."

"That's what *you* think."

Young women rode balanced on the hoods of jeeps, holding on to windshields and soldiers, light skirts flapping over their knees. People sang and cheered and wept. From the windows of brothels weary-faced, painted women waved, and the soldiers whooped back. Two nuns were running like schoolgirls, hand in hand, to be the first in the square when the papal window opened.

The boy of the cigarettes, having stuffed his pockets with them, showed some scribbling on his arm to a friend. "And what's that, a tattoo?" the other boy asked.

"Are you stupid? It's my sister's address."

"You haven't got a sister!"

"What do the Americans know?"

Guidi fell out of the crowd little by little, by slowing down his pace; still he was nearly sucked onward by inertia.

"The Pope's coming out at seven!"

"Let's go see the Pope!"

The bells began to ring, a myriad bells from over four hundred churches. People called to one another in the stream, became lost and reunited.

"Francesca!" someone cried out, and Guidi was tempted to turn and look, but did not.

At the bridge, where the crowd funneled nearly to a stop, he turned back, and slowly, bustled by the wave still mounting the opposite way, over rose-carpeted streets he retraced his steps home.

THE MARTIN BORA SERIES

by Ben Pastor

LUMEN

£8.99/$14.95 • ISBN PB 978-1904738-664 • eB 978-1904738-695

October 1939, Cracow, Nazi-occupied Poland. Wehrmacht Captain Martin Bora discovers the abbess, Mother Kazimierza, shot dead in her convent garden. Her alleged power to see the future has brought her a devoted following. But her work and motto, "Lumen Christi Adiuva Nos", appear also, it transpires, to have brought her some enemies. Stunned by the violence of the occupation and the ideology of his colleagues, Bora's sense of Prussian duty is tested to breaking point. The interference of seductive actress Ewa Kowalska does not help matters.

"Pastor's plot is well crafted, her prose sharp... a disturbing mix of detection and reflection." *Publishers Weekly*

LIAR MOON

£8.99/$14.95 • ISBN PB 978-1904738-824 • eB 978-1904738-831

September 1943. The Italian government has switched sides and declared war on Germany. Italy is divided, the North controlled by the Fascists, the South liberated by Allied forces slowly fighting their way up the peninsula. Wehrmacht major and aristocrat Martin Bora is ordered to investigate the murder of a local Fascist: a bizarre death, threatening to discredit the regime's public image. The prime suspect is the victim's twenty-eight-year-old widow Clara.

"Atmospheric, ambitious and cleverly plotted, *Liar Moon* is an original and memorable crime thriller." *Crime Time*